PROCESSED CHEESE

ALSO BY STEPHEN WRIGHT

Meditations in Green
M31: A Family Romance
Going Native
The Amalgamation Polka

PROCESSED CHEESE

STEPHEN WRIGHT

Little, Brown and Company

New York   Boston   London

Copyright © 2020 by Stephen Wright

Hachette Book Group supports the right to free expression and the value of copyright. The purpose of copyright is to encourage writers and artists to produce the creative works that enrich our culture.

The scanning, uploading, and distribution of this book without permission is a theft of the author's intellectual property. If you would like permission to use material from the book (other than for review purposes), please contact permissions@hbgusa.com. Thank you for your support of the author's rights.

Little, Brown and Company
Hachette Book Group
1290 Avenue of the Americas, New York, NY 10104
littlebrown.com

First Edition: January 2020

Little, Brown and Company is a division of Hachette Book Group, Inc. The Little, Brown name and logo are trademarks of Hachette Book Group, Inc.

The publisher is not responsible for websites (or their content) that are not owned by the publisher.

The Hachette Speakers Bureau provides a wide range of authors for speaking events. To find out more, go to hachettespeakersbureau.com or call (866) 376-6591.

Portions of this book originally appeared in different form in the short story "Brain Jelly" in Conjunctions 52: Spring 2009.

Book designed by Marie Mundaca

ISBN 978-0-316-04337-3
LCCN 2019937209

10 9 8 7 6 5 4 3 2 1

LSC-C

Printed in the United States of America

PROCESSED CHEESE

CHAPTER 1

A WINDFALL

THE DAY WAS HOT. The sky was blue. Graveyard was tired. He'd been pounding the pavement for hours. He was looking for work. He had no job. He had no money. He was flat broke. You know how that is. Sweetbreads and applesauce, he said to himself, I need some cash real bad.

Just then a big canvas bag came sailing down out of nowhere and crashed into the sidewalk inches from his feet. Graveyard looked up. The tall buildings looked silently down. The bag sat upright in the middle of the bright, astonishing day. People walked around as if nothing had happened. Clams and sourdough, he said to himself, I coulda been killed. Graveyard knelt down. He tried to open the bag. It was fastened at the top by a lot of tricked-out leather and metal doohickeys. He had trouble making his fingers work. Everything around him looked like a mirage. Hard melons and soda water, he said to himself, I coulda been killed. And this time he really believed it. He focused his mind. He focused his fingers. He tried to open the bag again. He unbuckled the buckles. He unstrapped the straps. He looked inside. His mind went around like a pinwheel. The bag was packed to the brim with plastic-wrapped bricks of fresh one-hundred-dollar bills. He buckled the buckles. He strapped up the straps. People walked around as if nothing had happened. Graveyard felt drunk. Then he felt hellasmacked. Then he felt like he was going to have a heart attack or something. Slowly, he got to his feet. Slowly, he picked up the bag. It was big. It was heavy. It was like trying to pick up a child who didn't want to be picked up. He pretended to look calm. Then, without a glance in any direction, he just rushed off up the street. Just rushed off. Hugging the bag to his chest. As if it were his. As if it had always been his.

Ambience was in bed. In the current era she was almost always in bed. She wasn't sick. She wasn't tired. She just wasn't feeling good about herself. She'd been feeling this way for a long time now. She didn't know why.

This was a good day. So far. She'd only cried once. Even if it had lasted on and off for more than three hours. She wiped her face with her blue sob rag. It was actually a prayer cloth she'd ordered once from a televangelist who was a dead ringer for BubbleWrap, the famous stand-up comic. To Ambience, tears were sacred. They were the juice life squeezed out of you.

She was propped up on giant pillows a rancid shade of orange she couldn't quite believe was decorating her life at the moment. She was watching television. Whenever she was down she watched television. Lots of television. *E. coli* contaminations. School shootings. Child predators. Any television.

Right now the set was tuned to *The Go-Boom Hour* on The Happy Channel. Sixty crankin' minutes of all kinds of crap being blown up in super x-mo. Her favorite segment was the ratings blockbuster "Exploding Cart O' Meat." The detonated beef seemed to actually blossom. Like flowers.

Her good buddy on these daily voyages on a mattress was her aloof cat, NippersPumpkinClaws. Nippers lay sprawled at the foot of the bed in a careless bundle of regal grandeur. His whiskey-colored face fixed in a permanent expression of sour disapproval. Was there any pleasing this cat? Not likely. And the slightest movement Ambience made was instantly absorbed into those spooky green owl-like eyes. Not that Ambience even moved around all that much. A trip to the john was a regular safari. Her favorite animal, in fact, was the turtle.

For all the obvious reasons. She wanted to be a turtle in her next life. Or even in this one.

She was nibbling on something sweet and sticky she had found in an uncovered bowl in the refrigerator. One of Graveyard's dubious leftovers. She didn't know what it was, but it tasted good. Was it good for her? She didn't know. How many things could a person worry about in a day?

She was also—the ever-dutiful multitasker—leafing through a week-old edition of one of the last hard-copy newspapers, *The Mammoth City Muffler* ("If It Ain't In The *Muffler*, It Ain't The Truth"). Every now and then she liked actually holding the news between her hands. She liked rattling its pages. It seemed more real, more true. She never knew much about what was going on in the world outside her head. Mostly, she didn't care. Why should she? Sometimes, though, she did feel a bit squidgy about being so dumb. But then, any time she made the rare effort to actually find out what was going on in the world outside her head, she only found the same stuff that had been going on the last time she had dared to look. People screwing each other, people screwing each other over, people screwing each other up.

These were not good things to be saying to oneself. They gave her a bad case of the hurries. Like there was a secret sender planted somewhere deep inside her, hacking into her system an endless stream of malware to make her sick. She'd been searching for the Off switch for years. No luck. Other not-so-good things to say to oneself: Am I fat? How are we going to pay next month's rent? Why do I have to die?

Suddenly Nippers's head jerked up and froze. All fine feline attention converging on the open doorway and beyond. Then, in a furry blur, the cat was gone over the edge and under the bed. That was easy to read. Graveyard was home. Nippers didn't trust Graveyard. Graveyard didn't trust Nippers. They had a dysfunctional relationship.

Then there he was, filling the doorway and grinning. Seriously grinning. This surprised Ambience. She hadn't seen Graveyard so much as smile in... well, she didn't know how long. These were not smiley times.

"What's with you?" she said. He looked exactly like the "damn fool" her father had always claimed he was.

Graveyard held up a dirty old canvas sack. Grinning and grinning.

"You got a job," she said. "As a mailman." She could believe just about anything about him at this point.

The bag thudded to the floor. "You know I can't work for the government," he said.

"Why not?" She hated it when people made grand pronouncements about themselves. They were almost always lying.

"Principles," Graveyard said.

"Don't make me laugh," she said. Then she laughed.

"You'll see," he said. "Oh, boy, will you see."

He bent over. He opened the bag. A lot easier the second time around. He pulled out a brick. He tossed the brick onto the bed. "Choke on this," he said.

Ambience studied the curious object for a moment. Then she picked it up. She looked at it in her hand. She looked at it from top to bottom. She looked at it from side to side. She lifted it to her nose and smelled it. "Is this real?" she said.

Graveyard was busy opening several packs of money with his teeth. He appeared to be swept up in the sort of common frenzy usually induced by a visit from the landlord or a call from a collection agency. "As real as a six a.m. knock on the door," he said. He kissed the stack of bills in his right hand. He kissed the stack of bills in his left hand. "Sweeter than the pope's ring," he said. He thrust a stack up to her mouth. "You kiss," he said.

So she did.

"Lick," he said.

So she did. And it was icky and gross, but she couldn't help herself—she began to experience the first flickerings of heat from down in her boiler room. And that was good.

Then Ambience picked up the knife lying on the nightstand among her various prescription vials, her various combs and brushes, and her collection of various small stones and rock chips no one but her knew what the hell to make of. The knife was long and thin and impressively glittery. It had a handle made of narwhal horn. She kept it nearby because she was afraid of things in the dark. And a lot of things in the light, too.

This was an important distinction. The knife had once belonged to ThreeWood, an old boyfriend of hers who had used it to threaten her and to open new DVDs. He also once used it to open both wrists and bleed to death on her birthday, an occasion she had not really celebrated since. It was still quite sharp. The blade slipped easily into the plastic-wrapped brick. Then, in a blink, hundreds of hundreds were spilling across her lap. Like she had just given birth to a green mess of fresh cash.

For the moment, Graveyard was totally gooned. Wrapped hopelessly into the bouquets of pretty currency clutched tightly in each fist. Had he leaned over, opened his mouth, and actually begun chewing on the crispy stuff, it would not have surprised Ambience. He didn't look like himself anymore. He looked like someone who had forgotten who he was.

Ambience picked up some bills, let them slide through her fingers. She picked them up, let them slide. She tossed the bills into the air. They fluttered down like leaves. Like petals. Like promises.

Now Graveyard was stuffing hundreds down into the crotch of his pants. He was making a bulge out of bucks. He posed sideways in front of her. "How do I look?" he said.

Ambience gave him a courtesy glance. "Savage," she said. She began gathering up the bills scattered among the sheets. "All right," she said, "we've had our fun. Whose money is it?"

Graveyard was studying himself in the full-length mirror behind the door. "Whose do you think it is, sweet taffy?"

"Tell me."

Graveyard rolled up some bills and stuck them in his nostrils and both ears. "Look at me," he said. "I'm Mister Moolah." He held up his hands, palms outward, hundreds between his fingers. Then he began hopping mechanically from one foot to the other, doing that silly dance of his he sometimes used to try to tease her into sex when she would almost rather be sticking hot pins into her eyeballs. Sometimes, though, his ploy worked. Sometimes, strangely enough, silliness was sexy. Not today.

"Don't make me scream," she said.

"Good," he said. He sat down on the edge of the bed. "Now that I've got your attention, pick a card, any card." He extended a fan of pristine bills in her direction. "C'mon, luscious lady, whaddya want, whaddya need?"

Ambience was starting to feel the first flickering stages of her famous jalapeño belly. Last time she'd had jalapeño belly she was convinced she was pregnant and Graveyard had kept her up all night plotting how they could sell the baby (jokingly, of course, he said later) to a couple of sterile millionaires for a bag of beans that might, just might, redeem their paltry lives.

"Tell me one thing," she said. "Are we in more trouble now than we've ever been before?"

"No," he said. Then he paused. "At least I don't think so."

"You didn't jack it?"

"Are you kidding? I wouldn't know where to go to even look at an amount of money this large, let alone boost it."

"You didn't scheme it?"

"Do you believe I'm that smart?"

"No."

"I didn't think so."

"You and Herringbone didn't run these off on that fancy Second-GenerationBestGeneration copier of his? And thinking what? How punk it would be to make your own money? I can hear him now."

"It may be punk, but that's not what happened."

"Then tell me."

So he did.

"I'm going to sit here," said Ambience, when he was done, "and I'm going to wait and no one's going to leave this room until you explain to me just where this fucking money really came from and I don't care how long it takes."

Graveyard told her again.

"I said I would wait."

"It's the truth."

"From the sky?"

"Yes."

"From the Chicken Little sky?"

"Yes."

"Chicken Little was a chicken," said Ambience. "A fairy-tale chicken. And nothing fell anyway."

"Or did it?" He waved the paper proof in her face.

"I don't know," she said. "It's got to be somebody's."

"It is," he said. "Ours."

"Somebody who's not gonna be too happy they don't have it anymore."

"Maybe it fell out of a plane."

"What? The money plane?"

"We don't know what's going on up there. Probably tons of cash every day flying right over our ignorant heads. Or maybe it just fell out an open window."

"Sure. Or was pushed. Maybe it even jumped. It couldn't take it anymore. It was heartbroken. Unloved, unwanted, nothing to buy in this cruel, cruel world."

She gave Graveyard her pointy look. "Are you sure you weren't followed?"

"I took three different cabs. In three different directions."

"You took cabs?"

"Today was one day I figured I could afford it."

"How much you think is in there?" She eyed the bag as if it were radioactive.

"Oh, well, considering the magnitude of the denominations, the volume of the bag, I'd say what we have here is, roughly, about an even gazillion dollars, give or take a bazillion or two."

"And how many pissed-off nut jobs running around looking for it?"

"I'll buy more guns." Graveyard had a special locked closet in their apartment where he stored his precious weapons collection. No one was allowed in there. Especially not Nippers.

"Seriously," she said.

"Lots of guns."

Money is a magnet for guns, Ambience said to herself. She hoped that wasn't true.

Graveyard took a single banknote and held it up over his head. He pretended to stare through it. "Know what this is?" he said. "This is a window. A magic window. Know what I can see through it? The future. Guess the color of our future, beefcheeks."

"Uh, green?"

"Four-leaf clover, Statue of Liberty, traffic-go-light green." He stood, unzipped his pants, let them drop to the floor.

"What are you doing?" said Ambience.

"Getting clean." He stepped out of his underwear. He peeled off his shirt. He picked up handfuls of bills. He began rubbing them vigorously all over his body. As though he were showering and money were soap.

In spite of herself, Ambience was amused. Graveyard hadn't looked this fine to her in years. She could see the molecules dancing across the surface of his skin. The sight felt good. It made something in the dark inside of her break, come apart in a soft rain of little sparkly pieces. That felt good, too.

Graveyard was laughing and rubbing and, frankly, growing visibly erect. "Washing out the past," he said. "The grime of history. My history. Your history. This is Day One. Understand?"

She understood.

He wrapped a roll of bills around his penis and pretended to fuck it.

Ambience enjoyed the show. She hadn't felt this nice since

Grandma FlightSuit died and left her exactly $7,346.12 no one knew she even had. That was the money Ambience used to get herself a boob job. That had made her happy, too.

"Come over here," she said, "and stick that big nasty thing inside me."

So he did.

It was the best orgasm either of them had ever had.

CHAPTER 2

THAT'S WHAT I'M TALKING ABOUT

MONEY MONEY MONEY MONEY MONEY MONEY MONEY
MONEY MONEY MONEY MONEY MONEY MONEY MONEY
MONEY MONEY MONEY MONEY MONEY MONEY MONEY
MONEY MONEY MONEY MONEY MONEY MONEY MONEY
MONEY MONEY MONEY MONEY MONEY MONEY MONEY
MONEY MONEY MONEY MONEY MONEY MONEY MONEY
MONEY MONEY MONEY MONEY MONEY MONEY MONEY
MONEY MONEY MONEY MONEY MONEY MONEY MONEY
MONEY MONEY MONEY MONEY MONEY MONEY MONEY
MONEY MONEY MONEY MONEY MONEY MONEY MONEY
MONEY MONEY MONEY MONEY MONEY MONEY MONEY
MONEY MONEY MONEY MONEY MONEY MONEY MONEY
MONEY MONEY MONEY MONEY MONEY MONEY MONEY
MONEY MONEY MONEY MONEY MONEY MONEY MONEY
MONEY MONEY MONEY MONEY MONEY MONEY MONEY
MONEY MONEY MONEY MONEY MONEY MONEY MONEY
MONEY MONEY MONEY MONEY MONEY MONEY MONEY
MONEY MONEY MONEY MONEY MONEY MONEY MONEY
MONEY MONEY MONEY MONEY MONEY MONEY MONEY
MONEY MONEY MONEY MONEY MONEY MONEY MONEY
MONEY MONEY MONEY MONEY MONEY MONEY MONEY
MONEY MONEY MONEY MONEY MONEY MONEY MONEY
MONEY MONEY MONEY MONEY MONEY MONEY MONEY
MONEY MONEY MONEY MONEY MONEY MONEY MONEY

CHAPTER 3

HALLUCINATING ROACHES

MISTERMENU SAT IN THE shade of the popcorn tree on the grand terrace of his duplex penthouse. He lived high atop the Eyedropper Building, fifty-two stories above the hullabaloo. He had a view of the ReadyToWear River. He had a view of the LookAway Harbor. He had a view of other buildings. He had lots of views. And he'd paid plenty for 'em, too.

He was sipping goosenut water out of what was called a libation vessel back in the old coca-leaf-and-obsidian-knife times. At least that's what the glossy catalog claimed. The "vessel" had been purchased at auction from the fabled house of SoBuyMe for—never mind how much. More than you got. How badly you want a stinky old cup used in certain "dark and cruel practices," anyway? People back then actually loved to attend spectacles of public bloodletting. And they went as often as they could. The shows made them feel cozy and prosperous.

MisterMenu was obviously prosperous. Did he feel cozy? What was the question again? He had his bloated income. He had his hot wife. He had his extravagant digs. He had other properties in other places. He had big monies deposited in this bank and in that bank. He had fancy cars. He had fancy boats. He had rare master-works by both Wisenheimer and Mucilage. He had two beautiful, relatively obedient daughters. Chrysalis went to Mistletoe College. NoDeposit went to LayAbout University. He had his foxy live-in maid, Mix'N'Match. He had his foxy live-away mistress, Chloride.

Whenever he wanted lipstick on his dick, he checked in with Mix'N'Match. When he wanted a finger up his ass, he stuck with Chloride. He was a very busy man. He didn't like to look at himself as wealthy, though he was—fantastically so. That was crass. He regarded himself as exceptional. And he was. And a prominent member of the exceptional class.

So what was he doing home in the middle of the afternoon? Guess. He was already stepping out of his pants as he came off the elevator. But the wide, open spaces of his big, big apartment were disappointingly empty. Where was Mix'N'Match? Probably out hunting and gathering for tonight's dinner. He'd wait.

So here he was, then, on the terrace in his underwear. His laptop on his lap. He clicked. He stroked a couple of keys. He stared at the screen. The markets went up. The markets went down. The money went round and round. Not that MisterMenu had anything to worry about. He was founder, president, and CEO of NationalProcedures, a division of GlobularSystems, which was an affiliate of The-ConsternationGroup, a branch of ProjectileStrategies, which was a wholly owned subsidiary of Divinicom, which owned everything. World economies could crash and burn. MisterMenu's financials were always sound. Count on it.

Slight problem: the job was mostly all headwork. Mostly all numbers. The numbers skittered around in there like fireflies in the dark. MisterMenu loved his job. Didn't everyone? But the whole enterprise was so damn abstract. So invisible. And he, so he told himself, was such a sensuous guy. He liked objects, the world of things. He liked to look at things. He liked to touch things. He liked to surround himself with things, especially things that provided tangible evidence of his kickin' success in life. And what could be more tangible than actual money in its actual grubby ink-on-paper three-dimensional format? Bags of real money, positioned at strategic intervals throughout his rooms, offered a specific comfort and solidity he'd been unable to find anywhere else. He liked to look at them. He liked to touch them. Visitors to the penthouse often mistook the upright, bulging sacks for pieces of pop sculpture, amusing works of contemporary art. Which, of course, they were.

Now, though, the moving lights on the screen momentarily commanded his attention. He clicked. He stared. He clicked again. A dozen more bags. Just like that.

Suddenly, he looked up. MissusMenu had abruptly materialized in the open doorway. She was a former supermodel, aspiring actress-ette, and the face of CellarDoorCosmetics. She maintained her unearthly gorgeosity through a combination of sheer will and the frequent application of fresh banknotes. She always looked good.

"What are you doing here?" she said. She had just come from IMeMine. Later, she would go to TheHouseOfFineness. In between, she had planned on a long, lazy session of intense mastur-bation. Her best parts were already tingling. Shopping for new clothes, trying on new clothes, simply being near new clothes always made her feel so insanely horny. Now this. Fatboy was home.

"Don't start," said MisterMenu. He recognized the voice she was doing. He'd heard it before. Too many times before.

MissusMenu glared at him for a moment. Then she wheeled about and went click-clacking away. In another moment she was back again.

"And why," she said, "are you sitting out here in full view of the entire world in your underwear?" Now she was doing her are-you-really-a-moron-or-what? voice.

"I was hot."

She glared at him. Her eyes like cinders. She turned and left.

MisterMenu had MissusMenu problems. He wasn't always sure exactly what those problems were, but obviously there were a lot of them. Once he and MissusMenu had actually liked each other. Really. Now, not so much. What had happened? He didn't know.

He went back to his clicking and stroking. Streaming numbers, bar graphs, pie charts were instantly replaced by a low-resolution image of a room, a bed, a woman asleep. Her name was Linoleum, and this was her site. One of MisterMenu's favorites.

He was an annual subscriber. If she were awake right now, he'd probably order her to do something NSFW with some hard vegetables, a couple of eggs, and a few clothespins. And she'd do it, too. There was a reason hers was one of the top ten highest-grossing sites in the overheated virtual sex slave community. He watched her sleep. He imagined lying down next to her. He imagined and imagined.

"What are you doing now?" said MissusMenu. She was back.

MisterMenu hit a key. The screen flipped to pictures of foreign people rioting in a foreign place. "Checking up on the news," he said. Study Says: Excessive Blinking Causes Cancer of the Eyelid.

"What's with the mess in the kitchen?" said MissusMenu.

"What mess?"

"The half-eaten melon on the counter. The broken crystal in the sink. The sticky red stuff all over the floor."

"MerryberryConserve," he said. "From the untrammeled, unpolluted slopes of the majestic Polyhedral Mountains."

"Why didn't you clean it up?"

"Leave it for Mix'N'Match."

"You know this is her day off."

"I know no such thing."

"Her schedule's been posted on the front of the refrigerator for the past three goddamn years."

"She can clean it up tomorrow." MisterMenu hated conversations like this. Hated them. They were too slippery-sliddery. With few handholds and no safety net.

"Or you can do it now," said MissusMenu.

"I don't think so."

"Why not?"

"I'm busy."

"Doing what?"

"Making money, what do you think? Making money for you, my sweet."

"I refuse to spend the night lying there in bed awake, thinking about those globs of jelly stuck to my floor."

"It's not jelly," said MisterMenu. "It's conserve."

"Do you have any idea how angry you make me? Any idea at all?"

"I was merely stating a fact."

"The entire kitchen will be overrun with cockroaches by morning."

MisterMenu emitted the short bark that passed for laughter with him. "Are you serious? On the fifty-second floor? What do they do, take the elevator up?"

"I saw at least a dozen running under the stove last week."

"You were probably hallucinating."

"They carry thirty-one different types of infectious disease. Thirty-one."

"Who says?"

"I saw it on the internoodle."

"Oh," said MisterMenu, "then of course it must be true."

"I hate you," said MissusMenu. She went back inside and re-appeared a moment later, clutching a bulging duffel of cash.

"Don't." He got up out of his chair to take control of this ridiculous situation.

MissusMenu went to the MuscleBarn every morning, no matter what. Of course, she had a bangin' body. And if she wanted to beat her husband to a pulp, she probably could. So hefting a sack of money and hurling it at his head was a cinch. But the toss was high and wide. MisterMenu reached up to make a dramatic catch, but his hands couldn't get a grip, and the bag was merely deflected. It flew over the parapet. It flew out into the anonymous city.

"Do you know how much was in that bag?"

"I couldn't care less."

"I'm sure you couldn't." He picked up the nearest phone. "You wouldn't know the value of an umbrella in the middle of a shitstorm." He spoke into the phone. "Yes, WindSock, this is MisterMenu. We've had a bit of a mishap up here. Yes. A large

17

canvas bag has accidentally fallen from our terrace and I wonder if you could possibly go out and retrieve it for us. Yes, that's right. On the Q side near the intersection with J. And WindSock, let me know if anyone was hurt. We don't want any unpleasant repercussions over this. Thank you." He put the phone down. He looked at his wife. She looked back at him. He really wanted to hit her. Bad. But he'd paid too much for that face to wreck it himself.

"We'll be lucky if no one was killed," he said.

"I hope they all were," said MissusMenu. "I hope everyone walking innocently down the block was killed. And I hope everyone who wasn't killed was maimed and crippled. By your money falling on their heads."

"If that bag is lost..."

"Oh, what do you care? One bag. One pathetic bag. It means nothing. None of them means anything. Here, let's toss another one over." She advanced on an untouched bag in the corner by the popcorn tree. "Feed it to the sharks," she said. "Feed all of it to the fucking sharks." She picked the bag up and began carrying it toward the parapet. MisterMenu grabbed her by the arm.

"What's wrong with you?" he said. "What the fuck do you think you're doing?"

"Taking out the trash," she said. She tried to pull away from him. He held on.

They wrestled. The bag fell to the floor. They wrestled some more. Not very serious wrestling, but MisterMenu still had some surprising strength in those untoned limbs. He managed to get a leg behind her and push her back down hard onto the MercyMe outdoor sectional they had once had sex on one distant memorable night. He stood panting over her.

"You're making me sweat," he said. "I don't like to sweat."

"Actually feeling something for a change? Unpleasant, isn't it?"

"I hope for your sake that that money has not gone missing."

"Yeah?" said MissusMenu. "What then? Tell me. I want to know."

"I might get angry."

"You don't frighten me."

"That may not be the most productive position to be in."

"Is that a threat?"

"Take it how you will."

"You know, at first, I thought you were just ignorant, and then, after a while, I thought you were stupid, but now, you know, I see you're just plain evil. You're MisterBullshit. You should change your name."

"You're the one who needs a name change. To MissusWhatever-YouWantToPutInHere."

"I'd clean you out. You know that."

"The prenup is fireproof, waterproof, bulletproof, and witchproof."

"I hate you."

"So you mentioned." MisterMenu went back to his chair, sat down, picked up his laptop, and clicked. Linoleum was awake. He wondered what she smelled like.

MissusMenu sat up and reached around under the sofa for one of her heels, which had come off during the struggle. She slipped the shoe back on and stood up and walked away without a word. She slammed the terrace door behind her as hard as she could. The glass panel exploded in a spectacular shower of shards and splinters. Was that her life tinkling in pieces to the floor?

"Go kill some roaches," said MisterMenu. "Kill 'em dead."

CHAPTER 4

MORE PACKAGING THAN PRODUCT

"SO," SAID AMBIENCE, "how long you think we can go without sleep?"

The shades were pulled. The curtains were drawn. Was it light outside? Was it dark? Who knew? Who cared?

"Beats me," said Graveyard. He hit Pause on the clicker. The electronic squall of digitized mayhem abruptly ceased. They were watching *Eschatology Force II: Cry Me A River*. (Even better than the original.) They were watching the movie on their brand new 103-inch HootchieCootchie flat screen. The picture was so sharp and clear it made real reality look muddy and out of focus. "What day's today?"

"I forget," said Ambience. She was slumped in the corner in her favorite puffy chair. She was scarfing down an entire carton of Pat & Pending's RoyaleMuddyDrawerSurprise. "What day'd you find the money?" She licked the spoon. It was chocolicious.

On her feet was a brand new pair of eight-hundred-dollar Loubotomy fuck-me stilettos. She couldn't take them off. She couldn't stop looking at them.

"I guess," said Graveyard, "that would had to have been Manna-day. Then came Doughday, Endsday, and Skrilladay, so that means this must be Cheddarday." He took the roll of bills in his fist and rubbed the paper edges back and forth across the stubble on his cheek. His hand now always seemed to be clutching a roll of bills. Like a good luck charm. Or a lollipop. "So, my treat, I'd guess we've been up for what—five, six days?"

"We must have slept sometime, but I don't remember doing it."

"What do you care? This is us now. We're off the clock. We're not in time anymore. We're flying above it." At the moment he lay sprawled across the black buttery expanse of a brand new emperor-length arcadian leather sofa that had cost twice as much as all their old furniture put together. Strapped to his left wrist was his latest prime purchase, a brand new glittery watch. And not just any watch. This was a signature Tri-Gem Elaboration from PattyCake, Ltd., featuring the exclusive anthracite and freshwater pearl dial and scratch-resistant blue platinum casing engineered to withstand not only the inconveniences of deep space exploration but also high-speed impacts of up to two hundred miles per hour. He couldn't stop looking at it.

"I think there were some missing periods somewhere in there," said Ambience. "I don't like missing periods." She paused. "Hey, I made a pun. I never make a pun."

"See? It's working already."

"What's working?"

"Why, the wunnerful, wunnerful, fabulous, fantastical mojo of money. From now on our lives are gonna be exploding with all sorts of spooky flavors. Coincidences, enchantments, charms, jokes, prophecies, puns. And cake. Lots of cake. You'll see. And you know what?—thought of it just this second—something else I want to buy today: a magic wand. And not some cheap juvenile licorice stick, either. I want the deluxe professional model, lacquered and encrusted with diamonds."

"What the fuck you want that for?"

"To perform diamond-encrusted illusions and stuff with, what do you think? I always wanted to be a magician. Make elephants appear, disappear. You know, magic shit."

"But what do you need a wand for? You already pulled a fortune out of thin air without one."

"Yeah, I did, didn't I? I must be good."

"You know it, babe. And guess what? You ain't the only one. I'm so damn good I really don't think I can stop myself from rewarding me, too, with a very special treat on this very special day."

"Treat away."

"I'm thinking gold. I'm thinking platinum. I'm also thinking diamonds of the also encrusted variety. I'm gonna be looking so fucking mint in my brand new tiara."

"Flapjacks and vinegar."

"Well, I always wanted to be a princess. It's been a lifelong ambition."

"But you already are a princess. You don't need a stupid hunk of metal to prove it."

"Princess of what?"

"I don't know. Rabidiya? Quagistan? Make one up."

"Then I'd be a made-up princess. I want to be a real one."

"Then you're gonna have to go out and find yourself a real prince."

"Well, maybe I will."

"Fine. Good luck to you." He hit Play. The Eschatology Force sprang back into action.

She had to shout to be heard over the clamor of Sensosound. "The world is full of princes, you know."

"That so?"

"They're all over the place."

"Like germs?"

"Don't make me want to punish you."

"Oh, would you, please?"

"How pathetic. Listen, you little worm, you're gonna have to beg harder than that."

"I'm already hard."

Well, you know, this sort of entertaining banter could have gone on for hours. And often did. What they were really doing was mostly just hanging out until the stores opened again in the morning. There was lots more stuff to buy. Where exactly they would put more stuff was another issue. The original used clutter of their desperately cramped apartment had been all but buried beneath an avalanche of new clutter from their recent shopping rampages. They could barely see each other over the mounds, the piles, the heaps, the tottering towers of bags, boxes, cartons, and crates—many of them still unopened—loot from the more or less constant spending spree they'd been on for however many days it had been now. PumpkinClaws ran up and down the narrow aisles between the fresh merch as if she were on catnip. She pounced on the plastic packaging. She rolled around in the wrapping paper. For everyone, man and beast, it was Christmas in July.

They had refurbished their dilapidated lives with product purchased almost exclusively in the TooGoodForYou District. They spent hour after hour trolling giddily through shops—shops, mind you, not stores—that would not have dared buzz them in in their previous incarnations. They went to KidMeNot & Sons, jewelers to the bejeweled. The damage? You don't wanna know. They went to TheTaintedBarrel, where not even the staff could explain most of the merchandise. Ambience bought an old cast-iron thingy called a quarrel. She didn't know what it was. Neither did the clerk.

She had to have it. Who else had one? They went to Fracas. Kitsch for the rich. They qualified. Of course, they dropped a bundle. They went to Clawfoot&Residue. Who cared how much a silver nutcracker cost? They bought a dozen. They went to the HouseOfNoRegrets, clothiers to the stars and nearby orbiting planets who wanted to bathe in the reflected radiance. They loaded up. Good thing, too. They no longer "did" laundry. When they were done with what they were wearing, they'd simply toss those rags into the trash, tear open a couple of boxes, and put on new. And, of course, they had to drop in to Graveyard's favorite browsing nook, AlliterativeAlchemy, where you could purchase philosopher's pizzles, eidolon elixirs, umbonic unicorns, allotropic alembics, plenitude panaceas, and lots of other neat stuff to fulfill all your transformative needs. They went to Methodology, a hidden unmarked-door erotic emporium catering almost solely to the discreet well-heeled sensualist. They left with two shopping bags each. They got G-spot stimulators and vibrating cock rings with multiple pulsating patterns. They got variously sized and shaped dildos in glass, silicone, and acrylic. They got anal beads. They got clit pleasurizers and penis sleeves and prostate massagers. They got a couple of Deluxe Condom Samplers, ultra-thin, ultra-ribbed, ultra-dotted, ultra-silky. They got oils and lubes and arousing gels in twelve colors and five flavors, enough to slick a world-class orgy. Could they possibly wait till they got home before busting out their new toys? What do you think? They wanted to get each other real nice real fast. They got busy about an hour later in a locked stall of the women's room at TheRestOfTheStory, a private club for students and alumni of Porcupine University (of which Graveyard was one, believe it or not), a secluded midtown oasis where knowing people traditionally allowed other knowing people to do what they know. They fucked and they sucked. They rinsed and repeated. Their new appliance friends offering encouragement to exceed all expectations. Then Graveyard got baby batter all over Ambience's face. Whoops. Boy, was she pissed. And she let him know about it. He apologized. He was sorry. She pretended to forgive him. But later, she had to ask herself, was that true? Was that really true? Or did some teensy messed-up part of herself actually like it? What the fuck. She didn't know.

After they repaired the damage and spruced up their mirrored selves as best they could, they went for dinner to TheInnerSequence. Where, for the moment, all the famous rich thin people were supposed to go to eat. The specialty of the place was arranging the food on the plate in alphabetical order. Whenever anyone ordered the SuperSimulatedDiamondButterSteakForTwo, the chef rang a little bell. Graveyard and Ambience didn't cook anymore. The top of their brand new BurntOfferings dual-fuel range with ten different cooking modes and digital everything was piled high with glossy boxes of cutting-edge electronics everyone could live without. The interior of the oven was stuffed with snacks. They liked snacks. All things salt and sugary. They had Snooker-Chips. They had BangoNuts. They had CheesySubs. They had ToastedPepperWhackers. And FruityPatooties. And LoopyCrisps. And FudgieWudgiePudgies. Their favorite. A cookie inside a cookie. Munching on all this nasty fun kept their glucose levels up until their next restaurant debauch. They went out for every meal. They went to all the places they would've been going to for years if they'd had the money. They went to DoNotAttempt. They had the EarlyRunoffSoup. The SpatchcockedGooneyBird with a HornyNutGremolata. LickMyFingerlings. JollifiedGreens. BreadSpindles. And WhereberryPie in a zesty HardLuckSauce. They went to TheSuperiorCowCo. BurnedBlackenedButteredAnd-Bruised. They went to TenderHydraulics. They had the WeaselRolls and the hibiscus-dusted laser-seared CapeBuffaloDelight and the GrilledJimsonStalks and the RandomGlacéedPears in a puddle of ArmoredMelonGastrique. Then back to DoNotAttempt. That melty mouthy bird. Those tingly taters.

After the gluttony, the lust. Clubbing every single night. They couldn't get enough. They went to Contagion. They went to ThrashingLimb. They went to ExplodedDiagram. At DigitalAb-straction they got totally whacked on who knew how many rounds of FuzzyQuilts. Then each popped a little blue pill (what the hell, they were rich) out of a paper cup offered them by a sketchy old guy in a wheelchair. He looked as if he were wearing a rubber mask. He wasn't.

"What is it?" said Graveyard, after he'd already swallowed.

"Ellipsis," said the old guy, as if you should have known.

"Oh, yeah," said Graveyard. He'd read about the ex–chem grad student who'd developed it out of utter boredom with the contents of his own mind. Now on the run from the substance cops in a faraway land with a bad reputation. Interesting drug. It turned your life into a movie with a lot of sudden jump cuts. One minute you're packed in the middle of a sweaty throng of funseekers all throbbing softly to the basic beats of DJMasterMasterChef, the next minute you're in the back seat of a speeding cab arguing with your wife about something vitally important you're going to forget in a second because now you're in the Up elevator at ArchaicMoon wondering why the building is slowly descending into the ground. The doors opened. On a total party blast of noise and light they could actually feel on their skin. On the wall opposite in poison-green neon: WELCOME TO THE MOMENT. The place was packed. There was barely enough room to step off the elevator. Everyone was dancing or trying to dance or pretending to try. Everyone was shouting enthusiastically to everyone else.

Ambience smiled. "I love it," she shouted.

"What?" shouted Graveyard.

"Why didn't we ever come here before?"

Graveyard shouted something.

She shouted something back.

Graveyard grabbed her hand and began shouldering his way through the crowd. Turned out this was the drop party for pop-ster Effigy's latest release, *BeatMeKickMeHoldMe*. So what were Graveyard and Ambience doing there? Seemed Graveyard was maybe, if you squinted hard enough, a smeared but passable copy of RascalCoupons. You know, the guy who played the quirky motel clerk in *ADoubleClutchLife*. Plus, to be perfectly candid, Ambience was this evening lookin'—there is no other word for it—totally hellified.

Then the ellipsis must have kicked in for a moment or two because all at once they found themselves seated at a prized table in a corner where the decibel levels were almost bearable. They ordered a couple of MentalCuffs. Great drink. A lemonhorseradish-peppermintschnapps combo. They looked around. Everybody seemed to be somebody who wanted to be seen. And every face you saw was a face you recognized or seemed to recognize or wanted to recognize. Up on the balcony, behind shiny chrome bars and surrounded by a babe posse of unreal boobitude, reigned the grand manipulator of the night, DJAcquisitionFee. He was jazzing on Effigy's tracks. He not only had his finger on the pulse, he was also regulating the actual heart rate of the room. The crowd vibrated in a sort of civilized frenzy. The lights strobed. The walls shook. If it were possible for a building to have an orgasm, this one was close to it. Then Effigy herself got up on top of a table and began gyrating in sync with her own vocals and her own images, which were being projected on the hi-def Humongotron overhead. Effigy's crew shrieked with laughter. They jumped up and began stuffing wads of cash into the tighty-tight waistband of her bush-low salt-and-pepper cigarette lowriders. When she finished, she applauded herself. Five minutes later she was in a secluded booth playing tonsil hockey with VelvetRope, the former MissDriveThru and unrepentant convicted felon.

Graveyard and Ambience ordered a round of FlyingBarbarians. Then another. Neither one, at this point, exactly sure which club they were actually in. But what the hell. They were having fun. Then they might have had, might have imagined, probably actually did have sex of one variety or another, either at the table, under the table, behind the bar, or in the john (again). Whatever. Something good happened this night. They were sure of that.

When they were back in their seats, Ambience reached out for Graveyard's hand. She said nothing. She just liked interlocking fingers with him. She liked feeling his heat.

"Look at that total tool over there," said Ambience. "Isn't that TastyAshes?"

And so it was. The nutso one-eyed director of such b.o. gold as *The Water's Fine* and *Lucifer by Starlight* was scuttling about the sticky floor on all fours, catching coins in his mouth tossed by an out-of-control table of movie people with emo hair and narrow rectangular glasses with black frames to show everyone how smart they were.

"Is he drunk?"

"Let's hope so," said Graveyard.

The music stopped. A drumroll sounded. A spot came on, catching the dramatic descent of a giant piñata in the shape of Senator HillAndDale being slowly lowered from the scaffolding overhead. The crowd shrieked. The crowd jumped up and down. The senior senator from BadgerPaw hated, or pretended to hate, most everything people at the ArchaicMoon liked. A long line quickly formed. Everyone eager to take a crack at the papier-mâché politician.

"I wanna beat on the rat with a baseball bat," said Ambience. She hated HillAndDale's meanie politics. She hated his face. She hated his voice. And she hated the way he reminded her, all too vividly, of her own absconded father.

"Go for it," said Graveyard. He watched her go. Watched the back of her head bobbing away into the crowd. Watched her take her place at the back of the line. She saw him looking. She waved. He waved back. Inside a minute, two ugly guys in ugly clothes were hitting on her. Lemon meringue and angel food, said Graveyard to himself, she is so...well, everything. She looked like someone he'd like to pick up. Why can't I see her every second of every day the way I'm seeing her now? Cash goggles? He didn't know.

Meanwhile, down on the floor, the wasted and blindfolded merrymakers were busy, one at a time, knocking major stuffing out of the wildly penduluming senator. And every healthy whack released a fresh shower of coins, candies, playing cards, steel washers, little plastic cocktail animals, fluttering bills of assorted denominations, bits of papier-mâché, and party packets of Hilarium, a fantastic designer drug so new no one had gotten around to criminalizing it yet. It was so potent it made you feel exactly how you wanted to feel. Get it while you can, folks. And boy, did they. Happy revelers scrambled around on the floor, completely ignoring the cash and bar-wrestling over the popular brain renovator. By the time it was Ambience's turn all four of the senator's limbs were gone and there was a serious indentation across his upper torso. She leaned back and let fly with a swing out of slugger's heaven. The sound on contact was like melon on pavement. HillAndDale's phony head shot across the room in a wicked line drive that bounced square off the back of some guy's real head. The guy was standing at the end of a long crowded table made entirely of glued-together cereal boxes. Like he was giving a toast or something. He turned around, rubbing his neck. It was MisterMenu. Holy moly. One of those new-money celebrities you see popping up everywhere nowadays. He looked at his hand. He smiled. He said something. Everyone laughed. MisterMenu's peeps: the former happy-to-see-ya Mayor GuardRails, whose deputy and police commissioner had just been indicted on charges of wire fraud, extortion conspiracy, and tax evasion; StutterStep, star quarterback for the Mammoth City Subprimes, currently under a restraining order obtained by his actor/singer/ dancer/stripper ex-wife, Extravaganza; the obscenely rich, almost mythological WheelPlay, CEO of everything this-and-that, generally disliked by the populace at large, universally loathed by the insiders at this table; the supposedly dying fashion designer Monogram, who always looked so incredibly vital, so incredibly tan; AllAccess, that shiny young appetite who'd won last year's Macadamia Award for her breakout performance as the hooker turned nun turned first female president in the rom-com juggernaut *One, Two, Four*, accompanied, as always, by that doofus boyfriend of hers, the three-fingered meth-lab-explosion guy she met in rehab; messy-divorce lawyer DoubleDown, of Softsoap&Dropcloth, who wouldn't even look at you if you weren't A-list famous; faded legendary songbird and marriage junkie BranchWater, so faded, in fact, that it was pretty freaky to even see her here tonight and even freakier to see that she was still happily numbered among the present and accounted for and apparently dating mega-agent AllRightsReserved, who brokered the deal that brought SordidBones to VulpineEntertainmentMist, and, well, the rest, as you know, is cinematic history; supermodel ScandalONova, of the electric-eel erotic charge, with her fifth appendage, the unendurably foxy BFF PipeCleaner, who couldn't stop pimping her latest top-tier fragrance, Cents, which came marketed, naturally, in a cent-sign-shaped bottle; the ubiquitous BuzzBomb, gossip columnist for the online *Eek!*; and, of course, the incandescent MissusMenu, the former Miss AllThat, who was inexplicably wearing a monster neck brace (rad new fashion statement or what? Who knew?). And, at the distant, Siberian end of the table, a random gaggle of plain-looking people Graveyard didn't recognize at all. Lost tourists? Contest winners? Relatives? A bunch of losers nevertheless.

He watched Ambience drop the bat. He watched Ambience rush across the room. To apologize, no doubt. He knew his girl. MisterMenu's entourage looked to be simultaneously shocked and amused. Wouldn't you be? She said something. She made my-bad gestures with her hands. Everyone was smiling, including MisterMenu himself. He was holding the papier-mâché head in his hands. He reached inside and pulled out a handful of bills. Everyone laughed. He displayed the bills. He put them in his pocket. More laughter. He was hosting his own show, starring himself. He lifted the fake head to his mouth and kissed the senator right on his brittle, painted lips. Then he drop-kicked the head back across the room, where it crashed into *The Weight of Her Hair*, a sculptural assemblage by media sensation and boy wonder MorningDew, most gossiped about for his stratospherically overpriced poster-paint-and-Magic-Marker diptych, the surprisingly underbaked *Vaginas 1 & 2*. Unfortunate funsters seated directly beneath "the work" were treated to a sudden cascade of broken glass, ceramic chunks, coils of razor wire, knotted plastic tubing, and actual vials of the artist's own blood. Too bad for them.

"Thank you," shouted an anonymous male voice. "I've always hated that fucking thing."

MisterMenu shook Ambience's hand. He gave her a long hug. He said something something something, and she was done. Several grinning celebs at the table also took the trouble to shake her hand as she left. Thanking her for the lucky line drive? Then

Graveyard lost her in the crowd. Then all at once there she was standing in front of him. Beaming like a blazin' member of the leaf community.

"What'd he say?" said Graveyard.

"He said I should be batting clean-up for the Capitalonians."

"Funny guy."

"He said I reminded him of his daughter. She plays lacrosse for Mistletoe College."

"That wasn't exactly a daughterly squeeze he gave you there at the end."

"Oh, he was just trying to be nice."

"But he's not a nice person."

"That's why he's trying." She watched him staring at her. She shrugged. "What can I say? Powerful man. His passions run high."

"And what would you know about powerful men and their passions?"

"I once saw a fascinating doc on the subject on the BadBoysAnd-Bimbos Channel."

"And your response, if he decided to act out that badness on you?"

"I don't know," she said. "I'd have to see the size of the check." She laughed. He didn't.

"You know," he said, "you don't have to see the size of anyone's check anymore."

"But I'm Little Miss Curious," she said. "I like to find out stuff."

"So become a detective."

"It was a joke," she said. "A stupid joke, all right? Whatever happened to your sense of humor?"

"I bought it out."

"Let me tell you something: whatever goes on in that nutty head of yours is not exactly what you think is going on in there."

"And what am I supposed to do with that sound bite?"

"Try it on for size and see if it fits," said Ambience. She paused. "You know I love you."

"Yes."

"And you know that whatever we're talking about right now doesn't really mean a whole fuck of a lot."

"Yes."

"You wanna go?"

Yeah, he wanna go. And so they did. Around the tables, between the clinging couples, down the thronging hallways, and out onto the street, where a cool crowd of smokers was smoking furiously, and Ambience and Graveyard had the same idea at precisely the same time. They crossed the street to the ValleyDellFreshFarm bodega, where they bought a pack of Daredevils. You know, the cigs with the pitchfork printed on every filter. They went around the corner and found a spot on the dank, greasy steps of some loading dock or other.

First there was the ritualistic opening of the pack. The musical crinkling of the cellophane. Then the rich dark aroma of fresh tobacco. Like raisins or dates or figs or all three at once. And the sparking up, the perennial mystique of the flame, the slow, concentrated inhale. The slow, extended exhale. Ambience studied the business end of her Daredevil. The little orange ember seemed alive, speaking to her in spirals of tender smoke. Neither of them had touched a cigarette in years.

"This is good," she said. "Why'd we ever quit?" She was feeling a bit dizzy. In a pleasant way, of course.

"I think we said to ourselves that we were gonna die."

"And now we're not?"

"No, now we don't care."

"Same thing," said Ambience. She took another long drag. She blew it out. A tremendous white plume went exploding away into the humid black night. It was beautiful. I made that, she said to herself. I'm a performance artist.

"You don't think they're gonna actually ban this sweet stuff outright, do you?" she said.

"Whaddya talking about? They practically already have."

"When are those rotten government bastards gonna get off our fucking backs?" she said. Then she laughed.

"Who cares?" said Graveyard. "Even if they outlaw cigarettes entirely, the rich will still smoke. The rich do what they want to do."

"Is that us?"

"Yes," he said. His voice as quiet as it ever got. "That's us."

CHAPTER 5

MAKIN' BANK

THAT WAS THE SUMMER everyone was supposed to be reading *It Is What It Is,* the gone-viral first novel by CuttyCrabCakes, author of the self-help book of the decade, *So You Can Get What You Want When You Want.* And they did. Read it, that is. And masturbated en masse to all the top ten highlighted scenes. Especially pages 42–45, 101–5, 126–31, 187–92, and so on. Even MisterMenu took a look, and he hadn't read anything as frivolous as a novel since his navel-gazing days at Weights & Measures University. Novels were for sissies. When he did open a book of any sort, which admittedly wasn't often these days, he preferred the heroic history-type stuff. He didn't like being "fooled" by fiction. But he was as susceptible as anyone else to the lures of genteel pornography. His favorite passage was everyone's favorite, the one in red type that began on page 263. He read it several times with great interest. He'd been trying to get MissusMenu to lick his taint for years. No luck.

So here he was, alone again with a book (a damn book) on another stale weeknight, waiting to get his pipes cleaned whenever Her Highness bothered to return from her latest charity ratfuck or other. He rarely attended such events. He was busy. He had a conflict. There were people he had no wish to see. Like Chorusline. Or worse, UnlimitedMessaging. Plus, MisterMenu had a headache.

He looked at *TastyNewsNuggets* online. Nothing new there. He read less than half of an article about himself. All wrong. He glanced through the latest spreadsheets. Nothing really new there, either. Company doing fine. Life was complicated; money was not. The economy was a pixie. You had to believe in it or it fell to the ground stone cold dead. And MisterMenu believed. Lord, did he believe. He hit a couple of buttons on the ol' keyboard. Made some more money. Lots more money. Ho hum. (Actually, he was thrilled. He always got a little thrill whenever he made some money.) He clicked on the FabuVision. Caught the last twenty minutes or so of some tarted-up pageant (possibly a rerun) where famous actors gave awards to other famous actors. Didn't everyone already have an award? How much love did these people need? Sometime after that he drifted off. He dreamed he was awake. But not awake enough to hear MissusMenu come home, slip into bed beside him. In the morning he told her not to speak to him the entire day. Suspiciously, she complied. Without complaint.

Then, seated in the back of the GalacticCloudTouringConfiguration, on his way to work, suddenly popping into his head, for no particular reason, the memory of one of the greatest—if not in fact the very greatest—blow job of his life. He'd met her his sophomore year in an uncharacteristic, at least for him, face-off about halfway through the second week of the centerpiece of the business school: Financial Engineering for Apprentice Wizards. What he remembered about her was her name (AccountsReceivable), her height (top of her head to the bottom of his chin), her eyes (were they all pupil or what?), her mouth (had anything ever been invented in the whole history of the globuverse that was as blah blah blah as someone else's hot lips and tongue drooling all over your precious jewels?). She'd worked that sweet spot on the underside of his dick, just below the mushroom cap. Until it felt like his whole dick was vibrating. And his whole being. And his whole fucking world. And when he came, or whatever that was, he went to a place he'd never been before. I love you, AccountsReceivable, he said to himself. Easy for him to say. They lived together for a couple of semesters. Until all the pretty vibrations went away. Where'd they go? Damned if he knew.

The DingleBerry rattled awake. It was InternalBundling, his CFO. His Clueless Fucking Onionhead, as MisterMenu liked to refer to him, especially to his face. Of course, he loved the guy dearly, though his understanding of the word *love* may not be the same as yours. There were apparently major discrepancies in the PissOnMe contract. The day's steeplechase already begun, and he hadn't even gotten out of the goddamn car. Actually, he didn't mind, really. He enjoyed the ride. Pretty much. Forty-five minutes of peace before the deluge. Not today. He told InternalBundling to take his thumb out of his ass and get ahold of NoRefrain over there in Dislocations & Infringements. He's got the 411 on all this crap. Did he (MisterMenu) have to think of everything himself? Now look at how hot he was running, and he hadn't even entered the building yet.

The NationalProcedures corporate HQ was located, naturally enough, in the BigPointyBuilding in the high-end, businessy part of town. NumberCrunchers, where all the tooth-capped aristocracy stuffed their faces, was just across the street. There was a dark old church of some antique denomination or other down on the corner. The fancy I. M. Me–designed world headquarters of Perpetua, Inc., on the next block. An upscale branch of the upscale Crumblecake & Sons, Ltd., right next door. It was a neighborhood where people made money. It was a neighborhood where people spent money. Lots of it.

The Galactic glided to a halt. MisterMenu instructed Trefoil, his chauffeur, to bring the machine back around at a quarter to one. What he neglected to inform Trefoil was that he was planning on lunching at LaLaLa's with EpoxyGrout Sr., the bloated head (egotistically, and, fittingly enough, physically) of MagnitudeNewsCorp, the self-proclaimed voice of the sick, the lame, and the lazy. Hefty demographic. Trefoil had no need to know. Much of anything.

On his way into the building and through the lobby to the elevator, MisterMenu dutifully said good morning to anyone who happened to look at him. He was famous for that. He had his own private elevator. A gold-plated express to the top, which opened directly into his office.

"I'm here," he said into the intercom.

"Very well," said MissyMiss.

MissyMiss'd been with him for ten, eleven, twelve years— whatever the hell it was—and he'd wanted to fire her about every other week for the whole ragged run. But he could never quite prod himself to finally bring down the hammer. Maybe because he just liked looking at her. He liked being in the same room with her. And she had a great smell. It was like having a living air freshener in the office. And sometimes, at home, he'd catch a whiff of that scent coming off his clothes, and he'd be transported to someplace else, where he was living with or married to MissyMiss instead of MissusMenu or, worse, the evil-smelling VelvetRope, mother of his children, former face of WhatYouLookingAt?Cosmetics, and all-around pain in the ass. How much she'd taken from him in the divorce settlement was a figure as closely guarded as the actual number of gold bars left stored in the national vault. Both numbers would probably surprise a lot of people.

He sat down at his desk. The very desk once owned by none other than the original Old King Cole. He'd gotten it for a steal from OptionalFeatures, who'd needed a quick cashfix to pay off the dream team of attorneys who'd gotten his securities fraud conviction reduced to a pinch and a whistle. MisterMenu went to work. Usual routine. Morons in and out. Phone clattering, clattering phone. Meetings morning, meetings night. Anytime he wanted, he could be "busy" every waking minute of every waking day. His choice. You guess. But this a.m., after just a few hours, the light from the computer screen had gotten inside his eyes. He barked at employees he didn't usually bark at. The data stream read like an alien language. Then he remembered. The honey bag. The missing honey bag.

"MissyMiss," he said into his intercom.

"Yes, MisterMenu."

"Get DelicateSear up here."

"Yes, MisterMenu."

"STAT."

"Yes, MisterMenu."

DelicateSear was the Executive Vice President for Context and Control. Nifty title, huh? MisterMenu made it up himself. He enjoyed being creative. What DelicateSear really was was the company wrangler. She put the boobs back in the bra. MisterMenu'd known her a long time. She was an ex-fuckbuddy, a current friend, and a general all-around screwaround. Deadass credentials, too. She'd graduated magma cum loud from PortOfSuccor College. She had a master's degree from the University of BlackToast. She'd been in the military. She'd been in the police. She'd been other places no one talked about. She'd been where you had to be. He'd met her on the leveraged buyout of PolkadotIndustries. She'd represented the other side. He'd bought *her* out. Of course they'd gone to bed together. She liked the sun in the morning and the moon at night. So did he. But it hadn't been a good fit. She liked her greasers plain. He doused his in slobbersauce. Her favorite TV show was *PickMe*. He couldn't stand that caterwauling, even when it was being done by CarbonatedDiva. She rooted for the Javelinas. He put his dime on the Subprimes. He liked getting blow jobs. She did not like giving them. He hadn't seen her in months. All quiet on the company front.

"You're looking well," she said, showing up about two and a half minutes after he'd asked to see her.

"Clean living," he said.

"How's the missus?"

"Getting it done." She had the kind of face you could look at for hours without getting tired.

"That bad, huh?"

He waited a beat. Then he said, "I'm not rising to that anymore."

"Oh? Not rising to what?" She speared him with her silkiest smile.

"Your bait."

"I'm not baiting you."

"Coulda fooled me."

"And you've always been such an astute reader of other people's fine print."

"I'm famous for it," he said. The longer she talked to him, the brighter she seemed. Or was he only imagining the effect? Who knew? "What's that you're wearing?" he said. "I can smell it from here."

"PrettyMe," she said. "The latest from ExquisiteEffluvia."

"Come over here," he said. "So I can give you a big yummy squeeze."

She did. And he did. And it felt as good and as comfortable as it always had. Bony, but comfortable.

"Oh, my," she said. When they finally unclinched. "How long has MissusMenu been gone? Was there something extra in that? Or am I imagining?"

"The missus hasn't gone anywhere. And she's as good as she needs to be. Have a seat. That's not what we're here to discuss."

DelicateSear sat down in one of the ergonomic chairs personally designed for MisterMenu by Eggwhite of Residuum. Your back will say thank you after mere minutes of such luscious lumbar support.

"Don't tell me this is only about some dreary company business. I changed my dress twice before running up here."

"It's about some dreary personal business."

"Better. Much better."

He told her about the bag. Omitting all references to MissusMenu. The bag fell, all right. Somehow. Done and done. He told her he wanted the bag back. He told her he wanted her to be the one who got the bag back.

"No problem," she said.

"Really? I would have thought there would be issues and complications. A verminous horde of issues and complications. I wouldn't even know where to begin."

"When I say no problem, it means there is no problem."

"That's what I've always liked about you. Your confidence. You are a supremely confident person."

"I know that."

MisterMenu laughed as loudly as it was possible for MisterMenu to laugh. "That's what I mean."

Two days later DelicateSear was back. She held in her manicured hand a transparent DVD jewel case.

"I'm sure somewhere amidst all this splendor you've got a bonehard player of some sort." She handed him the case.

MisterMenu pressed a button. A Hoo-Ray deck slid out of the wall. He pressed another button. A screen descended from a slot in the ceiling. MisterMenu put the disc in the machine. They sat back and watched.

"The first clip is from the surveillance camera in front of your building," said DelicateSear. They saw a busy street scene. Ordinaries walking back and forth. In the background cars and buses and cabs and bikes moving steadily from right to left. They saw the bag suddenly plummet from the sky, almost brain some nondescript nobody. They saw the nobody kneel down, examine the bag, open it, look inside, close the bag, and then just get up and brazenly walk off with it.

"He looks like he could use the dough," said MisterMenu.

"This next clip is from the MetaHealingBank branch on the next block," said DelicateSear. They watched the nobody with the bag struggle down the street through hordes of largely oblivious pedestrians. The screen went blank, then almost instantly came back on again. "The camera outside FontanelleJewelers," said DelicateSear. More struggling. "Time&TideLaundromat," said DelicateSear as another camera tracked the bag's slow progress. The nobody set the bag down and sat down on top of the bag. He glanced here. He glanced there. He glanced all around.

"Look at that idiot," said MisterMenu. "Guilty as hell. He's expecting the hand on his shoulder at any moment."

"Now there's a gap here of about half a block. We pick him up again in front of FlavorTown." The nobody set the bag down again, took a paper towel from his back pocket, and wiped his forehead. Looked around, appeared to ponder something important, then stepped boldly into traffic and hailed a cab. Nobody and bag got into a big yellow taxi, and they were gone. The screen went black.

"That's it," said DelicateSear. "If he had kept walking we could have followed him all the way up to his door."

"I'm astonished," said MisterMenu. "How'd you get access to all these cameras?"

"When I want something, I get it."

"Extraordinary. Well, I'm impressed; I'm goddamn impressed."

"Thank you."

"Now what?"

"As you could plainly see, the visual quality of the last clip is not anywhere near the high-tech spy quality we normally prefer. We're working on deciphering the cab number and the tag. When we get it, I'll tell you."

"Who's this 'we'?" He waited a moment. "Wait a minute, never mind, don't tell me. I don't want to know."

"My associates," said DelicateSear. "They're all on your payroll."

"Fine. But the less I know about payroll the better."

"Now you really surprise me. The poster boy for fervent micromanaging."

"I've got enough crap in my head at the moment."

"Yes, the missus's care and feeding and all."

"That's enough."

"Well," said DelicateSear. She got up out of the Eggwhite. "I'd better get to work."

"Nice seeing you again, D."

"Me, too."

"You're looking particularly—well, healthy."

"You, too."

MisterMenu walked her to the door. Breathing in her scent the whole way. Citrus and musk and something cinnamony. "I want to thank you in advance for the enormous expertise already expended on this project."

"You're welcome."

"You're one of the handful of people in this paranoid organization I can actually trust."

"It's not necessary to stroke me."

"I'm not. I'm simply relaying a basic fact." He tried to say something warm with his eyes, but he didn't know if that worked or not.

She patted him on the hand. "Don't worry," she said. "We gonna get your money."

"I know."

"I do, too."

And she was gone.

He watched her stride briskly away down the deeply carpeted aisle. A rare female creature of surpassing beauty and intelligence. Fine ass, too.

CHAPTER 6

BEST FRIENDS FOREVER

THE NIGHT WAS LONG. Graveyard and Ambience fell asleep.
Then they woke up. The TV was still on. Tuned to who knew
what. Did it even matter? As far as Ambience was concerned, all
contemporary flicks were pretty much the same. Bombs, boobs,
and bamboozlement. She had to admit, though, to an incurable
fondness for Last Girl cinema. You know, the flawed B-variety type
where a group of terrified young people is besieged by a scary gang
of monsters, vampires, zombies, gangsters, terrorists, or just plain
bad guys who systematically pick them off one by one in as original
or unoriginal and grotesque a manner as possible until only one
potential victim is left, the sole survivor, the Last Girl, who then
proceeds to kick major ass in a shitstorm of gory carnage, wreaking
total vengeance on all those clowns who dared to inflict harm on
her and her friends. At the end our heroine staggers off, bruised,
battered, and bleeding, into a beautifully grim sunrise. Could there
be a more satisfying finale in all of cursed moviedom? Thank you.
She didn't think so, either.

She and Graveyard broke out a box of DaffyDingles. Toasted
grain product stuffed with smart chocolate, chunky nutjob butter,
and vilified jelly. They washed those goodies down with a couple
of bottles of NothingCola. It had no calories, no vitamins, no
nutrients. It tasted real good. Ambience suggested that the media
fever be dampened a degree or two. Put on something quieter for
a change. It was almost dawn, for Christ's sake. So Graveyard did.

Some ridiculous confection about a hundred and fifty years old. And in black and white yet. Ambience hated black and white. She liked all things bright and sparkly. Black and white reminded her too much of death. But she sat and she watched, and after a while, strangely enough, this odd little antiquity began working its old-timey charm upon her captivated brain. She wanted in. She wanted to walk around in that lost land for a day or two. See what it would be like to have not only money but also manners and wit. Imagine that. The picture, of course, was *All the Diamonds in the Lode*, starring TangledWeb and LimitedQuantity. It was about a beautiful young woman in a shiny, tighty gown who wakes up one night in a creepy back-lot alley and finds herself in the middle of a big strange metropolis with no memory, no ID, and no money. What to do? How about suss out some super-rich folks and hang on for dear life? Lucky for her, every man she meets from then on is both rich and handsome. Some are nice. Some are not so nice. Problem: how to tell the difference and still get some beans into your jar. Ambience was mesmerized. The film's message seemed to be: good looks and cash go together. Niceness doesn't go with anything. Was that true? Ambience didn't know. What she did know was that most movies seemed to be about smokin' people you'd like to fuck who were locked in a thrill ride to nowhere that didn't require you to think about much of anything at all. The picture satisfied those requirements. There were a couple of suave creatures of the night here whose tuxedos she wouldn't mind getting inside. And just about the time our curiously undistressed heroine had wormed her way into the welcoming embrace of an aristocratic family of zany millionaires, Ambience thought she heard a weird sound coming from outside their door.

"Did you hear something?" she said.

"No," said Graveyard.

"Kill the volume."

He did. They listened. Then they did hear something. Was it an actual knock? They couldn't really be sure. It sounded like someone gingerly tapping a pencil on the wood. The eraser end. Who could possibly be calling at this hour?

Graveyard went to the peephole and peeped out. "Warranty," he said.

"Let her in," said Ambience. Warranty was Ambience's best friend. She lived with her boyfriend, Herringbone, in the same building as Graveyard and Ambience. Second floor. Apt. 6. Graveyard unlocked the three locks and undid the chain. He opened the door. Warranty was standing alone out in the hallway. She didn't look good. Her cheeks were red and wet. Her face seemed all blown out. She looked like she'd been crying for hours. "I saw the light under the door," she said. "I was hoping you guys'd be here and that you'd still be awake."

"Well, we are," said Graveyard, "and we are. C'mon in."

"You're not answering your phone. What's going on?"

"The cells are off. The landline's on mute. We're on telephonic hiatus."

"I've been up here a couple times in the last few days. No one's ever home."

"We've been busy."

"What's wrong?" said Ambience, rolling herself as best she could out of the sticky embrace of the puffy chair.

"It's Herringbone," Warranty said. Then she stopped. She'd just gotten a long, hard take at her friends' transformed apartment. It looked like backstage at a fantastically popular game show. "What the —"

"I'll explain later," said Ambience. She removed a pile of fancy Pothole&Paradigm boxes from their second-best brand new couch, an authentic HighPlainsSofa personally autographed by DustyTroubles. "Here, sit down," she said. "What's up?"

"Oh, you know, the usual." But Warranty couldn't stop looking around the room. "This is absolutely amazing. What'd you guys do, win the lottery?"

"Something like that," said Ambience. She'd been dreading this moment.

"Ambience's Uncle Parsnips died," said Graveyard.

"Oh, I'm sorry."

"He was a big hedge fund manager at Whatnot&Turnstile. He left Ambience everything."

"I didn't know you had an Uncle Parsnips."

"I didn't, either."

"Until he died," said Graveyard.

"Apparently," said Ambience, "I was his favorite."

"Had you ever even met him?" said Warranty.

"Yeah, I guess, but I was very little. I don't remember."

Warranty looked at both of them. She looked at one. Then she looked at the other. She squinted. She looked again. "All right," she said. "What'd you really do? Rob a bank or something?"

"You've got a suspicious heart, Warranty," said Graveyard.

"It's a fibbing world, Graveyard."

Ambience removed a pile of glossy black RegalRegalia boxes from the other end of the couch and sat down next to Warranty. "Okay, so tell me."

"No, no. No off-topic bullshit. What's going on with Herring-bone and me is just the same old, same old. But this"—she made a grand sweeping motion with her arm that took in the entire cluttered room—"this is crazy sick." In the mess atop the brand new BurningWillowCollection mirrored coffee table her startled eye settled instinctively on a familiar leopard-skin design. "Is that really a bottle of MaybeAraby?"

Ambience reached over, picked up the box, and handed it to her. "It's yours."

"What? Are you serious?"

"Of course, silly."

"No, really, I couldn't. This stuff costs...well, a lot."

"But I want you to have it. Really." She pressed the perfume into Warranty's hand. "It's a gift."

Warranty studied the box, ran her fingers over the embossed gold label. "No one's ever given me something this nice since— uh, never."

"Well, now someone has," said Ambience.

Graveyard knelt down in front of Warranty. He spread a fan of bills between his hands. "Pick a card, any card."

Warranty hesitated. "I'm not used to touching this shit without my gloves on." She worked as a toll booth clerk on the Conundrum Bridge over the ReadyToWear River. Choking on vehicle exhaust, blowing off drivers' insults, fondling all that filthy, filthy lucre. The stuff was practically alive, crawling with germs, bugs, cooties, all manner of vile nastiness. She might as well be spending her days scrubbing toilets in a roll-and-groan motel. Or, better yet, how about pulling an eight that didn't require suiting up in a pair of tight latex gloves? Happiness now would be a high-end situation that did not require the handling of any legal tender whatsoever. Probably she'd developed a disorder of some kind. Fundage Phobia.

"C'mon," said Graveyard. He kept flashing the bills in front of her face. "Whaddya want, whaddya need?"

Her hand came forward. Her hand went back. "I don't know, Graveyard, I'd like to, but—"

"It's brand new, Warranty. Farm fresh. Untouched by human hands—except for yours truly, of course. And we all know how squeaky I am."

She looked dubious, but she reached out, plucked a crisp one hundred from the pack as if drawing a lot for an execution. "Now what?" she said. "Do I memorize the denomination and then put it back?"

"No, what you do now is, you take that pretty piece of paper in your hot little fist and you rush down to that fancy store you've always wanted to go in but were afraid to and you give it to a clerk in exchange for something you would never even have dreamed of buying until now."

"She needs more," said Ambience.

"Right. Here, take another." Graveyard quickly peeled off a second bill. "In fact, take three, four, five more." He counted them out. He handed them over to Warranty.

She stared at the notes in her hand as if they were a newly discovered collection of alien artifacts from outer space. "Thanks, Graveyard. God, your generosity. It's kinda overwhelming, and I really appreciate it, but, please, I can't accept this."

"Why not?" said Ambience.

"I don't know. I didn't do anything to deserve it."

"Neither did we."

"And we don't deserve it," said Graveyard. He didn't actually mean this. Frankly, he felt he deserved everything. And more. Why not?

"Don't go girly on us now," said Ambience. "Don't erase yourself. Woman up."

"Think of it as a special offering from the universe to you," said Graveyard. "No strings attached. Simply for being you. That's how we look at it."

"And we want to share our good fortune as much as possible," said Ambience. "It's fun."

"Well, all right," said Warranty. She managed a faint smile. "You've talked me into it." She looked at the money one more time. As if it were barely real. Then she carefully folded the bills and stuffed them into her jeans pocket.

"There," said Ambience. "That wasn't so hard, was it?"

"Wait till you work up the grit to actually spend some of it," said Graveyard. "See how that feels."

A cat's paw darted out from under the couch, slapped at a crumpled ball of wrapping paper, then disappeared back under the couch.

"PumpkinClaws thinks all this stuff is just for her," said Ambience.

"Maybe it is," said Graveyard.

Warranty couldn't stop staring. Everywhere she turned there was something new to stare at. "Looks like the party's been going on for quite a while now. So how long have you guys been rich, anyway?"

"That's just what we've been trying to figure out," said Ambience.

"Your time sense gets so whacked when something like this happens."

"We're guessing about a week," said Graveyard.

"A week?" said Warranty. She looked at Ambience. "A *week*? Why didn't you tell me? You could've called, at least." She picked up an unopened box from StressCode. She looked at it. She put it down. With measured deliberation. As if it might explode if handled improperly.

"Sorry," said Ambience.

"So I don't get it. Still your best friend, right?"

"How can you even ask that? Of course you are. But you don't understand. You don't know what we've been through. This whole week has been so fucking sketchy."

"We've told no one," said Graveyard. "No one. Not a single soul."

"Not even our families," said Ambience.

"You know how, when somebody wins the lottery, no one knows who it is cause the winners don't reveal themselves for days sometimes. They're too freaked out. They don't know what to do. They're searching for the best face to put on to the world. Well, that's us."

"And we're not exactly the most stable people," said Ambience.

"Here, have another party favor." Graveyard pulled a bill out of the roll in his hand.

"No, thanks," said Warranty. "I've got more than enough."

"You say that now..."

"You're looking better than when you first came in," said Ambience.

"What?" said Warranty. Her head had apparently drifted off to someplace else for a second. "Yeah. Oh, that. That was me and Herringbone at it again. You know how we do."

"What was it this time?"

"Oh, the usual routine. He's restless. He can't sleep. He wants company. So he wakes me up to listen to him rag on and on about QuipsJulienne, the new head honcho at BeginTheCuisine. He's apparently none too happy with Herringbone's folding style.

Makes you wonder just what sort of skill set is required to be a stupid napkin technician. Then it's on to the fifty TamperProof owes him that he's never gonna see again. Or the shocking levels of sodium in HastyTreats, which he wolfs down by the pound bag anyway. Whatever it is, I'm nodding off. I gotta be up by six. He knows that. Does he care? Hardly. So then he wants his back massaged but says my hands are too cold. Then he wants soup, hot beetle snooze soup. No got. Then how about some dopa dusted down meal? No got that, either. Then the whining. Then the moaning. Then the screaming. I lasted about a minute and a half. Sometimes I can't help but wonder just what the fuck is wrong with him."

"He's a guy," said Ambience.

"Herringbone being Herringbone," said Graveyard. He regretted the words about one second after they left his mouth, but it was too late.

"You wanna get cut with a brand new heirloom-quality piece of EternalEdge flatware?" Ambience retrieved said item from an open box at her feet. She waved the ornamental knife around the way everyone does who's been to the movies a time or two. "And don't think I'm kidding. Cause I don't know if I am or not."

Graveyard leaned over and calmly lifted the blade from her hand. "You need sleep," he said.

"And you need some sense."

"Guys, please," said Warranty. "Let's not have a replay of what I just left downstairs."

"Have another hundred," said Graveyard. He passed her a fresh bill.

She hesitated, she hesitated, she hesitated, but she took it. Into the jeans pocket stuffed.

"Oh, yeah," said Ambience. "That solves everything."

"Prove me wrong."

Then came a series of knocks at the door that sounded like actual knocks. Bone on wood. Rat-a-tat-tat.

"I wonder who that could be," said Warranty.

"Let him in," said Ambience.

Graveyard did.

"Sorry to bother you guys at this hour," said Herringbone, "but did Warranty happen to—" Then he saw his girlfriend sitting calmly on the couch. Then he saw the rest of the room. "Holy fuck," he said. "What the hell happened in here? Looks like a mall exploded or something."

"We won the lottery," said Ambience.

"Ambience's rich Uncle Parsnips died," said Graveyard.

"And left you his lottery ticket?" said Herringbone.

"Something like that," said Graveyard. "Anyway, come in. Sit down." He patted a clear space on the big leather couch.

"You okay?" said Herringbone.

"Yeah," said Warranty.

"I'm sorry."

"Okay."

"I went off my meds."

"You're not on any meds."

"You know what I mean."

"Anyone care for a drink?" said Graveyard.

"Why not?" said Warranty. In two hours she had to leave for work. What a day this was turning out to be.

"Come in the kitchen," said Ambience. "See the new toys."

So they did. They gathered first around the brand new fridge, the don't-even-ask-the-price NorthernLightsCoolerator.

"It's got a glass window you can look in," said Warranty. She looked in. "Cool."

"LED interior lighting, too," said Graveyard. "Exterior temperature display, push-button shelves and storage bins, and built-in bacterial filters. Those spigots in the door. One's for GlacialEuphoriaReserve bottled water. The other's for limited-edition AllHailAle." He opened the door. There was nothing inside but champagne and chocolate. The champagne was vintage

BlackAndWhiteImperialConsortium, and the chocolate was, of course, TaprootAndJester's PremiumFlavanolIngots. He opened the freezer. It was full of brand new jewelry. Ambience's little joke. Ice on ice.

They sampled the champagne. They sampled the chocolate. They sampled the one. They sampled the other. Then they sampled again.

Next, drinks in hand (in the individually crafted Mandarin flutes from AzimuthHouse), they admired the brand new EnchantedScullery toaster with automatically adjustable bread cages, a one-slice option, and twelve brownness settings.

"I love the smell of toast," said Warranty.

"It has a tiny fan underneath," said Graveyard. "To waft the intoxicating aroma throughout your bedchambers."

"Really?"

"With a voice-activated control system that responds to instructions in fourteen different languages and then, at the end, butters your toast."

Warranty nudged Graveyard with her hip. Of course, there was a charge back and forth. There'd been a charge back and forth for years now. It was what made knowing each other so much fun for all this time. "You are such a weasel," she said. "But I want one anyway."

They looked at the GammaHosanna microwave. They looked at the WhirlyBurly blender. They looked at the BurntOfferings stove. Blah, blah, blah, blah, blah.

"Wanna see my new clothes?" said Ambience.

"Twist my arm, girl," said Warranty.

They left the kitchen. Edging sideways down the narrow hallway to the bedroom. Narrower than usual because the hallway was lined with stacked boxes of LaughFrogg, an aged single malt whiskey (cask strength) from an aged double-damned land. Graveyard's favorite. He didn't want to run out of that particular spirit ever again.

Graveyard and Herringbone refilled their flutes. They toasted each other. "Here's to your head, your heart, your glass, and your wallet," said Graveyard. "May they all be ever overflowing." They wandered back out into the living room. The BlackAndWhite-ImperialConsortium bottle clutched firmly in Graveyard's hand.

"A HootchieCootchie," said Herringbone, staring at the huge mounted TV. "Impressive. What'd that set you back?"

"Oh, a kopeck or two, I think."

"You don't know?"

"Frankly, Herringbone, if you'd have scattered as many notes as we have across the past howevermany days of the week, you'd have discovered, as we have, that numbers plus or minus tend to achieve a kind of hazy delirium in which everything blends with everything else to produce a pleasing rush you don't necessarily want to question. You know, the way it should be."

"Whatcha watching?"

"Oh, just some Stone Age crap Ambience wanted to see. Here, let me really show you something." He replaced *Diamonds* with *Eschatology Force II*. Hit the clicker a couple of times. Scene: two big guys in a little room, knocking the holy crap outta each other. One gets on top of the other. Close-up: a pair of stubby thumbs pressing down hard into the grimacing bottom guy's eyeballs. The thumbs keep pressing. The bottom guy screams. Suddenly the eyeballs pop into the air like a couple of bloody grapes.

"Whoa!" said Herringbone.

"And not a single detail lost on our exclusive all-encompassing MannaVision. But here, something even better." Graveyard bent down, rooted around in a plain brown box on the floor for a few seconds, then stood up, triumphantly displaying in his hand a pricey Better Day copy of the rare *Pork in Your Purse*.

"Is that the one with MelodyAssets?"

"The very same." He removed *Eschatology Force* from the player and inserted the legendary porn disc. "Now let's get right to it by jumping ahead to chapter three."

They stood there and watched in silence. For quite a while.

"Fuck," said Herringbone. "I think I can see the taste buds on her tongue."

"Multiple angles," said Graveyard. He hit a button on the clicker once, twice, thrice. And indeed there were multiple angles—one, two, three.

"They should have that on regular movies," said Herringbone.

"And in real life," said Graveyard.

They watched for a while.

"I didn't know that was physically possible," said Herringbone.

"Look—you can see her toe prints on the guy's skin."

The naked people did what naked people do when a camera is placed in front of them. The guys made the comments guys make when looking at naked people.

Then Graveyard said, "Wanna go look at some guns?"

"Aw," said Herringbone, "do I have to? Didn't I look at guns the last time I was up here? And the time before that, and et cetera, et cetera?"

"These are new guns. Some still in the box."

"What are those? Collectibles?"

"C'mon, man, you know you want to."

Graveyard liked guns. He wasn't supposed to. Not with his education, his politics, his assigned peer group. He wasn't supposed to, but he did. He couldn't help it. He liked looking at them. He liked holding them. He liked shooting them.

"Tell you what: give me a double shot of LaughFrogg and I'll go look at a howitzer with you. Provided you got one."

"Done."

"And, uh, oh, yeah, one other thing,"

"What's that?"

"Believe me when I say this. I hate to even bring it up."

"Yeah?"

"Hokum's vet bill was six hundred bucks." Hokum was their dog. She had heartworm disease.

Graveyard waited.

"That was a healthy chunk of our rent money. The size of the chunk that it's a chunk of, you don't want to know. Warranty and I, well, we're behind." He was smiling as well as he could.

"I knew you had balls," said Graveyard. "I didn't know how big. You and Warranty are the first and the only breathing souls we've even told about this eruption of freakin' luck into our lives, and not ten minutes after getting the news you're hitting on me. Unfuckingbelievable."

"What can I say?"

"How about, 'Could you spread those cheeks a little wider, please?'"

"That's not fair."

"What's fairness got to do with anything on this planet?"

"I'm sorry. I was desperate. I'm not myself these days."

"Who is?"

"You're a good friend. You've always been a good friend. I don't want to fuck that up. I just don't know anybody else who's got any excess cash lying around."

"You see any excess cash lying around here?"

"Uh, no, but I see plenty of the stuff that that cash gets you."

"What's the rent?"

Herringbone named a figure.

"You're kidding me. For that cramped shoe box? Worse than the extortion pried out of Ambience and me for the privilege of residing in our palatial digs."

"You've been here longer. You came in on a lower rate."

"Hold out your hand."

Herringbone did. Graveyard pulled the thick wad of hundreds from his pocket and counted them out, one at a time, into Herringbone's outstretched palm.

"Thank you," said Herringbone. "The words can't begin to express the actual sentiment. Thank you very much. I don't think you know how deeply I appreciate this."

"On the contrary," said Graveyard. "I think I know most certainly exactly how you feel. Now, can we go look at some guns, please?"

"I'm right behind you."

They went down the hallway to the walk-in closet. The door was locked. Of course. Graveyard fiddled with his ring of keys. He opened the door. They walked in.

Graveyard pulled down a box.

"Look," he said. "A MadderRose114 with moonscape sights and an insect-shell finish. Very light, very portable, yet packs a very severe punch."

"Should I be impressed?"

"Yeah, most definitely. They only made fifteen hundred of 'em to start with. I've got one. The Mystery Whispery Teams got the rest."

"Okay, nice, what else?"

Graveyard opened a cabinet. Pulled out one heavy meany weapon. "It's a HyperSniperM98 bolt action with a CosmicHiBeam scope and adjustable cheek piece, of course. Shoots emerald bullets, which, as you might imagine, are not exactly cheap. One just like this was used to kill BigBurden himself a couple of years back."

"What's that?" Herringbone pointed to an ugly mess of tubing that looked like some wacko plumber's failed art project.

"A GoldenShowerStreetWiper. On automatic, shoots five rounds a second. Supposedly can take out around twenty-five hundred people in about two minutes."

"Now you're really scaring me."

But wait, there was more. Lots more. The Humiliator. An over-and-under versatile platform highly effective at close ranges. The PocketDrillM180 with a secret reserve chamber containing five extra emergency rounds for those tight moments in tight places. And the LastJudgment, its silver-plated barrel engraved with life-like drawings of couples engaged in sexual positions most people couldn't even begin to imagine.

"That's pretty direct," said Herringbone.

"Yeah, and the gun's language is pretty blunt."

"What'd that cost ya?"

"I'm too embarrassed to say."

"I think if I didn't know you so well," said Herringbone, "I'd probably take you for one of those nutso skyfallers."

"Hell, who wouldn't? But don't forget, over this country the sky is always falling."

"That's why I don't go out much."

"And it's all just one big monster goof anyway. I've got the money. I've got the time. Why not indulge my goofiness? Isn't that what you'd do in my place? I mean, really."

"I suppose."

"So what is it?"

"What?"

"Your goof?"

"How should I know?"

"You're not used to thinking about flushing away mad money."

"I've never had any mad money to flush."

"Ah, but what if you did?"

"Well, if I really let myself go, I guess I'd probably travel some-where. Sky off to one of those orange-tiled-roof countries. They look nice. Quiet and clean. Good-looking light. The asshole ratio among the inhabitants probably lower than here. I would think everything moves along at a slower pace than it does here. Much slower. Pleas-antly slower. Probably they even move through time differently."

"Is this place real?"

"In my head it is. And when I got there, I betcha it'd be real in person, too."

"And that's where you'd write your book. Your great novel."

"Yeah. I guess."

Herringbone's not-so-secret secret. He'd always wanted to be a writer. Not quite as far-fetched a scheme as being a tinker or a tailor or a soldier or, yes, a rock star. But what do you want? He was an inmate of his times. Anyway, none of those earlier fantasies, he'd regretfully concluded, was ever going to pass over into experience. He supposed in some way that all he really wanted to do was just to make a mark of some kind, no matter how small, just one tiny scratch upon the great stone face of the world that said simply: I was here. He had a ratty folder in his desk at home filled with all the stories he'd ever written. He hated all of them. He'd twice tried writing something longer, but both times the tank had run dry in the same place, around page 50. Recently, though, he'd been gifted with a new idea: how about a book about an author writing a book about how to write a book? His own frustrations, blockages, and dejections would be the very stuff of the novel. The idea excited him. This I can make something of, he often said to himself. And, of course, he had before him the example of his favorite writer, OutOfPocket. OutOfPocket was one of the big-tent fictioneers of the day. His first novel, *Absorption!*, had won the ultra you're-the-top Pound Cake Prize and was zooming through multiple printings too numerous to count; his second, the wonderfully overwrought *Hope and Redemption Diet Cookbook*, a narrative in verse and recipes, had been, remarkably, baked into a steamy cinematic concoction starring both HotsieTotsie and SeldomAlone—box office bingo. And then, of course, there was the magisterial *Writers in Love*, which contained dozens of lifelike characters you could not only identify with but also want to invite to dinner. Today, OutOfPocket lived in a moated castle high atop Mount ShoeHorn. No visitors.

"We gotta get you out to the BulletBoutique and cut loose with these bad boys," said Graveyard. "Whaddya say?"

"You've been trying to get me to that range for years."

"And you always come up with some lame excuse."

"I'm a busy man."

"Doing what?"

"Folding napkins and fighting with my girlfriend."

"That doesn't even meet the criteria for 'lame.'"

Herringbone was studying the StreetWiper as if there were one particular way of looking at the gun that would suddenly reveal it for exactly what it was.

"C'mon, you know you want to. And listen, it might actually be fun."

"I'm not a gun guy."

"How do you know? I didn't think I was, either, until my roommate at Porcupine dragged me out once to this quarry in the country where we busted up a bunch of melons and empty vodka bottles. Turned out, amazingly enough, I wasn't half bad at target shooting. And that roommate's now—wait for it—Secretary of Rashes&Eruptions in the MadeForYou administration. So you never know."

"All right, you're getting to me."

"Tell you what: you don't find our little excursion into the wicked realm of glitzy weaponry the best crazy-ass time you've had since the last Gizmo and the BlowingChunks concert, I'll treat you to the BlueStar dinner at ForeignSubstancesOnTheSquare."

"I was high as a silkbird during that thing."

"So? Here's a chance to get off on propelling tiny bits of metal at three thousand feet per second into menacing paper people with numbered kill zones printed on their bodies."

"Peachy."

"You wait. You'll get over there, get locked in behind one of them state-of-the-art Tagged&Bagged variable power sights, Forma-Cushion stock hugging your shoulder like a contour pillow, tons of bangbang ready to be unleashed at the slightest twitch of your pointy finger, and you'll wonder where this mad dog experience has been all your life."

"I don't know. Where has it been? Let me guess. Hidden behind the target?"

"Beans and brie," said Graveyard. "Hidden behind the target."

Meanwhile, back at the ranch, behind the closed bedroom door, the women were talking clothes. Turned out the bed was piled seriously high with 'em.

"But where do you sleep?" said Warranty.

"Right here," said Ambience. "That's just stuff I bought yesterday.

We haven't even been to bed yet. Actually, we don't sleep all that much anymore. It's like money is speed, you know."

"Gotcha," said Warranty. She was fingering the unworldly sheen of the dresses. "ResidualWear, LiquoricePop, CausticCollective, even MemoriesOf. This place looks like the dressing room at Beggar&Peasant's."

"I did pretty well, didn't I?" said Ambience.

"I've never seen so much off-the-rack girly power gathered to-gether in any one place. Ever. I suppose this is what they mean by the Bomb."

"Yeah. I plan on taking out major cities with this stuff."

"Complete annihilation."

"Totally," said Ambience. "Look, we're the same size. See any-thing you like?"

"Are you kidding me?"

"Take whatever you want. There's plenty more where that came from."

"Well…"

She didn't need much encouragement. She picked out a MeowMeow and a La-di-dah. Maybe having money wasn't so bad. She was one of those people who felt they weren't supposed to, in this life, at least, have all that much of it. When she was done, Ambience gave her a big hug. They said they loved each other. Then they moved on to the shoe closet. The mother lode. Name a brand and Ambience had it. She had Atchoos and Bustershanks. She had OhNoNos.

"Same thing," said Ambience. "If the shoe fits, wear it."

"No, I can't. You've given me too much already."

"Not even close. Look, I see this as a share-the-wealth sort of deal, okay? Don't stress about money. Worry about what you like, what you don't like. Isn't that all that really matters, anyway?"

"God, how'd you get to be so smart, Ambience?"

"Dumb luck, I guess. Now, pick out some rockin' pumps."

So Warranty did. Right. Maybe having money wasn't so bad. If she said it often enough, she just might believe it. In fact, hooray for money. She needed plenty more of the fresh green in her life, that was for sure. She put on the SassyStomps. The ones with the famous amazing checkerboard soles. She paraded back and forth in front of the closet-door mirror, carefully eyeing her strut. She was definitely too fat, but still, she liked what she saw.

"You look good in those," said Ambience. "Real spankin'. They're yours."

Warranty started to say something.

"Don't say anything," said Ambience. "Don't spoil it."

"I was going to say I think you look good, too. Even without the pricey duds. Actually, it's kinda incredible. You look, I don't know, absolutely amazing. Like you swallowed a lightbulb or something. You are positively illuminated."

"Well, there is this." Ambience gestured helplessly at the ridiculous heaps of consumer goods.

"Yes, yes, but there's something else, too." She grabbed hold of Ambience's hand. She peered intently into Ambience's eyes. "Oh, my God," she said. The burned-circles look was gone. "You and Graveyard are having sex again, aren't you? C'mon, admit it. Can't fool me. You are, aren't you?"

"Like bunnies. We can't stop."

Warranty busted out a big smile. "Congratulations," she said.

"It's all this fucking dough," said Ambience. "It's like chocolate, oysters, and poppers all in one."

"Does everyone know this but me?"

"Look, I didn't know, either, till I was on the far side of the money moon."

"Sounds like a serious burn. How long you think it'll last?"

"I honestly don't care. I'm riding it to the end."

"You're my hero."

"But what about you, Warranty? You just got a bunch of new stuff. How do *you* feel right now?"

"I don't know. Good?"

"But you'd like to feel gooder, right?"

"Yeah, I suppose."

"Well."

"Thing is, I'm not feeling so kindly about Mr. Herringbone right now."

Ambience picked up a CoolHand skirt from off the bed. She handed it to Warranty. "How about now?"

"I don't know."

Ambience handed her a flashy pair of SweetAndHighUp slingbacks.

"Okay, I get it. I'll give you a full report later."

"Of course, this is all well and good," said Ambience. "But isn't there something else, something you've always wanted really, really badly, but so badly you were afraid to ask because you always knew deep down you were never going to get it anyway?"

"Well, there is one thing."

"What's that?"

"I can't. You'll think it's silly or stupid."

"No, I won't. Promise. And the evidence of my own silly and stupid desires lies pretty plainly all around us."

"Well…"

"Go ahead."

"Something I've always wanted ever since I was a little girl."

"Yeah?"

"And I still want it."

"Yeah?"

"A pony."

Warranty looked at Ambience. Ambience looked at Warranty. One laughed. The other laughed. They both laughed. Then they couldn't stop laughing.

CHAPTER 7

A COUPLE OF FUCKS

DELICATESEAR HAD GREAT FEET and she knew it. How many people could say that? And she'd seduced a fair number of sexual stooges with those dainty assets. They'd been caressed, fondled, stroked, licked, sucked, whispered to, and manjuiced on. Consumer satisfaction guaranteed. Unfortunately, the Mr. Pig she was sharing her sheets with at the present moment was obviously not a foot man. He didn't appear to be a tits or ass man, either. Despite her epic boobs. He was interested in only one thing: her vaguery. (Well, that was what she called it.) Ordinarily, this wouldn't be an issue. It should be, of course, a yummy plus plus benefits. Except that this guy's head looked like a potato, he hadn't shaved in three days, his tongue felt like a dying slug, and he smelled like the terrarium she'd kept her pet turtle in when she was nine. She'd picked him up at the IPO party the day GlobalCompass announced the introduction of the BlowHorn8G. He, of course, thought he'd picked her up. Typical. These shithole keypunchers couldn't tell bacon from baloney. Which made the whole school of 'em easy prey for someone like DelicateSear, who trolled the well-stocked corporate waters on a weekly, if not daily, basis, searching for the minnows who regularly mistook themselves for whales. Rich harvest. Lucrative as hell. Unfortunately, one tended to encounter an irritating number of throwbacks. This was one of 'em. He'd already dumped a load of warm paste on her thigh. Now he was displaying for her another pathetic erection. And expecting compliments, no doubt.

She couldn't even remember the dude's name. Estuary or Actuary or some such shit. She excused herself, wrapped herself in a sheet, and made her way to the bathroom. She looked at herself in the mirror. Not good. The face wasn't the one she remembered having last time she looked in a mirror. This version was the discontinued, marked-down variety. The one you picked up on a whim to wear to a low-rent costume party where everyone was slumming for the night and enjoying the relief from the usual required gorgeosity. Also, she was too fat.

She sat on the toilet seat for about ten minutes. Nothing. Mr. Pig yelled something. She couldn't understand a word. After a while, she got up, splashed some cold water on her face, and returned to the arena.

Mr. Pig was sitting up in bed and actually flossing his teeth.

"Make yourself at home," DelicateSear said.

"Do you have any GlacialEuphoriaReserve?"

"I only drink tap."

"Get me a glass."

So she did. Still wrapped in the sheet, trying not to trip over herself, she made her clumsy way to the kitchen, flipped on the light. What she wouldn't do for unlove. See, she hadn't quite decided yet whether she was actually done with this guy. You could never really know. She filled a glass, carried it back to the bedroom.

He took a sip. "I can taste the crud in this," he said, putting the glass down. "Do yourself a favor. Don't subject your body to such swill. Use a filter, like me. And a good one, not one of those shitty loose-carbon jobs, either. They're breeding grounds for all kind of exotic bacteria you don't even want to think about. Get yourself a solid carbon block reverse-osmosis system. The BioElite is pretty good. That's what I've got. Pricey, but what's your health worth to you, anyway? Otherwise, you're just hosing down your internals with a sweet cocktail of germs, viruses, cysts, chemicals like lead and arsenic, industrial pollutants like nitrate and trihalomethane, and, of course, every drug ever invented in the history of the world—

all the uppers, all the downers, all the steroids, all the hormones. Even estrogen—can you believe it? The goddamn fish are getting feminized. It's a wonder we're not all walking around totally cataloged just from what we're pouring into our bellies from the tap. And don't forget defocaine, tons of defocaine. You know, everything you drink, eat, and touch in this country, including all our money, carries traces of defocaine. Not many people know that."

"That's why I lick everything twice before touching it."

"I never go near the stuff myself. I've seen what it can do to people."

"What? Talons and horns?"

"You know. You lose track of what's important."

"Which would be?"

"Making money, of course. Now get over here and make me some happy."

So she did. He'd told her earlier that he worshipped his penis and that she should, too. She tried and she tried. No go. She figured she probably wasn't much of an idolator. He finally managed to get the thing inside without spilling any cargo on the landing strip. For which they were both grateful. And then it (whatever it was) was, thankfully, over. The verdict? Well, not the best, but not the worst, either. Wait a minute. What was she saying? Of course it was the worst. The worst of the worst. She hoped to never have to undergo such an experience again. In minutes he was snoring like a walrus. And she was in the john cleaning herself up. One of those fun head-to-toe jobs. Every adult bathroom should come equipped with a special chamber you step inside of after sex where you are magically dry-cleaned and disinfected in mere instamoments, and, and most important, relieved of any psychic parasites your partner may have, wittingly or not, infected you with. A function equally effective, of course, for deleting the troubling aftereffects of septic social encounters. The Expungerator. Go invent that, somebody. She looked at herself in the mirror. She had previously noted that how you appeared to yourself in an unforgiving mirror was directly proportional to how you were feeling at that particular moment. She wasn't feeling good. Period.

Two hours later Mr. Pig was gone. She'd wakened him up. With all apologies. She didn't want to be rude, but she had to be at an important confab at some ridiculously early hour. Which was true, or partly true, or whatever portion of true she wanted it to be. Plus she found it nearly impossible to get a decent night's rest lying in bed next to a virtual stranger. Or even lying in bed next to a good friend, for that matter. Mr. Pig was not happy. He gathered up his bulk and his clothes. He called her names. She didn't respond. She'd heard them all before. Whatever it took to get this stiff outta here. He huffed. He puffed. But in the end he went away like a good little boy.

She changed the sheets. She sprayed the room with GrottoGusto. She popped a couple tabs of Oblivia. While waiting for the chemicals to get up to her brain, she clicked through a mental review of her exes. What a rogues' gallery. A few good, too many not so good. Why'd he do that? Why'd she do this? The permutations of blame were infinite. Her version of counting sheep. And finally, who were they all, anyway? She wasn't sure she even knew. Oh, she was acutely aware of everyone's internoodle crap, those minutely managed likes and dislikes. But was that all anyone was? A collection of superficial tics? Maybe. She didn't know. Yet there was some shiny stuff amidst the wreckage. Paraphernalia, for instance. He was kind. Relatively. He was generous. Relatively. He never got on her nerves too much. Except for that thankfully brief period when he got fed up with investment banking and decided to try cooking, on a purely experimental basis only, and habitually left the kitchen looking like a high school chemistry lab after a fire drill. And DigitalNoise. Her first husband. He carried some good memories she could wallow around in for a while. This was in Bludgeontown, across the river, when they were poor and everyone had a scraggly lawn and lived in a crumbling house and no one had any money. Odd little moments of such seeming insignificance you wouldn't think they'd be remembered by anyone at all. He was sitting across from her at dinner in a restaurant they really couldn't afford. She looked at him. She asked him if he was happy. He said he wasn't sure anymore what that meant. She asked him if he was happy right now, sitting there with her. He looked at her. She looked at him. There was so much going on in his face she couldn't take it all in. No one moved. No one spoke. That's all. A handful of seconds so loaded with meaning they never really went away. Was that love? She suspected it probably was. Then she slept.

Later, somewhere in the dankest well of the night, she was asleep, then she was awake, passing instantly from nothingness to every-thingness, eyelids snapping abruptly open on a pair of human legs standing right next to her bed, not a foot away from her head.

"What the—" she said, her panicked self pulling quickly away.

"You're outta milk," said a voice. Okay, relax. It was only BlisterPac.

"Give me a heart attack, why don't you?"

"You're tough. You can take it."

She had her hand on her chest and appeared to be listening down into herself. "I can hear my pulse in my head."

"Oh, chill out. This was a good exercise. Keeps those reflexes toned."

"Ever consider the possibility you might get shot?"

"Frankly, no. It never occurs to me I might get shot. And you told me once you refuse to keep a gun in your apartment. You said it would be like owning a venomous snake."

"I don't always tell the truth."

"Good M.O."

"How do I ever forgive you for this?"

"Prayer and contemplation?"

"I'm not going to get angry. I'm done with that. And I don't drink milk."

"Then what do you put on your KrunchyChunks here?" He had a bowl of them in one hand, a spoon in the other.

"I eat 'em raw. With my hands. Like a wild animal."

"So primal. Who would've thunk?" He sat down on the end of the bed and began shoveling the gravel-shaped confections into his mouth.

"I can be a lot of things," she said. "A lot of strange, wild things."

"Tell me."

She watched him eat. Then she said, "Just what, may I ask, are you doing here, exactly?"

"I had some free time."

She glanced at the clock. "At four thirty-seven in the a.m."

BlisterPac shrugged. "I was up."

"Priceless, you know," she said. "That's what you are."

"So people tell me."

"Okay, out. Let me get myself together. And close the door on your way."

She was naked under the covers. So she got up and threw on a popping-blue silk bathrobe she had had custom made for her in the gated district of a really expensive city really far away. She ran a brush through her hair and then checked the mirror to see which face she happened to be wearing at the moment. She approved.

In the living room she found BlisterPac sprawled across the bone-white Comber&Wrack sectional in front of the God-knows-how-many-inches optical platform. He was watching an extremely loud infomercial for DemonBeGone. Is your house talking back to you? Are precious loved ones changing shape before your very eyes? Pets refusing to come indoors, even out of the rain? Do you feel as if your own personal body is not really yours? If so, you may be suffering the symptoms of a total demon infestation. And we can help. A century's worth of proven techniques. We are licensed to eradicate demons, sprites, spooks, fairies, ghosts, poltergeists, banshees, gremlins, apparitions of every order, exotics like jinn, incubi, succubi, lamia, lemures, and countless miscellaneous manifestations that don't even have proper names. Satisfaction guaranteed. Call 1-666-666-6666. Why wait? Be demon-free now.

"Pretty cheap," said BlisterPac. "Considering. Your entire soul gets a thorough wash and rinse. And they do pets and children under five for free."

"My soul's been out on loan for years."

"Yeah?"

"Don't look at me like that. I'm not talking about it."

"You're such a tease."

"That's how I make my living."

"Look, man," said BlisterPac, pointing to the screen, "if you act now, you also get as a free bonus gift a convenient travel-size tube of DemonBalm for those unexpected paranormal encounters on the road."

"I thought we were supposed to be doing this tomorrow... well, actually, today at ten a.m."

"Business? Already? So cold and impersonal. I like it."

"I'd like it better if we were kicking back in a private power booth at Bassinet. Enjoying a couple large flagons of Militarized-Peninsulas."

"Who says we can't?"

"Yeah, what would be the point? You decided you had to see me now. For reasons known, or perhaps unknown, only to you. Kinda selfish and thoughtless, don't you think?"

"I was under the impression this job was important."

"It is. But okay, you win, you're right, why waste breath arguing about date and time? You're on your own schedule. You've always been on your own schedule."

They'd met when both had ended up together on the Mammoth City Police Department's Special Anti-NastyBusiness Unit. By then BlisterPac was already a known commodity for certain redacted achievements on behalf of various acronymic organizations. Known at least within the secret inner circles of secret circles. He'd been a member of the teams that assassinated RootieKazootie and abducted MercyMe from the ThinOzoneGang. He'd helped thwart the SackTiedInMiddleReservoirContamination. He was involved in the toxic little-green-apples scare and tracking down the source of the OoLaLa virus. Ever hear of any of these operations? Few people have. No news is good news. Now, thanks to DelicateSear, he was a "paid business consultant" to NationalProcedures, Inc., where he did less, much less, for more, much more.

"Maybe I got a bit excited. No calls in eight months. Ever since the PrettyShards fiasco. I'm an old horse. I heard the fire bells."

"Well, this probably isn't any bigger than a two-alarm blaze. If that."

She explained the MisterMenu matter. It didn't take long.

"I don't see much of a problem here," said BlisterPac.

"Neither do I."

"How hard you want me to lean on the guy?"

"You'd be a better judge of that than I. He'll probably give up the bag if you just ask. Politely, of course."

"I'm always polite."

"Not OffLine and BreakfastNook polite."

"What was I supposed to do? They were OffLine and BreakfastNook."

"I've seen the surveillance on this guy. Just ease on down."

"My smile is devastating. As you well know." Then he provided a sample.

"Killer."

"Listen," said BlisterPac, "you wanna fuck?"

DelicateSear considered for a moment. "Why not?" she said.

So they did. His dick was as gnarly as she remembered it. All stubby and veiny and exceedingly hairy. Kinda sexy, though, in a mildly perverse sort of way. She didn't orgasm, but she might have come close. Even through the condom, she could feel him squirting into her. Kinda nice.

CHAPTER 8

TROLLING FOR TREATS

"WHERE YOU GOING?" said Ambience.

"Out," said Graveyard. He had his keys in his hand. He was headed toward the door.

"Unacceptable."

"I don't know where I'm going. All right?" Sometimes, lately, he had so much energy knocking up against his walls he just had to get out and walk. Just go. Go anywhere. Burn off the excess. "Wanna come?" Sometimes Ambience came with him. Sometimes she didn't.

"How long you gonna be?"

"I don't know."

"Bring me something."

"What?"

"Surprise me."

"Don't I always?"

Graveyard and Ambience lived in a part of town that started the weekend on Wednesday night. Okay by Graveyard. Fine with him if every day was a weekend day. Without clocks, without demands, especially without bosses. He wanted to go to bed when he wanted. He wanted to get up when he wanted. In between he wanted to do what he wanted. An attitude not notably congruent with the demands of the corporate plantation everyone was now happily born into. You can't say he hadn't tried to pull his weight. A distinguished graduate of Porcupine University, he applied for and was typically granted a

slot within every position for which his degree in Advanced Marketing Me had more than adequately prepared him. A partial résumé:
apprentice weed puller for WeedsAin'tYou; professional desktop
arranger for the harried executive who, frankly, couldn't be bothered; bottle turner at the BetterThanVinegar wine company; official
counter at the trials of the GuessTheNumberOfJellyBeansInTheJar
Contest world championships; toupee handler for ImmaNoFool
of LearnToBeAsFilthyRichAsMe Enterprises; happy cup chemist;
living sculpture to brighten up a spartan business office; ticket
taker at FreaksOnTheBeach; and, his best job so far, assistant to
the personal assistant to BrazenRodentCheeks (before the disgrace-
ment), the controlling owner of every scrap of that valuable strip
of suburban lawn located between the sidewalk and the street from
coast to coast and there's nothing you can do about it. And, of
course, there was also the fab tentacled world of the computer
godhead, where he served variously as a compubandageroller, a
compupageturner, a compub.s.artist, a compupipejockey, a compu-
caddy, a compupolesitter, a compubottlewasher, a compugroomer,
a compuhandmodel, and, his favorite, a computrashcollector, a
gig that allowed him to keep whatever valuables he happened to
find in pursuit of his duties. Curiously enough, not one of these
golden opportunities had ever blossomed into full-time permanent
employment. Maybe he was still trying to find himself. That's what
people said. He tended to agree. Though whoever was running this
show had managed to hide him away from himself so thoroughly
he was still searching after more than twenty years on the hunt and
could report little success. The only occupation he had discovered
so far that he actually enjoyed was the one he presently held:
good-for-nothing idler. A leisure style requiring, of course, a comfy
cushion of coin. Like maybe having a bag of the good stuff fall
out of the sky onto your head. The moment kept going round and
round in his skull. Like a tune he couldn't shake. In the city you
often heard about the dangers of falling objects: bricks, tiles, pieces
of scaffolding, flowerpots, air conditioners. And when a pedestrian

took a direct hit, the resulting splat was not usually very pretty. And look how close he himself had come to being reduced to little more than a stain on the sidewalk. Actually, factually, dead. Miracle number one: he was still above ground. Miracle number two: what had nearly flattened him had made him impossibly rich. Was there a meaning in all this? Damned if he knew. Of one thing he was certain: his gain was someone else's loss and that someone was probably quite agitated by now and that what was in the bag was no doubt dirty and now he was dirty, too. Why not? People who had sacks of loot lying around their apartments were probably not "nice" people. They had probably acquired their "proceeds" in not very "nice" ways. And when they lost their acquisitions, particularly large sums of acquisition, they tended to get less nice. He had gone over the ground dozens of times. So far he didn't see any way he could possibly be traced. Anonymity was the best disguise. Just another innocuous number in a teeming hive of numbers. Money? What money? I don't got no money.

Everyone outside today looked bright and vivid. Everyone looked new, as if they had just been freshly minted. All their edges had been enhanced. A remarkable sight he'd never really experienced before. He didn't know it was possible for skin and hair to appear so well packaged. Today everyone looked famous. Even the well-scrubbed hipsters stuffing their faces at fenced-in sidewalk tables outside the Colloidium appeared to be actually enjoying their lives. Graveyard'd sit down and join them, order something obscenely pricey, like the cup of a half dozen handpicked duffelberries for $17.95 or the Standing Water Consommé for twenty-five dollars, but he was in no mood for sitting or eating. He needed to get out of his neighborhood, where everything reminded him of something in his life he didn't want to be reminded of.

He needed to travel to another country. He hailed a cab—he could afford it—and hopped uptown to the exotic TooGoodForYou district. Formerly the Forbidden Zone, now his favorite twenty blocks. Except for the occasional flash of fine tailoring, folks here looked pretty much like folks anywhere. They just had fatter wallets. And skinnier bodies. And noses expertly tuned for grace and comfort. Even the streets seemed air-conditioned. Veteran residents of these consecrated blocks had always known what Graveyard had just learned: happiness is a warm coat of money. A thick, a doubly thick coat. To live here, which admittedly might be fun, he'd still need another bag or two or three of the long green. Wait—what was he saying? He'd need a virtual bombardment of bags. An intense carpet bombing. What he could do now, though, was wander around the antechambers of the wealthy, soaking up the gravid atmosphere where everyone who was rich and well tended was looking at everyone else who was rich and well tended and disapproving of what they saw. Graveyard fit right in. He looked in a window. I can buy this, he said to himself. He looked in that window. I can buy that, he said to himself. And sometimes, just to prove he could, he rushed into a store and bought something he couldn't give a rat's ass about simply because it was priced beyond all limits of reason. What pleasure that gave him.

And there were real famous people, too, all over the place. On just this one afternoon he saw Cartwheel and FancyPants. They were holding hands. Must've patched things up since that very public brawl last spring on the island of Boolaboola. Graveyard had seen the full story on the celeb-besotted InYourEar cable channel. He liked to pretend otherwise, but to be embarrassingly candid, that's where he got most of his news. He saw OverAge. He was wearing white shorts. He had a rally-red tattoo on his right calf depicting a devil nun with horns and a tail giving the finger with one hand and smoking a cigarette with the other. Who would've thunk? And he saw NasalBags. All alone and in disguise. The phony beard looked so phony it couldn't possibly be fooling anyone. With his dough you'd think he could afford to have a makeup artist on staff who could do him up in a professional camera-ready manner.

All around him hard-charging exceptionals babbled away to one another in a medley of foreign tongues. Graveyard was lucky to even recognize the accents, let alone understand the words themselves. This was a space where money in all its wondrous incarnations came to mingle with other monies.

Graveyard went into I$Me. A leather-scented store for the privileged that sold pricey stuff the privileged couldn't get anywhere else. Graveyard bought a set of sterling silver corn holders and a platinum pen that wrote upside down and under water and a liquid clock, an assemblage of glass cylinders containing varying amounts of different colored fluids Graveyard hadn't a clue how to read. Very chic. And who said the exceptionals had no taste?

Rounding a corner, Graveyard was abruptly confronted by a camera crew, a mob, a story in progress, lights and microphones trained on a hapless uniformed doorman. He recognized the luxury building everyone was gathered in front of. It was the famous MontMont, which, Graveyard happened to know—he was a treasury of pop trivia—housed the palatial quarters of both SprinkledCupcake and LowToleranceComponent. What's going on? he asked a bystander. Turned out this particular building also contained the three-story digs of super financier AluminumCliff. Apparently, he'd been pretty bad lately. Another one of those tedious scandals the megarich were always getting wrapped up in. It was either sex or it was money or it was sex and money combined in salaciously inventive ways. Graveyard moved on.

Ambience was on his mind. He was worried. He didn't like the direction she seemed to be going in. The dollar high was fading much too quickly. Too much talk about not being worthy of all this good luck. It was starting to bring him down, too. Now she wanted something. She wanted to be surprised. But by what? What could she possibly want that she hadn't gotten for herself in the last two weeks?

Bang, zoom. It hit him out of the blue. A car. A brand new car. Like right now. He wanted a car. She wanted a car. They both needed a car. He flagged a cab and rode right on over to the classy showrooms on the far west West Side, which were full of obscenely priced engineering marvels designed just for people-like-you. The sales staff took him for a messenger or a delivery guy. What with the long unwashed hair, the torn jeans, the scuffed hip-hop sneakers and all. He hadn't yet converted his wardrobe to suit his present circumstances. But he asked to see the best, and, reluctantly, they showed him the best. I'll take this one, he said. I'll pay in cash, he said. All four of his pockets were stuffed with the sweet green that puts a smile on everyone's face. He signed the paperwork. He drove the car off the lot. What was he feeling? A sensation beyond words. Chicken feet and razor clams, Graveyard said to himself.

Now he needed a drink. He headed downtown and ended, as on some level he always knew he would, back in his own hood, headed inexorably toward Why?, his favorite bar. And even here in his (relatively) low-rent pretend "ghetto" the day's good fortune continued dispensing its welcome smiles. There was, astonishingly, an open parking space waiting just for him three blocks from the bar, directly in front of the WiltedLettuce grocery store. And perched atop a trash can in his usual spot was the store's unofficial greeter, an apparently homeless man whose name, even after exchanging hellos with him for more than six or seven years, Graveyard still did not know. "All we ask is a penny," the man said. "No one should go hungry." Graveyard always gave him something, dutifully emptying his pockets of whatever change he happened to be carrying that day. This day, though, was this day. He gave him paper. One whole pocket's worth of paper. "Thank you, kind sir," the man said. Which is what he always said. But the startled expression on his face was not what his face usually expressed. "Bless you," he said. "You're welcome," Graveyard said. Immediately saying to himself, this guy probably lives in a fine apartment better than mine and takes a monthlong vacation to BurnishMe Island every winter. Graveyard couldn't help it. He was as human as everyone else passing by, running the same thoughts through his overloaded noggin.

Why? was a second home to Graveyard, the adult equivalent of a kids' backyard clubhouse. He knew the owners and everyone who worked there, including the kitchen crew, and most of the regulars. He knew both bartenders, MasterPlaster and EndZone. MasterPlaster was writing a screenplay about a zombie hospital where damaged zombies went to have other zombies put them back together again. She was also a serious ballroom dancer. EndZone was a wannabe actress when she wasn't an actual pourer of drinks. She was currently appearing in the infamous *Panties in a Bunch* at the Crumpled Door, a hundred-seat theater a couple of blocks away. She was topless through most of the second act for reasons no one quite comprehended but could still appreciate. Sometimes MasterPlaster and EndZone went home together after work. Sometimes they didn't. Graveyard also knew most of the rest of the waitstaff—P, Q, and R. They were all just marking time.

And wouldn't you know it, the first people he saw coming through the door were the very rub-a-dub-dub LimitedEdition and the reliably "as is" PocketPool.

"Hey," said LimitedEdition. "There he is, the Man Who Wasn't Here. Long time no see."

"Yeah? I been around."

"Haven't seen you in days."

"I been busy."

"Busy? Doing what?"

"Shopping," said Graveyard.

"Shopping? You kidding me?"

"It's my new hobby."

"I think what we probably got here is a case of the ol' Mr. Pussywhipped," said PocketPool.

"You should be so lucky," said Graveyard.

"So what'd you buy, shopping?" said LimitedEdition.

"Odds and ends."

"Anything you care to share with your good buds?"

"Ends and odds."

"Thought you were having trouble meeting the monthly nut," said PocketPool.

"I was, but, lucky for us, Ambience has come into a little unexpected legacy."

"How little?" said PocketPool.

"Ambience and money are like oil and water," said Limited-Edition. "How'd she manage to get her fingers on a dollar without it getting away?"

"Well, you're not gonna believe this, but a rich uncle died."

Everyone laughed.

"Really? Like in the movies?"

"Just like."

"So how much?"

"That's her business. Ask her."

"Where is that girl, anyway? Haven't seen her around much, either."

"She's been out buying neon beer signs and antique medical equipment. She wants to redecorate the apartment."

"Into what—Dr. Ygor's underground med lab?"

"She likes to entertain her eye."

"Why not a whole new apartment?" said PocketPool.

"We're considering."

"Then this must be more than a little little money."

"A little more."

"Substantially more."

"In that general area."

"You're not gonna tell me, are you?"

"Don't believe I am, no."

"Well, then, the least you could do is buy all us luckless dead-beats a round of drinks."

"My pleasure," said Graveyard.

So he did. A shot of BlackPeat and a beer back for all. Then he did it again. Then he lost count. Everyone got drunk, and those who were already drunk got drunker.

"Why couldn't this happen to me?" said PocketPool. "Nothing ever happens to me."

Not true. Stuff had been happening to PocketPool his whole life. Only problem: hardly any of it was good.

"What are you talking about?" said LimitedEdition. "You won the lottery."

"Yeah. Once."

"Still, a win's a win."

"Yeah. Fifty dollars of win."

"Well, that's fifty you didn't have before."

"And by the next day, fifty I'd never see again."

"Don't blame us if you're so careless with your dough."

"You ever think about how much money there is in the whole wide world?" said PocketPool.

"No."

"Well, think about it sometime. It's a lot."

"So?"

"So why isn't more of it flowing in my general direction?"

"Cause you just haven't lived the right and just life. Only those who deserve the money get the money. You know that. The foundation of the culture."

"So I'm not worthy?"

"Apparently not."

"And I am," said Graveyard.

"Apparently, yes."

"Well, what a crappy way to divvy up the goods."

"You got a better way?"

"Yeah," said PocketPool. "Everyone gets what they need. Not what they want, what they need. There's plenty to go around."

"And who would be in charge of this magical redistribution?"

"Benevolent souls who dress in rags and live in caves on faraway mountains."

"There you go. Problem solved."

"And how much would you expect to take home under this new regime?" said Graveyard.

"Oh, only a couple million or three."

Everyone laughed again. Loudly.

"Well," said PocketPool. "It's what I need."

You never heard such laughter.

PocketPool had a few issues. Drug issues, mostly. He'd experimented, dabbled, and indulged from the eighth grade on. He'd never met a drug he didn't like. He didn't know why. His favorites were Luridonin and OverEasy. Luridonin made his head feel as if it were packed in gunpowder. OverEasy made him feel like an egg. They were his real friends. They'd never let him down. In fact, he wished that at least one of them was with him right now.

"Anyone seen *Five Wet Rats on a Log*?" said LimitedEdition.

"Is that the one about the plot to corner the world market in pandemonium?" said Graveyard.

"Yeah."

"What's pandemonium?" said PocketPool.

"It's some kind of sacred mineral that's inside every cell phone, every computer, every electronic device."

"Corner that and you control everything."

"That's why the evil Dr. Vitus and his hunchbacked minions are busy kidnapping, torturing, and assassinating every Quasiland government official whose face they don't like. Quasiland's the place where this pandemonium is dug out of the ground by the oppressed masses."

"Who are the wet rats?"

"They're the elite force of do-gooder ex-cons sent into Quasiland to liberate our pandemonium. We want our pandemonium, and we want it now. Get the fuck out of our way."

"Don't tell me. The leader of the pack is none other than BurlyMuffins."

"Fresh from saving the world in *Interstitial*."

"Isn't he getting a bit old for the muscle-and-gun routine?"

"It's called experience."

"Have you checked out his face lately? He looks like a practice dummy for plastic surgery students."

"Who's the babe?" said PocketPool.

"VernalMist," said LimitedEdition.

Everyone groaned in unison. Which is what everyone was supposed to do whenever this particular actress was mentioned.

"You haven't lived till you've seen her suck the poison out of BurlyMuffins's trigger finger. Dr. Vitus, see, shoots a dart from his badass helmet gun. Happens to hit our hero right on that delicate spot. And boy, does she know how to work a finger. Disappointment is, there's been some obvious editing."

"Maybe we'll get to see the whole thing on the DVD extras," said PocketPool.

"One can only hope," said Graveyard.

"Oh, no," said LimitedEdition. "Don't try and pretend you're above it all. You'll be drooling over that scene same as the rest of us."

Graveyard looked at LimitedEdition. Then he smiled with his eyes. "All right," he said. "Got me."

Graveyard and LimitedEdition had known each other since their fabled-in-their-own-minds brew-and-smoke days back at old Tip O' The Wedge High. They never got in any actual trouble anyone ever found out about. Well, except for that time they pranked the school. Snuck in one night and proceeded to glue about two hundred in nickels, dimes, and quarters to the floor of the main hallway and another two hundred in dollar bills to the ceiling. With a scattering of tens and twenties at strategic intervals just to make it interesting. When school opened in the morning, the ensuing melee resulted in multiple bruises and contusions and a couple of torn fingernails and one broken arm. Everyone involved was suspended and barred from attending the prom. They held their own prom in the back room of WoeIsMe's BakeShack. Superior refreshments for all. And everyone in attendance had sex of one kind or another before the night was through. School-day memories.

LimitedEdition worked at StandUpAndCheer in computer cubicle Q5872Y. They were the gold standard in wealth management. They took your money, rubbed it up against other people's money, and ringadingding, the stuff multiplied like bacteria. More sugar for everybody. LimitedEdition's job was to sit and stare at a screen for ten, eleven, twelve hours a day. When the majority of numbers on the screen had a little + sign in front of them, LimitedEdition could go home. You can imagine how many days a year he got home early. Graveyard worked there once, too. He lasted about a week. His head always felt as if there were a thick, tight belt wrapped around it and as if at the end of each hour the belt were systematically tightened a notch. Graveyard felt that way on a lot of jobs.

"Shouldn't you guys be at work or something?" said Graveyard.

"It's Saturday," said PocketPool.

"Oh."

"How could you possibly not know that?"

"Men of leisure don't have to know the day of the week. In fact, men of leisure don't want to know the day of the week."

"One less aggravation," said LimitedEdition.

"Yes, and isn't it interesting that how much dough you have or don't have affects your perception of time?"

"So how does time look to you now, Mr. Aristocrat?"

"It goes slower and I've got more of it."

"Money in the bank."

"Bingo."

"Effigy's getting fat," said PocketPool, just to say something, let everyone know he was still there, still in the game. He pointed to the television screen up behind the bar. "Fat and old. Look at her." It was the video for "Cat In A Box." She was dressed in body-tight snakeskin and writhing around on a metal grate suspended over the CGI flames of an impressively phony CGI hell. Every male gaze in the bar zeroed in on the dancing screen in the way testosterone-flooded eyes everywhere tended to do whenever Effigy's image, in any medium, was placed directly before them.

"I'd tap that," said LimitedEdition.

"She's already spoken for," said Graveyard. "Devil's already got her under his management. Look, here he comes now."

Some skinny half-naked guy painted candy-apple red and wearing horns and batwings and a rubber tail flew up out of the pit, seized the popster in his long shredded arms, and dragged her, still warbling, down into his infernal throne room, where she was crowned queen of the underworld as all the denizens of hell broke out into a mad, krumpin' frenzy.

"How ridiculous," said LimitedEdition.

"It's supposed to be ridiculous," said Graveyard. "You remember it better."

"Who's gonna forget that body?" said PocketPool.

"I've seen better," said LimitedEdition.

"Yeah, where?"

"At work."

"Oh, yeah, who?" said Graveyard. He wondered if he'd known anybody LimitedEdition was talking about during his brief stint at StandUpAndCheer.

"Well, LoadedDice for one. Once she even got a personal wardrobe warning from NoWaivers himself."

"What'd she look like?"

"Stacked, packed, and whacked. She eventually got fired for putting xenofoam into the break-room coffeepot."

"Never met her."

"And PrivateIssue, down in Disinformation and Insecurities. She had half the entire Human Capital team. I mean, she literally had them."

"You actually make the corporate life sound busy and fun."

"Yeah, well, what do I know?"

"How's that Resolve of yours?"

"Oh, good. Real good, as a matter of fact. You know her, she's always good." He paused. He paused again. "I think we might be coming apart," he said. The line just popped out. On its own. Big surprise for both him and his friends.

"Oh, shit," said PocketPool.

"You can't come apart," said Graveyard. "You're a team."

"How do you know you're coming apart?" said PocketPool.

"Her girlfriends look at me funny," said LimitedEdition.

"Uh-oh," said Graveyard.

"It's never anything terribly overt. More like I've got some terrible disease and they're sorry, but they can't do anything about it. Sometimes I feel like I'm being attended to by nurses. Nurses who're studying me for further symptoms."

"So how'd you come to be the patient in all this?"

"Beats me. If you ever get a good read on Resolve, let me know, cause you'd be a better detective than I am. I think this was probably a long time coming, but you know how she is. What's the message? What's the static? I can't tell the difference anymore. I'm too this, I'm too that. I talk too much, I'm too quiet. I'm too close, I'm too far away. I make strange birdlike noises when I eat. Hyenalike barks when I come. I don't make enough money."

"Sounds pretty much like your normal relationship to me," said PocketPool.

"And just in the last month, she's begun developing allergies to things I've never even heard of."

"Like what?"

"I don't know. Castaway seeds and bitterheart and crisscross grain. And, oh, yeah, yobodia. Apparently that's something really bad found in all gingum flour."

"Sunchokes and adzuki beans," said Graveyard.

"I'd hate to have to give up gingum cookies for life," said PocketPool.

"She's making her own meals now. Separate from mine."

"Maybe she just needs a brief vacay or something," said PocketPool.

LimitedEdition waited a moment, then he said, "I think she might be seeing someone else."

"Here we go," said Graveyard.

"What makes you think that?" said PocketPool.

"She goes out at night. She doesn't get back till dawn. She's all ellipsised up. She won't tell me where she's been."

"Okay," said Graveyard, "but what else? Where's the smoking gun?"

"It's not funny."

"I know it's not. Sorry."

"I keep waiting for that 'we have to talk' moment."

"Maybe she took on another job without telling you," said PocketPool.

"Yeah. The horizontal kind."

"I think we need more drinks," said Graveyard. He called over Q. He decided they required an urgent upgrade in alcohol percentage. A round of Brainpoppers. Hold the Tabasco.

"Sorry, guys," said LimitedEdition. "I didn't mean to dump all this crap on you two. I don't know what happened."

"Who else you gonna dump it on?" said Graveyard.

"You've got problems of your own."

"Not as bad as yours," said PocketPool.

"Thanks," said LimitedEdition.

They sat in silence for a while. No one knew what to say. Graveyard was thinking about Ambience. Where she was. What she was doing.

"Sorry," LimitedEdition said again.

"Forget it," said Graveyard.

"Make her jealous," said PocketPool. "Your time to party."

"Does that work?"

"Who knows? But at least you'll be getting some fun out of this mess."

"I don't know anyone who's getting any fun out of anything."

Next thing Graveyard knew he was staring out the front window and gradually realizing it was getting dark outside. What? How'd that happen?

"What time is it?" he said.

"I don't wear a watch on the weekend," said LimitedEdition. "This is when I pretend I don't work for a living." PocketPool never wore a watch.

Graveyard caught Q on her way by. She wasn't wearing a watch, either. She didn't like to be reminded how slowly time was passing on this shitty scumbag job of hers. Thanks, Q.

"Well, no matter what the time is," said Graveyard, "I think I've got to be shoving off."

"You know what she wanted?" said LimitedEdition. "What she's always wanted real bad? A pair of those Lance&Fester shoes. I always said they were too expensive. If only I'd gotten her those shoes, maybe none of this would be happening."

"How much are they?" said Graveyard, reaching into his pocket.

"I don't know. A lot. Five hundred or so."

Graveyard counted it off the roll in his hand. He passed the bills over to LimitedEdition. "Pick her up a pair on your way home."

"I couldn't." He tried handing the money back.

"Yes, you can." Graveyard pushed the bills away.

LimitedEdition looked at the new green notes in his hand. Then he folded them and put them in his pocket. "Thank you," he said.

Graveyard turned to PocketPool. "That boyfriend of yours need anything?" he said. "Before he leaves?"

PocketPool was an alternating-current kind of dater. He'd take up with a woman for a while and whenever that ended he'd find himself with a man until he left and it was back to a woman. He was obviously looking for something. He didn't know what it was. At the moment he was on the male half of the cycle.

PocketPool looked at the money in Graveyard's hand. "We're good," he said.

"Have a party favor anyway." Graveyard crumpled up a few bills, stuffed them into PocketPool's shirt pocket. Then he pushed back his chair and stood up. "I'm afraid, gentlemen, that I must now take my leave. Got to get back to the hacienda to prepare for the evening's repast."

"And what do rich bastards like you eat, anyway?" said PocketPool.

"What all rich bastards eat: barbecued angel wings and unicorn steaks."

He gave a mock salute and he was gone.

Out on the street he suddenly remembered. I bought a brand new car today. Amaranth and watermelon, he said to himself. Hard to believe that monstrous contraption parked halfway up the next block was actually his. He coulda bragged about it to the guys. Given them an up-close view of what an exceptional's ride looks like. But then he realized he hadn't really wanted to show off before his friends. He hadn't wanted to feel what they'd be feeling when they salivated over the priceless machinery. He hadn't wanted to feel what he'd be feeling watching them. He popped the locks with the remote and got in behind the wheel. That heady new-car smell. Leather and money. He drove the dozen blocks home with studied care, worrying the whole time about getting even a single scratch on the car before Ambience could take a look. He wanted her to get the full, unadulterated impact. Then, miracle of miracles, there, before his disbelieving eyes, was an empty space right in front of his brownstone. He didn't know how much more parking luck he could stand in one day. He carefully maneuvered the massive vehicle into the spot (a smooth, easy fit), raced up the stairs, calling for Ambience as he rushed through the door. She was in the bedroom, trying on jewelry before the mirror.

"Where the hell have you been?" she said.

Graveyard grabbed her hand. "Don't say another word. Just come with me." He hurriedly dragged her down the stairs and out the door and posed her in front of the new car.

"What?" she said in blinking disbelief. "You bought that?"

He nodded.

"You bought that."

He nodded again.

"We own that?"

"Incredible, isn't it?"

"It's a HomoDebonaire."

"The HomoDebonaire3000. Top of the line. Runs on sunshine and fresh breezes. It's greenly green."

"No," she said. "No." She walked around, examining the bright, shiny thing in an apparent daze. "I never thought I'd own a car this expensive, this nice, in my entire life."

"Well, now you do."

"Can we go for a ride?"

"Certainly." He stepped forward, opened the passenger-side door for her. "After you, miss. Step into the Homo, please."

They took the LookyLou Drive up along the ReadyToWear River, over the Conundrum Bridge, and in half an hour they were out of the city. The normal, ludicrously heavy traffic seemed to move aside at their approach.

"Didn't this insane purchase take quite a hefty chunk out of our assets?"

"You'd think."

"Why I asked."

"But no matter how much I take out of the bag, the amount left behind *in* the bag seems to remain pretty much the same."

"Like in a fairy tale?"

"Exactly."

"How is that possible?"

"Maybe this is a fairy tale. A real fairy tale."

"As opposed to a made-up fairy tale?"

"You need to get with the program, Ambience."

"I am with the program. I just don't know why."

"Give me a kiss."

"You're driving."

"A kiss so deep I might even lose control of the car."

She leaned over and planted a major tongue sucker right on him. The car swerved to the left. The car swerved to the right. It settled back into its proper lane. Everything about the moment was thrillingly otherworldly. After it was over, they pretended as if nothing had happened.

"At least the traffic's not too bad," said Ambience.

"They knew we were coming. They cleared out."

"I can't even hear the engine."

"Acoustical baffling. Standard issue on this model."

"And the ride. So smooth. If you didn't look out the window, you wouldn't even know we were moving."

"Mattress-quality engineering. Standard issue on this model."

"Well, whatever the standard issue is, the whole experience is making me standardly horny."

"There's plenty of motels around here. Look, there's a Highway Hideaway, and on the right a Bogus Inn. Vacancies at both."

"I'm not talking about motels, you simp, I'm talking about the car. Fucking in the fucking car."

He pulled off the interstate at the first opportunity. The Governor RoundAbout Memorial Rest Area. Parked in the shadows, away from the all-illuminating sodium vapor lights. They climbed into the spacious leather back seat and went to work. This time there was more oral than there had ever been before. And Graveyard felt he could do what he was doing for hours, or so he liked to imagine.

"What's that?" Ambience said, squirming around on the tip of his tongue.

"Don't know," he said. "Invented the move just this instant."

"Me like," she said. "Keep doing that."

So he did.

She tasted like something primeval, something you kept tasting and tasting yet still couldn't quite get.

"You know what's wrong with the world?" she said. "I just realized."

"Tell me," said Graveyard, trying to keep up.

"Pleasure," she said in a strange voice, half groan, half grunt. She was obviously somewhere far beyond the stupid rational world. "Pleasure deficits...all of us...too damn many." She got quiet. Then she said, "Could you do that thing you just did?"

"I don't know what I just did."

"Let me help you remember." She shifted her hips.

"It's coming back to me." He felt that right now, in this momentary moment, he was making up for years of deficits.

"Could you go a bit lower, please?"

He went lower.

"Little to the right."

He went right.

"There," she said. "Now, don't stop. Please, don't stop."

Okay by Graveyard. He wanted to go and go and go until he was spent.

CHAPTER 9

THE ART OF THE FUCK

ON THE ELEVENTH FLOOR of the sleekly styled BigPointy-Building, in midtown, was located the beating heart of the NationalProcedures organization, an officeless open space divided into more than a hundred cubicles, each occupied by a bonded Gatekeeper whose job it was to bring into the company as much asset as possible during every 24-7 work cycle. The floor was known within the company—and throughout the industry, for that matter—as the Comb. Where the worker bees deposited and stored the honey. Score was kept by means of a stadium-size electronic board mounted to the wall at the front end of the floor. Each employee's position in the hive could be read at a glance by anyone who cared to look.

At the moment Gatekeeper 65, in row K, cubicle 8, was listed at number 47 on the company's flickering box card—not too horrible, not too great. UnauthorizedReproduction's personal goal for the day was to close at 40, a level he had come tantalizingly near but never quite attained before. The most important part of the job, he'd learned quickly enough, both professionally and personally, lay in eavesdropping on conversations in nearby cubicles and the treasure trove of the break room and turning the overheard data to lucrative advantage for himself and the company. He'd scored big today, overhearing a convo in cubicle 10 relating to significant updrafts at MurmurLow, one of NationalProcedures' major competitors. So he punched in a handful of letters and numbers and made the company two million dollars justlikethat.

But the best advantage to pilfering personals on his colleagues, both professionally and personally—though at this point, what was the difference?—lay in discovering who was fucking whom, the company's most sensitive intel. What he knew so far: MisterMenu was fucking both NeedlePliers and DelicateSear and many more employees than anyone could keep accurate track of, including TearDrop, who was fucking BlisterPac, who of course was also fucking DelicateSear, who was also fucking EmeryBoard, who was fucking TrollFarm, who was fucking CapsaicinPod, who was fucking SlapHappy, and DigitalSignage, who was fucking...and on and on (you get the drift), so the sugar noogies were passed ever and steadily downward, sweetening the firm from top to bottom. Of course, there was always a sourpuss or two who didn't enjoy the same candy the others did, and these people would try to get their gummies wherever they could. Outcome: not good.

Occasionally MisterMenu himself made an appearance on the floor. He'd stand at the front of the room, engage in a brief face-to-face with SpringLoaded, the Comb's floor pimp, let his eyes roam unseeingly over the roomful of bad-postured employees, then depart. And sometimes, after one of these cursory check-ins, a female Gatekeeper would casually rise and exit, as discreetly as possible, by the same door. Rumor had it that MisterMenu maintained a capacious boudoir off his executive suite, which got significant play. UnauthorizedReproduction didn't know whether to believe the rumor or not. MisterMenu had to be smarter than that. Or did he? Nevertheless, UnauthorizedReproduction kept watch. And, based on his careful scrutinies, he couldn't help but fantasize about fucking his own way to the top. And why not? He'd seen the movies, too. Of course the preferred lead of those pictures was almost always a woman. But why couldn't a guy successfully crawl over a few willing female execs? Maybe he could if he were as gorgeous, well built, and all-around studly as PumiceStone or CordialLips and had a slick screenwriter draft the script for him. So in his mind that's what he was. And when that particular scenario had been brought to a satisfying conclusion he'd dissolve into the next long-running feature: *Doughnuts to Dollars*, in which he, UnauthorizedReproduction, played this time by CocktailRepartee, seduces TearDrop, played, of course, by the irrepressible PageTurner, and, in a memorable scene of hilariously staged pillow talk, learns that the all-time favorite doughnut of MisterMenu, impeccably impersonated by the ever-fluid KingClover, is the GlazedLumbarCluster, available only on Tuesdays until product runs out from the CrustToneBakery in Chyron Heights. Next Tuesday the image of Unauthorized gets up at dawn, makes the hurried trek to the Heights, buys a box of a dozen Clusters, and, back at a reasonable facsimile of the BigPointyBuilding, stations himself in the stage-set lobby until KingClover arrives, then boldly fast-talks his way into a convincing connection with the great man, who, naturally, invites him up into the executive aerie, where, after a bit of comical business with the farcical staff, installs him as prime doughnut procurer for the entire corporation at a thousandfold increase in salary. Maybe he marries the boss's daughter, NoDeposit; maybe he doesn't. What does it matter? Curious how much of his on-the-clock was consumed by these absurd brain flicks, which, transformed into the prevailing script format of the day, would simply expire unnoticed because of funding deprivation in the ward for terminal long shots. He had already been briefly cast in a real movie in the real world (he'd fucked the casting director's assistant in high school) as an underpaid, defeated peon in a national epic of consuming self-love, unglued greed, and emotional slaughter entitled *Fat Chance in a Slim Boat.*

But what the hell, it was lunchtime. He fervently prayed that today, at least, OnDelivery, row I, cubicle 8, would please, please, please take her lunch break somewhere outside. If she had her carton of yogurt at her desk again he honestly did not know if he would be able to restrain himself from getting up, barging down the row, and strangling her to death with his bare trembling hands. It was the scraping, the constant, endless, nails-on-the-blackboard scraping of her plastic spoon against the plastic container, relentlessly, screechingly, tormentingly determined to extract each damn speck of the precious curdled milk from the walls of the precious damn cup. Obviously she was locked inside a perpetual diet, like every other woman at this and every other corporate infirmary in the whole doomed town, and was hence perpetually hungry. If he did indeed put her out of her misery, that one act of lunatic violence would make up for a year or more of sitting chained to this rigid chair while waiting for the earthquake, tidal wave, towering inferno, or inevitable catastrophe that would permanently erase the BigPointyBuilding from the face of the big bad earth.

At 12:23 p.m., more or less, OnDelivery, crumpled paper bag in hand, departed her station and exited the floor. She returned at 1:04, more or less, sans bag. For UnauthorizedReproduction this simple event signaled a successful workday. The closing buzzer sounded at exactly at 6:00 p.m., but no one moved. NationalProcedures employees were expected to set their own hours, preferably to the point where each pixel wrangler could no longer bear one single second more of profitable activity, and try to go beyond that. Today, for some reason or other, UnauthorizedReproduction determined he could endure at least thirty more minutes of desk posture. Which he did. At precisely 6:30 he looked up, checked the tote. His final score for the day stood at 45, a grand improvement of 2. In the afternoon he'd added another five million or so to NationalProcedures' already obscenely bulging vault. Was that enough? Hardly. Even after bringing in for the day what he calculated was a net of roughly eight million. A drop in the profits bucket. He got up and left the floor. First one out the door on this particular Friday.

What he needed now was a drink. His favorite bar: the PastelLoon, over on Cosset Street. He walked in and, whaddya know, failed to encounter a single face he knew. Which was fine by him. He took a table in back and ordered his usual, a double GoldenLariat. To his slight surprise, he'd only been seated about ten minutes when he began mulling over in his head the feasibility of purchasing a boat. Why? He'd never wanted a boat before. They were notorious money pits. And what would he do with one, anyway? Where would he go in a frigging boat? He didn't know. Destinations would come to mind. That was the thing about minds. They were always coming up with something.

He was on his second GoldenLariat and staring at a girl who looked just like BonusCash, his first steady back in high school, waiting on line for the ladies' room. He wondered if that could actually be her. He wondered where she was, how she was doing. He wished they were still in touch. Then he heard somebody talking to him. He turned around. It was CyberLawn. He worked over at ManagedSpill. He had the same sort of job as Unauthorized, doing stupid shit all day to make money for some asshole who didn't need any more money.

"The joys of the mogul life," said CyberLawn.

"We love it," said UnRepro.

Then they proceeded to get blind drunk and try to top each other with stories of the most egregious piece of bullshit they'd had to handle in the past eight hours. Today the contest was declared a tie. They'd each had to fudge at least one financial regulation by noon. Two hours and who knew how many doubles later, CyberLawn tried to pick a fight with some execubrat-in-training posing at the bar who seemed to be exuding in almost visible particles the stink that he enjoyed his phony-baloney job just a shade too much, and he and UnRepro were both kicked out of the joint. They reassembled themselves at TheFracturedHorn, on the next block. They made their unsteady way to the closest vacant table and plunked themselves rather noisily into disappointingly unchic chairs.

"Now," said CyberLawn, "what was it we were drinking at the Loon?"

"I believe those were GoldenLariats. Why?"

"Never mix your liquors. A famous wino once told me that.

Can really fuck you up. Always stay true to your brand." Which, incidentally, was the corporate motto at ManagedSpill. He looked around, casing the house. "Now," he said. He spoke in a drunken stage whisper. "Who in here do you want to fuck?"

UnRepro looked around. "The blonde in the green. Over at the bar."

CyberLawn turned around and checked said quarry for one extended second. "Me, too." He reached in his pocket and pulled out a quarter. "Flip you for her."

"Heads."

The coin dropped tails.

"See you back at the ranch." CyberLawn struggled to his feet and made his wobbly way to the bar. After a few minutes of whatever alcohol-steeped palaver he was capable of serving this girl, the two turned simultaneously, as if attached to connected strings, and directed toward UnRepro a pair of identical smiles, as if they'd just shared a big secret about his personal life. Drinks in hand, they then began marching in comic step toward him.

"This is RiderAgreement," CyberLawn said. "She just got fired from KanisterCan. Can you believe it? For taking too many piss breaks. I mean, can you fucking believe it?"

"What can I say?" she said. "I have a weak bladder." She took a seat between them. Up close she looked like a once-trending product that had been left in the window too long.

"Takes an iron bladder to man a sentry post in the eternal struggle against quarterly deficit numbers," said CyberLawn.

"You're smart," said RiderAgreement. "Never thought about it that way."

"Welcome to the real world," said CyberLawn. "Fuck the real world. Let's go to my place."

So they did.

CyberLawn lived in the renowned KrinkleTowers. He was only able to afford such digs because his parents, whom he hated with a politically correct hostility, owned a significant share of the building. He had a view of the ReadyToWear River and the LookAway Harbor, a private chef, and daily maid service made up of unbearably polite and efficient illegal immigrants he didn't talk about. His parents were major contributors to the Frightened White Man's Flying Freedom Freedom Party. He didn't talk about them, either. He worked at a routine loser's job at a company his father owned, where he was supposed to be diligently working his way up to that platinum turret in the sky. He could care less. The job was well beneath him, intellectually, physically, sexually, aesthetically, and, most important, financially. Other than injecting as many millimeters of concentrated hell into his parents' sniveling lives as possible, he hadn't a clue how he wanted to occupy his portion of existence on the planet. The only useful function that had occurred to him so far was to become a connoisseur of boredom. Sometimes, in mockery of his family's genealogical pretensions, he'd even refer to himself as the Duke of Ennui.

The inebriated trio made their tottering way as best they could over to the guarded entrance on Kalpa Street, where CyberLawn genially greeted the armed doorman, who blessed them all back with a defiantly impertinent stinkeye. They stumbled across the thickly carpeted lobby, accompanied by their own a cappella rendition of "Wishes and Fishes." CyberLawn led his raucous party over to an elevator door in a niche separate from the others. He pressed his palm against a pane of glass, the door magically opened, and they fell into the elevator as a more or less coordinated group, where RiderAgreement promptly threw up on the imported parquet. CyberLawn lived on the sixty-fifth floor, which seemed to take at least three hours to arrive at. They celebrated their triumphant disembarkation into the entryway of CyberLawn's ridiculously grand apartment by knocking over every expensive-looking table bearing every expensive-looking vase holding every expensive-looking bouquet of every expensive-looking flower to be found in the entire expensive-looking world.

Somewhat stunned by the opulence, they passed more or less

silently into the living room. The sunlight cascading through the wall of windows was so radiantly real it seemed fake. As did the room itself. The furnishings, so numerous and ornate, appeared as objects fashioned out of buttery icing for an exotic splendiferous cake no one was ever really going to eat.

RiderAgreement was visibly impressed and ran through her own private store of adjectives exclaiming over what she was seeing. "Why do you work at all, living in a palace like this?" she said.

"I like to keep busy," CyberLawn said. He led them on into the bedroom. Unauthorized had seen it all before so had no need or inclination to add to the shower of compliments RiderAg was sprinkling throughout the place. RiderAgreement asked to use the john. CyberLawn showed her to the proper door. She entered and remained for about five minutes, then exited and said, "How do you turn the water on? There's no handles."

"You think it. If you want cold, think cold; hot, think hot."

She let herself absorb that fascinating piece of info for about half a minute, nodded sagely, and said, "Cool. Ultra cool." She disappeared back inside, where she remained for about half an hour.

"What the fuck she doing in there?" Unauthorized said. He and CyberLawn had adjourned to the entertainment center on the other side of the apartment, where they'd been sampling Cyber's extensive liquor cabinet and flipping through the two hundred channels available on his massive Himalayan-size TV.

"I better check." CyberLawn excused himself, and then he, too, was gone for about half an hour. Later Unauthorized managed to tear himself away from a rerun of the last episode of *BloodOnTheKeypad*, the one where it is finally revealed who killed DoctorOakenBucket. He wandered through the rooms, discovered the john door open, and then, in the bedroom, CyberLawn passed out fully clothed on the spacious bed and RiderAgreement, fully unclothed, going methodically through his pockets.

"He'd probably give you the money if you asked," UnRepro said.

"I'd be too embarrassed to ask for a handout."

"But not too embarrassed to steal."

"Guess not." She sat up with her bare legs folded under her but opened wide enough to display fully all her charms. Without a hint of self-consciousness. She studied him for a while. "So," she said, "you wanna fuck?'

He studied her for a while. "Sure," he said. She scooted over to the other side of the bed, spread her (this time) fully extended legs. He got undressed and climbed aboard.

"Beautiful appendages," he said.

"So I've been told."

"You've been told right." He lay down and began gently stroking them. They were incredibly soft. They felt incredibly good. "Mmmm," she said. "Mmmm," she said again. He moved forward and began kissing them. It was like kissing rose petals, or so he believed at the moment. "Baby like," she said. "Don't stop." So he didn't. After a while he shifted his body upward so he could get himself into a favorable position to apply his horizontal lips to her vertical ones. Which he did. She began moaning and writhing around. A fine current began running pleasantly through both of them. For a while there they were floating together through a cloud of pink cotton candy. Or so they liked to imagine. They'd been released into that agreeable lostness sharing bodies can generate. Then abruptly his probing tongue encountered something unexpected up inside her. Something foreign and inorganic. He retracted his tongue, then cautiously extended it bit by careful bit. Again he touched something, some strange inhuman object that should not be where he had found it. He abruptly backed out of her and sat up. "What's wrong?" she said. He reached in with the forefinger of his right hand, felt around for a moment, and pulled out what he'd discovered: a wadded-up condom. Used. He held it up on display. "Oops," she said. UnRepro rolled off the bed and rushed to the john. He opened the cabinet, frantically searched the contents, and finally found what he was looking for: a family-size bottle of CootiesBeGone medically approved mouthwash. He took a healthy slug, swished it around in his mouth for a moment, spit it out into the sink. Then he repeated the procedure. He returned to the bedroom. "Sorry," she said.

"You should take better care of yourself."

"I'm sorry. It happened today at lunch break in the women's room. Didn't know there was anything left inside."

"Not too in touch with your body?"

"Thought I was."

"You might want to reassess."

She stared down at her fingers, which were playing idly with the end of a bedsheet. "I can't look at you," she said.

"I gotta sky," he said. "Listen, take care of yourself, okay?" And he turned and left the room, left the apartment, left the building, and hoped he'd left her for the remainder of his life.

Outside, he decided to splurge and take a cab home. First one he tried hailing stopped immediately for him. Miracle of the day. He settled into the back seat, gave the driver the address, and tried to enjoy the ride. He stared out the dirty window at the passing phantasmagoria. The city itself looked used, too. What didn't appear interestingly preowned had been demolished and replaced with the steel and glass equivalents of plastic. Money has ruined this town, he said to himself, trying not to replay the scene he'd just escaped. Whatever it touches turns to lead. The tired city looked like a copy of something for which there had been no original. And the people living in it, too. End of the day on Friday thoughts. End of casual sex with random strangers day. Maybe he'd feel better in the morning. Then he was back on his own safe street in what had once been his own safe, comfortable neighborhood. No more. Aside from a few grizzled veterans like himself, only those coming into town with pockets stuffed with cash or those lucky enough to have fallen into jobs whose employers didn't mind stuffing their pockets lived there now. Rents were obscenely high and still climbing. Sidewalks jammed every night with drunken hordes of rampaging trust-fund barbarians. He'd seen storefronts go from art galleries to restaurants to banks. He'd been in the area for more than a dozen years, and all the friends he'd made in those first years were long gone, priced out. But gone where? Seemed the places left in which to hide were becoming fewer and fewer. Money ruined everything. Shut up, he said to himself. Pay the driver and go upstairs. So he did.

InvoiceEnclosed was in the kitchen. Puttering around doing some kind of kitchen activity.

"Where were you?" she said.

"Having a drink with CyberLawn."

"Well, you could have called."

"Sorry."

"I made that baitwurst pie you like. With callowbeans."

"Lickety-fine. Any beer?"

"Picked up a six-pack of StormThunderLite on the way home." She was Effigy's current bra groomer and, besides being well reimbursed for her talents, got to travel the world with the pop star whenever she was on tour, which was almost always.

"How's Effigy today?"

"Usual. This afternoon she tore a custom-made SpottedRambler in half cause it was supposedly pinching her side boobs, and those things are pricey and hard to find. Then just for good measure she fired CalamityFeet cause, supposedly, he was looking at her, and I quote, 'funny.'"

"Wow. Hasn't he been with her for years?"

"Since the *Burning Cake* album."

"These people are all so terribly spoiled."

"News flash. Anyway, after he got the swipe left, he went out to the parking lot and keyed her CloudRemedy."

UnRepro laughed heartily for the first time that day. "She probably won't even notice."

"Or care. Listen, I already ate. Want a plate?"

"I can get it."

"No problem. I'm already up. Just sit down." So he did. She served him a steaming platter of baitwurst and a sweating bottle of cold StormThunder. After he finished eating (it was all good, better than he deserved) they flaked out in bed for a while watching the last half of *CelebrityCroquet*. Tonight's message: celebs suck at croquet. Then they distracted themselves playing with each other's genitals, leavened by a couple of halfhearted fucks.

"Well, that was decidedly bleh," InvoiceEnclosed said. "Did you get fucked on the way home?"

"No. I can't believe you'd even ask me that."

"You're just not in your usual let's-take-Vaginagrad mode."

"Work," he said, as if that were enough of an explanation. And it was. They lay there for another while discussing for the umpteenth time whether he should finally walk from his high-flying lameass job. And for the umpteenth time arrived at no clear conclusion. When they grew tired of that burned-out topic, they decided, on the madcap spur of the moment, to try to catch the last showing of *Apocalypticus* at the nearby HappyMore. Even though it was well past midnight and the picture was already ten minutes in, there were only a few seats left and they were lucky to get them. In the empty lobby they bought a tub of VolleyCorn, a couple of bars of NixNo, and a large NothingCola, which they shared. In case the theater collapsed during the show they'd have sufficient supplies to survive on until they were dug out of the rubble. Wildly popular, the picture was the boffo smash of the summer and seemed primed to gross out (in more ways than one) all the other wannabes in a heavy wannabe year. It was the ridiculously entertaining story of a drug, LeanLove, the diet pill gone bad. The reducing aid had been formulated from by-products discovered during the manufacture of plastic garbage bags. Ingesting just a single pill a day resulted in almost immediate and visible weight loss without requiring any change whatsoever in diet or exercise regimen. Big pharma rushed in. Unfortunately, the pill also reduced the volume of the average adult cerebral cortex to a throbbing knob of nerve endings about the size of a walnut. Major side effect: irrepressible urge to kill anything that moved, skinny or fat. Big firearms rushed in. But by then zillions of the miracle tablets had already been sold and consumed. The world erupted into a frenzy of murderous rage. A CGI wet dream. And when not slaughtering the innocent outright, the twigs, as they were called—because of their generally emaciated, sticklike appearance—got busy spiking all unattended stores of food and drink with the horrific supplement. Amidst the carnage, though, real love found purchase and bloomed, if only briefly. Which made for a couple of diverting sex scenes involving actors inside cartoon bodies you wish you had. By the time the film ended, humanity itself had been reduced to an embattled enclave of a couple hundred survivors, none of whom could trust each other not to try to kill them. Prognosis for mankind and the planet looked undeniably grim. Here it was at last: the end of everything. But wait, not to worry, socko trailer coming up, there was a big-budget sequel already in the works.

CHAPTER 10

FORTUNE HUNTERS

AMBIENCE WAS UP. AMBIENCE was down. Ambience was up and down. She didn't know why. Internal weather. Today's forecast: more of the same. Stuff just happened. All that funky chemistry popping and fizzing through your vitals. Making you happy, making you sad. Is that all everything truly was? Everything? Really?

Big event of the day: we're out of cat food.

She grabbed a wad of cash from the honey bag that Graveyard insisted be kept "hidden" in a corner of the bedroom closet under a smelly pile of his dirty clothes. For easy access, he claimed. She sniffed the money. It seemed to be still retaining that swoony, fresh vault odor. And in her hand, it looked good and felt good, too. But best of all, of course, was watching it leave your hand. You passed out these strange little scraps of paper, and what did you get in return? Your own desires, magically materialized and solidified into shiny things you could hold, look at, fondle, ride, eat, put on and take off, talk back to, caress, break, forget about, or even toss in the trash. Every transaction a little miracle. She still couldn't seem to get over the sheer wonder of it all. Okay, she felt better now. Ready for the expedition to the corner deli. She practically skipped down the five flights of stairs and out into the surprise of a Mammoth City August. Who knew it could be so damn sweltering outside the refrigerated extravagance of her apartment, its pleasant autumn atmosphere created and controlled by the newly installed Air Process System by Tundra? She broke into a messy sweat after just a couple of blocks. If she'd known it was this jungly out on the street, she would have called. Had the cans of VarmintVittles delivered. She reached the corner, held her hand for one singular second on the front-door push strip of the HappyFarmSunnyPasturesBigCountry bodega, and then, for some reason or other, abruptly turned and went right on past. She didn't know where she was going. She just followed her feet. Took a left at Short Alley, cut across Paling Lane, went on down to Stile Street, and then took another left at Round-about Square. All these old-fashioned twisty streets with old-timey names made up of real letters, not numbers. Hadn't taken her long to realize that her favorite parts of her favorite town were the twisty parts. People told her (the people who are usually described as friends and family) not to move to that horrid sewer. Ever. When she first blew into Mammoth City, about a hundred million years ago now, bursting with pop fantasies, dumb yearnings, and a fanny pack full of nutso hope, she was told repeatedly, don't ever, on the street or in the subway, ever dare to look anyone directly in the eye. It's like provoking the bull. But everywhere she went everybody was looking at everybody else. Real hard. So she joined the crowd. And no one seemed to mind. People liked being looked at. As did she. And most of the lookers appeared fairly reasonable and fairly satisfied. And people who looked reasonable and satisfied were people you probably need not fear. Or so she liked to believe. Plus she really loved the whole crazy cultural gumbo that made up her big, loud city. All these wonderful hungry souls, pushing and shoving against life, crawling and climbing all over each other. One big-top flavor mash-up. It made her feel connected. To what, she wasn't sure. But she liked the feel. She knew, of course, that there were plenty of folks who hated what she liked. Too many originals for them, not enough copies. Too much of you know. All the dissonance made them feel angry. Too bad for them. Her city, the city she loved, was obviously a preview, for everyone, of the future, of, like it or not, the life to come on this spinning mudball, if there was ever to be a to-be.

When her feet finally stopped, she found herself in front of Pirates&Prostitutes, a wilderness outpost owned and operated by her other BFF, CarnyDoll. All product in the store related, in ways both obvious and arcane, to standard consumer fantasias of those two perennially popular occupations. All your pirate and prostitute needs conveniently located in one nearby outlet. Out of the back room CarnyDoll ran a side business selling marked-down knockoffs of the brainiacPhone8 for a tidy profit. She did what she had to do. Where'd she get the cells? Don't ask. These were troubled times.

In her weaker moments Ambience wanted to be CarnyDoll. In her stronger moments, or whatever kind of moments those were, she kinda hated her. Mostly, though, she just liked her a lot.

CarnyDoll was wearing a T-shirt that said: PRAY FOR BEAUTY. She had just been unpacking her latest shipment: a box of black leather bustiers with nasty white leather skulls sewn across each cup. She held one up to her chest.

"For the ultimate slut," she said. She laughed her husky, whiskey-soaked laugh. "We should sell a ton of these."

She showed Ambience her latest acquisitions: thigh-high boots that laced up the back, white silk puffy shirts, miniature treasure chests crammed with magnum-size black condoms, eye patches you could see through, a lavishly illustrated coffee-table book entitled *Whore Culture*, recent street fragrances from the House of Sweet Delay—GutterBalm and the trending AlleyOops—and suede-lined shackles for the delicate masochist.

"I plan on getting His Nibs into these tonight," said CarnyDoll. "And losing the key."

She had already worked her way through two loser husbands and was now looking to ditch the latest loser boyfriend.

"He's a real barnacle," she said. "I feel I have to pry him off with a stick."

"Where in God's name do you find these dickheads?"

"Where you usually find 'em. In the dicking place."

Ambience figured she had probably come over here to tell CarnyDoll about the recent and amazing improvement in her financial health. So she did. The Uncle Parsnips version.

"Nice," said CarnyDoll.

"What?" said Ambience. "That's all? That's your total reaction? That's all you're gonna say?"

"What do you want me to say?"

"The whole thing is kinda mind-blowing, don'tcha think?"

CarnyDoll shrugged. "People die," she said. "None of 'em's yet figured out a way to take it with 'em. Dough's gotta go someplace. Looks like it was your turn."

"You jealous?"

"Should I be?"

"But it's money. Lots and lots of money. It's a bunch of magic paper you never expected to have that you can trade for some fun you were never gonna have."

"I'm happy for you."

"Well, you don't look it."

"Whaddya want me to do? Squeal and clap my hands?"

"You certainly don't have to hop up and down, but a hug would have been nice."

So CarnyDoll hugged her.

"Thanks," said Ambience.

"Let's say we shut this sucker down," said CarnyDoll. She walked over to the front door. She turned the sign in the window to CLOSED. She locked the door.

"Every time I come over you shut the store," said Ambience. "How good can that be for business?"

"Probably not very. But you know what? For me, personally, it's pretty damn great." She pulled a bottle of MistyBog and a couple of shot glasses out from under the counter and filled them both.

"I haven't even eaten anything yet today," said Ambience.

"All the better," said CarnyDoll. She raised her glass. "Pennies from heaven," she said. "For you and for me." They clinked glasses.

They had another shot. And another. And another. And after that, who cared?

"Know what we should do?" said CarnyDoll.

"What?"

"Get our palms read."

"You're shitting me."

"I never joke about the future."

"Seriously?"

"Yeah, I think so."

"You honestly believe in that old con?"

"Define *believe*."

"So why should we do this again?"

"Cause we don't believe in any of it, and we're drunk?"

"This where I'm supposed to say, 'Sounds good to me'?"

"Well, yeah."

"Okay. 'Sounds good to me.'"

They covered the five and a half blocks to Palms, Cards, and Balls in record time. When they were drunk, they walked faster. Though Ambience found herself struggling to keep up with CarnyDoll's surprisingly ferocious pace.

"I don't see how you can move so fast in those spikes," she said. CarnyDoll liked to parade around in the high-altitude footwear generally favored by women in show business and/or street business. That's how she styled.

"My dogs be barkin' if they ain't in 'em," she said. She pressed the painted blue buzzer next to the painted red door. From inside they could hear a lot of screaming and crying. From numerous age groups. They waited.

"Maybe we should leave," said Ambience.

CarnyDoll hit the buzzer again. After another minute or so, they heard a female voice from inside. "Coming at'cha," it said, getting louder. "Coming at'cha."

Then the sound of one lock being opened, a second lock being opened, a third lock being opened, and the door opening. It was

Madame Doodah herself. All six impossible feet of her. She was dark and bony and looked exactly like someone who had crossed a big ocean under unspeakable conditions in order to one day pose in all her majestic grandeur in this specific narrow doorway before a couple of suitably impressed white girls. Around her head were wrapped five or six scarves of colors there were probably no proper names for. She had serious door-knocker earrings. She had a light mustache that appeared to have been actually penciled in. She spoke in an intermittently thick guttural accent of no recognizable origin. She was the whole package. Ambience was thrilled.

"Welcome," Madame Doodah said, and to CarnyDoll, "Good to see you again."

Ambience looked at CarnyDoll. CarnyDoll shrugged.

"Please, please, enter," Madame Doodah said, ushering them into a cramped room with heavy purple velvet drapes covering every wall. "Excuse, please," she said, plucking at the frayed lapel of the faded blue bathrobe she wore. Bits of crumpled tissue protruded from every pocket and every sleeve and from between her family-size lady lumps. "I feel better than I look," she said.

"We can come back," said Ambience.

"No, no, pay no mind," said Madame Doodah. "All's okay. Please, have a seat." She pointed to a beat-up pair of metal folding chairs. They sat. Madame Doodah lowered herself into a massive mahogany throne, its high backboard decorated with a carved hodgepodge of indecipherable signs and symbols.

"Who's first?" said Madame Doodah.

CarnyDoll plopped her arm down on the card table between them as if dropping a lamb shank onto a butcher's block.

"So eager," said Madame Doodah.

"I've got places to go."

Madame Doodah took CarnyDoll's hand and peered into the palm. She muttered. She sighed. She peered harder. Finally she leaned back and looked CarnyDoll in the face. "Same," she said.

"Same, same, same." She brushed the hand away. "Nothing but same. Why do you keep coming back here?"

"I'm an optimist," said CarnyDoll. "I keep hoping you'll find something different."

"What different? The lines never lie. You understand? Once the lines are written, they are written forever. Nothing I can do."

"I've been doing hand exercises," said CarnyDoll.

"Nothing."

"I think I've been developing some new wrinkles. They're faint, but I think there's something there. Baby squiggles. Wanna see?"

Madame Doodah waved her off. "No babies. No squiggles."

"You could at least take a look."

"No need."

"Your attitude doesn't seem too professional to me."

"I am top professional in Mammoth City area."

"And this is how you retain clients? By ignoring and insulting them? What kind of businesswoman are you?"

"You keep coming back."

"I'm an idiot."

"Well." Madame Doodah rolled her big bloodshot eyes.

"Aren't you supposed to tell people what they want to hear? What they're paying to hear? Isn't that how everyone makes money?"

"I'm not everyone. I am a prophetess."

"And a damn poor one. In both senses of the word."

"Tell a lie and you chip at the heart. Tell too many lies and you break your Ouija board. Where you are in the world you cannot find ever again. You truly want to be that lost?"

"A con artist with integrity. I admire that."

"If you possess integrity, you cannot be a con artist."

"Well, good luck in business with that attitude."

"I am not in business. I am in navigation. You understand?"

"You wouldn't even fudge the truth one tiny bit to make a quick buck?"

"No."

"Not the teensiest, weensiest little fib?"

"No."

"I can see why you live in a storefront."

"I live where circumstances suit me best. I will not put my talent in danger."

"What's wrong with your palm?" said Ambience, slightly freaked by the exchange. A superstitious side of her friend she'd never seen before. The girl was a constant carnival.

"Ask her," said CarnyDoll. "Apparently all my critical crap connects to all my other critical crap. And in all the wrong places. It's like a road map to hell."

"Hardly," said Madame Doodah. "You exaggerate, I think."

"What'd she tell you that was so awful?" said Ambience.

"Oh, I don't know. Something about my Goody line being abnormally short to begin with and right before it ends it intersects with my Needy line and that can't be good, can it? Also, my Want line steers totally clear of my Credit mound. So you can see where that leaves me. Somewhere around loveless, friendless, penniless."

"It's more complicated than that," said Madame Doodah. "You have a very nice Liability line."

"Thank you, Madame Sunbeam," said CarnyDoll. "I don't think I'm coming back here again."

"Fine. Your choice. Now, may I read your sister?"

"She's not my sister."

"So you say," said Madame Doodah. She turned to Ambience. "Now, let's see what we have here. Give me your outer hand, darling."

"Which one is that?"

"The one you write with."

"My right."

"Let's see that one."

She took Ambience's right hand, pressed gently a couple of times into the pad of flesh beneath her thumb. "Oh," she said. "Very pretty. Very nice."

"What? My lines?"

"Your hand. It's quite beautiful. So soft. The fingers so well shaped."

"Thanks. I try to use them as little as possible."

"But they shake so."

"I guess I'm a bit nervous."

"What are you afraid of?"

"You, I think."

"How silly."

"I think I'm afraid of what you're going to tell me."

"Oh, nonsense. What I say to you, you already know. You know that."

"Okay."

"You like boys, I see."

"Yeah, I guess."

"Several islands here on your Valentine line."

"Is that good?"

"Let's skip over those for the moment. You have a problem with money, yes?"

Ambience looked at CarnyDoll. "I don't think so. I mean, I like money. Doesn't everyone?"

"Maybe she'll have to break up with it," said CarnyDoll, giving her the bad boyfriend smirk.

"Not unheard of."

"That's a good one. How do you break up with money?"

"Abracadabra. You quit touching it."

"What? Like, physically?"

Madame Doodah nodded.

"Why would you want to do that?" said CarnyDoll.

"Money is vile," said Madame Doodah. "Full of the history. Old quarrels, old diseases, old curses."

"I notice you don't seem to have much of a problem handling the stuff."

"I know the secrets. That old stink don't stick to me."

"How lucky for you. Where can I get a deodorant like that?"

"Not for sale."

"Okay," said CarnyDoll. "I'm done. Let's get outta here."

"But I haven't even heard my fortune," said Ambience.

"You really want to?" said CarnyDoll.

"How bad could it be?"

"Fine. Your funeral."

Madame Doodah took up Ambience's hand again and peered into its sweaty palm. "You will have a long and prosperous life," she said.

"Okay," said Ambience. "As long as it's not accompanied by too much pain."

"There are no promises in prophecy."

"Too bad for me."

"How much?" said CarnyDoll.

"Wait," said Ambience. "That's it? 'A long and prosperous life?' I could get that outta a fortune cookie."

"You want cookie fortune," said Madame Doodah, "you get cookie future. I give you honest future."

"Really?" A bit surprised by how badly she wanted to believe her.

"What did I say? Madame Doodah tells no lies."

"If I were you," said CarnyDoll, "I'd settle for the 'long and prosperous' angle. Once she starts rooting around in your creases, no knowing what she'll find. Now, how much was that again?"

"Special," said Madame Doodah. "For you, today only. For both, one hundred dollars. No one gets such a price."

"A hundred bucks to tell us I'm fucked and she's going to Fantasy Island?"

"Many apologies. I didn't invent the world."

"Let me get it," said Ambience.

"I'm the one who dragged you here," said CarnyDoll.

"But I'm the one with the mad money. Why not spend what I've got till it's gone? Or until I am. Whichever comes first."

She counted out the bills and even left Madame Doodah a siz-able tip—out of compulsive politeness, not because she wanted to. She was such a stump. She hated herself.

"Now what?" said Ambience, as they stood outside blinking into the unexpectedly bright exterior.

"Don't know about you, but I, for one, could certainly use a drink," said CarnyDoll. "Let's try that shithole over there." She pointed across the street to a joint called Juggernauts. CarnyDoll, leading the way, walked in and, without a pause, made a perfectly graceful U-turn and walked right back out again, Ambience close behind.

"What's wrong?" said Ambience once they were safely outside.

"Jackholes," said CarnyDoll. "Serious jackholes. Whole infesta-tion of 'em. You notice? Clustered around the bar like a bunch of sickass flies."

"Wanna try the Hideyhole?"

"Forget the drink," said CarnyDoll. "How about the zoo? Go look at some real animals. When was the last time you were even there?"

"With my nephews about a century and a half ago."

"Perfect. Let's do it."

They hopped the next train north to the Mammoth City Zoolog-ical Gardens. Ambience couldn't believe the admission fee. More than double what it was the last time she'd visited, however many years ago that had been. The Age of Paying More and More for Less and Less. Of course, they had to first go to CarnyDoll's favorite: the gabled and fabled Reptile House. And just in time for the midday feeding. They watched live mice being dropped into cages where they had a life expectancy of about thirty seconds. The spectacle left Ambience feeling raw and unfinished. Everything stuffing every-thing else into its big collective mouth. Gobble, gobble, gobble. What was that all about? She didn't know.

They went to Monkey Mountain, Ambience's choice. They watched the monkeys picking bugs out of one another's fur and popping them into their mouths. They watched the monkeys watching you. They watched the monkeys masturbating. Right out in the wide-open air. Food for thought.

"Energetic little devils, aren't they?" said Ambience.

"This is making me horny," said CarnyDoll.

"You're even sicker than I thought you were."

"Tiny dicks, big loads. Look over there. That's as much spunk as any of my boyfriends ever put out."

"TMI."

"You're such a prude, Ambience. You don't get into the juice, all of the juices, you're just a looky-lou at the scene of the crime."

"I ride the rides, girl. Don't tell me. And I've screamed, I've cried, I've laughed, I've gotten sick."

"Yeah. Me, too. Sure is fucked, ain't it?"

"What?"

"Fucking."

"Oh, that. I thought we were talking about spending the day at Whirly World."

"Oh, you," said CarnyDoll, playfully punching Ambience in the arm. "You're such a punkster."

"Think I've had about as much monkey love as I can take in one afternoon."

"Me, too," said CarnyDoll. "What say we hike on over to a FlavorCabana and get ourselves rehydrated pronto?"

So they did. They found one of the famous "energy stations" cannily positioned right next to the popular Elephant Park. Carny-Doll had a Papaya Plié, Ambience a Banana Disaster. They both felt instantly invigorated. The elephants looked bored. They looked like they were waiting for something momentous to happen. The girls left them waiting.

Outside the Freedom of Flight Aviary they stopped to watch the birds. All that fluttering color. A whole wild spectrum in motion. The display was exhilarating.

"Makes you wish we had wings, doesn't it?" said some total

stranger standing next to her. Very next to her. She hadn't even noticed he was there. Quickly, she gave him the complete head-to-heels check. Oh, my. Here was a rush she hadn't experienced in a long, long time. And his face. So close to the genie face that usually appeared to her whenever she worked her Magic Button. Oh, my. He was big. He was broad. He radiated IQ. He was looking her in the eye. Steadily.

"You read my mind," she said.

"Not so hard."

"Really?"

"Yeah. All you have to do is pay attention."

"That easy?"

"Sometimes it is."

She wondered about Graveyard. Where was he? What was he doing? How was he feeling?

"You like zoos?"

"They're okay."

"My last girlfriend hated 'em. She said they reminded her of concentration camps."

"Except a lot of these animals would probably be extinct without them."

"That's the big picture. My girlfriend liked to look real squinty at things extremely close and extremely small."

"Sounds like that could probably be pretty exhausting."

"Tell me about it. That's why she's no longer my girlfriend."

"Smooth," said Ambience.

"Not really. I just try to be honest."

"Ambience," she said, extending her hand.

"PowerPoint," he said, extending his. They formally shook hands.

"Have we ever met before?"

"Oh, no," she said. "And it was going so well, too."

"No, no, it's not a line. Really. It happened, didn't it? Crossing paths, you and I. Something, somewhere."

"Some guy told me that once. Of course, I didn't believe him.

Turned out we had. He had sat behind me in EarthSkills class at ColdStone High. I don't know that I'd ever even looked at him once."

"Bet he looked at you."

"His loss."

"Don't sell yourself short."

"I do tend to do that."

"Diminishes the value of the product."

"And I certainly wouldn't want to end up in the damaged goods bin."

"That's not gonna happen."

He was looking into her eyes again. Searching, searching. For what? She had no answers. But what did that matter? Their bodies were talking to each other now. And he looked, well, silky. Probably his dick felt the same, too: silky. She kept looking at his hands. She had read once that the size of a guy's penis was directly related to the length of—what was it, now? The ring finger or the middle finger? She couldn't remember which. So she was checking out all his fingers. They were all of a goodly stature.

They looked at the birds for a while. The birds flew from tree to tree and back again. They perched on their roosts and talked to one another in weird sci-fi sounds.

"They're so bright and graceful," said PowerPoint. "It looks fake. So mediaesque."

Suddenly he pulled out a metal flask from some sort of secret pocket somewhere. It appeared to be made of silver.

"Silver," he said.

"I see," she said. "Cool."

"Scotch. My favorite. LaughFrogg."

"You're kidding, right? It's my favorite, too."

He took a hit. He passed the flask to her. She took a hit. And repeat.

"Doesn't have that rotten, boggy flavor," said Ambience.

"No. Not that rotten and boggy don't have their places. I've had quite a few great whiskeys where I felt I was kneeling down and sucking the stuff right outta the ground."

"You're right," she said. He was looking at her mouth. She was looking at his mouth. Next thing she knew her lips were on his and she felt as if the entire contents of the flask were suddenly roaring through her body in some delirious riptide. She felt as if she were standing on tiptoe when she wasn't. What the hell was happening here?

"You kiss good," he said.

"Not so bad yourself."

"Let's try that again."

So they did.

Interesting. He reminded her of Graveyard. He reminded her of Trapezoid. Her first real boyfriend. Who once, after a long, sweaty, memorable night, proposed to her. In a cemetery, of all places. Actually, she thought that was pretty brilliant. She'd almost said yes. But she hadn't. Her bad? Maybe, maybe not. Whatever. This guy, though, was making connections in all the right sockets.

She looked at CarnyDoll with a girly help-me face. No dice there. CarnyDoll was too busy macking on the other guy, whoever he was, to even notice. The friend. Of course there was a friend. Wasn't there always? Goofy-looking dude with a melon head and bad skin but a body that might be interesting under the jeans and the INVEST IN ME tank top. CarnyDoll had obviously been on him in half an instant. Ambience knew what she was doing. The ol' CarnyDoll seduction trick. Lock eyes, lock smiles. Then get on down into your cooch, the floral fruit of it, the sugary sweetness, the primal perfume. Pack all that into your gaze and beam directly into the troll-like male brain. Pussy power. He'll fall into your lap like a poisoned bird off a branch. If you want a dead bird in your lap.

This PowerPoint's lips were like Magic Fingers. Exploring all her secret spaces. In his arms she was just *in his arms*. She was just *herself*.

"Come here," he said. Okay. She liked the command in his

voice. He took her hand and she let him and he led her off into the bushes behind a FlavorCabana. Behind an overflowing Dumpster that reeked of fermenting oranges and week-old meat and all of yesterday. Guarded by fat iridescent flies as big and loud as bumblebees.

They made out for a while. He tasted like peppermint candy. Her whole body was vibrating. He wanted a mouth party. She could see it in his eyes. All big and burny. What did she want? She didn't know. Sometimes she just couldn't believe herself. He started unzipping his jeans.

"Isn't this a little fast?" she said.

"Maybe not fast enough."

All right, Ambience said to herself, what can we do with this? A situation. This situation. Know what? She could do whatever the fuck she wanted. She was rich. She got down on her knees and pulled down his pants. He was wearing Krazy Klown boxers. She pulled down the boxers. His fingers had told no lies. She took his dick into her mouth. He smelled like a stale sponge. She could feel his pulse on her tongue. She hadn't been in this position since whenever. The emotions resurfacing were peculiar and complex. Reading them was like trying to decode the innards of some fresh-off-the-line electronic device she'd been introduced to in a signal corps class back in her intro-to-war days at good ol' Ft. WhyMe: too many different colored wires connected to too many unidentifiable doohickeys. But now, just as it did then, her sense of pride and skilled confidence kicked in, as well as a mounting force of irresistible pleasure, and despite the fact that her knees were beginning to hurt (she was getting so old), she unashamedly bent to the job and worked it like a pro. For a moment or two, she actually forgot who she was. That was nice. When he started to cum, she pulled away and let him anoint the blacktop with his pudding.

"Thanks," he said. He stuffed his pug stick back into his pants, zipped up, wiped his hand on his thigh, and, without another word, walked away.

WTF. WTF. WTF. Whatever happened to her stupid vow: won't-get-fooled-again? Something was wrong with her, something definitely and deeply wrong. She really wanted to hurt someone or something real bad. The flies buzzed. The garbage stank. Slowly she stood, brushed the grit from her knees, and staggered out into the light. CarnyDoll was all alone, leaning against the rail surrounding the aviary.

"Where's your buddy?" Ambience said.

"Aw, you know. He was a hump. Yours?"

"Ditto."

"Ditto, ditto, and ditto," said CarnyDoll.

"I suppose there are very few original assholes."

"No. You gotta have even a fragment of a brain to pioneer in creepiness."

On the long ride back into the city, Ambience filled CarnyDoll in on all the thrills not to be had behind a FlavorCabana.

"I'm sorry," said CarnyDoll. "I'm crazy sorry."

"S'all right. What was I expecting? Dinner and drinks?"

"Well, you always were an old-fashioned girl."

They rode for minutes in silence. Wheels and wheels.

"Guys," said CarnyDoll.

"I know," said Ambience. "At least I tell myself I know."

"No one put a gun to your head."

"No, just a flesh one."

"So you blew some cretin at the zoo, right? Happens to the best of us. Could've been better, could've been worse. Any buzz in it at all?"

"Maybe." She paused. "I don't know."

"There. See? Not a total write-off."

"Too bad there isn't a tax deduction for asshole encounters."

"If that were the case, no one would have to pay any taxes at all."

"You know," said Ambience, "I love you."

"Love you, too," said CarnyDoll.

They hugged. A genuine buzz this time. They got off at the same stop.

"Sorry," said CarnyDoll again.

"Not your fault," said Ambience.

"Give me a call."

"I will."

"We can't let the assholes win."

"No," said Ambience, "but they're real quick sprinters."

"Then we just have to run faster."

They hugged again. Ambience ambled on home. The afternoon's highlights on a mad loop in her head. Despite herself a certain mood had settled over her. It was like being trapped inside one of her mother's canning jars—cramped, airless, contents on full display.

And the day was not, as CarnyDoll had helpfully pointed out, a total loss, a date to be permanently expunged from Ambience's Book of Days, but rather the occasion for a valuable teaching moment, which we're all waiting for—the hard lesson that there is indeed something from which money, for all its considerable supernatural power, cannot protect you: yourself.

CHAPTER 11

420

FARRAGO WAS ALONE IN her room doing ghost hits off her favorite bubbler, watching *Vampire Chef* on her ForbiddenFruit laptop, and texting stupid-ass brain shit to her bestie, Anagram—she was multitasking—when her mom started banging on the door like a crazy lady.

"What?" said Farrago.

"Open up!"

"No."

"Open this door right this instant!"

"Go away."

"You think I don't know what you're doing in there!"

"That's right. That's what I think."

"You want to be grounded again? That it? Try me. I'll ground you in a Mammoth City second."

"I thought I was."

"What?"

"Grounded."

"I'm not talking to you through a locked door. Open it. Now."

"I don't think so."

"I'll stand out here all night! All right? Don't think I won't. Cause I can stand out here a long, long time."

"Knock yourself out."

Her mother pounded. The door rattled in its frame. The wall shook. After a while the pounding stopped.

Silence. More silence. Then, "I won't be insulted like this. Your behavior—it's childish, it's unacceptable."

"Whatever."

"Tell me this, then. One thing. Why do you enjoy tormenting me so? Can you just answer me that?"

"No."

"You know I'm only concerned for your welfare. Ever since your brother left, you're the only one I worry about. You're my baby. You know that. I care about your well-being, your safety, your life. I care about you."

"In your head."

"And I think you're spending way too much time cooped up in that room. It's not healthy. Go outside, feel the sun, talk to people. Get out and do. There's a whole world out there. It's like you're just hibernating or something."

"How do you spell *hibernating*?" Farrago was texting play-by-play commentary to Anagram, who was loving every detail. Anagram hated her own mother, too.

"Now, don't make me lose my temper again. Please don't do that. You know how I hate to lose my temper."

"You tell me often enough."

"That's not fair."

"Can I go back to Dad's tomorrow?"

"You've still got two more days left with me. But maybe, if your father's free, and you open this damn door."

"Guess I'll tough it out in here, then."

"You really disappoint me sometimes, Farrago. What goes on under that dome of yours I'm sure I haven't the foggiest. If I didn't know better, I'd wonder if you were actually mine." And back went the tiny little mom feet, clump-clump-clump like big heavy I-want-you-to-hear-every-serious-step feet, back down the hallway, back down the stairs.

"What a hosebag," said Farrago to herself. Then she said it again, out loud: "hosebag." She'd always been a passenger trapped on her mother's struggle bus. She texted Anagram what had just happened. RBUs, Anagram texted back. She had always liked Anagram's sense of humor. But why not? They were the same height, the same weight, the same age, the same coloring, the same aliens in similar earthsuits. Only difference, major though it was, was that Anagram had recently become a star and a celebrity, a celebrity and a star, by posting for months on MooTube her fashion dos and don'ts, made up out of stuff you could find in your refrigerator. I mean, could you believe it? Farrago was so mad crazy jealous she could just die. Wouldn't you?

They'd met on the first day of fourth grade at Munch & Crunch Elementary. Their teacher, Miss Gazump, in an effort to demonstrate how much "fun" she was and how much "fun" they were all going to have in the coming year, dismissed the class at the end of the day according to eye color. Blue went first, then brown, green, gray, and finally hazel. That left Farrago and Anagram. They had tried to go out on green and then hazel, but Miss Gazump, after checking their respective irises, had held them back. They didn't know the color of their eyes. Miss Gazump didn't know, either. The issue never seemed to have come up before. Finally, after all the other kids with real colors had gone, Miss Gazump squatted down, gave the offending organs an up-close, extended scrutiny. At last she sighed, straightened up, and said, "You two are special. You have miscellaneous eyes." And with that they were dismissed. They'd been BFFs ever since.

Mothers, of course, were a major topic, online and off. They seemed not so much a wholly different species as an unfortunate, often irritating, sometimes scary mutation of their children, a message from the future: avoid, at all costs, becoming *this*. Talking about mothers seemed to help ward them (the mothers) and the possibilities off. Two main issues: (1) Who were these creatures, really? and (2) What did they, what could they possibly, want? Hours of conversational fun.

Latest mom bomb: Farrago's "role model" had been given for her birthday by one of her stupid friends a silver tiara, which she then proceeded to actually wear for an entire week, not just at home but also out in public, to the amusement of strangers and her daughter's utter mortification.

And Anagram's mom was somewhere in the middle of an interminable project to redecorate their home from top to bottom, which involved throwing out all the "junk."

She said she wanted her family to embark on a new "lean, mean" way of life. Anagram's dog, SpellChecker, had already run off weeks ago, spooked by the near-constant parade of painters, electricians, plumbers, and "living stylists." Her father, under whatever name he was using that week, had already decamped to a one-room hideaway at the FluorescentLinoleum Inn. Her brother, BatteryCharge, had put his own locks on his door and denied access to all but his most shady friends.

Farrago, at least, had the freedom, sort of, that allowed her to shift from one nutso parent to the other in accordance with the mysterious rotations of their respective mental issues. This week was Carousel's turn—no crisis, just part of the regular cycle. Farrago had no favorite, really, preferences exhibiting notoriously brief shelf lives. Sometimes one parent was crazy, sometimes the other, sometimes both were crazy at once. There was no predicting their nonsense.

Farrago signed off with Anagram. She had work to do, a dumbass paper for her Old Timey Times class, "Why Color Movies of Today Are So Superior to Antique Black and White." She'd done her research. She'd collected her examples. She just couldn't face the huge hassle of dragging a bunch of stupid words outta her brain. Who gives a fuck, anyway?

She refilled the bowl. She sparked up the bubbler. Leaf was a friend. Good and true. Leaf could always be counted on. It knew her. It knew what she liked. It knew where she wanted to go. And it took her there, without fail, each and every time. She liked traveling into the caramel. Where everything sharp and hard became soft and chewy. But even with a prime head on, her homework assignment remained naggingly in view, persistent, hovering. Just far away, so very far away. She'd rather watch her fish. She could stare at them for hours, gliding around in their lighted tank. So bright and smooth and alive. Some were quick. Flashes of cool neon. Some moved sooo slooowly. In no great hurry to go anywhere. That's because none of the fish were trying to get to any particular place at all. They knew what they were doing. They were making patterns. The fish were talking to one another. They were talking to her. And the message, it wasn't exactly verbal. It was something directed at the body. Something you knew without thinking. Something private. Fish knowledge. From the time when we, too, were little fishes. This is how the flying-saucer people in outer space communicated. This is how God spoke.

Sometime around there she fell asleep, or passed out, or whatever you want to call it. And when she came to, bad light was blooming behind the window curtains. Oh, shit. She was afraid to look at the clock: 11:11. Oh, God. She was supposed to be handing in her paper right about now. Fuckups like this were the reason she hadn't already graduated, been released from learning prison. She'd been held back twice, once in third grade and once in seventh. She'd had attendance problems. She'd had grade problems. She'd had attitude problems. She didn't seem to "get" school. What was the point, exactly? Only reason for the entire system's existence, as she saw it, was to provide an elaborate baby-sitting service for parents who weren't there, weren't ever going to be there. Who knew what to do with her? So she'd been recycled. Now, with her freedom date from Tip O' The Wedge High in actual sight, she was in major trouble again. She looked at the clock again. She ran through her options, her lack of options. She sat up quietly in bed for a moment. WTF. She reached for the bubbler. Wake 'n' Bake time. All hail the leaf.

An hour later she had managed to get into most of her clothes. Same ones as yesterday, natch. But she still couldn't find her StompYou boots. So she had another couple of hits. Searched around some more. Found missing boots in wastepaper basket. How the fuck had they ever gotten there? She went to the bathroom. She brushed her teeth. She washed her face. She looked at herself in the mirror. No consolation there.

She stepped out into the Haunted Hallway. Black walls covered in phosphorescent green ghost stickers to help light your way to the john in the darkest of nights. She paused to listen. House strangely silent. Where the fuck was her mother? Where was the fucking door banging when she needed it? She descended the circular Staircase of Doom into the Free Association Family Space, a large open area decorated in a squeaky cacophony of styles that made no sense to anyone but its wacko architect. The banged-up sticks of mismatched furniture had been painstakingly gathered over the years from random yard sales, not without cost in time, money, and fumigatory annoyance. The whole curious collection presided over by handpicked wall displays of Artworks by JingleBell, metallic fashionings depicting hellish landscapes on imaginary planets. Her mother believed these monstrosities were actually "bee-you-tee-full." Of course, this was also a woman who tooled about town, to Farrago's enduring mortification, in a car-size fully operational bright green pickle, the centerpiece of a now defunct ad campaign for the Sons & Daughter Pickle Emporium, purchased at auction several years ago in an appalling, but not uncommon, lapse of parental judgment. "Mom?" she said. No answer. In the kitchen she found a note stuck by turtle magnet to the battered door of the old Cold Comfort refrigerator: "Gone to Porcelain Shebang in Skeeter Hill with CheddarBake and LooseEnd. Jelly beans in bowl on counter. NothingCola in fridge. Have a nice day at school. Love, Maw."

"What an asshat," she said. She ate the beans. She drank the cola. Her favorite breakfast, for the last couple of years, anyway. She texted Anagram. Anagram was zoning out in her Consumer Heroes class and wondering where Farrago was. She texted Loop-hole. He was, surprise surprise, dutifully seated in his assigned chair in CutNPaste class but so freaking buzzed and skittery he was ready to punch Mr. PinchNerve right in his putty clown nose. Mr. PinchNerve was the lord prime of all CutNPaste and easily the most despised teacher at Tip O' The Wedge. His car had been keyed (numerous times), his desk drawers painted shut, the sleeves of his suit jacket scissored off, and his spare toupee stolen from his briefcase and superglued to the bald bronze head atop the statue of the founder, Old White Guy, that stood outside the front entrance, perpetually blessing apprentice scholars past, present, and future. Loophole was ready to bolt. Where was she?

Loophole had transferred in halfway through the previous year. He'd been kicked out of half a dozen schools in High Falutin Heights for, among other offenses, chewing gum in a no-gum zone, calling his shop teacher a ten-thumbed monkey, throwing corn dodgers at the lunch ladies (yuk, yuk), heckling fellow students in BlushAndGrinSpeech class until the daughter of Principal Wigwam burst into tears and ran from the room, smearing dog shit inside the star quarterback's jockstrap, fronting a general unpleasant air of all-around Don'tGiveAFuckdom, and, oh, yeah, selling raze to an undercover narc in the senior class and "borrowing" Nurse Budget's car for a wild joyride that ended in emergency room visits for all participating revelers. What to do? His hapless parents exercised the nuclear option. They moved. And Tip O' The Wedge, they announced, was to be the very last stop on their son's erratic educational bus. After that, final destination: the Saint Fiduciary of the Bent Nail Home for Nasty Little Punks. Didn't sound half bad to Loophole. They had a heated pool.

Loophole and Farrago texted back and forth for a while. Blah, blah, blah. Then Loophole told Farrago to meet him in thirty at the Rock Pile. BackAlley's Rock Pile was a dark, dorky, smelly den of T-shirts, music memorabilia, and video games down at the west end of the Mess O' Stuff Mall, right next to the Shellack Shack. BackAlley was from one of those countries where the War had come for a brief visit and had liked the place so much that it decided on a lengthy stayover. So BackAlley bugged out while the bugging out was good. Most of his family had been killed the last time the War had been their guest. He'd left with a suitcase full of spare clothes and an ATM card to his dead uncle's account in a foreign no-questions-asked bank. The family money wasn't exactly clean, but then whose was? He'd used most of the funds as seed to finance his dream, this shrine to pop culture in the land that invented pop culture. He could see the hundreds and the thousands and the hundreds of thousands and—dare he even contemplate?—the millions rolling toward him, wave after green wave. He and all his castaway relatives finally redeemed from life and released from history. A reality, unfortunately, that never materialized. Location, no doubt, a major issue. But where else was he going to open a store? All he had ever wanted in life was to migrate to a sheltered oasis free of explosions and hot lead, where corruption was on the down low, the air smelled of trees, children played in the grass, and, in the enveloping quiet, he could be quietly stacking. So why not Randomburg (formerly DeficitFalls)? Home to the famous BigBadGorge, which thousands of tourists drove hundreds of miles in order to gawk at. Home to CorrugatedDreams, the nation's largest manufacturer of cardboard boxes. Two interstate exits from the Mess O' Stuff Mall, third largest in the world. And only 4.5 miles from the Shuttlecock Indian Casino and Hotel. But most important, the place where that classic golden age musical *Painted Clouds* (translated into BackAlley's language as *Drippy Sky*) had been shot, a film BackAlley happened to see at a very impressionable age on his rich cousin's giant XoLoTron. He'd never seen a TV screen so big or a movie so real that he thought he'd imagined it himself. Wherein a naive, cash-challenged foreign exchange student from Upper Maxistan travels to Mammoth Country, settles into the postcard perfection of Randomburg (formerly DeficitFalls), here called Goodyville, and naturally gets tangled up in the lives and loves of the adorable SteamGasket family he's staying with. All the characters smile a lot and burst into catchy song whenever they look at one another for too long. And in spite of the predictable series of comical misadventures (all massively entertaining), our hero ends up fucking all the right good-looking people, founds a wildly successful business making calibrated nibbins, gets elected mayor, and finally marries the achingly available daughter of the wealthiest man in Goodyville in a lavish production number involving most of the population of said town. Afterward, BackAlley couldn't sleep for a week and his mother scolded his cousin for showing him what she was sure must have been a horror movie. Today he could still sing all the tunes from the sound track and would if you looked at him too long. To Loophole and Farrago, though, he was a cool dude. They liked his accent and the crazy, off-the-dress-code clothes he wore. And he listened to the same music they did. He watched the same TV. Sometimes he even sparked up with them and let them play for free his rare collection of vintage video games. Burro Squash and Kosmic Karnivores and Froggy on Ice. This visit, though, was to make a score. BackAlley also sold beer and leaf out of his car to a select number of personal clients. Guess what? Loophole qualified.

Standing in the hot parking lot behind the mall, staring into the open trunk of BackAlley's powerful little Zoomzini, as if supposedly gazing upon museum treasures under glass, was not exactly how Farrago wanted to spend these precious few, unexpectedly "free" hours she was certainly going to get punished for. What she wanted to do was just get ultra wasted. As soon as possible. That was the necessity. What happened afterward was optional. Loophole was taking an eternity to button the deal. Talking and talking about nothing and nothing. And BackAlley, of course, was standing quite close to her. Very, very close. This was the downside to BackAlley. He liked to crowd your space. Within minutes of their first meeting Farrago could feel his invisible hand reaching out to touch her where she didn't want to be touched. She knew without really pulling up the visual that BackAlley wanted to fuck her in a creepy, cuddly, foreign sort of way. This was the sort of transmission from the testosterone zone she tried to ignore as best she could. But frankly, sometimes her nerves got a bit fried. She gave Loophole an elbow tap in the ribs. Finally Loophole handed over the cash. BackAlley handed over the "product." They left.

"Well, that took forever and a half," she said as they climbed into Loophole's XYZ, a muscle car on steroids.

"Whaddya want from me?" He was trying to open the plastic vial of BackAlley's leaf, which seemed to be secured by an excessive amount of cheap sticky tape.

"Where's the piece?" she said, rooting around in the glove box, stuffed with old parking tickets, old crinkled maps, old pizza rinds, and an old pair of black panties with a red skull sewn over the crotch. Hers? Probably.

"Under the dash," he said. "There's a box."

She felt around until her fingers located and retrieved a metal first aid kit with a couple of magnets glued to the bottom. "Cool," she said. "This is new. When'd you get it?"

"I don't remember." He still hadn't gotten the vial open. "Why all these fucking questions?"

"Just curious. I like to know what you do."

"Well, right now, see, what I'm doing is just trying to get into *this fucking lockbox!*" Exasperated, he chucked the vial over to her. "Why's he got to go and wrap it all up like that? It's like trying to peel a golf ball."

She passed the opened vial back to him.

"How'd you do that?"

She held up a hand. "Long, sharp nails," she said.

Piece loaded. Piece lit. And in seconds they were expelling endless plumes of sweet smoke. Hotboxin' in the parking lot of the Mess O' Stuff Mall. They watched the people, the stooges, jingling their car keys on the way in, pushing their carts of shiny crap on the way out.

"Look at that fucker," said Loophole. An elderly man with a cane came hobbling out of the building, stopped, stared out in apparent confusion at the vast glittering field of sunstruck metal and glass. "CurtainCall before the face-lift," he said. "Probably can't even remember which row he was in. Or which fucking black camper is his fucking black camper." Farrago started to laugh. She didn't want to, but she did.

"Oh, wait, wait, lookee here. Effigy and her pack of grotty rug rats." Young mother trying to balance two ridiculously overloaded shopping bags between her arms while simultaneously attempting to herd a couple of small, screaming offspring to their car. "Probably ran out of the kids' Temperall this morning."

"Stop," said Farrago, struggling to hold herself in. "I so don't want to laugh at them."

"Yes, you do. You know you do. Hey, man, check out this dude. NoName right around the time he got the lead in *Galactic Cowhand*." Slender guy in bunny sneakers, torn jeans, and a stained RoadBurn T-shirt. Acne scars and looked like he hadn't shaved in a couple of weeks.

Now her laughing machine had started, and once started, she couldn't stop it.

"Amazing," said Loophole. "Who'd have thunk it? All these rich celebs shopping at a crappy mall in Randomburg."

"How'd they even find this shithole?"

"They know bargains when they see 'em." The laughs kept coming.

"Who'd you take me for when you first spied me?" said Farrago.

"You? Easy peasy. Hiding out there in the back corner of Mr. OlivePit's Jolly Roger Democracy class hoping no one'll notice you, hoping you'll never get called on."

"Ever again in my whole fucking life."

"Yeah. You were a dead ringer for MissyMiss."

"The porn star?"

"The rock star."

"Before the Algorithms or after?"

"Before, of course. One look and I knew you were a penis paradise. That's where I wanted to vacay. And I knew I would."

"So confident," she said.

"Well. Look at me."

So she did. Then, without a word, she leaned over and kissed him. Hard. He kissed back. Hard. They mixed syrups. When they pulled apart, they looked at each other again and realized there was no apart.

"Let's bounce," said Loophole, turning the key in the ignition, turning to look at her. "Where to?"

"Spin the wheel," she said.

Loophole was famous for dramatic exits. His signature move. The louder, the faster, the better. They went roaring out of that parking lot, scattering pedestrians, screeching cars, panicked bicyclists, and nearly T-boning a transmission-plagued melon truck.

"Stash the piece," said Loophole, glancing at the mirror for telltale signs of revolving red lights.

Which Farrago did. Between her legs.

They cruised the town. They went up a street. They went down a street. They went down a street. They went up a street. Like that.

They toured the greater Randomburg metroplex area. All three blocks of it. Nothing, nothing, and nothing.

They checked out the major Kid Haunts. The KwikiKween. RestYourAss State Park. GameYou. No one haunting. No one else cutting school.

They scoped out Tip O' The Wedge. So still, so silent, so solid-looking from the outside. Hard to believe the pimpled turmoil caged within.

"Wonder what's going on in MinyMoe's class," said Loophole.

"No, you don't."

"You're right. I don't."

"You hungry?"

"Read my mind."

They drove over to LooseyJuicy's, the run-down one out on

CornView that got robbed last month by a couple of gunmen who were supposed to be degenerate illegal immigrants or something. Lunchtime. Place packed, line out the door. Even the drive-thru all jammed up.

"Wanna go somewhere else?" said Loophole.

"I didn't wanna come here in the first place."

"You like the BroccoliSliders."

"When I'm drunk."

"Wanna go somewhere else?"

"We're fucking here," Farrago said. "Let's fucking eat. Get in behind the teal Oracle. The one with the Yowsa plates. God, what are they doing all the way up here?" She picked up the piece, packed it, sparked it, ripped it, passed it on to Loophole. Until they were sitting inside their car, inside a cloud of burning leaf, going round and round until a space finally opened up. They got food of some sort. Later, neither one of them could remember exactly what sort, but they ate it. It was food. After a while the smoke pouring out their windows began to attract unwanted attention—knowing smiles from fellow leafers, scowls from mommies with kids.

"All right," said Loophole. "Now that we've done our duty, freaked out the normies at LooseyJuicy's, we can shove off."

"Do it," said Farrago.

Broke outta there like a bat from, well, somewhere else. They cruised around. Out on Route 73, clutching a DustyBoy in one hand, the piece in the other, Loophole made a clumsy right onto Old Windmill Road. He glanced at Farrago. He glanced away.

"What are you doing?" she said.

"Driving."

"Well, drive someplace else. Now!"

"Let's just check out the parking lot. The lunchtime crowd. For fun. See how ol' Pops is doing."

She started pounding on his shoulder with both fists.

"Hey, cut it. That hurts."

"Turn the fucking car around!" She continued to pound.

"All right, all right. Just stop with the fucking hands." He turned left into a DominationDonuts. Pulled up to the door. Parked. "Wanna Burpleberry Cream?" he said.

She glared at him.

"Fills your face," he said, quoting the ad.

She glared.

"Well, long as we're here, believe I'll snag me a couple of those Choco Grenades." He opened his door.

"I cannot believe how stupid you can be sometimes," she said. "I mean seriously, dangerously stupid. You think I want a replay of what happened last time he caught me with you?"

"Don't worry about it. He's inside counting up his receipts."

"Until he comes out."

"He ain't gonna see nothing in the two seconds it takes us to go by."

"I hate you."

Took some more leaf, some more beer, some more tooling around until some semblance of chill was restored.

They went out to the Spirit Mound. One bogus car in the gravel lot. A purple PavementEater with a bumper sticker that read: F@#% BUMPER STICKERS.

"Oh, my God," said Farrago. "It's RoamingMinute." She scrunched down in her seat. "You see him?"

"I'm looking," said Loophole, scoping left, right, front. "No nothing. He's probably down by the river. Taking a piss in it."

"Bet that skank Hollaback is with him, too." She and Hollaback hated each other. Neither knew why.

"Wait—I hear voices. Somebody's coming."

"Is it them?"

"Two people, looks like, coming out of the woods. Yeah, it's them. Uh-oh, they've seen the car. They're coming over."

"Oh, shit." Farrago sat back up again. She watched the couple cross the gravel lot. "Little Miss Hollaback. She walks like a truck driver."

"RoamingMinute looks like an extra from *White Line Washouts*."

They were still laughing as RoamingMinute and Hollaback approached their car, dividing up without a word, RoamingMinute toward the driver's side, Hollaback toward the passenger's, guy to guy, girl to girl, everybody happy.

"What's so funny?" said Hollaback, leaning her finely engineered boobs into the open window. Farrago took one look at her mask-like face. All she needed. Hollaback had "high" eyes. Well, good for her.

"Nothing much. Loophole and I like to laugh."

"So do I. Laughing, you know?"

"It's the best."

"Like looking at your ride," said RoamingMinute to Loophole, "every time I look at it." He patted the roof affectionately.

"A real beast," said Loophole. Which led into a private boy-stuff discussion on the subtleties under the hood.

Hollaback bent over, clawing at her bare calf. "Watch out," she said. "Skeeters are crazy bad over near the Mound."

"Those ain't skeeters," said Farrago.

"No?"

"Native juju. They're the souls of the Shuttlecock, come back to wreak their bloody revenge. On pasty heathens like you."

"Yeah? Like to see what'd they do against a can of PestOff. Got a cig?"

Farrago fished around in her bag for a pack of Daredevils. Handed her one, which Hollaback immediately lit and sucked on as if it were her first good, deep breath of the day.

"So what are you guys doing out here?" said Hollaback.

"Could ask you the same question. Aren't you supposed to be in class or something?"

"Not today. I'm at home right now, in case you haven't noticed. I'm sick. I've got the crud."

"Yikes." Farrago shrank back in her seat. "Then don't stand so fucking close."

"I'm not contagious."

"Right."

"Hear about PressOn?"

"Who hasn't?"

"Whaddya think'll happen to her?"

"Hope she likes jail."

"You know, she said to me once she didn't think God wanted her to be happy."

"Well, obviously, BallBearings didn't."

"'Smack that bitch up.'"

"Yeah. One of those."

"At least he's not dead."

"Yet."

"She just cut him up a little. Right?"

"She's my hero."

"What?" said Loophole suddenly, tearing himself away from a hard-core face-to-face with RoamingMinute on comparative compression ratios, the Mayflower head versus the Trillium head. "What'd you say?"

"Nothing you need to hear."

"I need to hear everything."

"She said she'd like to slice you up with a box cutter," said RoamingMinute.

"That's what I thought."

"It's nothing, all right? Just go back to your car crap and everything'll be fine. I'll explain it to you later."

"I'm not liking this."

"Who said you had to?"

RoamingMinute let out a half chuckle, half cough kind of sound. Loophole glared at him. "Hey," RoamingMinute said. "It's funny."

"So's your face."

"Paparazzi would kill to get a clear shot at my face."

"They're not the only ones."

"All right, boys," said Farrago. "Separate corners, huh?"

"Hey, Farrago," said RoamingMinute. "Know what a pussy is?"

"Let me guess. A box a penis comes in?"

"Oh, you heard it, huh?"

"Only about a century ago."

"Still funny," said Loophole.

"If you're twelve," said Farrago.

"She's got no sense of humor," said Loophole to RoamingMinute. "Neither does Hollaback."

"I hang with you, don't I?" said Hollaback.

"Why don't you two just go back to sucking off a piston rod or whatever?" said Farrago. "Everyone'll be happier."

So they did. Grumbling.

"Going to AloeVera's party Friday?" said Hollaback.

"Who's gonna be there?"

"The usuals, you know. SettingDefault and AnchorBolt and Luminaria, that bald witch she runs around with, all us cool kids, and a mess of her rat bastard friends from Saint Peppermint's. Plus the Fiscal Cliffs are playing, supposedly. Her mother's life coach has a son who's in the band."

"I don't know."

"She's even gonna have NutClusters the clown."

"Really? Doing what?"

"Clown stuff, I suppose."

"What's the occasion?"

"Her parents are throwing it, actually. Trying to make up for the last five years, when there were birthdays but no parties."

"Tell me about it. That girl's fucking cried her way through high school. So when'd the parents get back together?"

"Not sure that they have. But they're together enough at the moment to give her this whatever-it-is. So you coming?"

"When is it again?"

"Friday. Eight."

"I'll try. I may have something."

"You know the leaf she gets, right? Flowering tops. Heirloom quality. From Papa Presto."

"The good papa."

"Word is she's got raze, too."

"Raze? Really?"

"Last time I tried that shit, over at TaffyPull's house, I got double vision real bad and then I forgot who I was and then I forgot I was an actual person."

"What time'd you say?"

"Eight. But you know, you can show up whenever. Till dawn, practically."

"Might be worth checking out."

"Friday."

"Got it."

"Hey, babe," said Hollaback over the roof of the XYZ, "ready to split?" And to Farrago, "His mom wants us both for dinner tonight. She's making his favorite: fried husker balls with some kind of crazy-ass sweet sauce makes you wanna barf."

"Yum."

She shrugged. "Hey, he likes it." She looked at her phone. "C'mon, we gotta sky. BurningBush needs a ride to her Jiggle class."

"Right there," he said. And to Loophole, "*Gum Turpentine*. You can download it off of SplinterFlicks. Wait till you dig on what goes down at the end up in that fucking barn."

"Don't tell me."

"It's tight, man."

"Let's go already," said Hollaback. "She's gonna be late."

Farrago looked at her phone. "Yeah, we gotta slide, too."

"Parents?"

Farrago shook her head. "Meeting somebody."

"Laters."

"Peace."

"Blow out the candles," said Loophole.

"Got my wish on right here," said RoamingMinute, grabbing his crotch with his right hand, shaking it.

Loophole and Farrago watched the pair go crunching away across the gravel.

"What a couple of d-bags," said Loophole.

"Don't ever turn your back on either one of 'em."

"Got that right."

Loophole placed his hand on the ignition key. Turned and looked at Farrago. "Say the word, bird."

"Ka-ching!"

"Bangin'."

Twisted the key, crushed the pedal, went shrieking out of that lot like a demon loosed from a spell. Another grand exit. Hooting and hollering down the straightaway till the first major intersection, when Farrago warned him to lighten up.

"See the Persimmon Petroleum sign over there?" she said. "Sergeant Bicuspid likes to hide behind it with his radar gun on stun."

"What a dickwad."

"Even worse if he stops ya."

"Watch me now. Daddy Road Rules. See, I'm turning with my turning light on."

"Looks like he's not even there."

"Cameras, Farrago. You never know where the cameras are."

"Watching, watching, watching."

"Your mom home?"

"Who cares?"

"She doesn't exactly like me."

"Who cares?"

"I was thinking about you. Parental freakouts are a real buzzkill."

"No drama. We walk in the house. We go upstairs. We go in my room. We lock the door. End of mom story."

At the next red light he leaned over, wrapped his arm around her waist, pulled her to him. Their mouths always seemed to fit together so incredibly well. Tongues, too. When they heard honking, they pried themselves apart.

"What is wrong with people?" said Farrago. "Tell me a single place in this whole fucking town you need to get to that quickly."

"I love you, babe."

"Me, too." She looked at her phone. Scrolled through the most recent dozen-plus messages. Replies? Just to Anagram and Filibuster. The rest could wait.

At her house, amazingly enough, no mom car. Blessed be the spirit in the sky. Inside, past the perpetually unlocked door, they found, in a prearranged tableau on the kitchen table, a collection of detailed Mumbleware depicting each and every character of the whole lovably roguish cast of the infinite Corporverse: the two-headed, eight-armed CEOs, junior execs secretly operating elaborate multiplanet pyramid schemes, fetching assistants in black leather catsuits, one-eyed financial officers who each spoke a separate exotic language, accountants sweating real acid, security guards with ever-shifting allegiances, a cleaning staff running its own investment firm out of key toilet stalls, and assorted stooges of species both tellurian and cosmic, right down to an alarmingly lifelike rendering of—everyone's favorite—MarginCall, the wise-cracking monkey from the Huminahumina galaxy who actually happened to run the whole damn show. Amid this impressive display was propped a note: GONE TO MOUNT BARBELL FOR BIG AUCTION. LAST PIECES OF BUTTERMUFFIN ESTATE UP FOR BID. I SO WANT THE LORD PITTERPAT MUSING CHAIR, THE ENCHANTED POOL FOUNTAIN PEN, AND THE FAMOUS SET OF CRYSTAL CRUETS, A GIFT FROM PRESIDENT AND FIRST LADY BLADDERSTONE. WISH ME LUCK. (REALLY WANT THOSE LONG-LOST CRUETS.) MONEY FOR ZA ON COUNTER. LOVE, MOM.

Loophole grabbed the bills, stuffed them in his pocket. "Get some more leaf later," he said.

"Want a beer?"

"Sure."

Farrago opened the fridge, grabbed two DustyBoys, headed down the hallway to the stairs. "We can't go all night," she said. "I've got to finish this paper I was supposed to turn in today."

"What's it on?"

"I can't remember. The usual. Some bullshit or something."

"Well, I can help, then. I'm an expert on that topic."

She turned, stuck her tongue out at him.

Up in her room Farrago immediately disappeared into her closet. Loophole plopped his bony ass onto the cracked and split cushion marking his spot on the red leather couch in front of the big TV screen. Farrago had informed her mother several years earlier that she wasn't going to stay overnight ever again until she (the mother) bought her (the daughter) a no less than fifty-inch HootchieCootchie. Bazam. First the big bedroom, then the big TV. Say it and it shall appear.

"C'mon," said Loophole. "I'm in the mood for a real slaughter today." The controller was in his hand, the meDepot5 on, the superscreen fired up. Primed to enter the enchanted Dominion of MumboJumbodom, where the darkness was "stygian," the passage "parlous," the goal "ethereal." Beware the Shatterbeast, the wily Grimchocks. Farrago had already lost a leg in a battle with the vicious Razrface on Level VIII, which had necessitated a lengthy detour back to the Healing Chamber on Level II and then a further delay hunting for hidden prosthetic parts in the Wood of Mangled Dreams. But even on hobble speed she'd managed to dispatch 4,682 tiny X-shaped minions, double her Treasure Trove, and add to her collection of weaponry the difficult-to-access Meridian Blade and—everyone's favorite—the triple-barreled Destiny Maker.

"Let's go," said Loophole. "Smell the blood."

One of the places Farrago kept her stash was in the inside zippered pocket of an ugly old coat her mom had given her, which she, of course, had never worn. At least it was good for something. Carried the stash back to the couch and the great bubbler that sat regally on the coffee table in front of it. Fired up the bowl. Fired up the game.

Click-click-click. Kill-kill-kill.

"We keep playing this good," said Loophole, "we just might really make it to Level LXXXVIII."

"Yeah, so?"

"You know what happens when you hit Level LXXXVIII?"

"Uh...no."

"No one does."

"Has anyone ever reached this magic LXXXVIII?"

"No."

"How do you know?"

"What's with all the questions? Jeez."

"You win any money for getting there?"

"Of course you don't win any money."

"Then what's the fucking point?"

"The game, stupid—winning the fucking game."

"All right, then, let's win the fucking game."

Click-click-click. Kill-kill-kill.

A pizza was ordered, delivered, eaten. Somewhere in there.

Two hours later, when they had arrived at Level XXIII (where the Willomorphs acquire demented xenic weaponry and there's a three-minute time limit to clear each entered room), her mom started banging on her door like a you-know-what. "Don't think you're fooling anybody, young lady. I can smell that shit all the way downstairs."

"She's baaaaack," Farrago said to Loophole. To her mother, "Yeah? Stuff some tissues up your nose."

"Who've you got in there with you? It's not that Loophole boy, is it? Better not be that Loophole boy."

"Nobody. There's nobody in here with me."

"I'm sure I heard voices. As in more than one."

"I like to talk to myself. Don't you?"

Long pause. "You better not be lying to me."

"When have I ever lied to you?"

"Every time you open your mouth."

"Goodnight, Mother."

"Had a big day at the auction. Got those estate pieces I wanted. At a decent price, too."

"That's nice."

"Got you something. A special surprise. Wanna see it?"

"Not right now, Mother. I'm a bit preoccupied."

"With your homework?"

"Gotta get this paper done."

"I'll leave it on the kitchen table. It's the heavy object in the FlavorTown bag. Be real careful when you open it."

"I will, Mother."

"Goodnight, Farrago. And please, don't call me Mother. So formal. Makes me feel like your granny."

Silence. More silence.

"I think she's gone," said Farrago.

"You wish." He gave a nod toward the screen. "Watch out up ahead here. Possible ambush at the Wobblety Bridge."

"Don't worry. I see 'em."

"Look out—they're gathering. They're gathering!"

"This what you call a horde?"

"Kill the fuckers! Kill all of 'em!"

Both of them working their controllers as if the controllers themselves were living things trying frantically to escape the white-knuckled grip of their hands. Then all at once: sudden stillness. Battle over. On the screen, in the enchanted land, a field drenched in blood, strewn with stray body parts.

"Smoke break," said Farrago. She lifted the bubbler onto her lap. Loophole hit the Pause button. They smoked.

"So whaddya think your mom boughtcha?" said Loophole.

"I don't know. Heavy. What's heavy?"

"A big rock. This leaf."

"Hope it's better than that pickle peeler she got me at the Tri-Rivers swap meet."

"C'mon, now. Be fair. You love that pickle peeler. I saw you kissing it just the other day."

"You." She pushed him over onto his side, then got on top of him. She pretended to pummel his chest.

"Hey, watch it. We're gonna lose the level." He moved the controllers out of the way.

"Fuck the level." She pushed herself off Loophole's body. "Take your clothes off."

"Why? We're in the middle of a game."

"We're always in the middle of a game."

"Well, there you go."

"I'll tell ya what you're gonna do."

"Yeah?"

"Once we sign off here, you're gonna split, race on home to those slidey blacky satiny sheets of yours, start makin' mayo to the many me's on your digital frame." She knew the layout. She'd been to his place, the closet-size studio above Big Fat's Tats out on Knackerback Road, which his parents didn't even know he had. Actually there were two digital photo frames on the nightstand next to his bed. On one an impressive rotation of exes, currents, basted beauties, and random GIFs. On the other a seemingly endless slide show of favorite cum shots. His own. Lots of practice required to get camera click in sync with biological click. But by now he was an old hand at it. Fun fact: the greater the height, the greater the distance of the goop loop, the hotter the bust.

"Yeah?" said Loophole. "So?"

"So what's the point?"

"An orgasm."

"But you could have a real orgasm right now with a real me."

"We're in the middle of a game."

"We're always in the middle of a game."

He shrugged.

"Know what? You bug me." She went back to the bubbler.

Concentrated on that. And, after a while, everything just sort… of…drifted…off.

She was Altadora, superchick with a wicked twin-bladed star-sticker and a kickass bod, slicing and dicing her way through ravenous hordes of mechanized undead and gibbering mutant elves mistakenly released from their subterranean dens by the heroic klutz Loophole/Zantar, when at the labyrinthine House of Lachry-mals, instead of stealing a cup of magic longevity brew, which is what he was supposed to do, Loophole/Zantar impetuously decided to violate one of the cardinal rules of Level XXX: never piss in the cauldron. Beasties don't like that. They'll swarm you in half a sec. But what thrill-ride fun slaughtering the nasty pests left and right. Gave her a real bump. Added bonus: the diamondlike drops of sweat flying dramatically from Altadora's forehead at every twisty thrust and parry. Made her feel so savage hot. Those four-eyed obsessives at MediaKills were some slammin' perfectionists. Props to Art.

And on to Level XXXI. The wonder of Attitudinal Falls. The horror of the Movable Morass. And ever the all-consuming hunt. So she was happy, she guessed. At least for the moment. Bouncing around in her head. For she knew something her stupid parents and their fart-bag friends and all the fart bags of the world did not know, something important, something really important you should know, we should all know, and it was this: we are here to have fun. Period. That's it. End of big meaning. Over and out. Send. And the better you felt, the holier you were. How's that for kneelin' and mumblin'?

Time for a pee break.

"Pause it," said Farrago.

Loophole did.

She unlocked her door, padded unsteadily down the hallway to the famous Glass Shitbox, her mother-designed "comfort station" with floor-to-ceiling mirrors on each wall, providing brutally honest vistas in every direction. First-time visitors had been often known to exit the john wearing the sort of somber expressions usually seen at funeral-home viewings. Farrago actually liked looking at herself. Oh, there were some areas that needed tweaking—minor bulge reductions here and there, a slight enlargement of boobs—but over-all, the whole package still good enough to be snapped and posted on what she knew was Loophole's favorite website: Hottie Chicks Clicking Selfie Pics in Bathroom Mirrors. So far, 57,879 hits. Take that, Tip O' The Wedge haters. She sat down, peed, wiped herself, stood up, and, before leaving, carefully checked out her thigh gap in the door mirror. All right. Looking fine.

Back in her room she found Loophole with his head collapsed on the back of the couch, mouth wide open, making nasty snoring sounds.

"Hey, douche bag," she said. She kicked his leg.

"Huh?" He sat up. He looked around. He looked at her. "What?"

"Wake up, Sky Lord. Wake up and get killing."

"Where you been?"

"The crapper, asshole."

"Wow. You were gone so long."

"Well, you know, it's like so far away. You need a fucking passport to get there."

"Next time tell me where you're going."

"I did tell you."

"Tell me louder next time."

"Where's the bubbler?"

"I don't know. I thought you had it."

She looked around the room. "I don't see it."

He pointed. "Right there, shithead. On the table right in front of you."

"Oh. Silly me." She picked up the bubbler, sparked it up. When she exhaled, the smoke left her body in one long, long sugary stream. In quick fantastic seconds her head felt like cotton candy. And after that, she just slowly slid on down into herself.

She played the game some more. She killed some more monsters. She talked to Loophole. She couldn't remember about what.

Sometimes, after a while, she would get up, stumble over to a wall. She loved walls. All walls. She loved to lean against them. She loved to touch them, allow her own drowsy fingertips to wander aimlessly over the cool, waxy, electric surface of them. She pressed the skin of her cheek against the paint, light breaking across the pebbly face of it in such infinitely interesting patterns. Ridges. Shadows. All those dark, cozy places to hide in.

So she'd been staring at Loophole for over an eon now. He'd been staring back. Graveyard's eyes. So blue, so pointy, so crazy. In a good way. He had 'em.

"What?" she said.

"How you feeling?"

"Frosted," she said. Her smile was all over her face.

"Want some sprinkles on top?" He held up a small brown glass bottle he had magically produced from some pocket or other.

"What's that?"

"Secret killah dust."

"Holding out on me, huh?"

He unscrewed the cap, poured a tiny mound of grayish-white powder on top of the already packed bowl. He looked at Farrago. "You're gonna like how you feel wearing this." He clicked on the lighter. Fire. Smoke. Delirium.

Just then, right in the middle of a tricky-ass transposition to the realm of the Fog Sentients, where travel to other dimensions was not only possible but required, the meDepot5 abruptly died, and the TV went black.

"Fuck," said Loophole. "That you?"

"Probably." She had discovered some time ago during her journeys under the leaf that her mind or her body or whatever she was when she was really rockin' it became possessed by weird unconscious powers over the voodoo of technology. Televisions changed channels at random, computer screens froze, remotes failed. She figured she must put out some kind of witchy death ray that messed with electricity. Potent stuff, this leaf.

"Well," said Loophole. "Reset the fucker." But he certainly wasn't about to budge a single inch.

"You're closer."

"I ordered the pizza."

"I went down and got it."

"I loaded the last bowl."

Farrago looked at her fish. Back and forth. Round and round. Caged iridescence. She looked at the clock. 11:11.

"Okay," she said. "I don't think I wanna talk anymore."

And you know what? She didn't.

She was so faded.

CHAPTER 12

WHAT HAPPENS IN BULLIONVILLA

LATE AFTERNOON. GRAVEYARD AND Ambience hadn't been out of bed all day but for periodic bathroom breaks and to snag the latest delivery from ExcessExpress, today's indulgence consisting of one magnum of WalleyedMonks Champagne 1912 (Shipwrecked Edition); a baronial-size tin of Don'tAsk blue caviar especiale from the clean northern shores of the Spritzer Sea; and an executive platter of dragon-scale nachos topped with melted cave-aged auroch cheese, a generous shaving of the exceptionally rare white virgin trifola, and a healthy pinch of hand-coddled, lip-kissed epaulet red pepper flakes. What the hell. They were rich.

"Pleasant heat," said Ambience. "A gentle, lingering burn."

"Yes, and coupled with a deep, distinct note of briny dankness, the dish somehow, in spite of itself, manages to achieve a memorably piquant flavor profile. Wouldn't you agree?"

"A fine, complex finish. So unexpected. And in a delivery no less."

"You're forgetting, my olive, the size of the check. We could have the entire Twelve Feasts of the Wandering Gourmand trekked to our door along with Chef Bandanna himself to personally oversee it, long as we got the proper bills to pay the man."

"And have we got the bills," said Ambience. She fluttered a fan of happy paper under Graveyard's nose. "Smell it," she said. "Smell the bacon." She liked holding the money. She liked touching the money.

"Let's just dump the rest of the caviar on top of this mess and be done with it," said Graveyard, eyeing the sloppy remains of their Boardroom Refection.

"You're not supposed to do that."

"Do what?"

"Mix fish and cheese."

"Says who?"

"I don't know. The fish and cheese people."

"Oh, really? Well, here is my considered culinary opinion." He dumped the caviar. They dug in.

"Interesting combo," said Graveyard, chewing thoughtfully.

"Ocean cheese berries on a scale chip," said Ambience. "Loving it."

They licked the goo off their fingers. They licked each other's fingers. Then they found other places to lick. Then it was all limbs and lips.

"Who'da thunk?" said Ambience, pausing to suck the last fish egg out of Graveyard's navel. "That a few little nachos could be so…so inspirational?"

"Well, these ain't exactly your typical belly-bomb variety," said Graveyard. "Shift your ass a little to the right."

She did. "Mmmmm," said Ambience. "Mmmmm."

"What you said," said Graveyard.

When they finally managed to pry themselves apart, Ambience found herself actually panting. And she hadn't panted since, well—ever.

"That was cosmic," said Graveyard.

"What the f?" she said. She looked pretty blown out. "Why haven't we ever been told? Why hasn't anyone ever been told? Our lives have been one huge fraudulent joke. It's an inexcusable crime to have lived this long stumbling about in this much ignorance."

"Trade secrets of the rich and famous. God forbid the great un-washed should learn to steal even a moment's genuine satisfaction from the conditions of servitude prevailing on this planet. We might get ideas."

"Any of that Walleye left?"

Graveyard leaned out of bed, lifted the magnum up off the floor, raised it into the declining light. "About an inch."

"Gimme."

She drained the bottle in one noisy gulp.

The sex dust temporarily settled, Ambience turned to Graveyard and said, "Forgot to tell you, I gave ButterRoll a fifty-dollar tip the other day."

"Fifty? For what?"

"For nothing. I just felt like it."

"He give you a free lighter?"

"Of course."

"That must have cost him all of a dime."

"C'mon, Grave, be nice. Who else was willing to carry us through our numerous financial embarrassments? He gave us credit when no one else would."

"Always wondered what his problem was."

"Remember the days of stale crackers and tasteless noodle soup? Remember those? He saved our starving asses often enough. Who can forget that famous devil's-behind curry of his or whatever it was?"

"And those hard little green pellets of no recognizable food group."

"You gobbled 'em up quick enough."

"Never met a cuisine I didn't like."

"Grave, honey, why don't you be a dear and wander out to the kitchen and get me what's left of that box of Cherubim in the refrigerator?"

"More chocolate? How much of that stuff can you scarf down in a week?"

"Girl's gotta get her ganache. And post-fuck is one of the most recommended times for your daily dose. All the finest sex-diet experts agree."

"Next item on the agenda: a maid."

"If we had a maid, we couldn't run around naked anymore."

"Who said she had to be dressed?"

"Go."

"Save my place." He got up out of bed and headed toward the door. She liked watching his bare ass ambling provocatively out of the room. Made her blood feel like champagne. At least for this moment, right now. In their new, resurrected life they rarely bothered much with clothes anymore. They were in an almost constant state of quiet combustion, and at home, total nudity just seemed so much more, well, handy.

As soon as Graveyard was safely gone, NippersPumpkinClaws crawled out from under the bed and hopped up on top of it. He crept up to Ambience. He rubbed against her thigh. He began to purr. He had a loud purrer.

"Been missing our little talks, haven't you?" she said. She stroked his furry head. She stroked his neck, the underside of his chin. She'd been so busy lately, shopping, partying, and fucking, that her quiet times with the Nips had dwindled down to maybe once a week. In her B.C. (Before Cash) period, Ambience had conferred almost daily with her little buddy about various psychological aches and spiritual pains. By now Nippers knew all her secrets. He knew about the failed boyfriends, the fake girlfriends, the whole phony life. He knew about the cheating on the Numbers and Things final at Pantaloon University and the backpacking fiasco in South Agenda and the breakup by text with SafetyCap, which she had never really gotten over, and what she did after her father died. And no one knew that.

"Sorry," she said. "Got nothing for you today." Nippers looked at her, that green freakishly unblinking dead stare that said, "I see you. I see you all the way through." Which was why the people she knew who hated cats hated cats. When they chose to look at you, there was nowhere to hide. Suddenly Nippers stiffened, eyes locked on the open doorway. In an instant he was off the bed and back under it.

Graveyard was already talking before he entered the room.

"What's all this crap from this Flinders and Poach outfit?" he said, shuffling through a handful of mail. "Flinders and Poach. That don't sound good. That sounds like lawyers."

"They want to speak with you about some sort of legal issue."

"I don't have any legal issues. Do I want to open any of these and actually read them?"

"Probably not."

"That's what I thought." He tossed the envelopes into the wastepaper basket next to the door.

"I'm betting that's not a particularly good idea."

"Got a better one?"

"Aren't you even a tad curious to see what Filbert and Peaches want?"

"What do you think they want? What all lawyers want: money."

"Then why not call 'em before they, uh, elevate their inquiries?"

"Bad idea."

"Dealing with members of the legal profession is not necessarily always a negative."

"If it's anything truly important, they obviously know where to find me. And if they're looking for dough, why, I am merely a down-on-his-luck seeker who's got a couple hundred in the bank, a couple twenties in his pocket, and a head bursting with hope, okay? End of story."

"Guess that's my story, too."

"Word to the wise. And by the way, meant to ask, but have you happened to notice lately anything strikingly peculiar about the contents of our goody bag?"

"No denominations below a hundred?"

"How much do you think we've spent already?"

"Couldn't begin to say."

"To the nearest thousand."

"Well, there's all the dinners and the clubs. The clothes, the jewelry, the shoes."

"The alcohol. The drugs."

"The TV. The car, of course. A couple of ridiculously overpriced guns. I don't know. Fifty grand?"

"Hah. The car was more than that."

"You're kidding."

"One does not cruise the highways and byways of our great nation in HomoDebonaire style and comfort without shelling out a modest ransom for the privilege. No, my estimate would be easily quadruple that."

"Goes fast, doesn't it?"

"Maybe for the ordinaries, but you forget, we're exceptionals now. We live in the world of wonder. No matter how much we spend, our bag is always full."

"How can you be so certain? You never really counted it to begin with."

"This is an eyeball estimate."

"Well, don't obsess over it. If you question the power of the magic bag, all the money in it will disappear, and then everything you bought with the money will disappear, too."

"And where did you come up with that fun fact?"

"It's common knowledge."

"Yeah? Among whom?"

"Mystics and investment bankers. We discussed this in my book club when we read *Fairies and Finances*. Unexpected gifts from leprechauns, old crones, and talking animals always come with these weird conditions no one seems able to keep."

"What about manna from heaven?"

"There's a separate chapter on that."

"So they lose everything."

"Naturally. Every copper, silver coin, and golden nugget. But ultimately, of course, they're better off for it."

"How come?"

"They've learned to be happy and humble without being burdened by all that vile wealth."

"Yeah? Well I've got another hearthside homily for you."

"What's that?"

"Happiness can't buy you money."

That night, Ambience lying asleep in bed next to him, snoring, not snoring, whatever the hell she was doing, Graveyard, still awake at 4:47 in the a.m., stared up at the ceiling, watching the reflections of traffic passing nonsensically in reverse above him. Something about the confounding mysteries of light and physics he had absolutely no understanding of whatsoever. He couldn't sleep. He didn't know why. He tried to think of something he didn't have that he wanted to buy. No dice. At the moment the Want tray was curiously empty. What to do? Well, a change of scenery might be nice. Unfortunately, Graveyard hated traveling. He hated riding for long periods in cars, buses, trains, and planes. He hated schedules and timetables. He hated hotel rooms. But he did like being in different places, though. He liked seeing stuff he hadn't seen before. He liked buying stuff he hadn't bought before, too. And he liked meeting odd people in odd clothes. He liked being surrounded by languages he didn't understand. He guessed what he really wanted was to be an absurd tourist for a while.

"All in," said Ambience, after he told her of his plan when they got up later in the p.m. of the following day. (Who but miserable keyboard zombies ever rolled out of the sack before noon?) "Which one?"

"Which one what?"

"Which country?"

"I don't know. Someplace impossible. Colorful and far away and hideously expensive. With purple mountains and moldy museums, primo beaches and pretentious food and tiny taxis. Pastry and attitude. Gotta get me some."

"Plenty of candidates to choose from."

"And it's gotta be old. Really old and antiquey. I want to walk around on tons of old dirt."

"How about Quasiland? Remember? It's where BackDoorSlider

and FacetCut got married last year in that big haunted castle and no one worth less than ten mil was allowed on the invite list. In fact, double-digit millionaires were the rabble at that wedding."

"Didn't TwoForOne get arrested for donkey-punching the best man at the rehearsal dinner?"

"Yeah. And the happy bride had a herpes sore on her upper lip that her high-end makeup job couldn't quite conceal, so no one wanted to kiss her. And afterward they had two receptions: one regular and then later one all nude for the numerous freaks in attendance."

"Yeah, we saw that special together. *The Funning in the Dungeon.* Think they had that blowout in the winter, though. Probably too uncomfortably hot to go there now."

"PortPenny?"

"Two words: Doldrum's disease."

"Waa!BooHoo?"

"Well, the capital's supposed to be secure. For the moment, at least. Civil wars, though, they're so dicey. Probably we should only consider visiting places where the locals aren't tossing too many wild bullets at one another."

"That narrows it down somewhat."

"Temperate climate, contented populace, a minimum of loaded weaponry."

"Bullionvilla," said Ambience.

"Perfect."

"It's old."

"It's artsy-fartsy."

"Its architecture looks edible."

"It's flush-friendly."

"It's safe."

"Then in order to make this an official madcap getaway, I think we should probably leave, like, right now. Sky on outta here on a red-eye, get there in time for a fabulous continental breakfast at the fabulous Treasured Paw."

"The one on that show we watched the other night? The oldest surviving restaurant in the world?"

"Our pearl."

"Book it," she said.

Ambience retrieved her phone from under the bed and called FurryFarm to book an open-ended boarding reservation for Nippers. Who knew how long they'd be gone? Graveyard put a pair of locks on the magic bag, heaved the bag onto his shoulder, and struggled out of the building and into the street, where he turned left and proceeded somewhat unsteadily down the block.

PlexiBerryPunch lived in a five-story walk-up on TarPaper Alley, right around the corner from AardvarkBailBonds, whose services he had, unfortunately, been forced to avail himself of on more than one disappointing occasion. The Alley was one of a dwindling number of "bad" areas, swarming with "suspicious" types of every age and gender who had fewer and fewer places to go. If you wished to do something illegal, buy something illegal, or merely observe something illegal in progress, this was your spot. PlexiBerryPunch could certainly afford to go upscale, hunker down in a better part of town, but he plain liked the noise, the color, the drama of the edgy life. He wouldn't have moved if you paid him. An offer obviously contingent on how much, exactly, would be involved. Because his present address would be exceptionally painful to lose. There were just too many conveniences packed tightly together in tantalizing proximity: illicit substances of every variety easily available 24-7 just steps from his door; an endless parade of the more theatrical specimens of humanity you couldn't be entertained by anywhere else; cat food for sale at the corner bodega at 2:00 in the a.m., even if you didn't own a cat; and when your balls needed emptying, you simply grabbed the hand of the nearest curbside nymph, hauled her back to your digs, and screwed her until the screwing itch expired.

Graveyard knocked on a hard-used door with NO MENUS scrawled across it in phosphorescent lime.

"Yeah," came a sullen voice from inside.

"It's me, Graveyard. I just spoke to you on the phone."

"Who?"

"Graveyard, you stupid brain-sizzled toad licker."

Comical sound of too many locks to count being painstakingly unlocked.

"Took ya long enough," said Graveyard when the heavy metal door finally creaked expressively open. PlexiBerryPunch stood before him, all sixty-five and one-half solid inches of him. He was wearing a monk's habit and black tennis shoes. He looked like a husky child masquerading as a baby-faced adult member of some sort of bizarre underground religious order. He was also clutching a gun. Appeared to Graveyard's trained eye to be a rare variation of an early twentieth century gent popper, the infamous CarteBlanche's Iron Attaché.

"Whoa there, cowboy," said Graveyard, hands up in mock surrender. "Just a harmless tenderfoot from back East."

"That them?" Indicating with the barrel of the revolver the bag Graveyard had set down on the floor beside him.

"You mind?" Graveyard nodding at the still-leveled weapon.

"All apologies." The CarteBlanche disappeared somewhere beneath the ratty clerical drapery. "Old habits." From the dark period when he had fallen so hopelessly in love with raze that he rented a second apartment from which to deal the drug to customers both sweet and unsavory who responded best to persuaders in the higher calibers. In those rowdy days he famously favored the .56 CarpetKisser.

"Forget your meds today?"

"Get the fuck out of the hallway, you idiot."

Graveyard did. He then watched, fascinated, as PlexiBerryPunch secured the fortress, fiddling with seemingly twice as many bolts and locks as he had to let Graveyard in.

"Indians about to attack?"

"The natives are always restless. So what have you got for me?"

"Just the high-end stuff. A few rarities, a few antiques. The guns

I'd have trouble replacing should anything happen. Wouldn't even consider asking anyone but you to stand watch over them."

"I'm honored as fuck."

"Well, now, look, if it's too much trouble—"

"Just messing with you, Yard. Said I'd keep 'em, didn't I? That's my word. Know how valuable these shitsticks are to you. Goes without saying. They'll be as safe as baby kittens with me."

"I wish you hadn't used that particular simile. I remember what happened to Twinkletoes."

"Unfair. Not my fault. How was I supposed to know MemoryFoam was a wannabe magician? An uncommonly bad wannabe. You heard what happened to him, right? Got a vibrator stuck up his ass and refused to go to the emergency room. Whirring away for days in there. Thought he'd be okay once the battery wore out. He wasn't. Lesson for us all, right?"

Graveyard heaved the sack back up into his arms. "Where do you want these?"

"Follow me." They made their way through a narrow winding maze of handmade bookcases overflowing with thousands of esoteric volumes hard and soft, title after title even know-it-all literary types invariably failed to recognize. PlexiBerryPunch had dedicated his life to locating a solution to the "problem" of the universe. Which was good if you regarded the universe as a "problem." He did.

"I'm afraid I've come to the conclusion," he had once informed Graveyard, "that we are, in fact, quite alone."

Graveyard looked around. They were seated at the time at the raucous center of the downtown AuditoriumGrille. "You mean, as in lonely in a crowd?"

"I mean, as in drifting aimlessly through eternal solitary night. How's that for a vision? We are, unfortunately, finally and fatally, cosmically alone. At three in the morning we all know it's true. There's nothing else out there. Alien life forms, where are they? Billions and billions of stars, right? Billions and billions of planets. An infinity of possibilities in which to cook up other chances, and yet so far, nothing. Absolutely nothing. No riveting air show, no Great Lawn landing, not even the slightest radio peep. Nothing. Just deep deep-space silence."

"Yes, but what about UFOs?"

"What about Santa Claus?"

"Folks have seen them."

"They've seen Santa, too."

"They've gotten gifts from him."

"Still waiting for my puppy from Mama Martian. As yet, not even a measly chunk of comet coal. You want to know what's out there, what's really out there? I'll tell you: a badass cosmos of rainbow-flavored fantasies. So unfortunately, I'm afraid that all this"—his dismissive gesture encompassed the entire Grille and beyond—"is definitely it."

"If that's true, seems like quite a ludicrous and terribly inefficient waste of space."

"Only from our antlike perspective. Check this out. Universe is infinite, right? And what if, as so many have speculated, all those nasty black holes the universe is apparently riddled with are simply portals to other universes that are equally infinite? So what we're left with is an infinity of infinities. Which, of course, makes our universe about as common as a grain of sand in your eye at the beach. Like the man said, alter the scale and you alter the perception, right? Which leads us to one basic, inescapable truth: our planet and this whole living, breathing commotion and everything we see or don't see, in the sky, the stars, the scary, pulsating darkness, is here just for us. Us alone. Other forms we can't even begin to imagine inhabit their own separate and distinct universes. And no matter how much we might wish it otherwise, we'll never see those creatures, we'll never know them. We're not meant to. Clash of realities, you know. Very messy. Very, shall we say, apocalyptic."

"Am I supposed to be comforted or depressed?"

"Your choice."

Punch's bedroom was about the size of a pricegrabber cabin on a no-budget cruise line. Mattress on the floor, blank beige walls. No windows. The place reeked of male b.o. and a piney, indescribable incense from the distant past that took immediate hold of the back reaches of the sinus cavities, sending out sneezing signals that stopped just short of producing an actual sneeze. "In there," Punch said, pointing to an open closet, its musty, overpacked contents spilling out into the room like stuffing from a split couch cushion. Graveyard set the bag down with a grunt, shoved it as best he could in the general direction of a rear corner. "You're sure this—"

PlexiBerryPunch made a dismissive snorting sound. "You know the last time someone was in this shithole, let alone this room, let alone that closet?" From the floor of said closet he scooped up an armful of dirty laundry, draped the wrinkled T-shirts, the wadded briefs artfully over the bag. "There," he said. "All safe and tidy. No one's gonna mess with that stinky heap."

"You're a good guy, PlexiBerryPunch." Graveyard patted him on the shoulder like someone insincerely attempting, and failing to be, insincerely affectionate.

They'd first met some fifteen years ago or so, when both found themselves putting in time at SweetDigits—adding files, deleting files, adding files, toting up apples to arrive at oranges, then repeating the whole soul-abrading process in reverse. What remained of Graveyard's mind after six months of this merry-go-round was barely sufficient to successfully oversee the morning shoe-tying ritual. For PlexiBerryPunch the job hardly even qualified as a trifle. He could do it with one hand in his sleep. Or down his pants. And often did. He was some sort of incognito computer wiz, which enabled him now to only seek employment when he needed to, i.e., whenever the shekels ran low. He'd managed somehow, in his limited excursions into the wonderful world of wage slavery, to acquire a lucrative reputation as "the one consultant you must consult" whenever your computer stuff needed a "wash and rinse." But actually, PlexiBerryPunch, for all his wallet-fattening abilities, hated work. He hated the concept of work. He hated the actuality of work. He hated the sentimentalization of work. He hated the word *work*. He believed his fellow citizens were sadly deluded on the subject, as they were, in his opinion, on most subjects. His quotable quote on the worship of work: "You can run, but you can't hide."

Back out in the slight clearing in the stacks PlexiBerryPunch persisted in calling his living room—two kitchen chairs, milk-carton table, plastic lamp, and a clear glass ashtray containing a half-eaten enchilada resting atop an impressive mound of filterless cigarette butts (naughty naughty PlexiBerry)—he sat Graveyard down and offered him a couple of hits of powdered ellipsis.

"Ambience's favorite," said Graveyard. "But really, I can't. We're leaving in a couple hours."

"Yes, why?"

"Why what?"

"This ridiculous trip. I mean, really, in this day and age, why go anywhere at all? Who needs to? Just screen it. Click, click. There you are."

"We want the tastes, too. The smells. We want to get down and dirty with all that suggestive foreignness."

"Well, yes, the smells." He was nose-vacuuming the ellipsis off a hard-used copy of MediumRare's magisterial *The Isness of Is*. "Fun drug." He cleared his nose. "Comes in all formats. Powder, pill, crystal, and liquid. Sure you don't want a lick? It'll X out the flight."

"Tempting. But think I want to experience this one in all its aggravating glory. I haven't been anywhere in years."

"Suit yourself. But let me lay on you a fabulous parting gift for later. Just in case." His hand rummaged around inside his robe, emerged displaying on his palm what looked like a couple of pellets of grayish navel lint.

"Where, exactly, you been stashing this shit?"

"Over the hills and far away. Where do you think? What a squeamish lad. I'm as clean as your very own toilet seat. Which, interestingly enough, modern science has proved definitely to be the most sanitary spot in anyone's home."

"What are they?"

"Those?" Bending over to inspect the fuzzy objects as though he had never encountered them before in his entire curiosity-driven life. "Oh, I suspect those to be first cousins of the most extraordinary kind to our dear friend candylane. And you know how that do."

"Wish I didn't."

"Were you aware that ninety percent of the universe is composed of dark matter? Ninety percent. Do you know what dark matter is?"

"You've already told me this, not once but several times."

"Good. I love repeating myself. Do you know what dark matter is?"

"I'm sure I don't."

"Neither does anybody else. So you realize, then, what that means. All but a minuscule fraction, a tiny sliver, really, of the known universe is absolutely unknown. Nada, nothing. A frightening void at the very center of our comprehension. Science, our cleanup batter, has struck out. Little of any real consequence is understood in even the meanest way. And it's the bottom of the ninth and we're losing. In a shutout. Mystery wins. Anything is possible."

"Don't have to tell me that."

"The universe. Think about it."

"No subject is ever further from my mind."

"Well, that's why you're one of the special people."

"What special people?"

"The ones trying to save the planet with their thoughts."

"I'd hate to see what kind of world could be tossed together out of my used-up thoughts."

"Don't sell yourself short. How could your version of existence possibly be any worse than this squalid shithole we're all trapped in?"

"And, of course, we can all be comforted by the certainty that when thoughts fail us there's always the backup in the bag."

"Not to worry. I have zero interest in breaking into your precious armory, staining all your little toys with my grubby fingerprints."

"Never a doubt, Plexi."

"I mean, I don't even want to look in there. I could care less. Guns are icky."

"Yes, I've noticed your chronic aversion."

"I didn't say I didn't like ickiness. Of course, if while you're away, the zombie apocalypse should happen to descend upon us, well..." Plexi shrugged his shoulders like a waiter signaling that the kitchen was out of the special.

For no discernible reason, Bullionvilla seemed, at this particular confluence, to be an aggravatingly difficult destination to arrive at by air. They would have to cross an ocean, a sea, a continent, a ludicrous number of time zones, a couple of unhinged countries no one ever wanted to fly over, and several unpredictable weather patterns pilots would just as soon avoid. Plus *two* layovers, in Macabreb and Orthodontia. And booking reservations at the last minute landed them (big surprise) peasant's seats on the last flight of the day of that budgeteer's fave, TurboBusAirways. Their motto: Take a Flying Fuck.

Ten minutes into the flight and Graveyard was already squirming around on his narrow, thinly cushioned, plastic-wrapped Passenger Support Device. "There's more room in a coffin," he said.

"Curious," said Ambience, "how sometimes even money isn't the insulation it's cracked up to be."

"It's a goddamn outrage."

They looked at each other and they laughed.

When they finally landed in Bullionvilla, some eight and a half indescribably excruciating hours later, the air smelled of adhesive bandages and oven cleanser. Everyone yammering away in some sort of vowelly jibber-jabber neither Graveyard nor Ambience could make any sense out of whatsoever. Everyone with at least one hand out, if not two. Graveyard dutifully crossed every palm thrust his way. Which led, naturally enough, to an available and suspiciously agreeable cabbie Graveyard was able to trade enough meaningful grunts and shrugs with to establish a useful business connection. The ride into Bullionvilla was like being trapped in an amateur stock car rally in which even the most casual principles of self-preservation had been gaily abandoned. They did manage to glimpse through half-open windows, when not frantically seeking firmer handholds inside the lurching cab, several go-to destinations scattered about the fabled city: the granite polyhedron where hunted lovers in olden times sought refuge from the usual bands of nonlovers armed with the usual sticks and stones; the dried-up reflecting pool from which Ancient Guy delivered his famous treatises on the ineluctability of the world, the warts, the welts; Cleft Towers major and minor; the Dangling Gate; Bitter Hall, bolted seat of government through half a dozen energetic wars, three failed insurrections, and a couple of herd-thinning contagions; the architectural wonder of Busybee Cathedral, sole surviving structure of the Great Fire, which had virtually consumed the town, leaving the massive walls of the sanctuary permanently scorched and hard-boiling the sacred egg in the Holy Kettle; and, finally, the giant rutabaga sculpture in the center of Diatribe Park, which, for reasons not entirely clear to anyone, respectful citizens touched and kissed as they went about their citizenly business.

"This place fairly reeks of history," said Ambience.

Graveyard shot her a glance. "You don't honestly expect me to respond to that comment, do you?"

When the careering taxi at last lurched to an abrupt stop before the imposing edifice of the Cowled Castle, Graveyard, grateful that he and Ambience were still physically intact, pressed upon the beaming driver a pocketful of colorful currency whose actual value he still had barely a clue about. The driver let out an involuntary shriek, quickly composed himself, snapped to attention, and presented Graveyard with a smart salute, then scurried around the cab, waving the bills in the air, and showering upon amused onlookers a series of exclamations requiring no translation.

"I think you might have overtipped," Ambience said.

"Now that we've gotten the opening clichés out of the way...that's another thing I hate about traveling. Our roles are all so rigidly preprogrammed."

Mercifully free of the tiresome burdens of luggage, they strolled into the eye-popping lobby of the grand hotel. Back in the day a genuine castle with turrets, crenellations, and ramparts, home to generations of intimately related titled folk, dozens of national artistic treasures, wandering ghosts, and fascinating historical tales—some of them actually true—the site had been repurposed into a gleaming corporate representative of that ever-popular style: Gimcrack-a-Go-Go. Along the inner walls, banks of ringing, beeping slot machines, most of which were being worked with solemn vigor. The walls themselves were papered with reproductions of currencies from around the world. Overhead, darting multicolored lasers strobed in sync to the Nether Boys' "Don't Do That." Even with dawn no doubt breaking outside, the level of activity inside this windowless, atmospherically controlled pleasure zone was more reminiscent of midday anywhere else. The place was packed. With a herd of bad clothes. All denim and pastels or some tasteless mix thereof. T-shirts over heavily tattooed arms. Sweatpants covering a multitude of dietary mistakes, or not. Leisure suits on both sexes. And hats, plenty of hats, mainly baseball caps advertising various manufacturers of farming equipment. The scene resembled a block party at a trailer park.

"Comforting to see," said Graveyard, "the rest of the world just as cheesy and clueless as we are."

"Even the well-heeled contingent," said Ambience. "Must be a goof of some kind."

"What's going on?" Graveyard asked the desk clerk. He gestured toward the obnoxious stoogefest steadily unraveling behind him. The desk clerk looked just like the second hitman in *The Last Girl*. You know. The one with the lazy eye.

"Well, sir, you're in luck. Just in time for our annual SlamminSlumminSoiree." The desk clerk's name tag read: MR. SERVOMOTOR.

"Yes, and that is?"

"I'm sorry, sir. I thought you'd stayed here before. You looked familiar."

"First time."

"Our busiest night, frankly. As you can see. We're approaching capacity, and that rarely occurs."

"Everyone seems to be rather shamelessly dressing down."

"Part of the event, sir. Patrons, guests, and friends are all encouraged to arrive in costume, ready to indulge freely in—well, how shall I put it? Bottom-rung debauchery."

Graveyard looked at Ambience. Ambience looked at Graveyard. "We are in luck," said Graveyard.

"You wouldn't even have to change your clothes," said Mr. Servomotor.

"We don't require a formal occasion," said Ambience. "We enjoy going quote, slummin', unquote every goddamn day."

"As do several of our favorite guests," said Mr. Servomotor.

"Once everyone's all tacky'd up," said Graveyard, "then what do they do?"

"Well, where to begin? There are countless buffets of every type of fast food imaginable, hours of reality TV on screens conveniently situated throughout the hotel, and a multilane regulation-size bowling alley specially constructed in our basement for your ten-pin enjoyment. Also, those so inclined are encouraged to hook up with one another on whatever passing whim prevails. No guilt. No regrets. Just good clean fun, you know. Tonight at midnight we hold our annual Overdrafts, Pork Rinds, and Final Notice Lottery. First prize: a HowlinWell toaster oven. Second prize: a case of Blitzo beer. Third: a package of Sunshine & Clover hot dogs. All proceeds, of course, to charity."

"What charity?" said Graveyard.

"I'm not at liberty to reveal that particular information."

"Nice gig." Graveyard glanced at Ambience. Her face was stone.

"And, of course, there's always gambling."

"Of course, goes without saying, right? Well, let's check in. Don't want to waste a minute of that precious party time."

Again, due to their last-minute booking attempts, Graveyard and Ambience had been unable to secure the coveted Nabob's Roost (Graveyard's choice) and were forced to settle, on a much lower floor, for the slightly less luxe suites 253, 255, 257, and 259.

"And how will you be paying, sir?" said Mr. Servomotor.

Stashed on Graveyard's person was the ten thousand dollars in currency he and Ambience had been permitted to bring into the country, plus several well-loaded chip-and-PIN HappyWanderer travel cards he had picked up at OmniBank on his way back from Plexi's. He decided he wanted to impress this clown. "Cash," he said.

"How novel," said the clerk. "Haven't seen any of that stuff in days. You forget people actually carry it around in their pockets."

Their rooms offered the expected ooh-aah visual, especially considering the price point required for the satisfaction. They were spacious. The frescoed walls so tall you might have been able to insert another full story between floor and ceiling. They were aggressively opulent, the question "Guess how much I cost?" invisibly affixed to every table, chair, bed, and whirlpool bath, a plebe's fantasy of financial royalty. The furniture, upon closer examination, seemed to have been purchased wholesale from one of those discount marts catering to the kitsch-loving rich. The whole look, in fact, reminiscent of a movie set designed to wow the locals. Between suites 253 and 255, in a narrow potted-plant corridor, was an actual sunken marble pool of fairly good size for your private use only.

"Now, that's what I would call decadent," said Graveyard.

"I love it," said Ambience.

"Me, too," said Graveyard.

They decided to save the water fun for later and, for now, before heading out to join their fellow elites on a spree, lie down for a moment and rest on one of these soft, soft, criminally soft beds. When they awoke late in the afternoon of that impossibly long day, the western sun was busy working its way through every available crack and crevice in blinds and curtains.

"Oh, my God," said Graveyard. He took a squint at the Elaboration on his wrist. "We missed the masked paupers' picnic."

"There'll probably be some overflow. Events like that have a habit of not ending cleanly."

"Plenty of time, though, to load up on tickets for the lottery."

"Didn't we already win the lottery?"

"Listen, my tangerine, you can't win too many lotteries."

They got dressed and went downstairs to the Cowled Castle's massively hyped three-star eatery, the Velvet Oubliette. They had the sautéed checkerfin loony on a wilted bed of crushed lolly nuts accompanied by seasoned melody sticks, meh. Washed that overpriced presumption down with a couple of bottles of undistinguished white. And decided to make the day an all-out cultural assault.

The Museum of Big Art was conveniently located, as the snide desk clerk haughtily informed them, a mere five short "walking" blocks from the hotel. "As opposed to what?" said Graveyard, "Driving blocks?" So they went. They saw everything they were supposed to see. They saw *The Stoning of the Heterodox*; *Emperor LinenInABunch Receives Tribute from a Delegation of the Vanquished Twig People*; *Mother, Child, Apple, Dog*; *After Fortune's Fall, the Binding of the Wounds*; *Pail #29*; and the impressively monumental *View of Ditherydoo in Midwinter Storm from the StandandSee Bridge*.

"Jeeps," said Ambience. "You couldn't even begin to imagine its size from a reproduction in a book."

"And so bright," said Graveyard.

There was an entire separate room reserved for *The Collocation of the Mist*. The triptych covered three walls. A chattering, sharp-elbowed crowd of masterpiece consumers was busy clicking pics of each section with their ubiquitous cell phones.

"The paint's laid on so thick," said Ambience, "it looks like frosting. You want to lick every panel."

"And so bright," said Graveyard. He strolled through the rest of the museum behind the protection of his exclusive KMA sunglasses.

"But you're missing all this astonishing color," said Ambience.

"It still gets through," he said. "It still astonishes."

After absorbing the recommended dosage of cultural nutrients, they managed to book a lunch table at that nearby mega-go-to celeb hangout, the Quacking Duck. Nothing much to brag about there. Chef WindsorKnot was, unfortunately, out of town.

Which, despite the disappointing meal, somehow put them in the mood for an extended session of energetic water fun back at the hotel. They splashed around for an hour or so in their shamelessly private pool like a couple of horny porpoises. And then they fucked each other. And each other fucked them.

Then they took a nap.

When they woke, it was dark: a.m. or p.m.? They didn't know. They didn't care. They were rich. Time to drop some coin.

The Million Kisses Lifestyle and Casino was easily accessed from the Cowled Castle via an abrasively lit connecting tunnel lined with life-size photographs of notorious gamblers past and present, among them: TrickleDown, LintBrush, HogTheTrough, and RidingTheTrail, the guy who broke the bank twice at the Nugget Emporium (he was now banned for life) and manipulated Birches&Elms stock in an elaborate pump-and-dump scheme to get his wife a coveted position on the board of trustees ($250,000 fine, three years' probation).

So they exited into the bright, loud world of high-stakes professional gambling. The floor was teeming. The teemees wound up to the glittering edge of delirium. Pheromones were bouncing around off the walls like invisible Ping-Pong balls. Graveyard checked his Elaboration: 4:32. In the a.m. He assumed the don't-look-at-me-I'm-looking-at-you sort of face he imagined upper-level execs preferred to adopt while touring any of the plentiful lower orders.

"You know where I'm headed?" said Ambience.

"Try not to blow your whole wad in the first ten minutes."

"I'll wear a condom. What the fuck are you talking about? I wasn't aware we were on a budget."

"Just thinking of our total pleasure enhancement."

"I'll get off the way I want to get off, if it's okay with you."

"Fine."

"And if you're gonna helicopter-parent me, let's just pack up our marbles and go home."

"All right, all right. Do what you want."

"I will, thank you very much."

And off she walked. No backward glance. Farro and fiddleheads, he said to himself. Don't let the vibe step on our luck.

The Million Kisses Lifestyle and Casino offered all the usual slots, cards, wheels, and dice other casinos came fully equipped with but had added to the mix its own unique spin on going bust in endlessly entertaining variations. The pocket laundering took place in an amphitheater-size annex attached to the casino's east wing. Above the entrance a sign in firehouse-red neon script: A STOLEN KISS. Beneath the high domed radiant ceiling one could place a bet on anything from heads or tails and rock, paper, scissors to "traffic fatalities in latest twenty-four-hour period on the (pick your pike)" and the insanely popular Russian roulette. There were squibs, of course, and red-dye-splattered heads everywhere. Don't Like What You See? Devise Your Own Game At Our Customer Service Counter and Wet Bar. Where there was a rather lengthy line.

Graveyard's attention was immediately transfixed, as was everyone's upon first entering A Stolen Kiss, by a twenty-one-foot-high glass column into which a nimble attendant, perched on an adjoining ladder, delicately placed a single feather and let it drop. How many seconds until said feather touched bottom? Place your bets now. Graveyard passed. The feather descended and it descended and descended. Action too slack? Try our nearby staghhorn-beetle jousting tournaments and turtle obstacle runs.

She was standing alone over by the End of the World booth. In a crush of interesting faces, hers seemed at once the most interesting, the most dramatically lit, singled out for his, and only his, particular close attention. For an embarrassing number of minutes it was all that he could see. Even as her striking features did keep going in and out of focus. And her bearing. Indelible. Straight as a drill sergeant's. Such confidence, such pride.

She actually reminded him of someone of whom he was reminded too often. Her name was Aquatint. They'd met his junior year at Porcupine U. He was living in a crusty dive with five other confused punk wannabes.

He was standing at the sink one night washing a plate, mind busy exploring off-worlds, when suddenly out of nowhere this body materialized right next to him. A living human body. It was Aquatint. They'd been playing eye pong on and off since she'd moved in a couple of months ago.

"Whoa!" he said, trying to act as if he wasn't startled.

"What's up?" she said. Her eyes appeared to be as cooked as his.

He didn't know what to say. "Nothing," he said. "Nothing much."

"Think you're about done with that one," she said. Dry as vermouth. She pointed.

He looked down. One hand held a plate. One hand held a sponge. The sponge was going round and round on the plate. Then it stopped. "Need the sink?" he said.

"I'm good." Her eyes were going round and round, too. She was smirking at him just like FanFeed in her famous scene in the Planchette Award–winning *House of Ballyhoo*.

"I like a clean plate."

"So do I," she said. "It's sexier that way." She stepped closer. She touched him. Then he could feel her hand moving around down there in the fire zone. He was wearing sweatpants, commando-style.

"Watch out," he said.

"I do," she said.

"Keep rubbing that spot, you know what'll happen?"

"Tell me."

"The genie'll appear and grant your every wish."

She started rubbing harder.

The match fizzled out after about seven months or so. Neither of them knew why.

Maybe this casino girl could spark him up again. Maybe she couldn't. But what the hell.

She appeared to be studying the betting instructions posted in a tasteful font on the overhead menu board. She appeared to be amused by what she read. GUESS THE CORRECT TIME AND DATE OF THE WORLD'S END AND WIN—EVERYTHING! Then suddenly Graveyard found himself standing right beside her with no memory of having crossed the intervening space. He was certain he'd seen her before. He didn't know where. He didn't know when. He pretended to peruse the colorful signage. After a suitably studied pause, he produced a phony chuckle and said, "Wonder who dreamed this scheme up?"

She turned to inspect this bold stranger. Did she like what she saw? Who knew? "Somebody, I suppose, very smart and very evil."

"Because what's the point, anyway? I mean, look at the odds. Bet a dollar, win a million. So you get lucky. You pull in a hundred million or two or three or a billion, even, or why not a trillion? What difference does it make? You're rich, fantastically wealthy, but what, exactly, are you gonna do with that big pile of worthless paper? Where you gonna go, what're you gonna buy? It's over, the world and you. Final call for everyone. Making the last wager a horrible, terrifying joke."

"You're quite the talky boy, aren't you?"

"Just curious. The world's a curious place. It seems to demand comment."

"Well, I have a comment, too."

"Yeah?"

"Yes, everything's over and done with, true, but know what? You won. You collected the last bet. Ahead of everyone else. At the very very end you and only you actually won. Maybe all it's really about is being the final winner."

"Strange goal."

"Know people much?"

Graveyard found himself looking over this intriguing woman with what he hoped was not too much of a scientific leer. For a moment her face seemed to have become detached from its person and was actually floating in space before him like the shimmering mask of a genie conjured up to grant a wish he didn't even know he had. Or not. Visions of his marriage went fleetingly through his head. Everything was beginning to acquire a vaguely disorienting sense of unreality.

"How about you?" he said. "Throw away any ducats yet?"

"I was waiting for one of these venues to speak to me, but frankly, everything in this ludicrous arcade seems pretty silly. And actually, gambling itself's not even the best part. It's the faces. I like to look at the faces."

"Yeah? Spied anybody interesting yet?"

"Coupla dead ringers for StandardShipping over by Guess the Chameleon's Color."

"I can't get enough face."

She looked at him. He looked at her. They both laughed.

Graveyard kept looking around for a guy lurking nearby. Her ring finger was empty, but still, where was the guy? There's always a guy. "I thought the feather was kinda amusing," he said.

She gave him a look. "Lost a hundred on that foolishness last time I was here. Who knew a single feather could move so quickly?"

"One I saw certainly seemed to be taking its own sweet time reaching the bottom."

"It was probably on drugs."

At the sound of an amplified but discreet chime, a rather sizable mob of eager players began to gather around the well-manicured pen of OinkyDoink, the Pig with a Mind of Its Own. The clever porcine predicted the outcomes of sporting events, horse races, political elections, show-business awards ceremonies, and other contests with an accuracy rate well above that of chance. Today's issue: which slop bucket does OinkyDoink prefer, the gold, the silver, or the lead?

"So," said Graveyard, "what's your favorite metal? You most definitely look like a gold girl to me."

"Lead," she said. "Go with the lead. Watch, it'll turn to gold. Trust me."

"Your call." He produced from his pocket a crumpled ball of banknotes, which he slapped down on the square marked PB. A bell rang, the gate slammed open, and, once released, OinkyDoink made a frantic dash in one undeviating line straight to the dull gray bucket into which he inserted his bristly snout and began gobbling heartily away to the accompaniment of various snorting, sucking sounds meant to convey, no doubt, much piggy contentment.

She let out a yelp, jumped up and down a couple of times, then gave Graveyard a tight hug from which he received, he was absolutely certain, a distinct current. He collected his winnings, passed a handful of them over to her.

"But I didn't put anything down."

"Other than the winning tip."

"Just lucky, I guess. My world-famous luck." She paused to check the empty space around her. "Curious, too, my standard accompaniment of escorts seems to be somehow missing in action. They usually surround me with coolers in establishments like this."

"You know, I don't even know your name."

"LemonChiffon," she said. She smiled. "My parents. I know."

"Best damn name I've heard all day."

"Thank you." The hand she extended was so small, so delicate, that he was more than a bit startled by the unexpected force of its grip.

"Graveyard," he said. "Don't hold it against me."

They strolled for a while through this raucous celebration of human greed, entertained by the sights, the pleasure, the pain, the getting, the spending, the triumphant cashing out, the desolate tapping out. They sampled a few venues. At "?" Graveyard put down an even grand. He stuck his hand in a box. He felt around inside. "A sanding block?" he said. Wrong. It was a dried-up sponge. Goodbye, one thousand bucks.

And surprise, LemonChiffon had been born in BetterDoRight, a smudge of a town just over the BlueCorduroy Mountains (really, just big hills) from Randomburg. She lost her cherry in the parking lot of the Mess O' Stuff Mall. She went to Tip O' The Wedge four years after Graveyard had graduated. On junior prom night, underage, she'd even downed a half dozen or so DustyBoys at his father's bar. Now here they were, some four thousand miles from "the sweetest spot God's got," meeting for the first time.

"Back home we'd still be strangers," Graveyard said.

"My mom always used to say sometimes you have to travel half-way round the world to find the way to your own backyard."

"Well, what are mothers famous for, if not choking us with verbal chicken soup?"

"I believed her. I still believe her."

"See your house from here yet?"

"I wouldn't want to see my house. Don't expect to be dropping by there for a very very long time."

"Sorry."

"It's complicated. One of the tons of excuses why I'm here with ShrinkWrap. Or not here as the case may be."

She had come as a couple. She was probably going home a single. She didn't know where *he* was. Last she saw of him *he* was screaming at a cab driver for scratching the crafted deerskin of his NeoBandoleerTravelingCase. Thankfully *he* had left their duplex Sweetheart's Suite paid up through the week.

"Comfy digs. What's he do?"

"He's an entrepreneur."

"In what?"

"Entrepreneuring. It seemed so godawful boring I never bothered to ask."

"And, I suppose, very serious about the work."

"He was a very serious d-bag."

"Wicked combo."

"I haven't cried yet. Weird. I don't know why."

"Listen," said Graveyard, "let's blow this kiddie karnival and top off the morning with—it is morning, isn't it?"

"Something like it."

"We'll greet the dawn with a round of real grown-up gambling."

"Like a-pair-of-jacks-or-better-to-open type of gambling?"

"No stranger to the tables, I see."

"I've messed around some."

"I'll bet you have."

"Ex-ex-boyfriend. He belonged to this club, like a secret society, I guess. He'd go every weekend, different place every time. Sometimes I went with him. So boring, if you ask me, watching play you've got no stake in. But I watched. Picked up a few tricks."

"I suspect you may know more than a few."

"I make my way."

"Gotta say," he said. He was giving her the full-body scan. "Those are the tightest damn jeans I've ever seen."

"Touch them."

His hand hesitated.

"Go ahead."

He reached out. What he felt was skin.

"Yeah," she said. "It's painted on."

"Impressive piece of work."

"His parting 'gift' to me. He had an artist sent up to the room with a spray gun."

"Must cut down on wardrobe costs."

"Sexy, fashionable, frugal. The perfect garment."

"Let's steer this exercise in high style right on over to the poker room. How can I ever go wrong accompanied by the perfect garment?"

On the way they paused for a moment at a nearby blackjack table. In five straight hands Graveyard dropped five large.

"Bluepoints and truffle oil," he said. "Guess I should've rubbed the pants first to activate the luck."

"Wouldn't be the first time."

"Well, let's not grieve over a momentary setback. Onward."

"You seem so surprisingly free and loose with your tender."

"I retain a full team of creative accountants."

"If you wouldn't mind my asking, where, exactly, do you get your money from?"

He turned to look at her. "I pluck it out of thin air," he said.

CHAPTER 13

LOSS LEADERS

LEMONCHIFFON'S RENTED DIGS APPEARED as advertised: utterly money. Not quite as platinum as suites 253, 255, 257, and 259, but still.... The main room, the InterpersonalEntertainmentStation, had been designed in an aggressively moderne glass and stainless steel arrangement "suggested" by the lavish old-timey stylings of OleKingCandy's CountingHouse, at the nearby ChateauBent. (You know. The trendy hideaway with the "spirit" in the keep, the "dragon" in the bailey. Popular selfie locations prominently marked.) No throne, but enough shiny sparkly stuff to induce in even the dimmest wannabe vague fantasies of wealth and power. Massive bouquets of freshly cut flowers bursting from vases in every room. Hidden sensors silently detecting the number of warm bodies in the area and adjusting the temperature accordingly. On the white-on-white damask walls original digidots by the artists TemporaryAbsence and DorsalFin.

"So clean," said Graveyard.

"Every time I turn around there's a maid behind me with a rag in her hand, as if she's just about to wipe something down."

"'Elegance. Style. Finesse.' Isn't that the motto here?"

"She gives me the creeps."

"But if one wishes to eat dinner off the toilet seat one can do so in complete hygienic confidence."

"Wouldn't say the place is necessarily that spotless. What can I get you to drink?" She ambled over to the elaborate wet bar in the corner, stooped down behind it. A brief impatient clattering could be heard. "Gotta be some ice here somewhere. They bring a fresh bucket every morning."

"Got any LaughFrogg?" said Graveyard.

The clattering abruptly stopped, followed by the appearance of her beaming face above the countertop.

"What?"

"Are we related?" she said. "My exact favorite, too. Last year at Tip O' The Wedge that's practically all I drank. Kept me warm and toasty the whole winter. My boyfriend would steal extra fifths from his father's liquor cabinet. Which, I should tell you, was about the size of a walk-in closet. Used to get really skulled on that juice."

"Precocious drunk, were you?"

"Not any more advanced than anyone else I knew."

"Sorry. Just messing with you. I have a history of my own."

"And what was your happy head of choice?"

"Leaf, I suppose. With some rattletrap thrown in on top."

"Vicious."

Graveyard shrugged. "I ran with a callow crowd."

LemonChiffon had been scanning the well-stocked shelves on the wall behind the bar. "No LaughFrogg, I'm afraid." She reached up and pulled down a stout brown figural decanter that required both hands to set carefully on the bar. "But here's an interesting-looking jug of something called MacadamRose. It's shaped like a troll."

"Perfect."

She pulled out a couple of glasses and began to pour. "Neat?" she said.

"Of course."

She brought the drinks over and sat down next to him on the couch. He didn't want her to see him staring at her legs, but he couldn't help himself. He stared. Still absolutely peachy-keen.

LemonChiffon raised her glass. "Here's to blue skies, green lights, and, at the end of all our rainbows, a pot of gold." They clinked glasses and they drank.

"Rigorous burn," Graveyard said. He assumed a reflective air. He paused, then said, "Honey, most certainly; some fig; some orange peel, I think; burned campfire marshmallows; and stuff swept up off your grandma's carpet. It's a hug in a bottle."

"As good as life used to be," she said.

"Catchy. Another toast, right?"

"Dad's favorite. He couldn't pick up a glass without repeating exactly those same stupid words in a totally bad Irish accent. And I mean any glass. With alcohol or without."

"You know The Crevice, right? My father's place. Obviously, anyone who decides to open a bar is no stranger to raising a mug, but damn if I can remember a single interesting thing the man ever said with a drink in his hand. Except maybe 'Who the fuck's been at my damn Ballycock again? I swear I just opened this bottle last night.'" His visual field had begun to experience sudden reception problems.

"Parents. They're such funny creatures." She was a cartoon head now. A cartoon head speaking to him in a language he understood.

"But if you had to pay to see them in a show, you'd want your money back."

When Graveyard awoke some five hours later, facedown on the floor of a strange room he didn't quite recognize, a rhythmic pounding behind his eyeballs he assumed was his pulse, pants pulled down around his knees, pockets turned inside out, something wet running out of his nose, snot or blood, he wasn't ready to check, he found himself saying to himself, what the f? He tried to get up. Realized he couldn't. With an enormous effort, he did manage to roll over onto his back, where he lay for a while, throbbing, panting like a beached something or other. Time passed. Memory began to reassemble, stray images wandering in and out of the haze, pieces of a face that popped suddenly into alarming focus. He knew those lips. He knew those eyes. Cilantro oil and forbidden rice, he said to himself. Again he struggled to get up. On his second or third attempt, he was finally able to stagger clumsily to his feet and totter upright to the john. He wiped the goop off his upper lip with a wad of toilet paper. It was blood *and* snot. He looked at the face in the mirror. It was the exact face of someone who had just been drugged and robbed. He looked like a complete idiot. He didn't know how much he'd lost. He didn't want to think about that.

Somehow he made it down to his rooms with no recollection at all of how he had gotten there. He unlocked the door (the key, for some reason, having been, luckily, secreted in his shirt pocket) and entered as quietly as he could. No Ambience in sight. Good. He needed whatever alone time might be available to arrange in his mind the elements of a plausible story, any story. Then he heard the unmistakable sound of water running in the bathroom. She was in the shower. He briefly considered going right back out and not returning at all. The bathroom door clicked open. There she stood with a head of stringy wet hair and wearing, compliments of the Cowled Castle, a plush terry robe woven out of a silky blend of micro cotton and bamboo viscose fibers. She looked glamorous and rich.

"Exactly where the fuck have you been?" she said. She was wiping her ear with an equally luxurious Heaven'sCloud bath towel.

"In the Blackjack Room. You knew that."

"I checked the Blackjack Room. Twice. I also checked the Poker Room, where I was most of the night. The Baccarat Room. The Gin Rummy Room. And Slot Alley. No Graveyard."

"I moved around."

"I wondered if you'd flaked out and dragged yourself back here, so I called the room. And why didn't you answer your cell?"

"Who can deal with that nuisance, especially when I'm up to my eyeballs in the intricacies of the game? This gambling, you know, is a very delicate enterprise. The slightest variation in the atmosphere, of any kind, and you can go bust in an instant. So I turned the damn thing off. Electromagnetic fields, all those nasty invisible rays, affect the cards."

"You could at least have given me a call. I was worried."

"But I was winning."

"Could've fooled me. Cause frankly, right this minute you look like a goddamn loser. Have you been drinking, too?"

"Only what I was comped."

"You're drunk."

"Maybe a wee bit."

"So how much did you win?"

"I must've been ahead like ten, fifteen grand at some point."

"And?"

"I think too many people at that table had their electronic devices powered up. There was obviously a surge of some kind rolling through the casino ether."

"How much did you lose?"

He reached into his pockets and pulled them inside out.

"Oh, no," said Ambience. "How could you?"

"We can just go back to the well and get a refill."

"So you say." Still in her bathrobe, she slumped down onto the grand top-grain black leather sectional that occupied a good third of the room. She stared steadily at the interesting complexity of her bare foot.

Graveyard hurried over to sit beside her. "It's not that big a deal." He put his arm around her. "We're still rich, filthy rich. What's gone is just the tip of the tip. Remember—you've seen the evidence yourself—the bag is bountiful. This incident is merely a minor set-back, if that. We have no worries, understand? And zero financial issues. None, nada, zilch. The cash springs eternal."

"Are you just naturally this nuts or do you have to work extra hard at it?"

"The bag abides."

Ambience got up, went into the one of the four massive bed-rooms they happened to be occupying at the moment. Graveyard dutifully followed. She was pulling suitcases out of the closet, sling-ing them onto the bed. She was opening bureau drawers, gathering up clothes into her arms.

"Don't do this," he said.

"Well, guess what? While you were having fun breaking your own bank, I was throwing quite the celebration, too. And what a party it was. Hats and horns and chips flying through the air like confetti. Till all of a sudden the cheering and the laughing just evaporated. I was hoping to get a nice cash refill. From you."

"I'm sorry."

She slammed a suitcase shut, fastened the locks. "I'd advise you to get busy packing, too, buster. I think I may have just enough left to get us a cab to the airport and that's it. The bill here's been paid, right?"

"Through the end of the week."

"Then presumably we can get a refund on the remainder. For a handful of food and a cab to get us home."

"I'll make this up to you."

"What's the point of having money when you don't…have… the…money?"

Graveyard decided not to respond. Whatever he said would lead only to a futile round of complaint and countercomplaint and more lies than he had the energy to juggle at the moment. The flight home was a sullen affair. They each consumed the maximum number of drinks allowed, then traded furtive sips from the sometimes security cleared, sometimes not, plastic flask of sweet, clean, grape-forward TotallyVodka that Ambience was a little too fond of and that she had stashed in her brand new Croesus&RoughStuff indigo lambskin handbag, and the alcohol combined with the razorpin Ambience had been prescribed years ago for the chronic anxiety that had followed her around since puberty like a stray feral dog rendered the two of them relatively senseless. Not that they would have talked all that much had they been stone-cold sober.

Back home, still barely speaking. After a near-silent cab ride in, they split up, Ambience to FurryFarm to retrieve Nippers, Graveyard to Plexi's to retrieve the bag. When he hit the intercom, Graveyard could hear Plexi talking to someone else, someone else answering back. Fenugreek and mango pickle, he said to himself, Plexi has no friends. WTF? The buzzer buzzed. He went inside. He went up the stairs. He knocked on the door. He heard some scurrying around inside. "C'mon," said Graveyard. "You know who it is. Open up." More scurrying, more whispering. After some fumbling around at the lock, the door finally swung open and Graveyard found himself staring into the barrel of a piece he instantly recognized because he owned one himself: a Buster&Noggin 21D. The hand holding the weapon was attached to a little wired stranger with that indeterminate skin color that made many of those who preferred to regard themselves as white uneasy. There was an oil-like sheen of sweat coating his face. Standing still, he still trembled. Even his eyeballs seemed to be trembling. He looked like what Ambience liked to call a popcorn man—primed to explode at the touch of the nearest flame.

Graveyard raised his hands. "I give up," he said.

PlexiBerryPunch came hurrying from behind, pulled the stranger's arm away. "Now, now," he said. "Manners, manners." To Graveyard, "Forgive him, please. RealDeal here's a little frosted." To RealDeal, "Give me the bang-bang. It's rude."

"I'll give you the bang-bang." RealDeal turned and pointed the barrel toward the exact center of Plexi's forehead.

"Who is this guy?" said Graveyard.

"I'm this," RealDeal said. He waved the weapon around in front of Graveyard's startled face. "That's who I am."

"Don't do that," said Graveyard. "It's not nice, and even nice people have been known to get badly hurt doing that."

"Dial it down," said Plexi. "You can suck my dick later if you want."

"I don't like this guy," said RealDeal.

"He likes you. You like RealDeal, don't you, Graveyard?"

"Sure," said Graveyard. Then, getting his first good glimpse into the interior of the apartment, "Palm hearts and profiteroles, what the fuck is going on in here?" The floor was covered in money, scads of money, paper bills scattered carelessly about like autumn leaves, in some places ankle deep.

"We encountered a situation," Plexi said.

"It's our money," said RealDeal, still gesturing with the gun. He obviously loved the weapon, loved brandishing the weapon, loved watching himself brandishing the weapon, loved watching the effects of the brandishing on other people.

"Could you please?" said Graveyard. He pointed at the gun.

Plexi leaned over, whispered in Graveyard's ear. "It's not loaded."

"Sure," said Graveyard.

"It's our fucking money now," said RealDeal. "Every shitass dollar. Possession, motherfucker. Nine-tenths of the law."

"Who is this guy?"

Plexi took RealDeal by the elbow, steered him gently back toward command central, a once plush, now broken-down recliner set squarely before a ginormous Wondertron screen. "Here, sit here," he said as if guiding a game piece into position. "In the captain's chair." On the cluttered table between chair and TV was arranged an impressive assortment of game consoles and electronic devices surrounded by at least a dozen remotes, some of which presumably worked. "Play some FleshBlade. I need a private moment with my friend here."

"Five minutes," said RealDeal. "Then I'm coming for my money."

"Yes, yes," said Plexi.

"His money?" said Graveyard. "What's with all this *my* money shit?"

"Let's talk." Plexi led him down the cash-strewn hallway to the cash-strewn bedroom, where Graveyard's bag, thoroughly vandalized, was sitting upright in the center of a daisy-print bath mat Plexi used, for whatever Plexi reasons, as a throw rug. The lock, though still intact, was covered in ugly scratches and dents, but the canvas bag itself had been cut, slashed, and torn, crisp federal notes protruding from the openings like stuffing from a burst mattress.

"Party time, huh?" said Graveyard. "Have a lot of fun tossing around all this confetti?"

"We realmed out, man. There were creepy noises outside. Lots of 'em. Right at the door, too. Scratchy fingernail let-me-in kind of noises."

"Yeah, so what's so unusual about that in this building?"

"We could hear 'em, Graveyard. Zombies. A whole horde of 'em, clawing at the door. We were scared. We needed to defend ourselves."

"What were you going to do, throw money at them?"

"We were after the guns. That's what was supposed to be in there, not all this, this…" He gestured helplessly at the mess at their feet.

"So disappointing," said Graveyard. "I trusted you to keep my goods in, well, better condition than I find them."

"It's all there. Really. We haven't dared go outside, and what could we spend it on in here?"

Graveyard fished the key out of his pocket, opened the lock. "Got any of that duct tape?"

Of course Plexi had duct tape, since most of his ratty furniture seemed to have been repaired with ample layers of it. Graveyard, muttering all the while, patched the slashes on the bag as best he could. Then he got down on his knees and began gathering up handfuls of cash and stuffing them back into the bag. "You could help," said Graveyard. So Plexi did.

"Your 'friend' there's put together rather loosely, don't you think?" said Graveyard. "He gives me the yips. Where'd you meet this clown, anyway?"

"Don't get your doily in a crumple. He's as harmless as a baby in a crib. Followed me home one day. Oddly, can't remember when. Or where, for that matter. Actually, I think what he really wants is to commit suicide and just needs someone to witness the ceremony. You know, notarize the deed."

"Yeah? Well, looks like he might want to take some of his audience with him, too."

"He lives for an audience."

"Fine. Just don't expect me to be a member."

"You understand, of course, he regards at least half of your money as his."

"Whose is the other half?"

"That would be mine, of course. On the principle of finders keepers and all that."

"I don't believe that's settled law."

"Well, in his mind it is."

Plexi handed over a hefty bunch of bills he'd gathered up off the floor. "Where'd you get all these fucking bones, anyway? If you don't mind my asking."

"Ambience's uncle. He died. Some weird dude known to the family as Uncle Parsnips. Apparently he was quite loaded, and Ambience, I guess, was his favorite niece."

"Must have been an extra-special favorite."

"Oh, this?" Graveyard displayed a wad of wrinkled cash. "This is just a fraction of the pot. Everybody got something."

"Why didn't you tell me what was in the bag?"

"It's a lot of temptation."

"I don't care about money."

"That's why I brought the stuff to you. Figured even if you got curious—and I didn't think you would—and opened the bag, the stash would be safe, not scattered around the apartment like highway litter."

"Told you. We realmed out. The walking dead. You know. Real hairy."

"Okay, enough. I just want to pack up and go, but I did promise myself, before the gouda hit the fan, that I'd drop some sort of a party favor on you for your trouble, spread the wealth kind of thing. So here." He simply passed over the impressive double handfuls of loose currency he happened at the moment to be holding. "Don't know how much is there, but that's easily six months, a year, you don't have to work."

"How about not working for six years? How about that, huh?"

It was RealDeal. He was standing in the doorway, the imposing Buster&Noggin still firmly affixed to his hand.

"Beat FleshBlade already?" said Plexi.

"Fuck FleshBlade. What're you two ugly asshats whispering about in here?"

"Nothing much," said Plexi. "We were just conspiring how to best sneak this duffel out the door without your seeing it."

"You know I could just kill the two of you right now and take the whole shitpile for myself."

"No, you won't," said Plexi. "That's not you. You know that. Besides, we were actually just talking about your cut."

"Who said anything about a cut? I want it all."

"Well," said Graveyard, "that's going to be a bit of a problem."

"Yeah?" said RealDeal. "Funny: I don't see it that way. You close up the bag, you pick up the bag, you pass the bag over to me. No problem."

"RealDeal is kinda broke," said Plexi. "He's got pressing financial issues."

"Who doesn't?" said Graveyard. "My mother needs an operation, too. Tell you what I'll do, though. Five thousand in mad money. No strings. Spend it how you please. It's a gift. For your service."

"I want it all."

"Really?" said Graveyard. "It's not even my money. It's my wife's. Her inheritance. Was her uncle, not mine, who died."

"I'll leave you fifty bucks to buy flowers. Gimme the bag."

"Could I talk to you for a minute?" said Plexi.

"What for?"

"Just come. Just for a minute. Please." He put his arm around RealDeal's shoulders and walked him back into the gaming room.

Methodically, Graveyard picked up the remaining bills, shoved them into the bag as best he could, and stood there patiently waiting. He could hear the furious hissing of their voices back and forth at almost comical length, then a clear and distinct "Fuck that!" from RealDeal. An indistinguishable response from Plexi. Then the sounds of energetic struggle. Retrieving the scattered money in the hallway as he went, Graveyard entered the room to find the two "buddies" tangled all up in each other, thrashing about on the floor like some ridiculous hybrid creature in the midst of either giving birth or dying or both. They were shouting. They were cursing. They were trying with limited success to bite each other's ears, cheeks, fingers, whatever exposed body part was readily available. Then RealDeal began to beat Plexi on the side of the head with the butt of his gun to no discernible effect. Graveyard watched for a while. He was curious as to who would win. The struggle seemed to have settled into an exhausted draw. "Okay," said Graveyard finally. "You gentlemen can stop now. I have a plan."

"Get this fucking fucker the fuck off me!" Plexi said, punctuating the request with an ineffectual attempt at kneeing RealDeal rather seriously in the groin.

Graveyard tried to pull them apart. No go. So he leaned down and, employing the famous Venusian nerve pinch favored by Mr. FlavorAdditive, his ninety-pound-weakling high school chemistry teacher, who used it to instantly reduce insubordinate jocks to compliant heaps of cringing flesh, seized between thumb and forefinger that narrow muscle running along the top of RealDeal's right shoulder and squeezed. He squeezed hard. "Ow!" said RealDeal. He quickly rolled off of Plexi and as far away from the "death" grip as he could get. He rubbed his shoulder. "That fucking hurts!"

"It's meant to," said Graveyard. "What's the trouble here?" He started picking up the stray cash from the floor of the room.

"I believe you're familiar with the issues," said Plexi.

"Fine," said Graveyard. "So what sum would it take, exactly, for everyone to leave here, if not altogether euphoric, then at least well satisfied?"

"The very subject of our spirited discussion," said Plexi. "We have been unable to agree on a happy figure."

"How about fifty grand?" said Graveyard. "Seems fair and generous."

"The very number we were approaching," said Plexi. "Excellent choice."

"How's about I just cap the two of you," said RealDeal, "and take all of it?" The gun was somehow back in his hand. He waved it in their general direction.

"You know that's not loaded, right?" said Plexi.

RealDeal looked at the gun. He pointed it at Plexi. He pulled the trigger. Once. Twice. Click. Click. He looked at the gun. "Jokes," he said. "You like jokes. How's this for a joke? I'm sure there's at least one motherfucking bullet lying somewhere around this shithole. You find it, you put it in the gun, and we all play a fun game of Russian roulette. Last fucker left takes home everything. How's about that?"

"Sounds stupid to me," said Plexi.

"Ditto," said Graveyard.

"What happens we go around once, click, click, click, we're all still standing? What then? Divide it into thirds?"

"Whaddya think happens, shithead? We go again."

"And if still nothing?"

"Don't agitate me, Plexi. I'm getting agitated. Fucking agitated!"

"What does the survivor do about the bodies?" said Graveyard.

"Whaddya mean, what does he do? He grabs the fucking money and leaves the stiffs lying on the fucking floor."

"In my apartment? For me to clean up?"

"Well," said Graveyard, "you, of course, may not be among the sentient anymore."

"See?" said Plexi. "Proves what I was saying. Too many complications for this freaking scenario."

"What do you mean, complications?" said RealDeal. "There's no complications. It's clean. It's quick. It's sweet. No more dickhead arguments. No more shitass percentages. No more crunchy feelings. You put a round in the chamber. You put the gun to your head." He put the gun to his head. "You pull the trigger." He pulled the trigger.

It wasn't like in the movies. If there was a sudden special-effects explosion of body fluid and brain matter erupting from the far side of his skull, Graveyard didn't see it. All his attention was focused on the perfectly round entrance wound above RealDeal's right ear, from which streamed an astonishing torrent of real blood, real bright, real red, like colored water from a hose as the man's body, in a trippy kind of hypnotic super slow motion, slumped frame by agonizing frame onto the hard, immutable floor.

Graveyard and Plexi stared at each other. Wow, they mouthed together in silent unison.

"He's bleeding all over the rug!" said Plexi at last and hurried out of the room.

As Graveyard watched, oddly unable to move, mind stripped bare, the strings in his limbs all gone, the crimson fountain dwindled down to a small bubbling crater in the now toylike skull. The eyes were still open. Graveyard couldn't look at those. He didn't see any point in checking for a pulse, either, but he did and discovered he didn't need to do much of anything at all. Beets and balut, he finally managed to say to himself, this is gonna leave a mark.

Plexi returned, carrying an armful of towels and a bucket. "I paid five hundred bucks for that damn rug. Got a deal from a guy down on Razzleberry Street. Claimed it was on the last shipment out of Thingamadad right before the city fell. Notice all the fancy design work? Supposed to ward off evil spirits and other collateral crap."

"Back to the loom on that one."

"Well, you know," said Plexi. "Evil. It's pretty stubborn shit." He threw the towels onto the puddle of blood creeping slowly across the floor.

"Thought you said the gun wasn't loaded."

Plexi shrugged. "What do I know? Must've been a stray round left in the chamber somewhere."

"So what are we going to do with this guy?"

"Don't worry about it."

"What do you mean, don't worry about it? There's a body lying here in the middle of your apartment. A dead body." He glanced over at what used to be a guy named RealDeal. "A decidedly dead body."

"I know some people."

"Oh, really?"

"People in sanitation. Supposed to be good but they're pricey."

"How pricey?"

"I don't know. Maybe I can get removal and a squeegee for around five or so."

"And how do you happen to be acquainted with such enterprising individuals?"

"I'm a gregarious fellow. Look, uh, think you could help out a little here?"

"He was your friend. Or something."

"It was your money got us into this fix."

"Nothing would've happened if you hadn't ripped into that bag like a kid on Christmas morning."

"What about half? I think that's fair."

"I'm not even half responsible."

"You offered him a share."

"All right. Two thousand."

"Beautiful. You've helped make the world a better place."

"I'm a goddamn saint." Graveyard opened the bag and began counting out the bills.

"Yes," said Plexi. "The timeless sorcery of money." He extended his open palm. "It makes all the bad just go away."

"We can hope," Graveyard said. He peered over Plexi's shoulder to see if, in the last few minutes, the body had moved at all. It hadn't.

CHAPTER 14

THE MAN FROM THE UPPER FLOORS

FIRST OF ALL, NIPPERSPUMPKINCLAWS was not pleased. When the cage door was finally sprung, he stared attentively at the new opening. He sniffed the air. He stared again. He sniffed again. Then slowly, slowly, inch by careful inch, he crept warily out into the big beyond as if all this dubious space were a cage of a different order. All the while as Ambience enthusiastically called to him, appeals pointedly ignored. And when she picked him up, pressed him to her chest, cooed repeatedly in his ear, he refused to look her in the eye. Then, getting him in the carrier for the trip home required the gloved assistance of a trained FurryFarm tech. Ambience, who was by now feeling a jalapeño belly coming on, had never experienced such difficulty with Nippers, even on numerous traumatic visits to the vet. Obviously, he was hurt at being abandoned, locked up among strangers for all these days. But there was something more. Ambience knew her Nips. Her Nips knew her. He was reading her internal weather. All the static she'd been steadily transmitting since leaving Bullionvilla was not lost on him. Despite Ambience's near-constant efforts at providing vocal comfort, he complained loudly all the way home.

Halfway down the block she immediately picked up on the suspicious intruder, the what's-wrong-with-this-picture perched on her front stoop as if he belonged there when he obviously didn't, a fairly complete representation of the industrious corporate bee type. Standard-issue uniform, though the Harrogate charcoal suit was

195

too high end for government drone work. Oxblood quarter brogues obviously handmade and quite shiny. Impressive gold watchband peeking out of his left sleeve. Headful of closely cropped steel wool for hair. As she approached, she detected the distinctive reek of the played-out scent of Master&Manor's Eden Ambush, the gentleman's cologne for those who aren't. Only aliasing in the picture: he was also a dead ringer for XSquared. You know, the lovably wacky morgue attendant on *Here Come the Po-Po* who liked to draw smiley faces on cadaver foreheads. Pointedly ignoring him, she turned and started up the steps.

"Pardon me, miss," he said. "You don't happen to be, by any chance, a certain Ambience?"

"Who's asking?" she said.

"A friend."

She gave him her patented puzzled look. "Sorry, not her."

"Are you sure?" the man said. "'Cause frankly, you bear a remarkable resemblance to this particular individual." From his inner suit pocket he extracted a piece of paper, which he painstakingly unfolded and passed courteously to her. It was a copy of her last DMV photo, the one she refused to show anyone because, to herself, at least, she looked like a bloated body fished from a bad river. She pretended to look at the picture. She pretended to look at him.

"Who are you?" she said.

"I'm not gonna be so cliché as to say, 'My card,' but…" From his exotic-skin wallet he produced an off-blue business presentation that read simply:

BLISTERPAC
SENIOR INVESTIGATOR

"Shouldn't your name have a *k* at the end?"

"My parents," he said. "Creative types."

"Cute," said Ambience.

"Perhaps we could step inside so as to discuss this complication in comfort."

"Listen, what's this bullshit all about, anyway?"

"Financial concerns," he said. "Of a personal nature."

She looked into his eyes. Closed door after closed door after closed door.

"Please," he said, extending his arm invitingly toward the front entrance as if it were his residence. "No reason the entire neighborhood has to share in our business."

"I have no secrets." Nippers's meows were beginning to sound like the cries of a human baby.

"Oh, I think you might."

"I don't ordinarily allow strangers into my apartment."

"Good policy. I don't, either. But you know, exceptions to every rule." He was smiling like XSquared always did just when he was about to pull away the sheet on a gnarlyfest of a corpse. "I'm house-trained and I don't bite," he said.

She was looking at his fingers. Sorry. She couldn't help it. Meaty and stubby. Exceedingly hairy knuckles, too. "I hope I don't regret this," she said. She led him into the building and up the stairs. She unlocked the door. She paused. "Place is kinda messy."

BlisterPac laughed the laugh he was supposed to. "You oughta see mine."

She opened the door. They went in. Boxes of product, boxes of product, boxes of product. She set the cat carrier on the floor, stooped down, opened the wire gate. Nippers bolted out, dashed down the hallway, and went into the bedroom, where he could presumably be found hiding under the bed. "He's happy to be back home," Ambience said.

"Where's he been?"

"The vet."

"Anything wrong?"

"Not really. Just a routine neutering."

"Ouch."

"He wasn't conscious through it."

"Still."

Ambience removed some stray wrapping paper and shopping bags from the couch. "Have a seat."

BlisterPac sat. He looked around. "Nice," he said. Just like the bad guy in the movies you know is only pretending to be friendly.

Ambience watched him eyeing the loot. "Please. Excuse the clutter. Just had an insane baby shower in here."

"Killer haul."

"Yeah. I have a lot of friends, and I guess they're all pretty generous."

"All this. For you?"

She nodded.

"Congratulations. When's the big day?"

"December eighteenth."

"Really? How fortunate. Maybe you'll have a Christmas baby."

"We're hoping."

"Tough, though, for the kid. You know, to have your birthday and Christmas so close together. Don't get as much stuff."

"True. Listen, can I get you anything to drink?"

"Thanks, but no, I'm fine."

Ambience took a seat on the far end of the couch.

"Can't help but notice," said BlisterPac, pointing to one of the numerous unopened cartons. "Someone gave you a case of Premium OutlawGold for your baby shower?"

"I have weird friends."

"Well, don't we all. But you know, better to have the friends you've got than the ones you don't."

"Couldn't agree more."

"Pleasant place you've got here. Homey."

"Not exactly the word I'd use, but close enough."

"And you reside here with your current husband?"

"There's only ever been one."

"One what?"

"Husband."

"I'm sorry. I didn't mean to imply…" His voice trailed off for a moment, paused, then started up again. "That cat of yours, if you don't mind my asking, seemed rather big to just be getting neutered."

"He's a Northern Blue Bog Tatterdemalion. It's a famously large breed. About twice the size of an average house cat."

"Isn't a Blue Bog kinda pricey, too?"

"Normally, yes, but Nippers was a shelter rescue."

"A beautiful animal with that pedigree? Wonder who'd abandon a cat so expensive?"

"People, sad to say, can be quite carelessly cruel."

"You know, you're right. I'm constantly struck by what passes for courtesy in this daffy world of ours."

"You're sure you don't want something to drink?"

"No, no, I'm good. I suppose we might as well get down to business."

"Yes. Let's. Whatever this mysterious business could possibly be." She gave him a smile that, though it wasn't her intention, even she would have described as somewhat sickly.

"I represent a certain individual who wishes to remain anonymous, largely out of embarrassment. He's lost, you see, purely by accident, a rather substantial sum of money."

"How unfortunate."

"Yes. And of course he'd like to get it back."

"Makes sense. What sort of sum, exactly, are we talking about here?"

"Well, here's an odd detail about our situation. My client isn't certain of the total involved. It was a bag. A rather large bag."

"A bag of money?"

"Yes."

"Which your client has somehow mislaid?"

"Fell out of a window, actually."

"Excuse me, but out of a window?"

"Strange to say, but that's what happened."

"Must be a hell of a story there."

"Yes, but that's neither here nor there."

"So what does all this nonsense have to do with me?"

"My special client and I have reason to believe that you and your husband are in possession of crucial information about where these missing funds might be located."

"You do? But I haven't a clue what you're talking about."

"I understand. It's quite possible this matter concerns only your husband."

"You'd have to ask him."

"Are you aware, say, of any recent purchases on his part of perhaps a rather extravagant nature? Purchases he'd ordinarily find difficult, if not impossible, to make?" She noted the quick glance at the boxes and understood he wanted her to note that glance.

"Is that a crime?" she said. Occasionally, depending on her mood, Ambience would enjoy a healthy verbal spar with the minions of petty officialdom. This BlisterPac guy, though, was somewhat creeping her out. The voice was all tea and scalpels.

"No, but sometimes it's a tell. Sometimes not."

"Look, Mr. Pac, this is a big city full of big people and big cash. In case you haven't noticed, buying and selling seems to be the major, the only, activity going on around here. Dollars are everywhere. Why zero in on us? We barely scrape enough together to make the rent each month. And, besides, even if someone did happen to find your precious bag, how could you prove it was yours?"

"We have the video."

"What video?"

"Of your husband. Or videos, I should say. More than one. Many more."

"What do you mean?" She could actually hear her heart. She hoped he couldn't.

"Visual confirmation of your husband—his name is Graveyard, I believe?"

She nodded.

"Of Graveyard coming into possession of our assets."

"And where did this purported 'coming into possession' supposedly take place?"

"In front of the Eyedropper building, as a matter of fact. Busy location."

"Graveyard's rarely in that part of town. Too tight-assed for his taste. You're certain it's him?"

"Security cameras don't lie."

"Aren't they pretty low resolution?"

"Some are. Some aren't. In addition, we've run the images through our facial recognition program. A primo program. A classi-fied government program. There is no doubt."

"I don't know what to say. Graveyard is not a thief."

"Never said he was. Look, we're well aware that this entire event was simply an unhappy accident. The money was accidentally lost and then accidentally found by your husband. No one's blaming anybody for anything. We, understandably, just want it returned."

"I still think you've got the wrong people. I don't know anything about any lost money. I'm sure Graveyard doesn't, either."

"I understand. As I've already made clear, you may be a completely innocent party in this situation. Given that, let me inquire again whether you have been at all aware lately of any sudden bumps in your husband's personal finances, no matter how minor?"

She pretended to think. "Can't say that I have."

"Recent acquisitions of previously unaffordable luxury items?"

"Certainly not."

"I think I should probably confess to you that my client is deter-mined to bring this issue to a swift and satisfactory conclusion."

"I hate issues."

"Good. Then we're in agreement."

"If you say so."

"Then I should also admit that my client, in strenuous pursuit of his self-interests and legally justified ends, is concerned with neither circuits nor consequences. There will be no blowback on us. There never is. Do you understand?"

"I appreciate your candor."

"Then you can also applaud the seriousness of my offer."

"Count on it."

"I hope that you and your husband can resolve this matter in a fair and timely manner. What my anxious client demands is a prompt return of the remaining funds as soon as possible. Whatever has already been spent will be considered a reward for both finding and returning the bulk of—how should we put it?—the fallen misbegotten."

"I've told you, there's no 'misbegotten' here."

"No one is claiming anything. It's just that, let me repeat, my client believes you and your husband are, at present, in the best place to amicably resolve our current predicament."

"It's all about honesty."

"My sentiments exactly."

"Unfortunately, as I've repeatedly explained, I know nothing about any stray monies lost, mislaid, stolen, or whatever, and neither does my husband."

"You have my card," BlisterPac said. "We prefer a quick and painless solution to this matter as soon as possible."

"In preference to what?"

"Why don't we consider those options at the appropriate time, okay?" He gathered himself up off the couch. "I look forward to hearing from you." He offered his hand. She shook it.

Ambience followed him to the door. "Have a good day," he said.

"I always do."

She closed the door. She locked it. She double-locked it. Done. And she was done. Goodbye to Mr. Pustule and his employer. Goodbye to foreign travel. Goodbye to orange-tiled roofs in the rain. Goodbye to money with pictures of people she didn't recognize on it. Goodbye to shopping 24-7. Goodbye to the carefree, prodigal life. She got the vacuum cleaner out of the closet. She started vacuuming. In the bedroom, as if on cue, Nippers started crying. Nippers hated the vacuum cleaner. Ambience understood. She turned off the machine, cracked open a fresh bottle of OutlawGold (guzzling from half-empty liters lying randomly about the apartment was so déclassé), and poured herself a triple shot. She sat back down on the couch. She watched TV for a while. Some "reality" bullshit about a bunch of morons pretend-stranded on a desert island, killing time with fake flirts and fake arguments while armed only with spoons and jagged bits of glass, digging in the sand like deranged gophers for a buried pirate chest that might or might not be jammed full of enough glittery doubloons to finance a life. She liked the show a lot. The confrontations, the brawls, the tears. As she watched, she sipped her Scotch and consumed an entire pint of HoldMeClose chocolate butternut squash ice cream. Then she went into her room and began trying on new jewelry. That always made her feel better. And it did.

CHAPTER 15

BLOWING CHUNKS

THAT MONDAY THE ELEVENTH was not, for MisterMenu, at least, your typical blue Monday. NationalProcedures finally closed on the record-breaking SpiritualEquities deal and, frankly, had made a freaking killing, and an hour later he was informed he had won the monthly HoneyDrippers Screen Meet Lottery. He had forgotten he'd even entered the damn contest. And especially unusual for him, he'd even forgotten the precise amount he'd had to shell out for the privilege of claiming a ticket in the draw. He had to log in and check out the girl's image again. He was sure she'd be predictably stunning. He did. She was. Her name was LavenderLips. Her favorite fruit: the banana. Her favorite snack: cherry popsicles. Yeah, right. Nevertheless, MisterMenu was very excited. The clock would begin ticking in a week, at 0800 next Monday. More than enough time to get a crackerjack construction team over to the recently vacated PeerlessPolicies warehouse on the Lower West Side and prepare a suitable enclosure. What was required was a very specific look. Simple, spare, clean. And the walls, including floor and ceiling, had to be white, blindingly white, immaculately white. A solid door with a solid lock. The bag of money, the bottles of water, the roll of paper towels, and the bucket would be delivered to the room the morning of LavenderLips's arrival. He was guaranteed a full day with her, all the way until 1700—more than adequate to explore every twist and turn of your particular kink. He was very excited.

Meanwhile he had a company to run and money to make. Both

occupations he could manage in his sleep and sometimes did. He'd had several transformational experiences while asleep, going into sleep, and coming out of sleep. He had not the slightest doubt it was a magical place, well worth visiting frequently, even if it did eat up unfortunate tons of precious moneymaking hours. Solution: make money while sleeping. Learn to put your money into dark warm humid places conducive to the care and propagation of those marvelous little green notes, places like PDQParaphernalia, BurningBushCache, and XYZNut, all of which he owned and, frankly, contributed to the steady, ludicrous growth of his numerous bank accounts at a rate far greater than anything he ever did here at NationalProcedures while awake. Go figure. If only the living, breathing side of life could be managed so lucratively. If only emotions were dollars and could generate profits. What an overlord of the psyche he could be, standing astride all that mess like a god. The phone buzzed. It was the president calling.

"Tell him I'm busy," he said to PocketGuard, his administrative assistant for special assistance, whom he'd once had a fuck-buddy relationship with about three years ago. "Tell him I'm in a meeting, an important meeting, a very important meeting."

"You know he won't care. He'll insist you take it anyway. Like he's always done before."

"Tell him I'm in the damn john."

"But he knows you have a phone in there."

"Fucking catacombs," he said. He took the call. Nothing monumental. It was about a golfing engagement next Saturday. MisterMenu courteously declined. He had to be in Bugaboo that weekend, or so he said. His daughter NoDeposit was getting married Saturday to Filament, the competence-challenged son of Cravensworth, CEO of BolsterIndustries. Like father, like son. How any of these people managed to make even a single dime's worth of profit was a mystery of biblical proportions to MisterMenu. As was his style, the president pressed. DentalDam was scheduled to be in their foursome. His entourage, no doubt, in attendance at the clubhouse. You know, in all their flower-pussied glory. Postpone the wedding. Your daughter can get married any day of the week. A clam buffet of such splendor as this is served maybe once, twice per lifetime. MisterMenu agreed. He appreciated the invite and, to himself, regretted the lost opportunity to weasel something more useful out of this buffaloed chief executive than he already had—and believe me, he'd scarfed up plenty of tidbits wherever he found them. But no, his younger daughter, the wedding, you understand. The president pretended he did. They hung up. MisterMenu needed to look at some numbers—now. So he did. Illuminated figures scrolled across the screen in stately procession. The sight always comforted him. Even when the sums were not particularly beneficial either to him or NationalProcedures, the endless parade of 123s projected a sense of vibrancy, of invincibility, proof that no matter what happened to him or the firm, something in this porous world held fast, continued on undeterred. Something was eternal.

At 10:28 MattressTesterJr called. He and MisterMenu discussed the AutomatedCarnage deal.

At 11:52 ProvidentialWind called. They discussed the likely FerretHoldings acquisition.

At 1:11 MissusMenu called.

"Of course," she said, "you may leave me anytime you wish. You know that."

"What the hell are you talking about?" he said.

"I can persist in this charade as long as you can."

"What the hell are you talking about?"

"You and I both know the water's been draining out of the tub for six years now. It's just a matter of who's going to pull the plug first."

"We'll talk about this when I get home."

"I won't hold my breath."

"Fine. Don't."

He hung up first.

He went into his private bathroom and washed his face. He

looked at himself in the mirror. He looked pretty good for a man of his years. Slightly balding, slightly overweight, slightly handsome. He figured he could pass for someone half his age. He couldn't.

At 2:16 MisterMenu held an impromptu meeting of the innovative Guided Crash Team. Although he conducted the meeting with his usual perspicacity and vigor, a half hour later he couldn't recall much of what he'd said.

His day staggered on to its unacceptably serrated end somewhere around 8:38 p.m., when, instead of repairing to the MemoryFoam-Room of the trending ClusterClub for his customary workcapper of a pair of double BoltCutters on the rocks, he climbed into his chauffeured car for the interminable ride home.

Repeat with the usual variations for next four days.

Late Friday afternoon he was informed his fabled Bag O' Money was still somewhere at large in the wilderness of the world. BlisterPac hadn't been heard from in over a week. But what the hell. It was the weekend. Monday was only two days away. Until then he and MissusMenu rarely spoke. She stayed in her room. He stayed in his. Fine with him. He didn't like talking to her. He didn't like looking at her. He didn't like touching her. Or her touching him. And he didn't like her smell. And he especially couldn't care less about whatever the hell it was she doing in her room. Or even whether she was alone in her room or not. YOLO. Saturday night he went out with X from XAnalytics and Y from YBurdens. They all got stupid drunk and pretended they were twenty-one again. They insulted waiters, grabbed strange women's tits, picked fights with fellow assholes, broke assorted plates and highball glasses, got kicked out of two bars, threw up on the street in front of the HighHatHotel, and, before the night was over, each got a free hand job under a table at MadameUncertain's. They behaved like total jackasses. No apologies. What on earth had possessed them? he mused to himself later that morning. Humanity, he decided, being human, for a change, had ambushed them.

Sunday MisterMenu spent at the BobolinkRestHomeAndPetulanceCourse trying for four-plus hours to get a damn little ball into eighteen damn little holes. He was moderately successful. He shot a 98. When he got home he discovered the dirty breakfast dishes (all imported AddleWare china) he'd left in the sink were now broken and scattered across the kitchen floor. He and MissusMenu did not exchange a single word that entire day.

Monday morning arrived in a burst of glaring sunlight under the half-dropped blind, hitting his face directly in the eyes, but he didn't care. He'd been up since 6:00. In his room he locked the door, settled into his special custom-built PleasureForm eroto-gnomic chair, switched on the 103-inch HeebieJeebie, and tuned to HoneyDrippers4U/LOTTERY, where he typed in his secret winner's code, and blooming onto the screen came the channel's logo, a drawing of a cross section of a beehive with big cartoon bees circling around it and an exaggerated stream of thick honey leaking from the bottom in big heavy drops into a cartoon woman's outrageous receptacle-shaped mouth. He looked at that for a while. At precisely 0800 the image of his newly built room popped into focus, revealing the white walls, the white floor, the simple gray metal chair, but no LavenderLips, no female human anywhere in sight. He checked his watch. He stared at the screen. Nothing. He kept staring, as if attempting to will her appearance into view. He picked up his cell, preparing to call somebody, anybody, when abruptly a live woman stepped into the frame. She had arrived in total work costume: thigh-high boots, black leather miniskirt, biscuit-popping shiny metallic blue cutoff halter top, a fringed hippie-style suede shoulder bag. At first he wasn't entirely sure it was the real LavenderLips. She looked so different. Her hair was now a high-end boutique blond, and it was long, much longer than in her lottery-site photo. Fine with him. Makeup, obviously professionally applied, had also somewhat altered her face. It was now a glossy magazine face of devastating unreality. He felt an awakening in his pants. So he unzipped his fly, placed his hand inside. Her deep black eyebrows, obviously drawn in by a practiced hand, and her famous lips seemed even larger, the skin even creamier. But the major effect of all this perfect paint was to direct attention to the center of the picture: her eyes. They, too, had increased significantly in size: huge, alert, endless, they were like whole planets you could not avert your gaze from. They invited study, close study. They seemed made of glass, shining and clear, illuminated from within by an intense, sharp, hypnotic, almost unearthly deep yellow. It was the magnetic color of these irises that you could not pull yourself away from: a pure living gold, a gold that demanded to be mined. What was happening? He didn't know. He was obviously having a moment of some kind or other. He had never, not once in his long, narrow life, experienced the effects from the glance this woman seemed able to deliver so effortlessly. He was certainly glad he'd shelled out the cash to install a top-shelf HD camera capable of recording such a moment. And yes, he finally had to admit to himself, he did recognize her, the striking engrave-it-on-a-coin profile. And the dimples, he remembered the dimples, similar to the ones on NoDeposit's pink fuzzy cheeks. It was definitely the real LavenderLips. She looked around for a moment, noticed the camera, stared into it. She gave a little wave.

"Hi," she said. "Anyone there?"

"You find the place okay?" MisterMenu said.

"I'm here, ain't I?"

"You surely are. I take it my instructions were clear enough?"

She was still attempting to take in these strange new surroundings. "No problem," she said. She was looking around, nervously checking every corner, like a doe in a strange wood. "Don't worry about it."

"Good."

"What's up with this place, anyway? It's pretty creepy."

"A refuge from the distractions of the buzzing world," he said. "Have a seat."

She settled carefully into the gray metal folding chair, took in the objects arranged on the floor before her: an impressive stack of fifty-dollar bills, a half dozen family-size bottles of MountainMama volcanic-rock-filtered artisanal water, a clear plastic bucket, and a hefty roll of paper towels. There was a sudden clicking noise and she gave a start, turned toward the door. "What's that?" she said.

"I believe they're just locking the door. You're in there with a fair amount of money. We want to make sure it stays in there. My name, by the way, is MegaHyphenate."

"I can't see you. What do you look like?"

"If you want the physicals, okay. I'm six foot three, one hundred and eighty pounds. I've got medium-length dirty blond hair, a broken nose, but it's not too obvious, am in pretty good shape for my age but with the beginning of a slight pooch, kinda bowlegged with a hairy chest. Doesn't sound like much, I know, but the total package, I believe, is not entirely unappealing."

"How old are you?"

"Old enough to want to lie about it."

"So lie."

"Thirty-seven."

"Nice. You picked a good age."

"I have a confession."

"What's that?"

"I couldn't lie. That's my real age."

"Well, you know something?"

"What?"

"You sound honest."

"You can't have a good relationship without being honest."

He could literally watch her body visibly relax, slump comfortably into her uncomfortable chair. "You don't know how wired I was about all this. I mean, the instructions were so weird and all. You sounded like a total freak."

"So sorry. Didn't mean to frighten you in the least."

"You didn't. Well, maybe a little."

"Feel better?"

"Much."

He liked it when she tilted her head, the way she was doing now. It reminded him of DustBunny. One drunken night back in his twenties, he had fallen into a pontification about string theory or some such bullshit and fancied himself a physicist for about a day and a half, though of the decidedly junior variety. The blue light from DustBunny's computer screen fell across her neck, the side of her smooth cheek, did something pleasant to his dick.

"Let me see your fingers."

She held up her hands.

"Spread 'em."

She did. Her fingers were beautiful.

"Lick 'em."

She did. They were wet and shiny. Something pleasant was starting to happen in MisterMenu's down there. She continued sucking them, one slick finger after another.

"I like that."

"Thought you might. What's all this money here for?" She gestured toward the pile of bills stacked neatly on the floor in front of her.

"I want you to eat them. One at a time. They're fifties, aren't they?"

She checked. "Yes."

"Well, I'd like you to devour them, one by one, till they're all gone."

She regarded the size of the pile. "I've never eaten money before."

"Some folks find it right tasty. You've got the bucket, right?"

"Yes."

"Is it transparent?"

She held the bucket up before the camera.

"Any reversals of fortune," he said, "you may deposit in there."

She looked skeptically at the camera, then back at the bucket. "I don't know," she said.

"You know more than you think you do. And each bill you eat you get to keep, metaphorically speaking, of course. You earn that amount in untouched notes, which will be awarded you at the conclusion of our day. So go ahead, savor your adventure. You might even discover you enjoy munching on money."

"Chew it and swallow it?"

"Yes, of course."

She granted the camera a wary look. "So weird," she said.

"Indulge me."

"I thought this was supposed to be about something sexual or something."

"We're getting there."

She studied the pile with an appraiser's eye, as if gauging the feasibility of the task. Then, delicately, she lifted a single fifty from the pile. She looked into the camera. She looked at the crisp new note. Then she stared into the camera again and, abruptly, defiantly, balled up the bill, stuffed it into her mouth, and began chewing vigorously. Immediately she leaned over and spit a wad of wet green paper out into the bucket.

"Tastes like a dirty rag," she said. She glared at the camera and shook her head.

"You'll get used to it. Try another."

"I don't know."

"But I won the lottery. You're supposed to do what I say."

So she did. She spit that one out, too.

"C'mon now, don't disappoint me."

"Well, you dig it, Mr. Hyphenate. It's like trying to choke down a handful of dead dry leaves. Stuff should be colored brown, not green."

"But they're new. All clean. Fresh from the vault. And I'm paying you to eat them. There's two thousand dollars' worth of fifties on the top of the pile. Get those down and all the rest are shiny hundreds. As many as you can chew and swallow you get to keep."

Dubiously, she eyed the stack in front of her, and, after a pronounced pause, reached down, lifted a fresh fifty off the top of the pile, placed it cautiously into her mouth, and began slowly to chew. And chew and chew and chew.

"Swallow," MisterMenu said.

So she did. And made a pained face. "I've had cough syrup that was easier to get down than this crap."

"Very good. Another."

She did. Another face. Another complaint. And so on for another couple hundred or so. But then something happened. She had either, unaccountably, developed a taste for the bills or suddenly glimpsed the true possibility of making a quick bundle of easy cash. She was soon popping one after another crumpled fifty into her mouth. Chewing. And swallowing. And on and on.

"You're making me very happy."

"I'm doing my best."

"I know you are. And don't forget, however much you manage to ingest, you get that total as bonus cash in addition to whatever you're being paid for this session. And by the way, what are you being paid?"

"Not anywhere near enough. But I think that's my business, thank you very much."

"Well, you're right, it is. But money happens to be my business and I'm always naturally curious about how it's flowing in other people's business."

"Could always be better."

MisterMenu let out a phony chuckle. "Popped the pimple with that one, young lady. 'Could always be better.' What we all say, isn't it? Speaking of which, where are we now at the bottom line? Seem to have lost track in all this excitement."

"I think it's six fifty so far."

"Now, that's yours, understand? Hopefully, though, it's just the beginning. Let's see just how high you can truly go."

She picked up another bill, stuffed it in her mouth, and almost immediately began to gag.

"You have water, I presume?"

She lifted the bottle of MountainMama into view, unscrewed the top, and eagerly drank about half of it.

"That last one go down?"

She opened her mouth. It was empty.

"Seven hundred," he said.

She picked up another bill, stared at it for a moment, continued holding it in her hand, contemplating her next move. She had long vampire nails that were painted a glossy dark plum, contrasting strikingly against the almost unearthly paleness of her skin. It looked, in fact, as if the tips of her artistically long fingers had been dipped in congealed blood. MisterMenu couldn't help but picture those elegant fingers wrapped around his attentive dick. Then he happened to notice that the end of the nail on the ring finger of her right hand had been torn off and, instantly, he didn't know why, the realization flashed through his mind: she has a kid. Air began to leak out of the carnal balloon. But no, he said to himself, he had imagined this scene so minutely for so long now, almost an entire week, and he was not about to have the experience ruined by random baseline thoughts that may or may not be true. The best was yet to come, to coin a phrase. Then LavenderLips, who had been dutifully and silently ingesting bill after bill (he'd lost track of how many) suddenly pitched forward, grabbed the bucket, and directed a powerful stream of belly water and clots of money into it, stopped for a moment, then noisily heaved again. Unbidden, MisterMenu's hand had stealthily ended up inside his shorts. He was surprised to find himself audibly panting.

LavenderLips pulled off a wad of paper towels from the roll that had been placed on the floor before her and swabbed at her mouth. "Sorry," she said. She had tears in her eyes.

"No problem. That's what the bucket's for. What's the sum so far?"

"I think about a thousand or so. I guess."

"You okay?"

"I guess."

"Can we continue on?"

She nodded without acknowledging the camera.

"You're awfully close to the hundreds."

"Not close enough. You know, I'm sorry, but frankly, I really don't know how much longer I can manage this gig."

"But you've been doing a bang-up job."

"Sure. When do we get to the sexual part?"

"Now," he said abruptly. "Take off your clothes."

"Well, if you don't want me to, I won't."

"No, no. I want you to. Please."

"You don't sound all that into it."

"You wouldn't say that if you could see me."

"You want the whole taco or what?"

"Down to the molding. And do it slowly."

So she did. She removed her clothes as if she were a little girl who'd been sent to bed early as punishment for some minor parental infraction too absurd to be taken seriously by anyone. She took her sweet time. She peeled off her halter, her thigh-high boots as if each separate article were a piece of dressing covering a wound. There was an exaggerated degree of pain in every move.

"I want some boom-pah," MisterMenu said.

"Do I get a free fifty for that?"

"Take it."

She plucked a bill from the stack and stuffed it into the fringed bag lying on the floor next to her chair. Then she stood, displaying an endless pair of admirable legs, turned, and, flashing a practiced stage glance toward the camera, proceeded to detach her crimson-red bra as if unwrapping a coiled snake from around her chest. The magnificent breasts that now plopped into view were of a size and shape MisterMenu had only ever observed in his imagination. Save yourself for later, he told himself. LavenderLips now directed her attention to her leather miniskirt and began fiddling, in a deliberately languorous manner, with the back zipper for so long it seemed as though it were something she had to find first before she could be freed from the garment. But suddenly, success, and the skirt dropped to her feet. Underneath she was wearing a pair of leopard-print panties, and on her unbelievably flat abdomen rested, strangely enough, an elaborate tattoo of a giant turtle in crazy psychedelic colors, its shell an eye-popping checkerboard of neon inks. And with that the spell was crudely broken.

"Oh, no," MisterMenu said. "What's that? What's that thing there on your belly?"

"The tat?" she said. "It's not a thing. It's a tortoise." She looked offended. "He's a symbol of the earth. He brings peace and good luck. He protects me. His name is PhyloxBox. I couldn't live without him."

"Why'd you do that to your body, desecrating it up like that? I just don't—"

"Most guys seem to get off on it."

"I'm not most guys."

"Like you have to tell me."

"All right. I'll try to ignore this, this…daub. Let's get back to business, shall we? Sit down."

"I thought we were done with that."

"Baby, we're just getting started."

She made a little-girl pouty face.

"Remove the panties."

She did.

"Sit."

She sat. She was looking at the camera now, as if it were a camera and not another person.

"Open your legs."

She did. He stared for a while at the spot where the rubber met the road, on his face an unreadable expression, data being dutifully processed. When the operation concluded, his expression changed.

"Now," he said, "where were we?"

"Eleven hundred."

"Right. Pick it up from there."

She crumpled up a fifty-dollar note, inserted it carefully into her waiting mouth, looked defiantly into the lens, and swallowed.

"Eleven fifty," she said.

"Good. Eight fifty to go."

Then suddenly she wadded up two more bills and swallowed those quickly. Then two more. She took a pause. She took a drink.

"Only thirteen more fifties and you break into the hundreds."

She looked at him as if she'd just been presented with a dare she couldn't possibly refuse. She picked up two fifties from the pile and, never for a moment taking her eyes off the camera, rolled them together between her hands into a single paper ball, which she proceeded to toss casually into her mouth as if it were nothing more than a big piece of candy. She choked it down and smiled for the camera as if to say, see, mister, it ain't nothing, I can gobble down this stuff all the fuck-long day. Then she balled up two more fifties and swallowed those.

"I do like what I'm seeing," said MisterMenu.

LavenderLips stared quizzically into the lens as if she were far away and thinking of something entirely different. Then abruptly she leaned over and casually vomited, only a portion of which made it into the bucket, the rest splattering violently onto the floor.

She looked up at him. "Sorry," she said. She ripped off a couple of sheets of paper towel and sheepishly wiped her mouth.

"S'okay," he said. "S'stuff happens."

"Do the last two still count?"

"Of course they do. Raw dough don't always go down so sweet."

She was studying the tower of money in front of her. She looked into the camera. "I don't believe I can go on."

"What do you mean?"

"I mean, I quit."

"You can't quit. You haven't even broken into the hundreds."

"There's not enough hundreds even in all that stupid pile to make me eat even one more of those nasty bills." Something new had come into her large, explosive eyes, something serious and dead.

"But you're forgetting. You were hired for eight hours today to honor my requests, not yours."

"But I think you're forgetting a key phrase in that clause, 'within reason.' All requests 'within reason.' Forcing someone to eat a pile of money is not 'reasonable.'"

"How about ordering you to open up your twat, jam your fingers inside, and then suck them clean? Is that within reason? Masturbate with a plastic bottle? Stick your middle finger up your ass? Reasonable? Eat your own shit and smile while doing it? Reasonable? And I'll bet you've heard all those requests, and honored them, too. So let's make a deal. You need money or you wouldn't be here. Everybody needs money or they wouldn't be where they are. So let's get down to the metal. How much do you need? How much to open up some space around your life?"

"Oh, a couple million, probably."

"I said some space, not a country retreat."

"A million, then. Just one."

"The minimum."

"I suppose two hundred and fifty would do."

"The bare minimum."

"A hundred grand?"

"How much do you need right now, right this minute, to alleviate the pressure that's squeezing you the tightest?"

"Five thousand dollars."

"What's it for?"

"Living expenses."

"Such as?"

She gazed off to her left.

"You don't have to tell me if you don't want to."

"Okay."

"Your business."

She looked back at the camera. "Rent," she said. "I'm a couple months behind."

"And what does that entail, exactly?"

"Seven hundred a month."

"The other three thousand?"

"Food and stuff."

"What stuff?"

"You know, car payments, loans, electric, clothes, that sort of stuff."

"And I suppose you're behind in all those areas, too?"

She nodded.

"Tell you what, let's make a deal here. You continue on with our little project, polish off, say, another two grand or so, and again that's added on to the total you get to keep, of course, plus whatever HoneyDrippers is paying you, and on top of that, I'll throw in...how about an extra ten thousand? How's that sound? You can handle that, can't you?"

She nodded.

"Excellent. Let's get back to business."

She looked for a moment as if she weren't wearing makeup anymore and a glimpse of her real face came up for air. The face was unrecognizable. The sight disturbed MisterMenu for a second, but the second passed and he saw her again as he'd always seen her since she first stepped into camera range. Now she was intently studying the pile of money as if she hadn't noticed it before and was wondering who put it there and what specifically he wanted.

"Makes me gag just looking at it," she said.

"So close your eyes and take one, just one, and place it carefully in your mouth without looking at it or thinking about it. God, don't think about it. Just pick one up and stick it in your mouth. But do it quickly, okay? Got to do it quickly. Don't think, try one right now. Just as a test. Don't think."

So she did. And before she knew it the bill was gone. And she hadn't felt a thing. Swiftly she moved on to another and another after that and soon she was popping note after note into her receptive mouth as if they were all no more than cocktail peanuts and announcing the new grand total after each swallow in the brisk matter-of-fact tone of a track announcer reading off the payouts after each race. She had reached seventeen hundred dollars and two full bottles of water when her body initiated another rebellion.

It began with her holding up a finger as if to signal a slight pause in the morning's activities, on her face a serious focused expression as if she were attending to a dim, faraway sound at the very edge of audibility, then suddenly a volcanic explosion of ejecta, a fire-hose-caliber torrent of water and bits of paper money and whatever else was still in there, shooting out from her in an opulent display of unadulterated rejection.

"Not on the money!" MisterMenu said. He was barking at her now, concerned about the spray.

And once she finally did stop, she couldn't stop. The retching seemed to have assumed a mind of its own. It possessed her body and wouldn't let go until it had wrung every speck of loose matter and every drop of loose water from her spastic interior. Those goals achieved, the heaving mercifully subsided at last. Eyes bloodshot, panting like a dog, she stared imploringly into the camera, body goo dripping from her chin. "I can't go on," she said. She tore a wad of paper towels from the roll and wiped her face. "Sorry," she said.

MisterMenu stood, unbuttoned his pants, let them fall to the floor. He stepped out of his boxers. He sat back down. "Ten thousand dollars!" he said. "Ten thousand dollars!" He was practically screaming.

After a significant pause, she lifted one of the MountainMama bottles to her mouth, took a sizable gulp and paused, and then vomited that up. She took a smaller sip. It stayed down. Then, never taking her eyes from the camera, she plucked a bill from the pile, wadded it up, and swallowed without chewing. Immediately she was seized by a major internal contraction. She clutched at her stomach, bent over, and spewed out whatever little remained in her guts. The bucket, having been kicked out of the way long ago, and being more or less irrelevant by this time anyway, left the result to go splattering in every direction.

"Not on the money!" MisterMenu said. "Don't do it on the money!"

She slipped off her chair and onto the wet floor. On her hands and knees she continued to heave even though she had long ago been thoroughly emptied out. In an interval between spasms she tried taking another taste of water and that, too, came instantly back up. She was little more now than a brutal upchuck machine.

MisterMenu was laid out fully flat on his back in his fancy erotognomic reclining device. His eyes were closed. A hint of a smile going in and out of focus around his thin lips. A gleaming puddle of fresh ejaculate smeared across his hairy abdominal bulge. He had just experienced an event he didn't even think possible: the achievement of a completely spontaneous, mirabile dictu!, look-ma-no-hands orgasm. And it had been better than even the best of the humdrum coital variety. He bathed in the afterglow.

Naked, sitting in her own slime, LavenderLips, whose body seemed to have settled at last into some momentary simulacrum of physical peace, was toweling off her wet face with one hand, caressing her belly with the other. "My stomach hurts," she said.

MisterMenu sat up, wiped himself with his boxers, and said, "You've been magnificent. Better than you even know. In addition to the ten grand plus the substantial amount you've already ingested, you deserve a tip, a big fat tip. Off the top of the pile, however much you can fit in one hand, take it, it's yours."

"Really?"

"When I speak, people generally do what I say."

She cleaned off her right hand with a fresh paper towel, contemplated the stack of cash for a moment, then reached over and seized about a three-inch-thick bundle of hundreds. She showed the camera what she'd done.

MisterMenu said nothing. Which she took as approval.

"Are we done here?"

"Yes," MisterMenu said, "we're done here."

CHAPTER 16

THE RIVER...THE WOODS...
AND ALL THAT

"I'VE AN IDEA," said Graveyard. It had been a week since
BlisterPac's surprise visit. Since then a new dunning letter from
Flinders and Poach had punctually arrived each and every day, the
threatening tone escalating predictably. And now their cell phones
had become infected.

"Fine," said Ambience. "I'm listening." She was scrolling through
the morning's text messages, searching for the icky ones. "Here's the
latest," she said. She read: "'Wee Willie Winkie runs thru the town /
Upstairs, downstairs, everywhere he'd root / Under the mattress, out
on the lawn / He'd never give up searching for that fucking loot.'
Signed: A Concerned Friend. Well, how frankly scented-ass cute."

"Poor Willie."

"Mommy Goose must be so frustrated."

"Cause that loot, gentlemen, it hath 'gone where the woodbine
twineth.'" They shared a hearty conspiratorial laugh. "Who'd have
thought our friend Mr. Pustule harbored such a hidden fondness
for verse?"

"Your average stooge is a more complicated critter than most
people think."

"That's how they work their way up to the valuable 'stooge'
position."

"What was your idea again?" Ambience said.

"I believe the time has indubitably arrived for us to make a hasty
exit before our next encounter with the human abscess."

"No shit, Sherlock."

"So it has occurred to me, caramel cluster: what say we drop everything right now, I mean everything, and I mean right this very minute, and sky on outta here on a second madcap holiday getaway?" He had that crafty boyish look that usually meant he just blurted out something he probably couldn't or shouldn't get away with.

Okay, she'd play along. "What holiday and where to?"

"Well, as you may or may not know, it's National Mortuary Month, and in honor of the occasion, I figured we could check in on the wonderful folks who buried my once promising youth under the stone of one sorry-ass name."

"Oh, please."

"What? Too much self-pity?"

"Uh, yeah."

"Can't I even be permitted one brief wallow?"

"No."

"For old times' sake, at least?"

"No."

"You're evil."

"And talk about travel, if we're planning on going anywhere at all, how about a long-overdue hop over to Flinchtown? I haven't seen Mom since we stopped by on our way to visit that loose-marbles friend of yours in WestTongue—how many years ago? Five? Six?"

"Best for last, lemon drop. Your mother's is a day at the beach compared to the domestic boot camp we'll be subjected to by my pack of wack jobs up north. So let's do the worst first. Get through all the internecine fun my family can deliver as quickly and painlessly as possible. Spread a touch of pecuniary cheer around Randomburg, you know, lay on that whaddya-want, whaddya-need sort of thing for a while. Then scoot on over to Flinchtown, take a breath, and sink into the pink padded pillows of Mama PlaitedHopes's ratty couch. I can already feel the kinks in my muscles letting go. Yum."

"You actually think running home to Mommy and Daddy can

save you from Mr. BlisterFuck and whoever else they may already have in on this ass hunt? Look how fast they tracked you down here, a total stranger to them. And now they've got your name and address. Plus your parents' personals and everyone else's you've ever spoken a single word to since you learned how to talk. We're all living ventilated lives now. You know that. Privacy? Odd word—what's it mean? Some antiquated notion from way back in antiquated times. Forget about it. Long gone, blown out, dust. Never to be seen again, if it ever even existed in the first place. Everyone's buck naked now 24-7. There are no secrets anymore. There are no places to hide. Have you lost your mind?"

"I know, I know, I know. But I need some time to think. At least we can snatch some time up there. Don't you agree?"

"I don't know. I think we're in a real ratfuck here. And we're the fuckees."

"Start packing."

They loaded the HomoDebonaire with more luggage than any two people would need to travel anywhere, plus, of course, the bag of money and the bag of assorted weaponry. They got in the car. They drove off. First stop, drop Nippers off again at FurryFarm, then on into the interminable stone labyrinth of the million right angles that made up the city, then the sudden bursting out onto the fast freedom of an expressway leading to a six-lane interstate and points north. It took Graveyard the usual thirty agonizing minutes to clear the congested town. It might have been a pleasant drive, tooling along through nice country under a pretty sky, but for the disturbing reappearance of his new familiar, the Red Hole, some ten miles past the city line, as if it had been lying hidden among all these innocent trees and hills, waiting to ambush him when he was least distracted. Even when not vehemently visible, the Red Hole had always been near, intimately close, ever since its first abrupt eruption on the side of RealDeal's head back in Plexi's apartment. And yet still he hadn't spoken a word about what he'd seen to Ambience. He didn't know why. Maybe he didn't want her to feel anything like what he'd felt witnessing the event. Maybe he felt guilty, that somehow he should have done something more. Maybe he was reminded too much of his own death. He didn't want Ambience to be reminded too much of hers. He didn't know. Of course, he hadn't told her anything about the LemonChiffon shellacking, either. He did know the reasons for that omission. So now he was storing two more secrets along with the usual mental garbage he was carting around from sun to sun like most people. No wonder he was exhausted much of the time.

The Red Hole was manifesting itself in the air about hood high a hundred feet or so ahead of the car. Then everywhere he looked, he saw the Red Hole. Saw it more clearly than any actual seeing could. It was vivid and raw and painfully wet. And deep inside lurked all the grand mysteries, a veritable honeycomb of them. And sooner or later, everything everywhere would enter the Red Hole. In manacled lockstep. Then he noticed he was about twenty miles an hour over the speed limit. He needed to slow down, way down. He glanced over at Ambience. She hadn't noticed. Her rigid profile looked engraved.

"Shouldn't we have called your parents, let them know we're coming?" she said.

"It's a surprise. They love surprises."

"So *you* say."

"Why give them any advance warning?"

"Cause they might redeploy their forces in a more effective pattern?"

"They're an uncommonly cagey lot."

"You make an ordinary drive to visit your own parents sound like a military engagement."

"Isn't it?"

Ambience sat silently for a while. She was watching pictures of her own mother in her own mind, moving quietly through her own life in faraway Flinchtown. Was she lonely? Was she sad? Ambience suspected she was. She wouldn't require a preplanned strategy to visit her.

"Perfect day, though, isn't it?" she heard Graveyard say.

"I've seen better."

"You hungry?"

"I'll let you know."

"I was just thinking, we left in kind of a hurry, neither of us has had any breakfast, so if you wanted, we could stop just about anywhere—"

"I'll let you know."

They were rolling along in the HomoDebonaire in comfortable traffic at a comfortable ten miles per hour above the posted limit somewhere north of BrokenGap, about halfway to Randomburg, when Graveyard noticed a late-model black StareCollector two cars back, one lane over. Ten minutes later it was still there. He changed lanes; the StareCollector changed lanes. He sped up; the StareCollector sped up. He slowed down; the StareCollector slowed down.

"Let's stop for a bite," he said.

"I'm not hungry," said Ambience.

"You can watch me eat."

"Fun," she said. "Here." She handed him half a ScooterTooter energy bar, one of several she'd purchased at a RoundTheClock next door to FurryFarm.

"I said I wanted something to *eat*. Not something to *chew*."

When he saw the sign advertising a Rustlers&Hustlers at the next exit, he followed the big orange arrow. It was lunchtime, and the stadium-size parking lot was jammed. "Satan's allergens," he said to himself as he drove around and around for about half an hour, looking for a space. Finally found one about a half mile from the door.

"I'll stay here in the car," said Ambience.

"Oh, no you won't. You know I can't stand eating alone."

"I'm not hungry."

"Have a mountain water and the ThinYou Platter of celery and carrot sticks with the famous protein-foam dipping sauce or whatever the hell it's supposed to be."

"Yuck," she said. "Ultra yuck."

"Fine. Then chew on a napkin. But I'd like you inside with me. The car'll watch over the cash. Shelled out an extra five grand for the LeaveItAndForgetIt security sequence. I need you inside with me." He opened his door.

"All right," she said. She turned to look at him. "You know I can't resist when you sweet-talk me like that." She opened her door and got out.

On the way up to the restaurant, Graveyard paused and turned around, scanning the parking lot behind him. Intently.

"What are you looking at?"

"Stop a second. See that guy walking over there past the BringItOn Oil truck?" He pointed to an ordinary man in ordinary gear.

"Yeah. What about him?"

"He look like your guy?"

She studied the man for a moment. "Yes," she said. "No," she said. "I don't know," she said.

"You'd be a fine witness at a police lineup."

"I was too busy trying to come up with appropriate lies to pay much attention to what the a-hole looked like. I've told you already. He reminded me of XSquared."

"I believe he's the driver of a black StareCollector that's been dogging us for the past fifty miles."

"BlisterPac's much heavier and has a full head of hair. Steely gray pubic hair hair. I think."

They watched the ordinary cross the lot and join the end of a growing line of other ordinaries collected at the restaurant's front door. "Let's get outta here," said Graveyard.

So they did.

An hour later found them some sixty miles away and seated in plastic chairs at a sticky plastic table inside a sticky half-empty JumboGutHouse. Graveyard was having the PizzleFries and Deluxe ScraperBurger. Ambience was gazing at her VegoramaPlatter, trying to determine what exact vegetables these oddly shaped and colored bits of plasticky stuff were supposed to represent. She sipped from her medium NothingCola, which, as a result of a recent breakthrough in food-product technology, now contained negative 250 calories. Each serving consumed automatically subtracted that amount from your body's caloric storehouse. Hooray! They were both listening to a family in a nearby booth—mother, father, two kids—competing with one another to make the loudest, grossest, most realistic farting sounds. The father definitely seemed to be the most skilled. Probably more time in grade.

"Well," said Graveyard, "that's as valid a response to the absurdities of life as any other."

"Kinda tempting, though, isn't it?" said Ambience.

"What is?"

"Just cutting loose altogether. Letting it all go. Fuck civility. Fuck the social contract."

"One sticky point, my asparagus. A refusal to John Hancock that contract pretty much guarantees a deficit of one important item in your life."

"What's that?"

"Money."

Thankfully, the farter family collected its various raucous members and left, but not before leaving behind, as a sort of parting gift for all remaining, the distinct aroma of a couple of authentic rim shots that lingered on way too long.

"Tasty," said Graveyard.

"Mingles well with the aroma of your whatever-it-is." She was staring morosely at the half-eaten wad of bread and meat clutched in Graveyard's greasy hand.

"I don't insult your food while you're trying to eat it."

"You don't have to," she said. "It insults itself."

"No one put a gun to your head…"

From the back pocket of her ass-hugging JustForYou jeans Ambience extracted her brand new WordToTheWise Tellurian Dictator cell phone and passed it over to Graveyard. "Call your parents," she said. "Now."

So he did. Graveyard had a what-me-worry? relationship with his cell phone. He never would have even bought the damn thing if he hadn't been told repeatedly by friends and utter strangers he absolutely had to own one of the irritating devices in order to participate fully in the modern carnival. He didn't care. He could be either in or out. So sometimes he remembered to pack his phone. Sometimes he didn't.

Ambience sat there and listened to half the conversation. There were lots of subjunctive clauses and extended pauses. After he hung up, Graveyard sat and looked at her for a long moment. "Happy?" he said.

"I've been better."

"They're thrilled. They're especially eager to lay their peepers on you again, butternut crunch. You're their favorite daughter-in-law."

"How many daughters-in-law are there?"

"You're the only one."

"Oh, my God," said Ambience. She was staring past her husband toward the entrance of the restaurant. Graveyard had barely half a second to respond with "Wha?" before a complete stranger had plopped down into the chair next to him like someone returning from the john to reclaim his place at the table. The intruder was strikingly well dressed for a joint like this and, yes, an absolute dead ringer for XSquared, the stiff scorekeeper on that moronically popular *Here Come the Po-Po* show. He, too, had a headful of pubic hair. Ambience's face looked like dried plaster. The man nodded to her. "Nice to see you again," he said. Ambience looked at Graveyard. "This is that guy I was telling you about," she said. "The fed."

"Not exactly." The man pulled out his wallet, removed a card, passed it to Graveyard. BLISTERPAC, the card read, SENIOR INVESTIGATOR. "No government affiliation whatsoever," he said. "So you can relax."

"I wasn't tense," said Graveyard.

"Didn't say you were."

"What do you investigate and who you investigate for?"

"I handle certain business and personal complications for a private employer who wishes to remain anonymous."

"How nice for him. What are you doing here at a rest stop in the middle of nowhere?"

"Pure coincidence. On my way to a Helpers Convention in ToughBorough, as a matter of fact, when I happened to spot your car. Aren't many Debonaires out on the road these days. Caught up to you to get a closer look, when who should I spy in the passenger seat but your lovely wife here? Pure coincidence, like I said. She and I have talked."

"So I understand."

"And have you had an opportunity to address the concerns I shared with her?"

"Sadly, no, Mr. Pac. Unfortunately, I've had other pressing issues taking up most of my time at work."

"And where do you work?"

"It's a sensitive job. I prefer to keep the details to myself."

"Well, I congratulate you. You must be doing extraordinarily well. Not many folks can afford a HomoDebonaire, and a new model at that."

"I do okay."

"Congratulations, too, on the coming attraction to your family."

"What attraction?"

"Why, your new baby, of course. Your wife told me all about it."

Graveyard and Ambience exchanged looks.

"Is that a sensitive detail, too?" said BlisterPac.

"We're a private family," said Graveyard.

"Well, perhaps it's best, then, I leave you two to yourselves. I would ask you both to consider a satisfactory response to the dilemma I raised at my last meeting with Ambience here. Since neither of you seems to answer your mail or your phone calls, I'm afraid face-to-faces may be the only adequate alternative from now on. We'll be in touch." He rapped his knuckles twice sharply on the table and stood. He looked down at the ketchup-drenched pile of Graveyard's PizzleFries. "Spare one?" he said and, without waiting for a reply, picked up a single fry and popped it into his mouth. He chewed. He swallowed. "Spudtastic," he said. He smiled. He walked away.

Forty minutes and seventy-plus miles later, after Graveyard had calmed down sufficiently enough to engage in rational discourse, Ambience said to him, "He never mentioned the money. Not once."

"He didn't have to."

"You think he'll follow us to your parents'?"

"No. He obviously knows the address."

"Imagine them mixed up in all this bullshit."

"A definite line would be crossed."

"You know there's a quick and simple way to exit this mess."

"Yeah?"

"Give 'em back the money."

"What money?"

They drove on. Graveyard glimpsed the black StareCollector in his rearview mirror, once, maybe twice more, again about two cars back. Or was it? One probable sighting turned out to be a dark blue, decidedly not black, FamilyHumpMobile full of generic family. Now he appeared to be hallucinating StareCollectors. He didn't mention any of these recent "sightings" to Ambience. Since leaving the JumboGutHouse, she'd dropped at least three ells that he knew of. At the five or more mark she tended to lapse into nonstop rambling monologues on whatever topics happened to be passing through her head at the moment. Mostly these mental downloads were mildly entertaining when they weren't obsessive, boring, or outright irritating. She hadn't talked much, though, since whatever it was that had passed for lunch. She had her neon-lime buds fixed firmly in her ears, her brand new paper-thin DustPad in her hand. She was in cruising mode.

Graveyard was trying to wipe his mind, wipe it clean of the dirt accumulated over the past few hours. He had discovered over the years that the less going on in your mind, the better you felt. The seed of religion. Driving was usually a pretty dependable crud eraser. The moving road seemed to induce a sort of alert hypnosis in which the world became unglued from language. The verbal fog dissipated. You saw clearly. You felt clearly. Not today. Today was an overflowing trash bin. Message from the wreckage: whenever you have money, other people want to take it from you.

"This is a really good tune," said Ambience. She was dancing around in her seat.

"What is?" said Graveyard.

"'You Fit Me Like a Spandex Onesie.'"

"I didn't know you liked TerminalSpace."

"Well, yeah."

"When did this happen?"

"I think there's a lot of things I like you don't know about."

"Like what?"

"If I told you, then you'd know about them."

"So what's wrong with that?"

"Mystery is the compost relationships grow out of."

"And where'd you get that gem?"

"I read it in *MadnessToday*."

"Then it must be true."

"Fuck you." She stuck the buds back in her ears. She hadn't meant to say "Fuck you," exactly, but she had and now she couldn't take it back and she didn't know that she wanted to take it back.

They settled back into silence until the big green sign bolted to an approaching overpass announced: RANDOMBURG NEXT EXIT. "Here we go," said Graveyard. He shifted over into the right lane. Ambience started rummaging around in her bag. Graveyard could hear the pills rattling around before he even saw the prescription bottle. "Are you sure?" he said.

"I've only had one today."

He looked at her and kept looking.

"I'm fine," she said. "Just need to soften the edges a little, round them off, you know."

"You look pretty circular to me."

"Your parents."

"You've met them before."

"Yes. I wonder if just one is enough." She studied the bottle in her hand.

"What do you care, anyway? They're not your family. And they'll be happy we came. They haven't seen us in ages. And they'll probably be well oiled on whatever the drink of the day happens to be."

"Maybe I should pop two more."

"You know those things don't mix well with booze."

"I won't drink."

"My father's a fucking bartender. He's going to want to fix you one of his patented BroomDusters."

"I can politely decline."

"He'll take that as an insult."

"I'll tell him I'm pregnant."

"Obviously," said Graveyard, "it didn't work all that well the last time you tried floating that line."

"S'all right. I'll keep peddling that counterfeit baby till someone buys it."

The family homestead, where Graveyard, his brother, SideEffects, and sister, Farrago, all grew up, was a two-hundred-year-old fixer-upper still in the process of being fixed up. The combination monster manse, haunted house, and carpentry shop was now occupied exclusively by his father. In lieu of a formal divorce, Mother had moved out years before to her own fairyland gingerbread cottage in the woods, Forevermore, which she had demanded Father build and pay for. And he had. Or so he claimed. Graveyard's feelings about the old homestead were all knotted up, impossible to untie. His head was full of soft memories and hard memories. His father was named Roulette. His mother was named Carousel. One spun one way. One spun the other. Graveyard had spent the rest of his life in a more or less constant state of vertigo.

He guided the HomoDebonaire carefully through the center of town, freshly amazed by how small the old place seemed now. And so bright, too. All the great shade trees lining the main drag of his youth had been cut down long ago. Why?

Then he turned right onto Burlap Court. For a moment the street seemed completely unfamiliar. He recognized nothing. Had he made a wrong turn? The houses were all wrong. The wrong cars were in the wrong driveways. The place had the look of a phony hometown, a TV set designed to fool you into thinking you were still safe on the good ol' mother planet when in fact you'd been captured and transported to an alien world whose inhabitants, it was soon to be revealed, had peculiar tastes in cuisine and popular entertainment. Then, as though a hidden switch had been thrown, the end of the street came into view and he recognized everything. He recognized *his* street. Everything in its proper place. And he was especially pleased to see that the old family hacienda was still shamelessly, beautifully, gloriously unfinished—the eyesore of the neighborhood. Seated on the second set of front steps, wearing big black sunglasses and, on this perfect sunny day, a large school-bus-yellow plastic raincoat, was a young girl smoking a blunt the size of a double corona.

"Isn't that Farrago?" said Ambience as they pulled up onto the crunchy gravelly driveway. It was, and as soon as she saw the car, Farrago bounded across the dry scraggly lawn to greet them. They hugged, they kissed, they examined each other for any changes in appearance since the last visit, which was at least five years ago now.

"What's with the raincoat?" said Graveyard.

"I'm washing my jeans."

"So? You don't have anything else to wear?"

"No."

"You expect me to buy that?"

"They're my favorite jeans."

"Okay. But it doesn't look like you've got anything on under that coat."

"I don't."

Ambience smiled. "I understand completely."

"Where is everybody?" Graveyard said.

"Dad's at work. Mom's I don't know where. SideEffects was just here about an hour ago looking for his baseball bat or some shit, I don't know."

"We staying in my old room?"

"What do you think? They didn't do a fucking thing to it, though. Said if you wanted better accommodations you could, and I quote, blow your wad on an overpriced shithole at the Stay 'N' Pay."

"Guess we're home," said Graveyard.

"Guess you are," said Farrago.

They left their luggage and the bags in the car and cautiously entered the house. A fragrant breeze was blowing through the living room from the tears in the curtain of rattling plastic covering the space where the back wall had been razed to accommodate the additional bedroom begun, by Graveyard's reckoning, some twenty years ago and still unfinished. No comment. They trudged upstairs to check out Graveyard's boy cave. The room was pretty much as he remembered. An indelible memory folded into each wrinkled guitar-god poster plastered to the walls, every chipped action figure and muscle-car miniature on the largely bookless bookcase, one entire shelf of which was devoted to a complete set of realistically rendered plastic critters from *Aster Feud*. Decorative strings of multi-colored Christmas lights were tacked to every wall. The windows were painted black. There was a green piñata in the shape of a pickle dangling from the center of the ceiling. An aquarium tank on the school desk in the corner was filled with cleaned animal bones of some kind. The closet door was open, revealing a cascade of clothes both hung and piled in heaps on the floor.

Ambience made an unclassifiable face. "This place should be preserved in amber," she said. "A major exhibit in the Museum of Arrested Adolescence."

"I don't think anyone's slept in here since you left," said Farrago. "Mom wouldn't let 'em."

"Who'd want to?" said Ambience.

Graveyard picked up a delicately painted toy planet warrior from the bedside table. He studied it for a moment. He put it down. "I don't know if I can do this," he said. Revisiting the past enshrined in this particular room was like sorting through an impossible mound of old smelly laundry.

"There's a tent in the garage," said Farrago. "You could pitch it in the backyard."

"There's always the pricey shithole," said Ambience.

"Maybe this wasn't such a good idea," Graveyard said. He looked around the room one last time. This is the last time I will see this space, these objects, he said to himself. This room, ever again. "Good thing we didn't unload the car."

"I could tell them you stopped by," said Farrago, "but there was, like, something wrong with your car, like an oil leak or something, and you had to get it fixed, like, right away."

"Not bad," said Ambience. She looked at Farrago with the sisterly admiration of a fellow accomplished liar. "We could go with that."

So they did.

At the nearby Stay 'N' Pay they naturally decided to opt for the best, the priciest—the deluxe Wayfarer's Delight suite, which actually consisted of little more than a couple of average-size rooms joined by a makeshift door cut into the adjoining beaverboard wall. The "suite" smelled faintly of mold and cigarette smoke, and the worn furnishings exuded a distinctly repurposed air.

"So what now?" said Graveyard.

"Let's fuck on these filthy sheets."

So they did. For Graveyard, entwining with Ambience was the

body equivalent of a palate cleanse. His boyhood faded like a photograph left too long in the sun. Plus, sex on a strange bed in a strange place added its own particular zesty seasoning to the event. Halfway through the proceedings Graveyard's dick seemed to detach itself from his body and become a separate object no one especially owned, a curious object they shared among themselves in a sweet space somewhere outside of time. Afterward they lay there side by side, panting, for a long while.

"Never felt that before," said Ambience.

"Me, neither," said Graveyard.

"I want to feel that again. As soon as possible."

"Know what I think?" said Graveyard.

"No. What do you think?"

"There's no end to this. There are no real boundaries anywhere. We feel as much as we can bear until we can't bear it anymore and then we stop, and wherever we stop, however incredibly good that may feel, something inside us knows there's more, there's always more. Unfortunately, arriving in that place doesn't seem to come naturally. It's like we have to learn how to feel good. Isn't that amazing?"

"That why the planet's so fucked?"

"Apparently so."

"How'd we escape?"

"On the money rocket."

They looked into each other's faces and for a prolonged interval they weren't seeing faces anymore but what the faces covered. Then they fell asleep. The ringing phone woke them around six. It was Roulette.

"Welcome back, stranger," he said.

"Hello, Dad," said Graveyard.

"Old homestead not good enough for you? Instead of staying here for the grand sum of absolutely nothing you'd rather go off and pay actual money for the privilege of rolling around on a pile of bedbugs?"

"It's the only exercise I get."

"They found a body over there sometime last year. Dead with a bunch of sticks, pencils, screwdrivers, what have you jammed up his ass. Door locked from the inside. Looks like he was planning on quite a fun weekend for himself."

"What was the room number?"

"What do you mean, what was the room number? How the hell am I supposed to know what the room number was?"

"Well, you sound like you're an authority on the case. I doubt we're in the same room."

"Your mother's here and she's already turned the whole kitchen into some kind of mad scientist's lab throwing together a special dinner for you. Your favorites: beef duds, potato spackles, braised fingerstalks, and those horrible little rolls with freshette marbling and those godawful catacomb seeds you like so much. So be sure to bring a competitive eater's appetite. You don't want to disappoint her. We expect you in an hour."

"I haven't eaten all day."

"Perfect. You know your grandmother always said that hunger was the best seasoning for any meal."

"Didn't she also say you should eat what you want when you want?"

"Your grandmother was a crazy bitch."

Roulette never said goodbye. He simply hung up the phone when he was finished talking. Which he did now.

"How'd that go?" said Ambience.

"Let's get on over there and get this fiasco over with."

CHAPTER 17

WINNER WINNER FAMILY DINNER

THEY WERE SETTLED AROUND the old familiar table in the old familiar dining room whose decor seemed grimmer and the walls closer together than memory had placed them. Even before Graveyard took his customary place at the table, his entire body was unexpectedly seized by a pervasive, under-the-hood, all but unscratchable itching sensation. Home. His parents had also shrunk appreciably in size since he'd last seen them, on one of their rare daring visits to Mammoth City some three years ago. Once they'd been giants. Now more dwarflike.

"House look any different?" said Carousel.

"No, strangely enough," Graveyard said. "Aside from an over-all surprising reduction in size, everything seems pretty much the same. Why? Was there something I was supposed to notice?"

"No, not really. Just can't remember what's changed since you were here last. It's been so long."

"Well, there is one thing."

"What's that?"

"That godawful reproduction hanging above the couch in the living room."

"*Angler's Afternoon*? Your father's favorite picture. I had to send away special for that."

It was a famous watercolor from BuffetPalette's late rustic period. It depicted a barefoot boy wearing a straw hat and seated beside his trusty Dalmatian at the end of a rickety wooden pier. He held a

239

bamboo fishing rod in his freckled hands, its thin white line dropping vertically into the dead center of a series of white concentric
circles spreading symmetrically across the mirrored surface of a
secluded country pond. The boy's cheeks were madder lake, the
dog yellow ocher, the pond sky blue number 1.

"Get rid of it," said Graveyard. "Immediately."

"It's a great work of art," said Roulette. He was already half
finished with whatever it was they'd all been first served on matching scalloped salad plates.

"It's not good for you," Graveyard said. "It'll make you sick
looking at it. It'll make you sick just sitting under it."

"I'll take my chances."

"I won't be responsible for the consequences."

"No one asked you to."

"Can we please just stop?" said Farrago. "We haven't even had
our jiggerydoo yet."

"Yes," Carousel said. "You know how much better it tastes before
the middenage wilts."

Everyone fell silent for several whole minutes. Studious scraping
of cutlery across the tableware.

"One thing I can tell you I certainly did notice," Graveyard said.
"The TV."

"What about it?" Carousel said.

"It's the same one I watched when I was ten."

"So?" said Roulette. "It still works fine."

"That may be. But it's too damn small. I don't know how you
manage to make out anything on that mini screen. It's like peeking
through a keyhole. You need a bigger set. A much bigger set."

"What I've been saying for years," said Carousel. "It's not good
for your eyes."

"My eyes are fine," said Roulette. "Good enough to catch all
your folderol."

No one spoke. More clinking and scraping.

"Isn't this wonderful?" said Carousel. "We haven't been all

together for a genuine sit-down dinner since I don't know when. Like a real family."

"Or a ghost facsimile of one," said Graveyard.

"Well, minus a member," said Farrago. She glanced meaningfully at the vacant chair beside her.

"Oh, please. You know your brother. When he says he'll be here, he'll be here."

"As if that promise ever means anything."

"He's got business," said Roulette. "He's making money. Pass that brown stuff in the green bowl."

"This reminds me of that famous dinner party in *Mountain Manna*," said Carousel. "Remember that scene where Prettybone, who's under a ton of makeup and looks ultra old and ultra ugly in this movie, invites all his relatives to a big farewell dinner in this huge mansion on the top of a hill where only rich people live cause he's dying and—"

"We've all seen the picture," said Roulette.

"The big surprise is that what he really wants is for them to simply enjoy one another's company and celebrate his life and their own lives and just life in general."

"So what's all that got to do with us?" said Farrago.

"The dinner scene, honey," said Carousel. "Remember, the entire scattered clan's back together for their first reunion in years and everyone's talking and laughing and having this fantastic time and gorging themselves on heaps of food that probably tastes as good as it looks and it's so perfect and homey and warm, it just makes me feel all wholesome and buzzy inside. Of course, that's before the knives come out, but still—"

"Piece of ridiculous crap," said Roulette.

"This is a fabulous dinner, Carousel," said Ambience. "And these astonishing potatoes. I don't believe I've ever had anything quite like them before."

"They're spackles, dear. No trouble at all. Wahoo indigo rounds parboiled in sugar water, then oven-poached in a creamy bath of frolic oil and wester butter. I swear Graveyard ate them just about every day for a whole year when he was little. Couldn't get enough."

"Well," said Graveyard, "tastes like candy, right?"

"I suppose," said Ambience. "But healthier."

"That's what I was raised on. Healthy candy."

"Guess I got the unhealthy kind," said Farrago.

"So dramatic," her mother said.

"You always jabbered on all the time about how good potatoes were for us, full of fiber and potassium and vitamin B and vitamin C and how they make you smart and lower your blood pressure and we should all eat them every day."

"Until the next day, when they tell us that was wrong, a big mistake, and we should never touch a potato again for the rest of our lives," said Carousel, as though she were reciting something she'd recently read. "Once that media light hits a fact of any kind it shrivels right up and dies. Truth only prospers in the dark."

"Uh-oh," said Farrago. "Here we go again."

"Where'd you get that?" Graveyard said. "Dad?"

"Where else?"

"Where does anyone in this family get anything useful?" said Roulette.

"What's SideEffects up to these days?" said Graveyard. "I've lost track of our brother these last few months."

"He's good," said Carousel. "Just sold a house over in Guffaw Estates for three hundred fifty thousand. That's a record in this area."

"I was offered a buy-in on the original investment in Guffaw," said Roulette. "Turned 'em down cold."

"Bet you regret that now," said Graveyard.

"Bunch of developers from Mammoth City. Coming up here to destroy Randomburg same as they did that town. Close-talking assholes, all of 'em."

"You did well on the CrossHair-BingoBango deal," said Carousel.

"Only because our nearest competitor, MahoganySands, got indicted a week before signing. And even then the payout wasn't all that stellar. Should have just taken that money and played the lottery." He looked at his son.

Graveyard refused the look. "So anything new in the neighborhood?" he said.

"Not much," said Carousel. "Old TireRetread finally died. You remember him. The man who wrote that nasty letter to President MadeForYou and next minute the street's swarming with Secret Service. With guns."

"The man was an idiot," said Roulette.

"Yes. Well, now he's gone. Mizzen's disease. The absolute worst. Took him forever and by the end he was licking the grapes off the wallpaper for breakfast. Horrible. I saw it and wished I hadn't."

"I hear the widow got three hundred for the house," Roulette said.

"She wishes she got that," said Carousel.

"SideEffects would probably know," said Farrago.

"Both sons on opioids, too. Terrible tragedy."

"Crankcase called," said Farrago.

"Yeah?" Graveyard said.

"He wants to see you."

"I haven't talked to him in years. How'd he know I was here?"

"In this town," said Roulette, "everyone knows everything."

"He still on over at Bullets 'N' Brunch?"

"He's the manager now."

"Maybe I'll drop by there sometime tomorrow."

"But you've got to tell us all about your trip," said Carousel. "We're dying to hear."

"What trip?" said Ambience.

"The one you and Graveyard took overseas. To Bullionvilla."

"Oh, that."

"Doesn't sound like you had much fun."

"We experienced various complications."

"Nothing too serious, I hope."

"I lost some money at the tables," said Graveyard.

"Depends on how you define *some*," Ambience said.

"But what were the people like?" said Farrago. "Do they really eat fried omicrons in red sauce for breakfast?"

"Yes," said Ambience. "With the beaks still on."

"Eeeeeew," said mother and daughter in unison.

"They wear shoes with soles made out of gold leaf?" said Roulette.

"Only the most flagrant assholes," said Graveyard.

"I'll bet the women all have mustaches," Farrago said.

"Just the ones who kiss toads and drink beer out of a glass."

"Don't they all follow that religion that demands all unbelievers be branded with an X on their foreheads?" said Roulette.

"No, they follow the other one."

"Is it true they can't pronounce the letter *t*?" said Carousel.

"The whole country is noted for its near-flawless elocution."

"They drunk pretty much around the clock?" Farrago said.

"Only in certain districts."

"They hate us, don't they?" Roulette said.

"Not really. They do, though, seem to regard us as a terminally silly people."

"What a deeply strange land," said Carousel.

"Sounds fun," said Farrago. "I want to go there tomorrow."

"Extraordinary crust on these beef duds," Ambience said. "Such perfection. I'd kill to get a crisp that flavorful."

"Oh, God," said Roulette. "Don't get her started."

"The crust is the least of it, honey. I rub them first with garlic, paprika, and sea salt. Then I boil them in a vacuum bag for about thirty minutes."

"In water?"

"It's something she saw on *Too Many Cooks*."

"I didn't notice anyone turning away from the table."

"We're afraid of getting something worse," Roulette said.

"Well, you're certainly free to tie on an apron and whip up a yummy feast for all of us any damn time you please."

"No, not that," said Farrago. "Last time Dad took over the kitchen he set a towel on fire and I got the pukes. He doesn't know how to cook a hot dog."

"Exsqueeze me," said Roulette. "I can prepare anything a master chef is capable of. Long as I got a written recipe."

"I saw a moving van parked outside the Crepehangers' the other day," Carousel said. "Looks like they've had enough. You know last spring he got fired from IncredulitySystems. I hear they're moving back to Morning Glory. Bought an avocado ranch or something."

"That that child molester with the withered arm?"

"No, that's TwelvePoint over on Ratchet Heights. He's still there. He never comes out of his house."

"Neighborhood's not what it used to be," said Roulette.

"What is?" said Graveyard.

"Did you hear they're laying off about five hundred workers at Corrugated this month?" Carousel said.

"Gee," said Farrago, "what'll I do? I was planning on applying there when I graduate. Looking forward to that liver cancer everyone gets who works there."

"By the time you graduate," Roulette said, "there won't even be a Corrugated plant to apply to."

"And it was my dream job, too, but you know, Dad, you always advised me to never go anywhere without a backup plan, so if worse comes to worst, I guess I'll always be able to get on at the Whirly Ball. They know me there. They like me."

"And a fine future for you in that prime establishment. I'll not have my own daughter working as a carny barker in a traveling show."

"Leave her alone," said Carousel.

"I could always go back to my first choice."

"And what was that again, dear? You've gone through so many occupations already."

"White sex slave."

"See?" said Roulette. "That's what I'm talking about. And I won't shut up until each and every member of this family achieves sufficient brainpower to realize that outside these walls existence is brutality and the only protection against painful and lasting damage is the cushion money provides. Life is poison. Cash is the antidote."

"Thank you, Dr. Warmth."

"If anyone at this table should be able to comprehend the hard truth of what I'm saying, it's you, Mr. WiseAss. With your mystery lotto. Your mystery win. How much was it, anyway? Your mystery haul?"

"Whaddya want?" said Graveyard. "A piece of sheer luck. I bought the ticket when I was drunk and didn't even remember I had it until Ambience reminded me."

"That's cute," said Carousel.

"So what was the total?" said Roulette.

"It's embarrassing," said Graveyard.

"It can't be all that much," said Carousel, "or we would have heard about it on the news."

"Or the internoodle," said Farrago. "I'll look it up right now." She whipped out her cell phone, a brand new chocolate-model BurningWonderPOS. She began punching buttons.

"Are these actual filigreed baby serpentines?" said Ambience. She pointed to a messy pile of green, slimy-looking, pastalike objects on her plate. "Haven't even seen any in ages. They're hard to find."

"Sure are," said Carousel. "I get mine from VeggiesToYourDoor. They're hydroponically grown in a secret greenhouse somewhere in AnglesBent."

"The few times I've managed to get my hands on a bundle they always ended up tasting like a kitchen sponge."

"Secret is to fry them in extra virgin hallelujah oil, then throw in a pinch of lemon quill about a minute before they're done. When the edges are turning up in that nice golden green curl."

"The ones she made for The Crevice employee picnic last month were better," said Roulette.

"You're not here," said Farrago, looking up from her screen. "On the winners list."

"Maybe he didn't win enough," said Carousel. "They do that sometimes. Only publicize the big winners."

"Well, what do you expect?" said Graveyard. "State bureaucracy. You know how well that works, huh, Dad? It's a wonder they get anything right. But I did win and win big."

"It's true," said Ambience. "I couldn't believe it, either. But really, we are now actual members of the 'filthy rich' club."

"How exciting," Carousel said. "Maybe some good luck's finally coming this family's way."

The wall phone in the kitchen started clattering and Roulette went to answer it.

"When's he gonna finally crack and spring for a cell phone?" said Graveyard.

"He doesn't want to throw away good money on a trinket he considers just a passing fad," said Carousel. "You know how he goes."

"The police were here last week," said Farrago.

"Yeah?" said Graveyard. "What was that about?"

Carousel sighed. "The property dispute with TimeDelay."

"He still on about that?"

"So weird," Farrago said. "They're talking out by the driveway, real neighborly friendly-like, when suddenly Dad comes back in, grabs his gun, and takes it out to show TimeDelay, tells him if he, his scraggly-ass wife, or his mangy dog sets one foot or one paw in our yard he'll give them an airing they won't forget or probably even survive."

"Was it loaded?" said Graveyard.

Carousel opened her mouth to respond when a sober-faced Roulette returned. "It's for you." He was looking at his son.

"Me?" said Graveyard. "Is it Crankcase?"

"I don't believe so."

"Who else knows I'm even here?"

"He does."

"Who?"

"The man on the phone waiting to speak with you."

247

Graveyard excused himself, walked into the kitchen, picked up the handset lying on the counter. "Hello," he said.

"Sounds like those beef duds must be mighty good," said the voice in his ear. "I'm jealous. Don't believe I've ever even had a beef dud myself. What is it, anyway—a bull testicle or something?" Followed by a snort of laughter. It was BlisterPac.

"How'd you get this number?"

"How's the family? Sound like good folks. I imagine they'd be plenty disappointed to learn that their favorite son and adored brother had acquired his newfound riches not by an impartial turn of a bureaucratic wheel but as the result of a fluke accident that can, must, and will be corrected. Understand? Let's repair my client's unfortunate loss, alleviate his suffering. He's in real pain, you know."

"Look, Mr. BlisterPac, if that even is your real name, I'm sorry about your so-called client's difficulties, but let me repeat, frankly, I don't know what the fuck you are talking about, and I'd greatly appreciate it if you quit badgering me and my family. Do *you* understand? Don't call here again."

"A person should own up to his debts, don't you think, Mr. Graveyard? Which, we both know, is indeed your real name, a name that shall be appearing shortly on several legal documents served personally to you."

Graveyard hung up the phone. He walked over to the sink, turned on the tap. The water, he noted, was a slightly off-beige color. He splashed some cold onto his face with hands he couldn't stop from trembling. He turned off the faucet and stood leaning stiff-armed against the kitchen counter. He looked out the window into the backyard and the woods beyond. Where he had played for infinite hours as a boy before he knew much of anything about money, its terrible demands, and the need to get some fast.

Back in the dining room Roulette and Carousel had descended into one of their circular arguments over who, exactly, had allowed their health insurance to expire a month before SideEffects took a nasty hit on the thirty-two-yard line during a Chisels homecoming game and suffered a major concussion, a broken collarbone, and a ruptured spleen and was partially paralyzed for half a year, requiring a four-month hospital stay.

"I wrote the check," said Carousel. "I put it in the envelope. I licked it. I left it on the side table in the hallway for all to see. I assumed you'd pick it up and mail it."

"It had no stamp on it."

"You can't go and buy a stamp?"

"When am I ever near a stamp-buying place?"

"You get in the car and you drive to one."

"I don't have time for that."

"Make time."

Graveyard retook his place at the table.

"Who was that?" said Roulette.

"A friend."

"Didn't sound particularly friendly."

"He wants some money I owe him."

"What friend?" said Ambience.

"I'll tell you about it later."

"You owe people money and you come waltzing in here like you've broken the bank at Monte Heighho or something?" said Roulette. "I don't believe it."

"He'll get what's coming to him."

"Never leave your creditors hanging, son. Extremely bad business form."

"Let's just drop it, okay? Where were we, anyway?"

"Trying to find your name on the list of winners," Farrago said.

"There were others who won much more than we did," said Ambience.

"Were those the ones who got on TV?" said Farrago.

"I don't know who got on TV," said Graveyard. "And who the fuck cares, anyway?"

"Stop," said Farrago, "or I'm leaving the table."

"We're discussing," Carousel said. "That's all. Nice and calm. Discussing."

"If your mother weren't so fond of certain obscenities, we might never talk at all."

"And is it always required that we all must be forced to bear witness to these demonstrations of 'love'?" Graveyard said.

"Public displays of affection are the bonds that hold the family together," said Roulette.

"Maybe we're better off just coming apart," said Farrago.

"Hasn't that already happened?" Graveyard said.

"For you, maybe. I'm still stuck here."

"Did everyone hear that SnowGlobe finally got her fat surgery?" said Carousel. "Last week. She had her stomach reduced by eighty percent. About the size of a walnut now. Wonder what she can eat with a belly that tiny."

"Birdseed," said Farrago.

"She's probably got the runs around the clock now," said Roulette. And to the assembled groans, "Well, I've read that happens."

"And for variety," said Graveyard, "a handful of multicolored paint chips. Especially the gourmet kind, the ones with the lead."

"That's just sick," Roulette said.

"No crazier than eating the moon."

"Well, what the hell else is it there for?"

"Same reason, I suppose, everything is there for you. To be consumed."

"Not the green cheese again," said Farrago. She pushed back her chair. "I'm outta here."

"You haven't had any dessert," said Carousel. "It's chocolate duffy. Yum, yum."

"I hate chocolate duffy." She stood up. She stomped off.

"Let her go," said Roulette. "She doesn't want to sit here with us, let her find people she does want to sit with."

"It's that pipe of hers she wants to hang out with," Carousel said.

"Did she say green cheese?" Ambience said.

Graveyard nodded toward his father. "Ask him."

"Facts are facts," said Roulette. "There's no disputing that." Roulette was a lifelong member of the Frightened White Man's Flying Freedom Freedom Party. There was no talking to him about anything.

"Depends on what you mean by the word *facts*."

"A fact is something that everyone knows to be true."

"Who's this 'everyone'?"

"A person who's woke, as the kids say. And let me tell you, there's precious few of us."

"But you've seen the pictures, right, the tapes?" Graveyard said.

"What you see is not necessarily what you get."

"But you saw men in space suits climb into a spaceship, blast off, jump a quarter of a million empty miles to this big empty rock in the middle of a vast emptiness, where they got out, hopped about for a while, schlepped around in a golf cart, planted a flag, snapped a few candid shots of each other, and—I want to italicize this detail—pressed their very real human footprints into the bright silvery sand. The mineral sand."

"Cheese dust," said Roulette.

"What did you say?"

"You heard me. Cheese dust. The stuff that flakes off a big block of cheese when it gets too dry. There's no water up there, in case you haven't heard."

"I've been informed. So tell me, Mr. Science, what possible reason is there for the moon, this huge, airless, lifeless object flying around us for no particular reason, to be constructed—and I can't believe I'm even saying this—out of a common foodstuff? And I assume, of course, it's colored green?"

"Why not?"

"Cheese is an organic product derived from the milk of living animals on the planet Earth. So it's degradable. It ages. It decays. It rots."

"Not in space. In space cheese is immortal. Preserved forever inside the cold vacuum of a giant refrigerator. It's soft. It's strong. It's pliable. The perfect building material. That's why they chose cheese to make the moon out of."

"Who's this mysterious 'they'?"

"Those who do everything in life you don't want to know about."

"Like tying a Windsor knot or filling out a tax return?"

"When you were a boy you couldn't get enough of my stories."

"I believed them then."

"Until you fell in with Crankcase and that crowd."

"You mean when I started learning how the world works and how the universe is actually put together?"

"Just opinions. Don't mean any of them are true. Besides, you know as well as I do they're all on the payroll anyway."

"Whose payroll?"

"Remember me talking about the Link?"

"No."

"The government behind government. Where all the decisions that really matter are cooked up. They're the ones built the moon."

"The moon's phony? It's not even a natural object?"

"Of course not. I'm surprised you're surprised. And it's not as far away as you think it is, either."

"How far away is it?"

"Couple hundred miles."

"That's preposterous. But I'll play along. Why so close?"

"For beaming down their rays."

"What rays?"

"It's the control room."

"For what? The Galactic Funnybone Network?"

"Pretty much everything."

"That's a lot of things."

"World's a big place."

"And who, exactly, sits at these mysterious controls?"

"Many you would recognize, but many you would not."

"So what does the Link get out of all this busybodying?"

"Gosh, I don't know. Money and power?"

"See?" Carousel said. "The story does make some kind of sense."

"Fractured rice and sticky beans," said Graveyard. "Don't tell me you subscribe to this nonsense, too."

"I don't know. The more you learn, the clearer everything becomes."

"Examples?"

"The Fickleburg Four conspiracy. CasterBlock was never really involved. He didn't even know the other three. That's just another internoodle doodle."

"The surprise installation of PilferBox as head honcho at Tatterdemalion Enterprises," said Roulette. "With, of course, the subsequent trickle-down at SullenGlobe."

"Remember the dirigible fish poison sex-gland assassination of MoebiusParfait? And right in the street in the middle of the capital in the middle of the day. Directly across from police headquarters. Horrifying."

"And, of course, the value-added oxygen tax on every individual over the age of twelve."

"You two having fun?" said Graveyard.

"And don't forget the ladies," Roulette said. "What about the well-regulated female body empowerment act?"

"How could I?" said Carousel. "Or the institution of national cheerleading liberty squads in every public school from elementary level through secondary?"

"When did all this happen?"

"As we speak."

"Well, pretty chilly picture you paint of our impending future," said Graveyard. "Guess we should all bundle up."

"Betcha that nice ol' man in the moon don't appear quite so kindly anymore," Roulette said.

"I've always done all my wishing on a star."

"You don't believe stars are real, do you?"

"What? They're not giant balls of flaming gas millions and millions and millions of miles away?"

"Hardly. It's a freaking light show to distract the monkeys."

"The monkeys?"

"Us."

"Oh. A fine job they did of it, too, I must say. And all part of an elaborate sinister plot to keep us from looking too closely into what's *really* going on, right? You realize how delusional this sounds?"

"Well," said Carousel, "reality's not as real as it used to be."

"So," Graveyard said, "while Ambience and I have been living it up in the big city, the two of you have been sitting up here quietly going bonkers."

"We're not all that different from our neighbors. You'd be surprised what's going on out here in the sticks."

"Frankly, what everyone in this area is in obvious urgent need of is money, lots and lots of money."

"That's what your father says," Carousel said.

"Looked awfully bleak driving in."

"Hang around for a while," said Roulette. "You'll have more than enough bleak to fill your plate."

"Is there a service fee for extra bitterness?"

"Listen, Mr. WiseAss, you and all your snotty friends are going to be absolutely blown away by what happens at the big reveal."

"What?" said Graveyard. "A giant mouse gonna come scurrying in from Mars and gobble the whole moon all up?"

"You won't be talking that way in the aftermath."

Catching Ambience's wandering eye, Graveyard said, "It's not everyone's father who has unlimited access to the secret vaults of the universe itself, all those classified folders that reveal how things *really* work."

"You asked," said Roulette.

"Well, no, actually I didn't, but thanks anyway for the info."

Roulette nodded. "You're welcome," he said.

Graveyard had long believed there were emotional viruses as

real, as potent, as the physical, cellular ones. Of unknown origin, they invaded families and grew and thrived through generations, feeding on the various hosts' unconscious, which provided the food for the viruses. There was no cure. There was only treatment, and the treatment was vigilance, constant and pitiless. Symptoms needed to be recognized and quarantined and allowed to wither. Every perception was an antibody. And with luck (whatever complex of obscure forces that curious word shielded), you might be able to produce a sufficient quantity of antibodies to at least weaken the virus, diminish the discomfort, liberate yourself from the most noxious strains of family. He had always hoped that if he ever had any children himself he would be able, through such a dedicated regime of inner attentiveness, to pass on to them a degraded form of the disease. And they in their turn would do the same for their children and then their children's children and over time, perhaps great swaths of time, the effects of the virus would be at last rendered less and less painful and destructive and finally, perhaps, harmless. Or so he liked to believe. As for himself, like everyone else, he was an ongoing, unfinished project. Prognosis uncertain.

"All right, everybody," said Carousel. "Time for the duffy. Unfortunately, I'm afraid it may not be exactly as you remember. They were all out of the Cavalier bittersweet at Bumblebee's. I had to get the Roundhead."

But when she brought out the plates there were the usual oohs and aahs. Graveyard had two servings.

"It's absolutely saporous," said Ambience.

"Saporous?" Graveyard said.

"I heard it on *Tell It to the Chef.*"

Roulette said she'd served a better version at The Crevice's thirtieth anniversary party.

"I used glamour fat in that one," Carousel said.

"Use it again," said Roulette.

They finished their desserts in glum silence.

"Who's for coffee?" Carousel said.

They all were. Dunking solvent for neighborhood gossip.

"Remember TeakVestibule?"

"The woman who won twenty million in the state lottery when I was a kid?" said Graveyard.

"Just like you," said Carousel.

"Twenty million's a hell of a lot of money. I haven't got quite that much."

"Well, anyway, after being so rich for most of her life she got curious about who she actually was. So couple years ago, she sent off five hundred dollars and a sample of her spit to FaceYourFounders and a month later discovered she was thirteen percent black. I mean, can you imagine?"

"Little dab'll do ya," said Graveyard.

"So she locked herself in her bedroom for the whole summer. With the shades drawn. Wouldn't come out until her mother died and she had to go to the funeral."

"She all better now?"

"Killed herself last spring. Came down with a cancer and then sat in her garage with her ChequeredRevenant running for about an hour and a half cause she couldn't bear the thought of being eaten alive by her bad body parts."

"What a colorful neighborhood you live in," Ambience said.

"Not really. We're a pretty average lot around here. Course there are exceptions. Like the LandGrabs. That horrid red barn at the end of Duvet Drive? You know they actually named their dog Dog? Can you believe it? Dog. D-O-G." She shook her head. "Some people."

"Hashbrown told me the other day," Roulette said, "that her son's preschool is considering a new rule to limit children's names to ten letters or less. Seems class lists are getting out of hand. Teachers are finding them almost impossible to read."

"We should all just be named BuyMyStuff," said Graveyard. "And be done with it."

"Like the LandGrabs," said Roulette. "Boy. Girl. Dog."

"I think there's already a lot of those," said Carousel. "Among, you know, the less affluent families."

"What?" said Graveyard. "They can't afford the extra letters?"

"You know what I mean."

"No. I don't."

"From the financial altitude he now occupies," Roulette said, "such distinctions are practically invisible."

"Rich people can't be bigoted?" said Graveyard.

"I think," said Ambience, "they tend to be even more prejudiced."

"Drop me a pile and I'll report back to you," said Roulette.

"I was getting to that," Graveyard said. "When Fortune smiles, says the gypsy, her blessings should fall indiscriminately. Why should Ambience and I be the only ones to enjoy this miraculous gift? Everybody gets something. So let's start with Mother. Okay, tell me, Mom, whaddya want, whaddya need? No holding back. Don't be shy."

"Well, gosh, Graveyard, really nothing, nothing at all. I've already been so blessed many times over. I don't need anything."

"All right, I haven't been clear. What do you want that you *don't* need? Open up that storeroom where all the stupid dead wishes are locked. What have you always secretly desired but never believed you'd ever actually get or deserve to get? Go nuts. Take a break from propriety. This is about that extra piece of pie. The hell with your waistline."

"Well, Graveyard, you put it that way, I guess I have to admit, and I'm embarrassed to say so, but I've always wanted to go on a luxury cruise to Cantaloupe."

"Cantaloupe?" Roulette said. "That tropical backwater ghetto driven into bankruptcy and ruin by a gang of coddled pirates who should've been chained and hanged decades ago? That Cantaloupe? Why the hell would you ever want to go there?"

"I don't know. The place has stuck in my mind ever since that miniseries *Encore Holiday!* You know, the one with Rattlesticks? From his book I read, *Roasted Nuts: My Life As an Ex–Comedy Legend*. Very funny book. I know it's not fashionable to like him, but when I was a little girl I thought he was funny, and I think he's still funny now. Anyway, what happens is, while he's on the road his beautiful wife leaves him for another, more successful, comic, and he starts drinking and living in his car and on stage starts forgetting his act so he doesn't get hired much anymore and just when he's about to throw himself into Lake Teardrop his shady grandfather dies and leaves him this rum factory in Cantaloupe that's also a front for a lucrative meth operation some not-so-nice people are disappointed they didn't get their hands on and, well, hilarity ensues. There's also some voodoo thrown in, and a couple unfortunate sex scenes and a great bit where Rattlesticks tries out a shift on the bottling line and you can imagine the zaniness. But the country's so painfully beautiful and basically so quiet, there's much less shouting than here, and the people move around much more slowly, naturally, like real people, and the weather is always nice. It made an impression. I just always wanted to go there. It seemed like a good time waiting to happen."

"And how much do you think you'd need for a good time down there?"

"How should I know, Grave? I'm so bad with money."

Graveyard pulled from his pocket a roll of bills larger than it seemed any pocket could contain. He began counting off the bills onto the table. "Five thousand?" He paused for a moment, then began dealing out in quick succession a large number of crisp hundreds. "Ten thousand? How's that? That seems like a reasonable good time's worth."

"Really, Graveyard, I wouldn't even know what to do with such a ridiculous sum. I can't take your money."

"Why not?"

"It's too much."

"Not for my own mother." He shoved the pile toward her.

"Take it," said Roulette.

Carousel cautiously eyed the thick stack of new bills. "But what does a woman like me do with a bundle of cash like that?"

"Spend it," said Roulette.

Graveyard took his mother's hand, pressed the green notes into her palm, and closed her fingers over them. "Send me a postcard from Cantaloupe."

"So what am I, chopped liver over here?" said Roulette.

"Best for last, naturally," Graveyard said.

"What about Farrago?" said Carousel. "Doesn't your sister deserve a goody or two also?"

"I was planning on something special for her—like how about a fresh bale of dank trainwreck?"

Roulette produced a short snorting sound his family had, over the years, learned to interpret charitably as a laugh.

"I'm not comfortable with that," Carousel said.

"*Novus ordo seclorum*," said Graveyard.

"And just what the hell is that foreign crap supposed to mean?" Roulette said.

"Read the back of your money sometime, Dad."

"Really, Graveyard," said Carousel, "I never thought I'd ever live to see my own son acting as a pusher for his baby sister."

"It's leaf," said Roulette. "Harmless enough."

"Maybe in your house. Not in mine," Carousel said.

"Let's not get on that merry-go-round again," said Roulette.

"Which one? We ride so many of them, sometimes simultaneously."

"Dizzy at any speed."

"I paid for Forevermore, me alone, every damn dime of it, with absolutely zero help from you, not that I would have ever wanted it, not a single one of your precious little pennies."

"Here we go with this story again."

"You're still arguing about that ancient business?" Graveyard said.

"We've never stopped," said Carousel.

Roulette continued. "And then to have the brainless gall to actually name the place Forevermore in order to apply an extra coat of pretension to that studs-up rehab is beyond forgiveness. Forevermore. What the fuck is that supposed to mean, anyway?"

"I like it."

"Well, good for you. You're the one living inside it."

"Dad," said Graveyard, "could we please, for the moment, return to the topic at hand, that is, making your dreams come true?"

"You don't have enough treasure to make my dreams come true."

"Try me."

"All right. Then what I want is a brand new KemosabeXL5000 in SolarGlide."

"C'mon, Rou, don't be so greedy," Carousel said.

"He asked."

"What's a beast like that go for these days?" said Graveyard.

"How should I know? Well out of my price range, I'm sure."

"Seventy, eighty, somewhere in that general vicinity?"

"So they say."

There was a slight pause, then, "Okay, back to the wall. You got it."

"Show me."

"I'm not buying the car. You are. I'll have the total for you sometime tonight."

"Why not just write out the check now?"

"I'm giving it to you in cash. Takes a while to count out a sum that large."

"You travel around with those kind of amounts on you?"

"Fat stacks, Dad. Fat stacks."

"You're a damn fool."

"Not so much. Never know when, on a mad whim, I might want to purchase some uselessly extravagant trinket like the twelve-year-old handle of Ballymoss Court's Devil's Offscourings I've been drooling over for three weeks or a bioluminescent wastepaper basket or a pair of jellyfish earrings for my Ambience, whose appetite for such baubles has, in recent days, enjoyed a remarkably healthy boost."

"You make it sound like I'm Lady Poofter or something."

"My mistake. You should, of course, be addressed as Duchess Poofter."

"You've bought tons more stuff than I have."

"That's why I'm the Duke of Poofter. And should I be abruptly seized by an overwhelming impulse to purchase some big-ticket tchotchke I don't really need, I have at my immediate disposal a more than adequate store of government-printed paper to provide in exchange for such an amenity."

"You only deal in cash?" said Roulette.

"I need to see my money. I need to hold my money."

"The whole world's moving on to cashless transactions."

"Good luck to them."

The ensuing silence was broken by the recognizable rattle, rumble, and roar of an approaching motorcycle, its plummy cry placing it instantly among the upper branches of cycling's genealogical tree.

"SideEffects," said Carousel. "I knew he wouldn't let us down."

There was the clap of a backfire, then ringing silence.

"Sounds serious," Graveyard said. "He get a new bike?"

"And already two accidents," said Carousel.

"Those were nothing," said Roulette.

"I would hardly call a broken wrist and three cracked ribs nothing."

"Nothing."

The back door slammed, followed by a series of heavy footsteps until the rider, clutching shiny black helmet, stood immanently before them. Yes, it was SideEffects.

"If it isn't the realtor from hell," said Graveyard. His brother was clad from neck to soles in tight, tailored black leather.

"Even demons have money," SideEffects said.

"Yes, I suppose. Stiff bridge and tunnel fees going to and fro. How you doing?"

"Okay."

"What's the bike? Sounds like a monster."

"WhangoDuran1400."

"Frankenstein. How's the ride?"

"Creampuffy."

"I'd like to give it a spin sometime."

"Just let me know when."

"You seem a bit skinnier than the last time I saw you."

"Maybe a few pounds."

"Diet?"

"What a waste of life."

"Allergies?"

"Basically just been having some trouble with the whole concept."

"Of what? Eating?"

"The deciding, the searching, the getting, the preparing, the cooking, the serving, and then all that damn chewing."

"He was always such a finicky boy," said Carousel.

"Hi, Ambience," said SideEffects. "You're looking especially fine."

"Thank you, SideEffects. But don't be too deceived. It's all a wonderful illusion. A masterly coating of UggAway. By PerfectAll." She paused, studied him closely. He was tall, about a head taller than she was, and, yes, relatively thin, with a strangely yellowish face that had a slightly used look about it, as if its repertoire of expressions had been exhausted some time ago. On the Fuck-O-Meter he registered at about a 5 or 6, with an extra point for the leather. "Didn't you used to wear glasses or something?" she said.

"Ditched those goggles last summer. These are new contacts. Here, check out the color." He bent down, moved his head to within inches of hers.

Ambience looked. "Mantis green," she said.

"They called it reseda at the optometrist's."

"That, too."

"You should see his clients," said Carousel. "All women. All beautiful."

"C'mon, now. There are a few guys."

"And they're all butt-ugly," Roulette said.

"But they've all got fat wallets." He scanned the wide assortment of dishes on the table. "See you're having Mom's famous beef duds. How are they?" He leaned over and scooped up a sample off

Ambience's plate. He popped it in his mouth and chewed. "Flavor explosion," he said. "Y'all be sure to scarf up each and every one of those, you hear? Crime to let a single dud go to the dump."

"She made better ones for the Founder's Day street fair," said Roulette.

"SideEffects, honey," said Carousel, "why don't you sit down and have a helping or two? Plenty for all."

"Like to, Mom, but unfortunately just got a minute or two to drop in and say hello to everyone. Big closing in an hour. I'm certainly up for leftovers, though. How long you two planning on staying, anyway?" This last directed at Graveyard and Ambience.

"Till you all get sick of us or we all get sick of you," Graveyard said.

"We're fluid," Ambience said.

"Until the money's gone," said Roulette.

"Yes," Carousel said to SideEffects, "you've missed the big excitement around here," and she proceeded to explain how Santa, in the form of Graveyard's sudden good fortune, had arrived early this year, each family member being offered the generous gift of a single heart's desire fulfilled. "Dad got a new Kemosabe. I'm going at last on my dream trip to Cantaloupe, so now it's your turn, honey. We all want to know, what's your secret wish?"

"This for real?" said SideEffects.

"Whaddya want, whaddya need?" said Graveyard.

"Okay." He considered his options for a moment. "All right, how about this? A get-out-of-jail-free card and four hundred dollars every time I pass Go."

"Sure. I can swing that. But isn't four hundred about double the usual amount?"

"Somebody's always got to have an edge."

"Merry Christmas."

CHAPTER 18

HUMPTY DUMPTY

A CLEAR SKY, A warm sun, a perfect day for gorge-peeping. In the morning Graveyard and Ambience left their "suite" at the Stay 'N' Pay, strolled outside, shared a smoke, remarked on the pleasant weather, and settled into the leather interior of their roomy Homo-Debonaire. Graveyard put the key into the ignition and turned it. On the configurable driver display the Body Integrity warning light began flashing red. "What now?" Graveyard said. Cursing, he got out. He walked around the car, inspecting the windows and frame. Twice. Around the door handle on the driver's side and the trunk lock there were numerous scratches defacing the perfect paint job. Cursing, he got back in the car.

"What's wrong?" Ambience said.

"Looks like someone's tried to jimmy the conveyance," he said. "Did a fuck of a job on the finish."

She didn't respond. She sat silently, staring out the window at the bleak institutional gray door to the motel. Finally she said, "Who do you think did it?"

"Three guesses," he said, "and the first two don't count."

"So what do we do now?"

"What do you think we do? We do what we do. Fuck him and his brainless client. If he can afford to throw thousands out the window like it's useless trash, he can afford to lose thousands. No fucking tears, okay? Now let's get on up to the fucking gorge and not think about this shit anymore." So they did.

After the mood-killing prelude, the drive itself turned out to be unexpectedly relaxing, the miles moving steadily away beneath them, leaving something stickily unpleasant far behind. Graveyard cruised easily along on what he'd always privately referred to as His Road, the local one whose various bumps and bends he knew by heart, the one that took him to most of the places he'd ever wanted to go. This morning, when he came to the first major intersection, he promptly turned off onto Their Road, the one he didn't know all that well, the one *other* people took to get to places he had little interest in. It was a noisy, nasty, heavily traveled multilane freeway that today, at least, transported them into an otherworldly country (trees, hills, fields, sky, like that) — the kind of place they only lately came into contact with by way of media representation. The scenery was so different from any they had personally experienced in years, so silently alive, that it even altered the landscape of their minds. All the nonhuman stuff parading nonstop across their eyeballs seemed to induce a kind of salutary calm. The thick trees pressed in so closely around the road that the air itself appeared to be green. It smelled green. Both Graveyard and Ambience wondering privately, to their unspoken surprise, was this a place they could possibly settle into someday? And actually like it? The windows were open and in the deep shade cast over the road they could feel themselves moving into and out of pleasant pockets of coolness scented with a refreshing brew of new leaves and old earth. The place seemed intensely familiar to Graveyard, filling his road-empty head with reanimated scenes from his past: standing in an open field around parked cars while his father and the friends with the guns talked quietly among themselves, then suddenly being bundled into a car and driven off while the men remained and hiked off into the woods in search of the game they had come for; the musty family cabin up on the hill in the trees, where the days were always cool even in the hottest summers and where his brother once choked on a chunk of watermelon and his face turned purple and Roulette picked him up, flipped him upside down, and slapped him on the back until the melon piece popped out; his grandfather clicking on the door-mounted spotlight during a late night drive one summer and aiming it off into a clearing in the darkness and conjuring into view the bright diamond eyes of a whole meadow full of startled deer; the twilight sky above their house alive with thousands of ravenous bats fluttering overhead like bits of blown ash from an overfired chimney. For several years of his childhood, at least, Randomburg was a breathing site of genuine wonder, of true color—as long as his father's bar, The Crevice, remained solvent and Roulette's mood stayed relatively agreeable. When profits ran low, though, so did the magic. And then town and country tended to turn to charcoal. But that wasn't a problem for him anymore, now, was it? He carried the spells with him. Whatever he called home would always be displayed in wide-screen Technicolor. Right?

Ambience liked the woods, too. She liked the shade, the relief from the unseasonably brutal sun. The area was okay, but that's all it was. A pleasant place to visit, to pass through, not a place to hang around in forever. She'd had her fill of small-town hokey-ness back in Flinchtown, where her mother still lived and where she still made fishing lures by hand in her kitchen—her mother being the inventor of the award-winning Black Duffle Wobble, best streamer fly east of the Canaugawonga—an activity she had taken up the year after Ambience's kind, quiet father, without the warn-ing prelude of a single fight, physical or verbal, or even a heated argument, quietly packed a bag and one cold winter night headed off into whatever place it was where escaping fathers disappear forever. Ambience had been nine years old at the time, a perilous age, she had observed. Effigy's mother had died when she was nine, as had MelodyRose's and SweetCustard's. SandyLoam's father had dropped from a heart attack, as had PedalTimp's and RollerDrum's, all with at least one of their children in his or her ninth year. At the age of nine, AdzukiBean, Ambience's best friend in grade school, lost both parents when they were hit by a bus on their way to choir practice. And there were many more. Ambience had been keeping track of such tragedies her entire life. She couldn't help wondering if there wasn't some mystical curse bound up, for some reason or other, with the number 9. She didn't know. What she did know was she wouldn't want to live through her ninth year ever again. If you survived the age of nine with both parents intact and still living amicably together in the same home, you were one fortunate child. And if you were still trapped in Palookaville or any of its numerous deformed twins at the age of nine and beyond, you were fucked. Unfortunately, it had taken her seventeen long years to get out of Flinchtown. She'd wanted people, traffic, lights, nightlife. And after a slight detour through the army fun house, she'd found them in Mammoth City. So while she certainly wouldn't mind occasionally vacationing in a chloroformed backwater like Randomburg, she found that after two weeks at most, all this oppressive greenery tended to blend into one big boring green backdrop. You could only look at a tree for so long before you started seeing it as an object to be chopped down and converted into something useful, like a door or a baseball bat. Once she realized what was actually scrolling through her mind, she knew she was more than ready to go home.

"So," she said, "any idea yet how long this trip down memory lane is going to last?"

"We only got here yesterday."

"I know. Just asking."

"You don't like Randomburg."

"It's okay."

"Oh, God."

"I'm here in the car with you, aren't I?"

"Yeah. All the time desperately wishing you were anywhere else."

"I liked your house and your funny little room and your wild-child sister."

"And my parents?"

"They were okay."

And then they both laughed.

"Just ahead is a turnoff onto a gravel road leading to the secluded family cabin where I lost my virginity about a hundred years ago. If it's even still there."

"What? The cabin or your virginity?"

"Which do you want it to be?"

She paused for a moment. "How about both?"

When they got to the turnoff, he turned off. The HomoDebonaire shook and rattled its way down the narrow bumpy gravel road, low-hanging branches scraping against the pricey body of the car. At the sound of each agonizing scrape, Graveyard made a wincing face. At the end of the road was a small clearing in which stood a modest-size cottage with eye-popping mauve shiplap siding and adorned with startling architectural embellishments not ordinarily seen on your typical cabin in the woods. It had a mansard roof with green tiling and fake dormer windows with bright yellow board-and-batten shutters, each with its own astral balcony baluster. There was a small blue-trimmed porch, its overhang supported by a series of orange spindles. The door was fire-engine red. The whole building was trimmed in elaborate white friezes, scrolls, brackets, and plaques. It was a structure not just to take shelter in but also to profitably study.

"Who built this cake?" said Ambience. "Elves?"

"Uncle GriddleCakes. It was an evolving 'project' he worked on sporadically for almost fifteen years in order to keep the growing tide of his 'nerves' from overwhelming the levee."

"It looks like something you could eat."

"Well, you think this is overwrought, wait till you see my mom's house, and it's a full-size construction. She's still at work on that 'project' after a couple decades or so. She calls it Forevermore."

"You have a very intense family."

"Thank you."

They parked. They got out. Graveyard walked around the car, checking the body for damage.

"Not bad," he said. "Hardly noticeable."

"Thank God," said Ambience. "Last thing we want is to be mistaken for run-down commoners."

"Fat chance of that. You even noticed a single HomoDebonaire since we've been here?"

"Can't say I have."

"League of our own, honeybread."

They walked over to the porch. At the door Graveyard started searching high and low. "Now, if I can just remember where they keep the damn key."

"Here," said Ambience. She pointed to a small key hanging from a nail on the jamb.

"Touch it."

She did. It was a painted picture of a nail and a key.

"One of Uncle GriddleCakes's little jokes," said Graveyard. He picked up the welcome mat, which said GO AWAY. There was nothing under it but dirt and wooden flooring. "Wait—how could I have been so stupid as to forget this?" On one of the orange spindles marking the entrance to the veranda was a remarkably realistic carving of the instantly recognizable face of beloved slapstick comedian RosinBag. Graveyard made a V with the first two fingers of his right hand, then pressed the tips into RosinBag's wooden eyes. The mouth opened, the tongue came out, and on it rested the key to the front door. "Voilà!" he said. "Comedy *is* king."

Thoroughly bedazzled by the full-spectrum exterior, Ambience was visibly startled by the in-your-face austerity on prominent display inside. Beyond the door was revealed a familiar middle-class interior just like any other, standard stuff in standard places, but all of it strikingly clean. The floor had been swept, the furniture dusted, even the walls washed. But there was no color. Almost every object was either black or white.

"Based on the outside," said Ambience, "I certainly didn't expect all this monochrome." She ran a finger over the ebony mantel. Checked the tip. Spotless. "Or all this nicey-nice."

"Who ever does? Interesting people are always more than one thing; that's why they're interesting."

There was one interesting exception to the severe art design. Ambience reached down and picked up a magazine from the discordantly polychromatic pile on the black coffee table. It was the latest issue of *Turtle Fancy*.

"Yes," Graveyard said, "the totemic animal of the family."

"What animal?"

"Totemic. The creature we all gather around and worship together as a group. Doesn't every family have one?"

"Only the ones living in tepees."

"My mom collects turtles, the figurine kind. Her house is full of 'em. She's president of the local TDL. Turtle Defense League."

"Your family. Who could make this stuff up? Is Uncle Griddle-Cakes still with us?"

"Unfortunately, no. Lasted an amazing ninety-two years, though. Joked and laughed his way through decades of crazy good health when suddenly, out of nowhere, his body just broke and that was that. It was a shock to all of us, especially Uncle GriddleCakes."

"So who's managing the upkeep on this historical site now?"

"I really don't know. My own parents never gave a damn about the place. My father called it a summer camp for rich fairies."

"Ever the charmer."

"I'd guess Aunt Tuffet's probably the one keeping everything all spick-and-span. She loved GriddleCakes. She loved this house. If there's still a garden out back, that'd be hers."

They wandered through the house. In the gleaming kitchen they found the dishes scrubbed, the counters bare, the pantry and refrigerator stocked with food, all the expiration dates recent. There was even a large liquor cabinet full of well-branded samples from every major spirit group.

"It's so weird," said Ambience. "I feel like we've stumbled onto a movie set."

"Except on a set," Graveyard said, "the food would be fake."

"Not always."

They went upstairs. There was a big bedroom and a little bedroom, both hotel fresh. Both beds were professionally made.

"I feel at any moment," Ambience said, "somebody's going to pop out and say, 'Surprise! You're on *Voyeur Voodoo.*'"

"Well, what are we waiting for? Let's fuck."

So they did. They took off their clothes and slid into the sheets on the big bed in the big bedroom. The sheets were crimson and woven of five-hundred-thread-count spun satin. Their luxurious color and touch made Graveyard and Ambience feel even hornier than usual. Then hands did what hands liked to do. Then there was a sudden commotion of liking.

"I feel the sheets are fucking me," Graveyard said.

"Then pull them in tighter." She reached up around him and pulled the top sheet down tight across his naked back. "Now make your little groan," she said. He did. She pulled the sheet tighter. "Now do it again." He did it again. When he came it was with such unexpected force she was startled into coming herself. Then it took a while for their breathing to calm down. "Wow," he said. "I never—"

"Don't talk," she said. They lay there quietly, their legs stretched out before them, his bare left leg lightly brushing the full length of her bare right leg. After a while their breathing returned to normal and when their breaths were in sync she turned to him and said, "So is this where the big event took place?"

"What big event?"

"Your epic deflowering."

"Are you kidding? We never even made it up here. It happened just inside the door, on the couch down in the living room."

"Was it good?"

"I've never forgotten it."

"That doesn't necessarily mean it was good."

"I've never forgotten it."

"What was she like?"

"I've told you about Borealis."

"Tell me again."

"Well, she had dark, dark hair, almost black, but not quite, just a dark, dark brown."

"Cut short, like SleekBreath."

"Yes. Like SleekBreath. But she didn't really look like her. Only the hair. And she had a bad temper, but when she got really angry her eyes would cross and she looked like a doofus and you couldn't help but laugh and she'd get crazy mad and hit you. And she liked mangleberry ice cream and bonzo rap and plinking buzzards on the internoodle."

"And she played the flute."

"Yes. She played the flute."

"Funny. Never saw you as a guy going for a flute player."

"I never did, either."

"What'd you like best about her?"

"She always smelled like fresh laundry."

"What do I smell like?"

"I don't know. Everything the goddesses on the mountain kept for themselves."

Her eyes were shining now and it was a long time before she spoke again. "Want a hit of ellipsis?" she said.

"I didn't know you had any."

"There's a lot of things you don't know."

"You holding out on me?"

"How'd you think I got through the big family dinner the other night?"

"Is that what got you through this afternoon, too?"

"Don't make me mad."

"Fork over the ellipsis."

She leaned over on her side of the bed, pulled her SenseiVander-Mess leather shoulder bag up off the floor. She rooted around in it for about half an hour.

"What is this," Graveyard said, "a treasure hunt?"

"It's a pricey HauteFemme pillbox I bought just for special drugs. I know it's here somewhere. Give me a sec." She continued to root. "Ah, success." She proudly showed him a tiny gold case tiled with emeralds.

"What's it hold, one pill?"

"More than enough to meet our needs." She opened the case, extracted one tiny white tab, which she handed over as if conferring upon him the last jewel from the last crown of the last kingdom. He immediately popped it into his mouth and swallowed. Ambience took one for herself and did the same. Then they sat back and they waited.

"Oh, look," Ambience said, "someone left an entire cake." They were in the kitchen now. She lifted the dome off the crystal cake stand sitting on the shiny too shiny kitchen counter.

"Oh, boy," said Graveyard. "Chocolate. Gimme some." There was a knife and plates and forks, too. They needed to eat two pieces each. Quickly. And drink two bottles each of StaggerBump beer, with the lovable bucktoothed beaver on the label, from the magic refrigerator that was perpetually full of everything they imagined they wanted.

In the garden they could feel the weight of the sun on their bodies. They weren't wearing clothes. Clothes were so heavy and scratchy. Under their bare feet were the growing things. Everything was immediate and alive. Antennae receiving messages from the outer realm. They pulled carrots from the ground and ate them raw. With the holy specks of dirt still clinging to them. Ambience's thigh looked like the juicy pulp of some new wondrous fruit. Graveyard leaned over and put his mouth on it. He licked and he sucked at the sweetness. For a long time. "Hmmmm," Ambience said. "Hmmm."

In the shower the water ran over their bare skin like a moving silk curtain that made them laugh.

"Have you peed yet?" Ambience said.

"No."

"Do you have to?"

"Give me a minute."

"Don't do it yet. I have to get into position." She got behind him, pressed herself up against his back, then reached around and took his penis in her right hand. "Ready," she said.

"What are you doing?"

"I've always wanted to see what it would be like to pee in the shower with a dick for a nozzle. Just let go when you're ready."

So he did. He could feel her hand feeling him, the steady surge coming from him. Her hand aimed the stream down toward their naked feet, first onto his feet, then onto hers. When the stream stopped, she shook him to free the last few drops.

"How was that?" Graveyard said.

"It was okay. You know, Effigy pees on her feet every time she showers. She says it's good for you. Prevents athlete's foot."

"I did not know that."

"Now you do."

The day was so sunny and clear even the pavement looked bright. There were plenty of parking places. Pick one. He did. He turned the engine off. They sat quietly together for a while. Neither of them said anything. They looked out the windows.

"Don't you think the grass is greener than usual today?" Graveyard said.

"I was just about to say the exact same thing," Ambience said.

"Our minds have melded."

"They've melted all right."

"I said melded, not melted."

"That, too."

"I have to say I think that's funny, but I don't feel like laughing."

"Perfectly okay."

They stopped talking again. Time revolved. The Red Hole popped unexpectedly into Graveyard's head. He never knew when it was going to show up again. It was always surprising him. He was learning to look at the Red Hole from a distance, regard it as something not too connected to him. Sometimes that worked, sometimes it didn't.

"So where's this fucking gorge?"

"Over there past that fence and those trees. It's what the bridge is for."

"What bridge?"

"The one that begins a little farther down the road here, where this parking lot ends. We haven't come to it yet. We stopped here on this side."

"Well, let's get out and take a gander at this glorious wonder of the ages. That's what we came for."

They went to the end of the parking lot and then out onto the pedestrian walkway of the bridge. Halfway across they stopped and leaned against the rail and stared down, contemplating the abyss.

"Is that a river at the bottom?" Ambience said.

"The Bangadrumga. Headwaters back up in the foothills of the Bric-A-Brac Range, original home of the Quidnunc. You know, the tribe that started the Burlap-Ragtag War. The one where General Hiccup famously declared, 'When we run out of shot, we'll fire acorns.'"

"I thought we were up in the AppleCore Mountains."

"No, I'm afraid that's south of here."

"So much geography to keep track of."

"If you don't want to get lost."

"So much history, too. Everything you grew up around is so creepy, so old."

"Yeah, I sprouted up out of some terribly old dirt."

"I can actually see the tops of trees," Ambience said. She was peering intently down into the gorge. "How deep is this thing, anyway?"

"They say fifteen hundred feet or more. The deepest gorge in the state."

Ambience abruptly turned away, pushed herself back from the rail, and slumped down on her heels. "Makes me woozy. I think I'm going to faint."

"You okay?" Graveyard bent down, studied her face. It had lost its normal face color.

"I'll be okay in a minute. I've got a stupid thing about heights."

"You know why people get vertigo? It's not so much from fear of falling as fear they're going to jump."

"Like you're being called."

"Or like some part of you is yelling, hey, I got to get down on solid ground as quick as possible."

"Solid ground," Ambience said. "That sounds mighty good right about now." She grabbed the railing, pulled herself up on wobbly legs. She followed Graveyard down the walkway off the bridge and toward the parking lot, but then he turned and led her onto the grass and toward the wire fence and the trees along the edge of the gorge. "Hey," she said, "where we going?"

"You'll see," he said. "One of the seven wonders of the natural world."

They went along the fence. "There's an opening here somewhere if they haven't fixed it yet. Ah," he said, stopping beside one of the metal poles supporting the fence, "here." He stooped down and pulled a loose section of wire aside. "See if you can squeeze in through there." She could and did. He followed. On the other side of the fence was a row of large trees and then the rim of the gorge. "This better be good," she said. "Trust me," he said. He led her over to an opening in the weeds bordering the edge and a worn dirt trail leading steeply downward.

"You're kidding me," she said.

"We've had six-year-old kids go down this path and they all did fine," he said.

"They were six," she said. "What do they know?"

"Don't worry," he said. "We're only going a couple hundred yards." Turned out the descent was relatively painless. Then Graveyard stopped and pointed to a striking-looking tree standing all alone in the center of a clearing. The tree was utterly leafless and stark white, a barren object in an undeveloped negative.

"Impressive, huh?" Graveyard said.

"Yeah," said Ambience. "What happened?"

"It's said that some eighty years ago, around the time of the Great Harrowing, a vicious storm moved in one summer and, out of all the possibilities in this whole dense forest, a single bolt of lightning came down and struck just this one particular tree, and in an instant, every speck of color was drained out of it forever. Became kind of a local landmark and tourist attraction. People came from all over the country to take pictures of it, to pose beside it, to touch it, and to wish on it. Supposed to give you good luck for seven years or something. They call it the Hankering Tree." The tree was largely an odd assortment of gnarly branches with a scattering of brittle leaves pasted to them.

"Looks like it grew up out of the ground already dead," Ambience said.

"And yet the sturdy sprout still thrives."

"Do you think the magic still works?"

"I wouldn't worry too much about it. We're probably already loaded up on enough luck to cover seven years and more."

"I'm going to make a wish anyway." She walked over to the tree and took her place beside it and closed her eyes for several seconds. "There," she said and opened her eyes. "Done."

"What'd you wish for?"

"I can't say. It won't come true."

"C'mon, it's just a tree. What'd you wish for?"

"All right, but this is on you. I wished we wouldn't get hit by lightning."

Graveyard laughed, then he said, "Look across the gorge here for a minute. See that giant boulder about halfway up on the opposite slope? What's that look like to you?"

"A fucking big rock."

"Doesn't remind you of anybody?"

"No. Should it?"

"Lots of folks claim to have seen the face of Jesus in that stone."

Ambience took another serious gander. She shrugged. "All it looks like to me is a drunken pirate."

"You're hopeless. So much for Randomburg's tourist attractions. Let's get out of here."

Slowly they climbed back up the same trail they had just come down, Ambience complaining only once. Up on top they were searching along the fence for the exit opening when out from behind the thick shaggy trunk of a tree none of them could identify with any certainty stepped—who else?—Mr. BlisterPac.

"Taking in the sights?" he said. He was wearing his trademark smirk.

"We were," Graveyard said, "till you showed up."

"I'm a curious fellow. I like to travel, see new places, meet new people. Fine community you've got here. Filled with good folks. Law-abiding, too. Pretty low tolerance for wrongdoing. Wrongdoers. Know what I mean?"

"You're wasting your breath on the wrong people."

"Really? On the contrary, I don't think I am. I think I'm addressing the exact right people. Don't you agree, Miss Ambience?"

"If I had a dick, I'd fuck you in the ass."

"Now, now, Miss Amb, watch the hostility, watch the gay slurs. What's that say about our friends in the gay community who regularly enjoy certain offline sexual practices? That the intimate act of love is actually a covert expression of outright hostility? I'm disappointed you'd even imply such an unfortunate notion." As he spoke he moved steadily toward her until he was only a couple of feet from her face. "But of course, what could one reasonably expect from a liar, a fraud, and a thief?"

Graveyard stepped between Ambience and BlisterPac. "That's my wife you're talking to."

"I'm well aware who I'm talking to. I wouldn't be saying these things to anyone else. And I'm not done talking."

"But that's where you're wrong." Graveyard made the first two fingers of his right hand as straight and rigid as it was possible for fingers to be made. He pictured them as metal rods. He then began poking them into BlisterPac's chest as hard as he could, emphasizing each word as he spoke: "You are done talking, understand?" At each poke BlisterPac took a step backwards.

"All right, you two cunts," BlisterPac said. "Let's cut to the weenie, and you two just come clean and cough up the cash that we all know you have and end the bullshit and you can go return to your lives, however squalid and petty they may be."

"No," said Graveyard. "How about you [poke; a step back] return [poke; a step back] to your monkey job [poke; a step back] and inform the head monkey [poke; a step back] that there's no money [poke; a step back], no people [poke; a step back], no—" [Poke, and then there were no more steps to take.] Blisterpac had vanished backwards over the side. Into the distant bottom of the gorge.

"Holy shit," Ambience said. They both rushed as close to the edge as they dared to get and peered over.

"He never made a sound," said Graveyard. "Not even a single scream."

"Can you see him?"

"I don't see anything."

"You think he's dead?"

"I can't imagine what other condition he could be in."

"Critical but alive?"

Graveyard took another peek into the gorge. "Not from this height. And look at all the rocks and trees he'd crash into on the way down. I don't know if he'd even still be in one piece by the time he hit the bottom."

"Well, now what?"

"Let's get back in the car and sort this out."

Though they recognized the sole HomoDebonaire in the lot as definitely the very vehicle they had driven in on, it looked odd, slightly different, enough for a flicker of doubt to register in both their minds: is this really our car? But of course it was. Inside they sat in silence for several minutes, staring out the window. The sky was the same blue, the grass the same green, and time ticked on in the same way time does.

Finally Graveyard spoke: "It was an accident. Just one of those unfortunate miscues that happens sometimes when a curious, inexperienced out-of-towner takes one chance too many."

"He'd heard about the Hankering Tree," Ambience said. "He was climbing down to take a close look, to make a wish."

"He slipped."

"Right. He never got his wish."

"Or maybe he did."

"We didn't know him. We never saw the man before."

"We're out-of-towners, too."

"Terrible tragedy."

"Our hearts go out to the family."

They sat in silence again for a couple of minutes.

"All right," Graveyard said. "I think we're ready."

"Yeah. Let's get the hell outta here."

So Graveyard turned the key in the ignition and they did.

CHAPTER 19

LOST IN THE WOOD

SIDEEFFECTS STOOD ALONE IN the twilight of the empty room in the empty house out on the western end of SinusoidDrive. It was fall and, though the day was unseasonably warm, the interior still retained an autumnal crispness from the recent cold spell whose effects had settled deep into the walls and the plumbing. Until today's break in the weather, SideEffects had been considering firing up the furnace for the first time since last winter just to save the pipes. He was staring out the scenic living-room picture window at the sloping front lawn of dead brown grass and the clotted edge of the TemperedWoods, which ended in the undeveloped lot just across the street. This was "the sticks" of suburbia, where the distension of Randomburg pressed up against all that was not Randomburg, all the not-human mess needlessly occupying space outside the city line. Though the area wasn't any more "elevated" than the surrounding land, this particular community had been dubbed, for marketing purposes, AspenHeights, even if there wasn't a single aspen tree anywhere in sight. SideEffects himself had contributed the word *aspen.*

He liked empty houses, especially the new ones, the unlived-in ones. He liked being in them. He liked the feel of virginal space, the distinctively clean aroma of untouched product. And he above all liked fucking in them, on the bare boards before the furniture was put down, before outsider feet scratched and stained the fresh flooring. And he especially liked afterward rubbing his spent semen into the wood. His secret mark, his way of christening the house for the new owners, wishing it a safe journey on its harrowing voyage through the storms of domestication. Or, better yet, rubbing two sets of mixed semen into the polished grain, his and his partner's, whoever that partner happened to be at the moment, concocting a whitish amalgam into which forefingers were sometimes solemnly dipped and solemnly tasted, two unrelated mates joining together as cumbrothers. He'd experienced the ritual several times with various partners in unoccupied houses all across the greater Randomburg metroplex. Often, as he tooled about town, he'd check off in his mind the houses that had been so blessed, sometimes recalling the particulars of each sexual adventure that had taken place within the walls. The house he was standing inside of now was still, unfortunately, a virgin. He had hoped to upgrade its condition last Wednesday—hump day, as a matter of fact—but he'd gotten into an excessive argument with WetCoasters earlier in the day over the previous evening's bar tab at VinylColonial's, and the mood, such as it was, had been broken beyond repair, as had, perhaps, the relationship with WetCoasters. Too bad, since he wouldn't mind fucking him, either. Curious how many guys he passed in the course of a day he did want to fuck. The world was full of them. And his mind rolled on, as it often did, into a dreamy soft-focus erotic reverie in which his fantasy self went wandering through a fairy-tale forest of enchanted erections where he remained lost for several minutes until he was abruptly interrupted by his cell. He glanced at the screen. It was the SkinTags. Finally. He'd already called them twice. Left messages twice. They were an affably aging couple who had been seeking to downgrade from their monster trilevel to a more comfortable and manageable single-story ranch. SideEffects had waited an hour for them this afternoon and was already attempting to rein in his impatience when he heard that the reason for their no-show was a home invasion they had suffered that very morning, when a couple of armed gunmen of a distinctly minority ethnic persuasion had forced their way inside after posing as RabbitExpress deliverymen. The SkinTags had been tied up, beaten, locked in a closet, and robbed of jewelry and cash on hand totaling at least twenty grand. SideEffects offered his own outrage, his condolences, and hung up, slightly shaken. He'd always been quite sensitive to any violations of the sanctity of the home, particularly those owned by clients of his. Well, Roulette always said everything was steadily falling apart and had been since the last time the country won a war, which was now so long ago that no one currently alive, including himself, could even remember the damn thing. He opened his briefcase, rummaged around inside for the fifth of LaughFrogg he always liked to have on hand for just such moments as these. Found the whiskey, unscrewed the cap, and downed a couple of healthy slugs straight from the bottle. Then he took another gander at the label, which he'd already read numerous times, to appreciate again the long and storied lore of this restorative spirit. And it worked. His clouded mind began clearing almost immediately. Then his cell rang again to the catchy theme from *Eschatology Force: Dander Zone*, his favorite TV show when he was a kid even though it came on well past his prescribed bedtime. He checked the screen. It was HuggerMugger. He took the call.

"Whatcha doing?" HuggerMugger said.

"Standing alone in an empty property staring out the window at a dead lawn."

"Need some company?"

"Naw. I'm cutting out of here in about half a sec. What's up?"

"Nothing much. Got a friend who's in the market for a house."

"Okay."

"The friend's also got friends. There's five of them. All good people, *comprende*?"

"Aren't we all?"

"So they're going in on this together. They need something roomy yet also cozy, but not too elaborate, you know. Price is highly flexible."

"So am I. Listen, I happen to have for a moment just the place they're looking for."

"Yeah, where's it at? Location, location, location."

"Out on Mangosteen Drive. About five minutes from the reservoir, ten from the airport. It's rustic with a quaint exterior. Probably needs some modest TLC, but what fine home doesn't?"

"Don't front me with your realtor bullshit. What is it, a broken-down shack not fit enough for a pack of stray dogs to roam through?"

"It's got good bones."

"When can we personally examine this buried treasure?"

"Next Saturday at ten."

"Done."

"The address is 1111 Mangosteen Drive."

He'd no sooner gotten off the phone with HuggerMugger than his cell rattled immediately to life again. It was Farrago.

"She's doing it again," she said at once without any preamble.

"Doing what?"

"Breaking into my room. Going through my stuff."

"I thought you changed the lock on the door."

"I did."

"Then how'd she get in?"

"I don't know. I don't know how she does anything."

"You tell Dad?"

"Yeah."

"What'd he say?"

"Nothing he can do. He doesn't care anyway."

"Anything missing?"

"I don't know. I haven't had time to check out everything."

"Then how'd you know she got in?"

"Two of my all-time favorite T-shirts were wadded up and tossed on the bed. One of 'em was the one with the PromissoryTears on the front. You know, the one I wore to the MadeForYou rally and caught holy hell for. And both of 'em stunk of that shitty perfume she always wears."

"You know what I think, Farrago?"

"No, what?"

"I think she's jealous of you."

"Yeah?"

"I think she wants to be you."

"But I'm her fucking daughter."

"All the more reason."

"That's insane."

"Think about it."

"I always knew this family was fucked up. I didn't know it was that fucked up."

"Shit happens. Don't know what else you can do but change the lock again."

"Last one cost me over fifty installed. I can't afford that again."

"Get a good one. I'll pay for it."

"Thanks. You're the best, bro."

"I try."

They hung up. SideEffects unscrewed the cap on the LaughFrogg again, lifted the bottle to his lips, and drank deeply. Family. What're you gonna do? As far as SideEffects was concerned, the whole arrangement, or whatever it was between his parents, had been, so he'd been told, pretty much of an ordeal from the start. A constant carnival of crises. Mismatched from the moment they met at the Shuttlecock Indian Casino and Hotel, over in WestGriddleCake, they celebrated their fortuitous collision by getting utterly shitfaced, losing every dime they had on them, trashing both their rooms, running up damages neither could afford to pay, and topping off the evening, or more likely the early morning, with a loud tussle both verbal and physical that ended with a nude swim in the Olympic-size indoor pool and then a vigorous boning in the kiddie wading pool that had supposedly resulted in Graveyard's conception, or so the family legend went. They got married the next day, separated two weeks later, and then embarked on a maddening yo-yo relationship that was still yo-yoing along some forty-plus years later, to the amazement of family and friends alike. And for SideEffects, who had grown up, more or less, inside the show, on intimate terms with many of the particulars, the entire thing was still a mystery to this day. He couldn't comprehend the relationship, if that's what it was. He couldn't even describe it adequately. Finally, he didn't even really know who his parents actually were. Each one seemed as foreign and enigmatic to him as planets in a distant galaxy or examples of carved monuments left behind by a long-gone ancient civilization whose meaning or purpose remained frustratingly un-decipherable. Still he had spent countless hours seated before these curious artifacts trying to read meaning into their overwhelming size and insistent presence. The code, even now, seemed impossible to break. They could have been casual strangers he met by chance on a stroll through Anytown, Mammoth Country, Inc. And then, of course, there were the products of this bizarre pairing, the siblings, each warped in his or her own specific way. Farrago already well em-barked on the path to her ultimate Farragohood, whatever bizarre brew of sprite and witch that would turn out to be. And Grave-yard, the mutant prince. How and why, against impossible odds, he should have won some preposterous sum in a public lottery was proof of an irreparable crack in the universe, a flaw in the design. What possible aberration could have permitted a chronic loser like Graveyard to stumble into such a monstrous change in fortune that such concepts as order, justice, fairness, and all that crap were rendered laughable? He couldn't even think of his brother's good luck without an accompanying feeling of bone-deep nausea. Why him? Why him? Why him? His brain rejected the very words themselves. He simply could not physically tolerate the truth of the event. It went round and round his mind in infinite closing circles until he felt, not for the first time in his life, dangerously near the outlying precincts of total cra-cra. Why did this have to happen to him? Why did anything have to happen to him? He unscrewed the cap again and he drank.

He was just locking the front door behind him when his cell

began sputtering again. It was his father. Against his better judgment he took the call.

"Dad," he said. "Wassup?"

"Before dinner, do I take the green capsule or the red tablet or both?"

"How should I know? I don't have the info in front of me. Check the chart taped to the back of the medicine-cabinet door. Which is what you should have done before calling me."

"I can't read that thing without my glasses."

"So? Put 'em on."

"Haven't been able to find 'em for three days."

"How have you been getting to work?"

"I don't have to read a mess of tiny print printed on the back of the road in order to drive a car."

"Then take whatever pills you think you should take," said SideEffects. "And find your damn glasses." And he hung up.

Then, abruptly, he found himself in his own car, a sleek, high-powered late-model Boomerang, the wannabe ride favored by cash-strapped wannabe-ers who couldn't quite manage the financials required to step behind the wheel of the sleeker, faster, ludicrously pricier Celeron3000, with no idea how he got there or even where he was going. It took only a moment for the proper day of the week to pop into his skull. It was Friday, folks, end-of-the-week Friday. That meant he would spend much of his night at either the Black Hole or the Dancing Baton. Or perhaps both. Why not? It was Friday.

Despite the recent cold it had been the warmest day in October in thirty years and the air-conditioning was on the blink at the Black Hole. Posted above the bar was a hand-lettered sign: FUCK CLIMATE CHANGE TONIGHT ONLY GOLDRESTITUTIONS AND SLURPERITAS HALF PRICE. The cramped bar was, for the evening, at least, little more than a miserable sweatbox. SideEffects knew most of the revelers packed into the place, had sold homes to about half of them, had

had sex with about a third. He liked the subway-style crush of squirming bodies on the floor, the smell of intoxicated flesh, the oppressive sense of claustrophobia the bar induced. He even liked the heat, the fine sheen of sweat on his and everyone else's face and arms. It reminded him of sex. It almost made him feel he was actually having sex. What he really needed right now, though, was a blow job from a stranger. It was one of those compelling impulses not worth questioning. He scanned the crowd, searching for a likely victim, found a couple of maybes but that was all. He was still distracted by the hunt when he realized the person standing in front of him was actually talking to him. He allowed his image to swim into view. It was DialTone. Once DialTone had been a pretty good-looking girl and was now, surprisingly enough, an even better-looking guy. SideEffects had first met him six years ago when his father had hired the female version to bartend weekends at The Crevice. In SideEffects's refracted opinion, the revised DialTone had also turned out to be a better person. He tended to remain in focus no matter how fuzzy the situation. Sometimes SideEffects wondered if we couldn't all be immeasurably improved by, after living our first twenty or thirty years as one sex, being magically transformed into our sexual opposites. Someone should one day make a sci-fi epic with such a miraculous reversal as the central plot device. *Cosmic Cosplay* or some such bullshit. He'd be there on opening day. SideEffects had sold a house to DialTone last winter over on Furrow Estates that DialTone had actually paid cash for. Rumor had it that DialTone was fronting the mob's footing into Randomburg. Okay by SideEffects. Money was money.

"I'm sorry," SideEffects said. "What were you saying?"

"I was just remarking how much I still like the house. Good space, good structure. And the flooring in the upstairs bedroom you warned us about, still holding up nicely. Not a single problem." He inserted a significant pause. "So far."

"Great. Always good to hear."

"Was wondering, though, if you have any other similar properties in the area. Got a couple friends new to the market."

"Certainly do, DialTone. Just give me a call whenever. Let me give you my card." He pulled out his wallet and extracted one of his brand new embossed sky-blue business cards ($2,300 for the design, one dollar each for the printing). "Love to do business with you again or any of your friends." And, surprising even himself, he leaned over and kissed DialTone on his amazingly soft cheek. He said goodbye to DialTone, gave the crowd one last cursory look-see, and headed off to the PurplePisser. He needed to take a leak real bad.

The men's room, the site of every manner of wonderful depravity you could imagine and many you couldn't, was illuminated by an overhead black light that gave everything inside a dark purple glow—except, of course, for the cum stains, the piss stains, and the bleached teeth, which all fluoresced a strikingly bright, vibrant white. And it was the teeth that drew him immediately to the young guy in front of the sinks who was receiving a thoroughly accomplished blow job from some old bald ugly guy SideEffects wouldn't ordinarily have even glanced at. But it was the teeth he couldn't take his eyes off of. The blowjobee had closed his eyes and was smiling so openly that his teeth were revealed in all their enameled glory. They were a complete set of perfect glowing choppers and SideEffects's reaction to them was somewhat of a revelation to himself. He hadn't ever been so attracted to someone's dental gift, at least that he was aware of. The novelty alone intrigued him. He stepped over to the row of urinals, unzipped, and, proceeding to ignore what was happening right behind him, took a leak himself. When he finished, he left himself dangling outside his pants and sauntered over to a sink, where he pretended to wash his hands. His stuff, in repose, measured four inches or so, eight in full bloom, or so he liked to imagine, numbers rounded up as such measurements usually are. He liked how the free air felt on his pent-up pubes, so he left the whole package on public display. Besides, the exposure

was a pretty effective way of saying hi. In fact, once the nearby
scene had concluded the blowjobee sauntered over to the sink next
to SideEffects and gave *his* hands a perfunctory soapless rinse.

"Hey, dude," he said to SideEffects from the corner of his mouth.
"Rare heirloom you got there. Does Daddy know it's out taking
a walk?"

"Junior's old enough to make his own rules." SideEffects grabbed
a paper towel and began casually drying his hands.

His new friend gave the poor evicted chub a second-over. "Mind
if I snag a pic?" he said.

"Be my guest."

The man pulled his phone from his back pocket, took careful
aim, and clicked. "One for my collection."

"Too bad it's only a photo."

"You never know. It might be trending."

An hour later they left together. It seemed a promising match. They
liked the same music, anything by SalamanderRose, FriedWater, or
DukeyButts, the same movies, the complete filmographies of both
CastorBean and GallopingShoes, and the same TV shows, particularly that sensation of the viewing year, the old-timey twelve-part
version of *Musical Chairs.*

SideEffects occupied a midrange apartment on a midlevel floor
of The Aspiration Tower, the second-tallest building in Randomburg or anywhere else, for that matter, in the entire northern tier
of the state. SideEffects had always wanted to live in a penthouse
surrounded by penthouse trappings. Since he couldn't afford such
splendor he had gone in the opposite direction. He'd had his entire
apartment designed by WrapAround of ContemporaryContempora-
neity, master of the trending Penitence-A-Lot lifestyle. The original
wooden floor had been sanded down and polished to a high sheen.
There was no furniture. SideEffects and his guests sat on colorful
bamboo mats. They ate and drank out of matching black enamel
bowls. The walls had all been painted in a uniform soothing and
gentle soft blue. No stray objects, no stray clothes. Everything was

spare and clean. There were no decorative effects of any kind what-soever. He couldn't believe how much he'd had to pay to make the place look as though he owned nothing. What he did have was a glorious view of the reliably picturesque Bric-A-Brac Range. That was free and unfortunately only available during the day.

Once SideEffects and his new buddy arrived they headed straight to the cell-like bedroom, stripped off their street clothes, and pro-ceed to test out the durability of the ten-inch CossetFoam futon (in SideEffects's mind a justifiable indulgence) with the latest stylings in gay gymnastics. Which they did. There were plenty of body fluids and body exploratories. The other guy's neck smelled of dick.

In the morning, when SideEffects was measuring out the grounds for his Hi-Testor Magna Dose Caffeine Delivery System, a luxury kept safely out of view in its own custom-made cabinet, he asked his guest his name.

"Loophole," the other man said. At which point the sprung innards of SideEffects's internal processing center creaked into motion like a broken windup toy with a click, a clack, a whir, and a wheeze, finally emitting a thin wisp of smoke to indicate the operation had been concluded.

"Acquainted at all with a girl named Farrago?" he said.

"Sure," Loophole said. "She's my girlfriend."

"She also happens to be my sister," SideEffects said.

"Well, what do you know? Small world, ain't it? Thought you looked a mite familiar. You've got a good sister."

"You've got a good girlfriend."

"I know." He laughed. "So what now? Is this the part where I'm supposed to offer an apology? Or the part where you hit me?"

SideEffects figured it was the part where it was his turn to laugh. So he did. Then both realized they had been staring into each other's eyes for well past the prescribed socially acceptable limit. "I'll beat you up later," SideEffects said. They returned to the bed-room. They returned to their bodies.

Two months later they were still together. And everyone knew it.

Or almost everyone. They were not exactly discreet in their distribution of PDAs about town and environs. Sometimes to an almost reckless degree, especially in SideEffects's case. In a community not particularly known for an open-arms policy on minorities of any kind, certainly not sexual ones, he risked a potentially substantial business loss. But he didn't seem to care. And it was common knowledge among social insiders that if you were interested in gay housing, SideEffects was the man to see. He probably figured whatever business he lost at one end by running with the "homo" crowd he made up for through the advertising at the other end. Or maybe he simply got exhausted with all the juggling of poses required to maintain good standing in the uptight look-at-me-I'm-a-running-hard-true-patriot-making-fistfuls-of-cash-and-you're-not-kind-of-guy club.

He and Loophole began a game he'd played with other people in other times in which the object was to fuck in as many public spaces as possible and not get caught or get caught. Either way was a win. They fucked in many different cars, their own and total strangers'. They fucked on trains. They fucked in planes. They fucked on other people's furniture and in other people's beds. They fucked in SideEffects's unoccupied properties, sold and unsold, territorial cumming on each separate site. They fucked in commercial stores—high end, discount, electronic, and grocery. They drove all the way to Whiteywhiteport and fucked on the white beach and in the blue water. They fucked in Loophole's boyhood tree house. They fucked in Granddaddy Park on Founder's Day.

They surrendered entirely to the seductive rom-com narrative tug, flowing dreamily through all the scenes couples in love or at least in high heat were supposed to enjoy. And enjoy them they did. They booked dinners at obscenely priced three- and four-star restaurants as far away as LogMinister, where they ordered exotic food they'd never even heard of and studied each other's shining eyes through warm candlelight. They took day trips on a whim to locations they never would have even considered visiting when they were single and sane. And no matter where they went, Loophole seemed endearingly out of place. Which for SideEffects upped his cuteness quotient almost immeasurably. They bought gifts for each other Loophole couldn't even begin to afford. They took to wearing each other's clothes. They even began to finish each other's sentences. Of course. Doesn't everyone in glow space? SideEffects took Loophole on his first golf game. He lost his temper on the third hole and wrapped SideEffects's five iron from his treasured SweetNutBlasterBlade set around a convenient tree neither of them knew the name of. Loophole kidconned SideEffects into buying the new upgraded version of meDepot5 "for your apartment," of course, and introduced him to the revolving realm of MumboJumbodom, but the graphics were too speedy, the tasks too involving, and SideEffects was never able to get his avatar moving at a rate quicker than FeenyTurtle mode or even advance beyond EasyClap Level I. After thirty minutes of uncoordinated futility, SideEffects threw his controller on the floor and stomped out of the room. They never played that game or golf ever again.

Finally, after what SideEffects considered a ludicrous amount of pleading, Loophole admitted him to the inner sanctum of LoopholeWorld: his apartment. It was a two-room efficiency above the GrinAndBearIt Medical Supply Store in a sad strip mall out on 101 east of the CorrugatedDreams plant. Notoriously low-rent area. Inside, though it did smell predictably of stale gym socks, the place wasn't as bad as SideEffects had imagined. It was cluttered but relatively clean and, amid numerous shelves stuffed with video-game cartridges, empty beer cans, and superhero action figures, there was even an actual book lying on its side in incongruous loneliness. SideEffects had to check the title. It was a copy of *How to Become Rich in Five Easy Lessons*. The bedroom was about the size of a good walk-in closet, the bed unmade, the white sheets gray. They immediately undressed and climbed aboard.

"This the bed you screwed Farrago in?" SideEffects said.

"The very same."

They tore into one another with fierce abandon.

They went on a cool luxury cruise to hot islands with un-pronounceable names. They danced in the foam. They baked in the sun. They met a pair of old queens in identical powder-blue jumpsuits who'd led fascinating lives as art dealers in the BooHoo district of Mammoth City. The couple had known PaperCut and ChinaTube and EverAfter when he was first making those clever little mad dogs out of pastel beanbags. They'd even had cameos in PaisleyButtercup's epic farce *Tonal Skies*. They were quite wealthy and loved to play cards, though they weren't particularly good at any game involving betting. Loophole financed the next year of his life playing Potter'sChoice against them. Neither seemed to mind very much. They held enough assets to buy the boat. After the cruise the two couples traded numbers. They promised to keep in touch. They never did.

Back home in good ol' Randomburg, SideEffects and Loophole had just finished fucking behind the Dumpster back of the SlurpyCream when they ran into Farrago on line out front.

"Believe you two know each other," SideEffects said.

Everyone pretended not to know what they all knew.

"What's up?" Farrago said. She side-eyed her brother.

"I'm in the market for a new place," Loophole said.

"Yeah?" She side-eyed Loophole.

"You know that apartment. It's so small."

"Seemed to fit you okay for ten years."

"Ten years is a long time."

"Listen. Where you been, anyway?"

"Around, okay? I got business, you know?"

"Yeah, I know your business. Listen, I want to see you. I'm coming over tonight."

"Yeah, sure, that'd be great, that's good. What time?"

"Seven?"

"Fine. Looking forward."

Farrago turned to her brother. "Get him a fantastic place, okay?"

"I will certainly do that."

She walked off to her car without looking back at either one of them.

"She forgot to get her cone," Loophole said.

"She is my sister. Treat her right."

"Always have."

It took almost a full week, but at last Loophole told SideEffects at an exclusive PretzelClub dinner celebrating the anniversary of their first full year together what had happened the night Farrago came over. They'd chilled, crossfaded, kissyfaced, slapped uglies all night long, and now she was good. Loophole's version. Which, as SideEffects had already begun to comprehend, was not necessarily of the real world. But of course SideEffects and Loophole were in the middle of their own translation and there was only so much energy available to devote to so much material. And besides, everything disintegrated anyway in the obsidian heart of each other's pupils. They moved on.

For six charged months the relationship remained otherworldly. It wasn't *like* a movie. It *was* the movie. They were stars and whoever was directing them deserved a Macadamia Award. The narrative glided professionally along through the warmth of a skillfully sustained dream, the spice of the expected crises arriving at precisely the perfect moments and resolving themselves after just the exactly proper amount of effort and suspense. They both knew as well as it was possible to know anything at all that they were being directed by fate or, more likely, something outside language toward the denouement they both desired, a place bursting with love and hope and redemption and all that good stuff no one ever really gets in real life. Things began to go bad in the cabin in the woods. They'd rented a place in the nearby Bric-A-Bracs for the summer, an exceptional's idea of a rustic hideaway complete with every convenience and appliance known to a happening, on-the-go lifestyle but still retaining the look and damp, earthy appeal of old rugged wood. It started, of course, with sex. Their sexual engine had been running in a lower gear for some time before SideEffects even took notice. He didn't say anything for fear of the potential shape of that conversation, so it wasn't the total mindfuck it might have been when, one morning as he lay in bed admiring the outright majesty of Loophole's sunlit erection, Loophole turned to him and proposed that the guest list for their next evening mattress party be expanded from none to who knew how many.

"No."

"It's a big bed."

"I know where this road ends and it's not a pretty spot."

"I've never been there before."

"You don't want to visit, believe me."

Loophole sulked the rest of the day. Dinner at PhineasPheasant that evening was ruined and the reservations had been just about impossible to get. So began the sad and prolonged Loophole subplot to SideEffects's personal melodrama. If one day he could only find the time for that crackling memoir he knew he could write. The relationship entered its chronic phase. Everyone knew the end result, but that didn't mean there weren't small compensatory pleasures to be found along the way. He and Loophole still enjoyed much of the time they shared together. They were civil. They joked around. Sometimes they even fucked. They pretended everything was the same even if it wasn't. And, after several months of this pantomime of indelible togetherness, they began to drift inevitably apart. Interestingly enough, it was SideEffects who first ended up falling into a stranger's bed. Or so he liked to believe. The stranger's name was FilmSprocket, or so he said. SideEffects met him online on SafetyCatch, a site he sometimes visited to scroll through the semicoherent advertisements that love-hungry looky-lous posted in the eternal quest for even the loosest of connections in a shoddily constructed world. He usually skimmed through the electronic pages, sneering internally at the sheer quantity of naked need on embarrassing display. What is wrong with these people? he'd say to himself. But then one especially energetic flag waver caught his roving eye. Read this or not, it said. I don't care. Email me or not, up to you. I don't like you anyway. I don't want to meet you. I don't want to have sex with you. So move on. You'll probably find someone better. But if you're tired of all this interminable shopping, flogging the infinite search, let me know. I am, too. SideEffects contacted him immediately. Unfortunately, FilmSprocket lived in CreosoteSprings, a small town just outside BigSack, home of ParleyMuffin bakeries, where all the flugelcremes in the world were manufactured. The following week he flew half-way across the country to BigSack—the air rich with the aroma of warm cinnamon bread—rented a car, and drove the thirty miles to CreosoteSprings. FilmSprocket lived in a bizarrely painted bunga-low that reminded him instantly of his mother's place. Its interior was crammed with thousands of miniature cartoon figurines drawn from the complete history of animation, a collection valued at, so FilmSprocket immediately informed him, a quarter of a bazillion dollars. FilmSprocket's own valuation, as far as SideEffects was concerned, on the traditional ten-point scale, could be found more toward the low end. That night FilmSprocket took him out to the local hot spot, a depressing dive called TheTaperedEnd, where they had a couple of SpongeShots, and after a couple of hours FilmSprocket informed SideEffects that he didn't like him, either. But they went back to FilmSprocket's place and had sex anyway. Of the decidedly generic variety. SideEffects flew out early the next morning. On the flight he reassessed the Loophole concept. Maybe it was something about him (SideEffects). Maybe he was at fault. You never knew. Why not try on that consideration for a while? See if it fit? His head instantly felt clearer. So he was in a good mood on the cab ride from the airport to The Aspiration Tower. He was in a good mood on the elevator ride up to his floor. He was in a good mood entering his apartment, calling out for Loophole, walking through the rooms, satisfied by their familiar orderliness, still calling, and on into the bedroom, where at last he found Loop-hole, his boyfriend, his lover, sprawled on their private futon in the hairy arms of a hairy man. He couldn't tell you what he screamed, but it was screaming and it was ugly and it went on for a long time. And from somewhere inside the screaming the strange man disappeared and maybe the cops were called. He seemed to have a memory of some imposingly stern people in uniforms trying to talk to him. But he wasn't certain. He wasn't certain where Loophole slept that night. He wasn't certain where he slept. They couldn't even sit down together, look each other in the face, and talk calmly and coherently for a couple of days.

"You weren't supposed to be back until Thursday," said Loophole.

"And that makes it better, that you could have gotten away with fucking someone else if only I hadn't come back early? Is that what you're saying? That it's really my fault? Is that the issue here?"

"I don't know."

"I'm sure you don't."

"Why're you so flamed about this? It's just sex."

"What do I know? Maybe I'm crazy."

"That's what I always liked about you."

And the halves of the piece inside SideEffects that had been broken began rubbing their jagged ends together. The mild discomfort actually felt good. And he was able to produce, for the first time since the lifequake, a replica of a smile, only half a one, of course, but still a passable facsimile. Then, without having planned it or considered the consequences, SideEffects revealed where he'd been the last two days and what he'd done. Loophole forgave him. What else could he do? So they declared a truce and entered into the third act of their relationship. It was the best period yet. They felt older, which they definitely were, and wiser, which they believed themselves to be. Each thought the other's looks had improved immeasurably. And they had. They'd started going to the local MuscleBarn together and running cardio contests together and hefting weights together and sweating together. They ate only PurityBureau-approved farm products. They made smoothies from high-end roadside weeds. Sex became dynamic, more athletic, longer-lasting. Orgasms were like exploding galaxies. They treated each other as fellow humans, with courtesy and respect. They enjoyed each other's company for unaccountable stretches of time. They each wanted to do the same things at the same time. They rarely argued, and when they did they were able to resolve the dispute in minutes. And for about a year and a half life went pretty well for both of them. Real estate in the area had never been better. Loophole got a job as assistant manager at PizzaMercy. Money was flowing through both their accounts and they were happy. And SideEffects had started Loophole on the journey to get his own realtor license. Aside from a substantial increase in Loophole's income, neither could have asked for more. There were no dramatic emotional storms, hardly any minor complaints, but whatever fragile bond they had managed to cobble together for these months began to wither in tiny unnoticeable stages. Neither knew why or even bothered to memorialize the erosion with a passing comment. Both men started working more hours and were home less often. Then came the missing long weekend, the three end-of-the-week days when Loophole just disappeared. And he wasn't at work when SideEffects called. He wasn't with Farrago, either, because she was in Mammoth City for the entire month with her bestie, Anagram, doing God knew what. At first SideEffects was irritated, then slightly angry, then he realized that in fact he simply did not care all that much, and when Loophole finally showed up without offering even a flimsy excuse SideEffects let it go. He realized that internally he had already left. Eventually Loophole returned to the fancy new apartment SideEffects had gotten for him and they didn't see each other all that much anymore. SideEffects did of course finally begin having sex with other people. There were other dicks, other holes. He found some. But some essential ingredient had gone missing from his life, something lighter than air that had helped elevate the leaden chain of days you drag behind you like an anchor.

Then for a while there was a pleasant bare patch, no fizzes, no splats, toothy civility and flashes of affection prevailed, while the last shred of whatever there had been between them seemed to have fallen into a crack and simply disappeared and walking away was practically painless. Eventually the time of Loophole twisted itself into a story SideEffects told to himself and others whenever it was time to tell those kinds of stories. And about life, he told himself, as do all patriotic Mammothonians, he had no regrets. He always did the right thing at the right time. Pretty much. And whatever happened to him happened for the best. Pretty much. But then he remembered, no, not true, it wasn't he, it was his brother who had won that damn lottery, actually taken the whole megillah, all of it. Out of how many untold millions of ticket holders, his own crazy loser brother. What were the idiot odds? He had never won a fucking thing.

CHAPTER 20

HOME ON THE RANGE

THE CURIOUS MIXTURE OF meat fried and gunpowder fired was
a smell not easily forgotten by those who experienced it at any age.
It took up stubborn residence high in the nostrils, back deep in the
sinus caverns. It wove itself into the fibers of shirts and blouses and
handkerchiefs stuffed into back pockets and seldom-explored purse
corners. They (Graveyard, Ambience, and his old friend Crankcase) weren't enjoying the famous brunch, exactly, but instead that
ever-popular meal located somewhere between lunch and dinner: a
lunner. They were each eating a rimfire patty melt with smallbore
sauce (the house specialty) and an order of loaded magnum fries
(fan favorite).

"For hamburger mixed with saltpeter," Graveyard said, chewing
heartily, "this ain't half bad." He'd already enthusiastically plowed
through half his sandwich and was seriously contemplating a
second.

"It's Chef Strudelstein's personal family recipe," said Crankcase.
"The choice of weapons aristocrats everywhere. He's from Lower
WellBeGone. The eastern side."

"It's okay," said Ambience. She'd taken two bites and put the
burger back down on her plate. She did not pick it up again. Today
she was buried inside her customary period funk, an annoying
personal she wasn't about to share with two guys, each of them
strange to her in different ways. Graveyard, of course, presented a
familiar strangeness. Her time in grade with him had rendered her

relatively immune to his numerous assorted oddities, though he was, of course, still capable of ambushing her at any moment with some fresh and unexpected twist in the backbone of his days. This new guy, Crankcase, Graveyard's famous bestie from high school, was something of an interesting puzzle to her. To start with, there were his looks: definitely in the lower digits on the Fuck-O-Meter. He appeared to be relatively fit, though that could be deceptive. She hadn't seen him naked. He shaved his head, yet there wasn't much hair to be shaved in the first place. Graveyard told her once he'd already lost most of it by his junior year in high school. *Quelle horreur.* Straight-ahead adolescence was bad enough without an additional comeliness crisis. And frankly, the head itself was not of sufficient shapeliness to be so glaringly exposed. It had numerous oddly placed bumps and depressions. It looked like a badly peeled potato. His dark, ferrety eyes were set exceedingly close together and basically he had no lips, just a long thin line across the lower third of his face signifying "mouth." There were other minor problems with his ears, chin, cheeks, but you get the picture. He did have a nice nose.

He was a stranger to her because she hadn't ever laid eyes on him until less than an hour ago. Graveyard was a stranger because she had been laying eyes on him for more than eleven years now. And she wasn't quite convinced that all that looking and subsequent touching had taught her enough to say for sure that she *knew* him. And she wasn't even certain what *knowing* anybody actually meant. Her life now and for almost the twelve years previous largely consisted of following Graveyard around, each day, each week, each month, always learning a little bit more but never enough. And so she had followed him here to this cheap grease joint clumsily affixed as a sort of tawdry extra enticement to the wonderful world of guns. It reminded her of another fry hole back in the War, MyHood's BBQ Market, where you could get bullets with your meat. The day she was reminded of, her second month at play in the sandbox, was also one on which she thought, she couldn't be sure, she had wasted her first human being. On a routine morning patrol somewhere in the Lower Jahbooty Valley they'd stumbled into a real soup sandwich. Everything everywhere just started blowing up real good. Jagged shit flying through the air. Ground littered with dominoes. Somehow she found herself flat on her stomach behind a hill or a dune or a fucking mound or whatever fucking piece of moon dust the entire colorless country was made out of. The mound was certainly of insufficient elevation to provide even minimal comfort and security while she was being shot at. The hajji shooting at her was crouched some fifty yards away behind the black carcass of a chewed-up deuce. Or maybe it had been a meat wagon. Something big that ran on wheels. He'd squirt off a few rounds, duck behind the wreckage, wait, and repeat. Ambience took careful aim at the spot where the head kept turkey-peeking. She waited. The head popped into view. She squeezed the trigger. The head disappeared in a cloud of pink mist. She waited. She waited. No more head. Maybe she had just killed a guy. Her first. Imagine that.

"Yes," Crankcase was saying, "business has, you might say, exploded. (Pun at no additional cost.) Male and female. Teenagers and old-agers. Whites, blacks, and browns. They're all gunning up."

"Why?" said Graveyard.

"They're scared."

"Of what?"

"You name it. Seem to be afraid of pretty much everything. Mainly, of course, one another. Anyone outside the box. You know. Then there's the whole fucking planet's condition, for example. We, and I mean every damn one of us, no matter what we may tell ourselves and others, know totally and deep down that conservationwise we're in serious trouble. We are shitting daily in our living room. And you know what? We don't care. We like shitting in our living room. It's easy. It's convenient. It's really fun. We don't even have to get up off the couch. And after a while, you learn to ignore the spectacle of it and the odor of it and just enjoy the sheer pleasure of it."

"A green gun nut," said Ambience. "Bet you could count the number of those on your fingers."

"You might be surprised. Not everyone is a cliché."

"Just the folks I know?"

"It's not who people actually are that matters. It's what you think about them."

"There's another one," said Ambience.

"Another what?"

"Pithy saying. They seem to come off you naturally. Like dandruff or something."

"It's a gift."

"Ever consider posting a collection of them, say, up on the wall back of the check-in desk?"

"No, but my wife has."

"Stuff could be quite instructive to some of your clientele. Who knows? They might even come to like them."

"You could call the list Barrel Wisdom," Graveyard said.

"Maybe there's even a book there," said Ambience.

"No, thanks. I knew a guy who wrote a book once. He barely got out of that bramble bush alive."

But Ambience was both listening and not listening. Her attention had been waylaid by a couple in the corner booth, a probable emotional cripple and his female caretaker and sperm can. The mister looked like the kind of blob who'd beat her whenever the mood struck and then rape her good. They were the types you'd expect to find in a place like this. But then she was here, too. What did that say about her?

"So we try to keep the temp here on the down low," Crankcase was saying. "As I was saying earlier, most everybody around these days seems to be about just one stick short of a major detonation, heads full of all sorts of primer to get riled about. Race, politics, religion, sex. You name it, you'll get busted in the face over it. So we not only practice weapons safety, we also practice conversational safety. There are certain topics strictly off-limits, on the firing line and in the restaurant. And, holy of holies, it's worked. At least so far. Course we've had to ban a few individuals permanently from the establishment, but aside from the gunfire, this is a relatively quiet zone."

"I'm sitting here," said Ambience, "and I hear nothing."

"HearNoEvil baffle curtains on the range walls and all along the tunnel. Top-shelf soundproofing."

"Amazing," Ambience said, "the ingenuity that goes into the care and feeding of the gun beast." The couple in the corner booth she had been steadily monitoring were now smiling giddily at each other. Then they leaned across the table and locked lips. Tightly. Enduringly. When they unglued, Ambience noticed that the woman's shoeless right foot was jammed up into her partner's crotch, where it appeared to be trying to work its way on up into the body itself. To her surprise, she found herself getting slightly aroused.

"We have just one hard and fast rule on the premises here," Crankcase was saying. "The gun is always loaded. Always. Understand?"

"Live by it," Graveyard said.

"Let me tell you, nothing leaves a more lasting impression than getting shot by your own empty weapon."

"So I've read."

"A terrible thing."

"Ever have something like that happen here?" Ambience said. For the moment the show in the corner was over. The two PDAers were back digging into their muzzle ribs and armor-piercing fries.

"No, thank God. We've had our share of incidents, of course, usual noob stuff, inadvertent line sweeps, minor racking injuries, nasty ricochets, hot-brass burns, nothing really major but for the two suicides, which, lucky for me, happened on days I had off. Last month guy comes in, rents an 1844, chooses a stall, fires just one round. Into the roof of his mouth. Heard it made quite a mess. Still some remarkable stains left on the ceiling tiles. You can check 'em out before you leave. Think a girl in a cropped black Death

Tourniquet shirt is in that stall now. You'll notice her right away as soon as we go in."

"You keep a close eye on all your clientele?" said Ambience.

"You have to. Morons with weapons. It's a volatile combo. Just last week we had a carload of 2A fucknuggets come rolling in in their Frightened White Man's caps, OC holsters, 5.11 pants, the whole shebang. Spent about twenty minutes preaching and grandstanding and parading around. One of 'em had a vintage LooseSmooch17 that he was creaming his jeans to impress his buds with. So after everybody gets a turn—and we're talking a good groupie-size mob here—this assclown sets the hot gun down on the bench and decides to stroll out onto the range to see how deep the bullets are buried into the backstop or some stupid shit and while he's out there the gun cooks off and a round tags him in the calf. He was already bragging about feeling no pain as they drove him to the hospital. That's my favorite range story. So far."

"Dramatic job," said Ambience.

"Not really. I'm sparing you the hours of dull edited-out stuff, the times when I sit on my ass, inventory the stock, and contemplate."

"Contemplate what?" said Graveyard.

"Oh, this, that, and the other. And the general idiocy of the human race."

"Pay well?"

"The contemplation, yes. The job, not so much. But certainly better now than my first years here, when I was just another stiff on the regular crew and had to work two gigs just to pay the rent, buy the groceries, and maintain my famous elevated lifestyle."

"What was the other job?" said Graveyard.

"Boob wrangler at Missy Pearl's House of Muff."

"No," said Graveyard. "You're kidding. I'd laugh, but I'm afraid I wouldn't be able to stop. Boob wrangler, my god. A high school boy's dream job. How in god's name did you land that gig?"

"Connections, how else? I do have 'em, you know. Remember ReverseMortgage?"

"The puffy kid who sold primo leaf out of his gym locker?"

"His uncle owns the joint. In fact, his uncle is Miss Pearl. Anyway, a couple years after you left town, I totaled my PikeBrat."

"No—not the one with the BillyBuck Oversquare?"

"The very same."

"What a loss."

"You're telling me. Anyway, ReverseMortgage put in the good word with Uncle HotTooth and next thing I know I'm up to my eyeballs in more half-dressed female flesh than my naive brain ever could have pictured."

"And what were your particular duties at this fine establishment?"

"Aw, you know. Little more than a kind of a glorified, or maybe not so glorified, house flunky."

"Ever wrangle any actual boobs?" said Ambience. Entertained by the amusing shape of the entire conversation.

"Now and then. Those show cuppers can be tricky to get into."

"You know my next question," Graveyard said.

"Once. Just once. Hard as it is to believe. I can't believe it myself. What a fool I was. But I guess those girls intimidated me more than I knew."

"How'd you ever cross the line?"

"I don't know. Thinking had nothing to do with it. It just happened. One day I was spraying glitter on her tits. Next day I was licking it off. It's like we knew each other, had known each other long before we even met. For a very, very long time before. She just made me feel, you know, that everything was okay, that I was supposed to be there."

"Sounds great."

"It was. Until her boyfriend got back from the War."

"Uh-oh."

"Right."

"You knew about this guy?"

"Unfortunately, yeah. She told me about him and I heard her, but I just couldn't quite believe the guy was actually real. I mean, how could he be? There we were, lips to lips, body to body, and between us not even the idea of another real person. And then one day there she is introducing him and I still couldn't believe it. This is the guy? He looked like trucker number two in a direct-to-cable road movie. I was outta there in less than a week. And that's the tale of how I ended up here at Bullets 'N' Brunch."

"Hope that wasn't the end of love, too."

"Remember Vaporine?"

"The movie-star prom queen?"

"Yeah. That one. Hottest chick in the senior class who slept with most of the senior class."

"Never even spoke to her."

"I married her."

"Gremolata and stewed plums," said Graveyard. "No, you didn't. You dog. How in hell did that ever happen?"

All right, Ambience was saying to herself. Enough dick measuring. Enough dick tedium. She had scant patience for this game in a world that was itself a male game. And those loofahs in the next booth staring at us are soaking up every word. They're smirking. They're judging. We're the afternoon's entertainment. We're tonight's story of the day.

"Sounds like quite the high school you two attended," Ambience said. "There a babelicious requirement to get in or what?"

"It's an ultrapatriotic charter high," said Graveyard. "It's not about grades. It's about how good you look."

"And just look at us," Crankcase said. "Graveyard and I were star graduates, and I think I can safely claim that both of us got everything we needed out of life on the basis of our good looks."

"Almost," said Graveyard.

A serious-looking door in the rear wall opened, and in came a serious-looking man who walked across the dining room directly up to Crankcase and waited silently until he was acknowledged. He was wearing a navy-blue short-sleeved shirt with the logo BULLETS 'N' BRUNCH embroidered in gold thread above his right tit. He

resembled almost exactly the funny fat comic who closed each episode of *A Brother, a Sister, Two Wives, and a Dad* with a witty recap.
Except that this guy was not fat and did not appear at all funny.

"Yeah," said Crankcase.

The man bent over and whispered in Crankcase's ear. Crankcase's face tightened. "I'm sorry," he said. "If you'll excuse me for
a moment. Something's come up." Then he stood and he and his
employee walked across the room and exited through the same
back door.

"So," Graveyard said, once he and Ambience were alone, "what
do you think?"

"About the range? I've been to ranges before."

"The Crank. What do you think of him?"

Ambience shrugged. "He's okay."

"Like the rimfire patty?"

"As in, would I eat him? No."

"All I asked was what you thought of him."

"And I told you."

"There's a world of opinion between okay and not wanting to
give him a blow job."

"Well, put my assessment somewhere in there."

"We had a lot of laughs together."

"That's good. Laughs are good."

"Sorry you didn't like him."

"I said I did."

"Not that much. He was my best friend back then."

"Look, he's the kind of guy who scores five hits of ellipsis and
tells you he's got one."

"Harsh."

"You asked."

The rear door opened and Crankcase entered and came back to
their booth and sat down. He did not look chuffed. "Fun times at
the range," he said. "Just had to escort UnauthorizedDuplication off
the premises. Again. He's a regular here. And a regular fortymeister.

And a regular turdbucket. He was on another tear, staggering around, cursing everyone around him, firing freely into other folks' lanes. He was absolutely untenable. We dragged him out, tossed him into the back seat of ColdCharge's BeaverRocket, and ColdCharge drove him home. Third time this month. Anyway, so where were we?"

"High school," Graveyard said. "Your wife."

"Of course. Vaporine."

"Yeah, you were saying. How'd that go again?"

So Crankcase told them about accidentally running into her one night just a couple of years ago at Trapezoid, a high-end punk club about a thousand miles away in stinky, sweaty Bel Louche, of all places, where she lived with PlasticPlatter, ex–class bully and current swimming-pool salesman who had married and impregnated her at seemingly the exact same instant and had immediately repeated the impregnation part in two quick successive years so she had a brand new husband and three brand new kids she hadn't at all planned on back at ol' Tip O' The Wedge, so she was happy to meet Crankcase at this utterly timely moment and happier still to enjoy a pricey steak dinner with him the following week and a deeply satisfying afterfuck. And one thing led to another and now they were living together back in Randomburg with two brand new kids of their own and one dog and one cat and a whole squeaking family of guinea pigs. And Vaporine even got her realtor's license and, amazingly, turned out to be pretty good at unloading houses no one really wanted onto rubes who didn't really want to buy and sometimes on the job actually ran now and then into SideEffects, notorious throughout the property biz for being a "real shit dog."

"No comment," said Graveyard.

"You got any kids?" Crankcase said.

"No," said Ambience. "And we're not looking for them, either."

"Of course," said Graveyard, "if we do happen to stumble across one or two along the way, that's fine. We'll pick 'em up and take 'em with us."

"From what I hear, you could hire a full care staff if you wanted to."

"The whole town knows?"

"The whole town knows everything."

"We're only modestly well off," Ambience said.

"What's that mean: kinda rich?"

"It means," said Graveyard, "we're exactly as rich as we need to be."

"My goal, too," Crankcase said.

"Whose is it not?" said Graveyard.

"Money money money money," said Ambience. "I'm sick of talking about it."

"We weren't talking about it," Graveyard said. "Until just now."

Ambience stared off through the front window at the bleak gray parking lot outside. Cars drove in. Cars backed out. "I'm sorry, then," she said. "Maybe it's just me. I can't seem to think about anything else. I look around. I don't see anything else. I listen. I don't hear anything else."

"Then done," Graveyard said. "Rest of the day money is off-limits. We'll enter a finance-free zone."

"You could drive around for a bit, catch some of the local sights," said Crankcase. "Fallen into any of the area's numerous tourist traps yet?"

"Not a one," Graveyard said. "We're still trying to clean the gunk out of our hair from last week's misadventures in the family tar pit."

"I hear ya, buddy."

"Thinking about taking in the big bad gorge later this afternoon. Ambience's never seen it."

They tried not to look at each other.

"Gotta do it, then. It's what we're famous for. Especially the bigness and the badness."

"And big holes in the ground," Ambience said, "are among the favorite sights of mine to peer into."

"Then you won't be disappointed," said Crankcase. He glanced

311

over at the bag Graveyard had carried in from the car and kept by his side ever since he'd entered the place. "Those your poppers?"

Graveyard nodded. "You assume correctly."

"Let's see whatcha got."

Graveyard leaned over and unzipped the bag. Crankcase started rooting with growing excitement among the magic tangle of exotic barrels and stocks. He let out a soft whistle. "You've got a LipLock40A and an NB30. Fucking unbelievable."

He picked up the LipLock. He shifted it around in his hands. He glanced at Graveyard. "Feels right."

"Yeah, don't it?" said Graveyard.

He put the LipLock back into the bag, traded it for another. "A goddamn Smashnikov500AK. How the hell did you ever score one of these babies? There's supposedly only about twenty left in the whole freaking world."

Graveyard pointed to his mouth. "Lips," he said. "They're sealed."

"All right, then, be like that." He pulled out of the bag a tricked-out assault rifle that resembled a toy water gun with enough add-ons to impress a child. "This is like Christmas morning at the Eastern District All-In Gun Club. A modified select BallBuster 480/90. I've only read about these. You know, you've got enough in here to outfit a world-class weapons museum."

"And you get the honor of first choice," said Graveyard. "Pick one."

"Actually think I'm going to need a full connoisseur's sampling. Hold on a sec." Crankcase left the dining room, came back immediately with a fistful of rolled-up paper targets. He unrolled them carefully, as if revealing a rare selection of ancient parchment. Each displayed a photo-real life-size portrait of a zombie in one of the more colorful and grotesque end stages of full zombiehood.

"Friends of the family," Crankcase said. "Okay, let's make this interesting. Tell me, who'd you like to kill?"

"Me?" said Graveyard.

"You're the one I'm looking at."

"Well, at the moment, no one really. I'm a peaceful soul."

"Cut the crap, Graveyard. I've known you too long. Everybody's got at least one person in their life they wouldn't mind taking a free shot at. For example, right now, if I could get away with it, I'd be happy to drill that piece of doo I just kicked out of here earlier today. Planet couldn't help but be a more agreeable place without his nonsense in it. So right now, who's the piece of gum on the bottom of your shoe?"

"Well, given no choice in the matter, I guess there might be a single special someone, now that I think of it."

Crankcase spread one of the zombie sheets across the top of the table. He took a black marker from his shirt pocket and bent over. "Name?"

"He calls himself Mr. BlisterPac."

Crankcase started printing in bold caps across the zombie's decaying forehead.

"Leave off the *k* at the end," said Ambience. "He's the product of creative spelling."

"I didn't know that," Graveyard said.

"It's what it said on his business card."

"Never noticed."

"All right," said Crankcase. "Your turn, Ambience." He pulled out a second sheet and prepared to write.

"You know, I think I'm most comfortable with just plain Anonymous," she said. "Anonymous Zombie." Crankcase wrote. Then he took a third sheet and printed across the top in big block letters: LOOP-HOLE. "Something personal for me," he said. He looked around as if to check that everyone was there who was supposed to be there. "All right, now, let's do her." He had them put in earplugs. He had them put on earmuffs. Then he led them from the cafeteria to a door into a tunnel that led to another door and then a third door after that and at last they entered the telltale musk and crack of the range itself. They each chose a lane and a gun out of Graveyard's bag. Crankcase, of course, opted for the Smashnikov. He let the gun settle into his arms, checked the heft and balance. "It's a good fit," he said.

"I'll stick with the BoxcarSystem 20/10," Graveyard said. His longtime favorite.

"The sniper's friend," said Crankcase.

Ambience chose the LampLighter 505, the weapon, incidentally, most favored by mass shooters in schools, office buildings, theaters, and churches. It did the job.

"Big firepower for the little lady," Crankcase said.

"Why take prisoners?" she said.

They found their various ammo boxes and stepped up to the line. Crankcase clipped the individual zombie portraits to the overhead carriers and ran each one out to about twenty-five yards.

"Fire when ready," he said. "Single rounds. Take out the head first. You know with zombies you got to go for the head."

So they assumed their positions and began. Plink, plink. Plink, plink, plink. Very measured. Very polite. Then they stopped and pressed the buttons and the paper targets came rattling back to them. Crankcase had a nice tight cluster in the middle of Loophole's decaying forehead. Graveyard's BlisterPac displayed a scattered acne of lethal hits all across his livid flat face. All Ambience's shots, however, were centered solely dead center on the hapless Anonymous's bulging bloodshot eyes.

"Wow!" said Crankcase. "Look at little Annie Oakley here." Both eye sockets had been completely obliterated. "Even if they're still alive after such quality shooting, they sure as hell can't see a damn thing."

"I hate zombies," said Ambience.

"When the apocalypse erupts," Crankcase said, "I want to be on your team."

"Sure. I'll put you on the waitlist."

"I look forward to the outbreak."

They reloaded with fresh magazines. "All right," Crankcase said. "Full automatic now. Tear the hell out of those zombies." They took their places. They began firing. Bam, bam, bam, bam, bam, bam, bam. The explosion of sound was so abrupt, so fierce, so continuous that everyone in the room not only heard it through their ear protection, they also felt it through their skin. People in other lanes stopped their own shooting and stepped back to get a clear look at whoever could be responsible for such monstrous firepower. But they could barely see through the thick, enveloping smoke. The din didn't cease until all the magazines were empty. And still the echo remained.

Crankcase let out a childish whoop and clapped his hands. "That was certainly something," he said. "Let's check the damage." They retracted the targets. Crankcase's and Graveyard's zombies were completely obliterated, shreds of paper dangling uselessly in the air. They congratulated each other on their shooting skills. Then they turned to Ambience's target. At first neither of them spoke. With the heavy LampLighter on full automatic she had managed to draw, as if with a powerful pen, a complete well-formed circle in hundreds of .308 rounds about the silently shrieking head of blind Anonymous.

"Hard-core," said Crankcase. He couldn't take his eyes off the mutilated photo. "Don't want to get in a gunfight with her."

"No," Graveyard said, "you certainly don't."

And Ambience stood there quietly among two guys with guns and ever so slowly, ever so dramatically unveiled the biggest, broadest smile anyone had seen on her face since its arrival in Randomburg some eleven long days before.

CHAPTER 21

DEEP IN THE CREVICE

OF COURSE, THERE WAS a deer's head mounted to the wall behind the bar. Why should Ambience have expected anything different? The cobwebs strung between the points of the antlers were no big surprise, either. The place was dark—definitely, defiantly dark. Dark reliably fake wood paneling covering the walls, dark espresso Dura-Bomb vinyl sheeting on the floor, dark tiles of an unknown midpriced brand forming an unexpectedly high drop ceiling. In fact, the place looked and felt more like the rustic lobby of a remote hunting lodge than a neighborhood watering hole. The only breaks in the general gloom were the impressive flat screen streaming the early local news from its perch on the wall under the deer's head and the spare, apartment-size year-round Christmas tree occupying a rear corner next to the entrance to the pissateriums. And even though the tree, too, was obviously fake, it simply looked tired. A sad string of miniature blue LED lights had been carelessly thrown atop the stiff aluminum branches. On the middle shelf behind the bar, which would ordinarily be stocked with bottles of liquor, was an eloquently arranged row of ceramic turtles in various sizes and colors. Very strange. What was that all about? It was early in the day, and The Crevice was relatively quiet, maybe a dozen or so customers scattered about the room, the sort of local types you'd expect to find hunkered down in a small-town bar, drinking an empty weekday afternoon away. Behind the bar, holding court and providing a steady flow of lubricant, was the owner, manager,

316

and self-proclaimed consummate mixologist, Roulette himself. He was also serving up a slightly modified version of the self that had been on display at the family dinner the other night. He was now occupying his workaday retail persona—the ruddy-cheeked, hail-fellow-well-met publican of story and song.

"Once the sun sets and the real drinking starts," he was saying, "you won't be able to move in here."

"It ain't drinking time yet?" said Graveyard, taking a sip from the freshly minted BroomDuster he held in his hand. The BroomDuster, Roulette's personal concoction, was the famous specialty of the house. It was a bizarre, fiery blend of closely guarded proportions of gin, vodka, tequila, white rum, lemon juice, white cranberry juice, and simple syrup, which, when completed, looked like a glass of water—"clear, clean, pure, innocent," Roulette liked to brag, "camouflage for the explosives hidden inside and guaranteed, believe me, to thoroughly dust your broom." Graveyard was just finishing his third of the day.

"How's that barn burner working for you?" Roulette said.

"I can feel the shape of my stomach."

"I can no longer feel anything," Ambience said. She was seated at the bar on a rickety stool next to her husband, their only company for the moment a solitary woman of indeterminate age at the far end of the bar who had faded ombré hair and a faded face. If this were a movie, she'd be precisely the type of barfly who'd have been hired to fill out this space, occupy that particular bar stool. Only this wasn't a movie and the woman was real. To Ambience she appeared to be someone it'd be good to know.

"Excellent," Roulette said. "Isn't that the point?"

"If you want it to be."

Listening to his thin country voice, looking at his asymmetrical face, left eye slightly lower than the right, nose broken probably some time ago, one ear sticking out, one ear not, cheeks so red the coloring appeared as artificial as cheap makeup, Ambience was struck even more forcibly by the same observation she'd had at the family dinner: what an odd little man. He seemed assembled out of discarded parts lifted from a Dumpster behind a movieland cyborg plant. Probably located somewhere on a distant planet with an unpronounceable name.

"Alcohol," he was saying. "The world's great lubricant. It keeps all the gears running smoothly. Reduces wear and corrosion. Maintains the crucial machinery in tip-top condition. Plus it's relaxing and just feels damn good. Imagine life without it. Unendurable."

"You've given quite a bit of thought to this," said Ambience.

"Only my life."

"What about the people who don't drink, not interested in it, never been interested in it? What about them? What about their machinery?"

"Sand in the wheels. Debris that needs to be filtered out."

"Who's going to be in charge of the filter?" Graveyard said.

"Who else? Drunks."

"That's your solution to everything, isn't it? Put the juiceheads in charge."

"Got a better idea?"

"No, but I believe Farrago does."

"What, that ridiculous Leaf Life Line of hers?"

"She's out to save the world, too, you know."

"Might help if she saved herself first."

"Well, a pox on all of us for not being as well put together as you are."

"Yeah, I don't know what happened, some glitch in the gene transmission with both of you."

"But SideEffects, I suppose, got all the proper goodies pure and unadulterated."

"He's working, ain't he?"

There was a long silence.

What could Ambience possibly say now to this man, she said to herself, that both of them could find even minimally interesting enough to sustain a conversational thread that might help kill another few minutes of this excruciatingly long afternoon? It was her turn. She hadn't a clue.

"I like your tree," she said, nodding toward the Xmas in the back.

"Put it up myself," Roulette said, as though the thoughtless placement of that unconvincing stick of wire and plastic were an achievement of which he could be justifiably proud.

"Been there since I was in preschool," said Graveyard.

"It's never come down?"

"I like to think," Roulette said, "that wherever I am, every day is Christmas."

"Saw the Kemosabe in the lot when we drove in," said Graveyard. "Looked to be taking up at least two spaces. Didn't they have a bigger model?"

"Well, you told me, bud, get what you want, and it was even a couple grand below the sticker, too. That's CosmicEye's place over on Flatpoint. You remember CosmicEye?"

"The guy who kept snakes in his bedroom until he woke up one night with a Red Barn Strangulator wrapped around his neck? That CosmicEye?"

"The very one."

On the screen above Roulette's head appeared a succession of images of the gorge. Standing in front of the actual rock wonder itself was a reporter talking into a microphone. Roulette picked up the remote and turned up the volume. "Randomburg authorities have identified the man who fell to his death last week from the western slope of the Randomburg Gorge," the reporter was intoning, "as one BlisterPac of Mammoth City. What he was doing on the other side of the guard fence and how he happened to fall are mysteries still being investigated. Any witnesses to this tragic event are asked to please contact the Randomburg police department. This is EpicBlowout reporting for Channel 6 Action News, Randomburg."

"Can you believe it?" said Roulette. "Imagine dying like that. Probably wasn't even conscious by the time he hit bottom. Body probably all tore up. People. They're all such idiots."

"How old was he?" Graveyard said.

"Old enough to know better. Say, weren't you out there that day?"

"I don't know. What day was it?"

"Don't recall, exactly. Last Thursday or Friday, I think. Tied up half the police and fire departments for most of the day."

"We saw nothing," Ambience said.

Graveyard assumed his time-tested concerned face. "Maybe we'd already left by the time he fell."

"No doubt the big event of our stay." Ambience matched her husband's furrowed expression. "And we missed it."

"We're always either too early or too late."

"Our luck."

"Not like it hasn't happened before," said Roulette. "Had some tourist from BadPortage go off the bridge couple months ago. But he was probably a suicide."

"Maybe this guy was, too," said Graveyard.

"Sheriff doubts it. They think if he was serious he would've taken a dive from a better spot, one with a clear path straight to the ground. All those trees from where he took the plunge, one of 'em could've broken the fall. No guarantee he'd be dead."

"What a disappointment," Ambience said.

"Such is life," Roulette said.

Ambience felt like laughing, but she didn't. Frankly, she often enjoyed being rude, but not now, not at this particular moment. The man was, after all, her father-in-law, and her feelings about him were far more complicated than could be handily untangled with an easy laugh. Almost from the first minute she'd laid eyes on him she had him pegged as a standardized parental dolt (male variation) and had seen or heard nothing since then to alter that original assessment. And, of course, she was not unaware of vestiges of that history woven into the fabric of his son's life, too. Sometimes she wished humans could recover from their families as easily as animals appeared to. Nippers, she knew, had been employed largely as an emotional garbage can by his previous owners during most of his harrowing kittenhood. He'd come into their life as a hard-used bundle of badly matted fur with a nasty open sore on his right side, a "weepy" eye, and a pronounced limp, also on his right side. But after just three months of tender care in their protective home, all the symptoms vanished. The medicine of a tranquil voice and a soothing touch. Too bad you couldn't bottle that.

"Where's the champion of the small businessman?" Roulette was saying. "That's what I'd like to know. Backbone of the country. What everything's all about. We've become society's trash heap. Where hope goes to rot. Try to make a decent living today for yourself and your family and watch your dream, along with a ton of cash, get flushed down the poop pipe."

"You don't seem to be in want of much," Graveyard said.

"How do you know what I want?"

"I don't. Course it does appear to me you got pretty much everything you need."

"Oh, listen up, boy, don't assume. I need a lot of stuff."

"Name one stuff."

"A Techno Vibrating Chair and Viewing Platform."

"What the hell is that?"

"The small businessman's instant staycation and nerve remedy."

Behind the conversation Ambience heard the ominous approach of a large rumbling bike. It sounded like an oncoming storm trying to work itself up into a single satisfying clap of thunder. A couple of minutes later the front door opened and in walked SideEffects in full rider-boy regalia. On the ever-present Fuck-O-Meter he had today moved up a notch or two since the initial evaluation at dinner. His skin had lost its vaguely jaundiced look and his features seemed sharper, more honed, and, consequently, older. At least that was how her memory was now replaying the difference. But maybe memory was wrong. In fact maybe nothing physical had changed at all except the mood and the lighting and the fact that they were all a couple of weeks older. In the same light Roulette was looking considerably more aged than he probably was. Lessons for today on the relentless grinding of time and the importance of proper lighting, not just on stage but in real life, too.

"Well, surprise, surprise," SideEffects said, dramatically extending his arms. "Look who's here." He came over and granted his brother a large theatrical hug. Then he proceeded to hug Ambience especially warmly before taking a step back and devoting himself to a full appraisal. Up and down he looked at her. Then he exposed a slight smile. "So," he said, as though he were actually thinking of something else entirely, "refugees from the urban inferno."

"Easy on the insults," said Graveyard. "We know you secretly love the nasty place."

"Never set foot in Mammoth City in my life. Never plan to, actually."

"You're just afraid if you ever did visit even once, you'd never be able to leave."

"I hear the real estate market is totally gangsta."

"Everything you love. Plus, money flows through the business like water."

"Polluted water."

"At least something is flowing."

"Oh, Dad," SideEffects said, "before I forget, I got something for you." He slipped off his backpack, unzipped it, and pulled out a thin blue plastic bag, which he handed with no small ceremony to his father.

"A present?" said Roulette. "Wonderful. You know how I love getting presents." He opened the bag and pulled out a comic book also sealed in plastic, which he proceeded to gape at in wonder. "A Crackerjack Comics number eleven. How the hell did you ever manage to snag one of these?"

"Complete fluke. BackAlley called me just the other day to talk some business and happened to mention in passing that this super-rare book had come in totally unexpectedly from a regular over in Squirreltown who needed money for a sudden divorce and so, reluctantly, had to break up his collection."

Roulette kept holding the book at arm's length and staring at the garish cover art, and he couldn't stop smiling—a rare reaction to reading material of any kind. In his entire life he had hardly ever cracked a book with a hard cover. Whenever he wanted to expose himself to some inert pages for a change, instead of to moving images on a screen, his immediate primo choices were superhero adventure comics and/or bar guides. Immersion in such fantastic worlds seemed to still the constant vibration in his inner engine mounting to a point where he was able to convince himself that no, despite how it sometimes seemed, he was not idling but steadily moving on, always traveling forward, and that the road was good and the direction true.

"What's so great about a Crackerjack number eleven?" Graveyard said.

"The holy grail of collectibles," Roulette said. "First appearance of Patchman. His origin story. One of the most sought-after issues in all of comicdom." He turned to SideEffects. "Hope you didn't have to mortgage the house for this baby."

SideEffects shook his head. "Talk about mortgages. BackAlley owes me a big solid. Don't worry about it."

"I think I've got some old Patchmans in my bedroom closet back home," Ambience said.

"Don't throw them out," said Roulette.

"Wonder if they're worth anything at all."

"Everything Patchman is worth something," said Roulette. "Let me put this away someplace special." Still gazing at the comic as if it were a framed photograph of an old girlfriend, he walked out from behind the bar and disappeared into his back office.

"Scored several lasting points with that one," said Graveyard.

"Leave it to you to keep track."

"Surprised you're not doing the same. Considering your lifelong infatuation with numbers."

SideEffects ignored his brother's comment and turned his attention to the silent wife. "So Ambience," he said, "how you doing these days?"

She shrugged. "Wish I could complain, but I'm fine."

"This jagoff treating you okay?" he said, glancing at Graveyard.

"Now that the daily beatings have stopped, yeah."

Roulette emerged from his inner sanctum, wiping his hands on an old bar towel.

"What were you doing back there?" SideEffects said.

"I don't know. My hands just felt dirty. I had to wash them off. Sometimes they just get that way. All the filth in this place. You never know what you're touching."

"Didn't get any crap on the Patch, did you?" said SideEffects.

"Are you kidding? Of course not. Thank God for protective plastic." He slapped his right palm hard against the counter. "Now, what can I get you?"

"What are they having?"

"What do you think?"

"BroomDusters?"

"Of course."

"Hard-core. Hit me with the same."

Roulette quickly mixed up three specials with his usual polish and set them carefully on the bar.

"Why don't we retire to a nice cozy booth?" SideEffects said. He picked up his drink and turned to go. "Need something firm to prop my aching back against."

"That still paining you?" Graveyard said.

"Oh, off and on. Mostly when I get tired. Like I am now. We'll be over in the corner, Dad."

Roulette nodded, his attention now thoroughly absorbed by the afternoon's live broadcast of the hearing before the Tumbledown House Select Committee on Foreign Footsie Play under the Green Baize. It was in its fourth continuous week and already there'd been half a dozen resignations at the highest level, a couple of arrests, and a deep stock market decline that left investors like Roulette helplessly affixed to the daily news feed.

The three of them settled into a booth with sticky seats and a wobbly table.

"Classy," Ambience said.

"What do you want?" said SideEffects. "It's a dive."

"Better not let Dad hear you say that," said Graveyard.

"You think he doesn't know? He likes it like this."

"That may be, but I don't think he necessarily wants such an opinion being bandied about in public by his own kids."

"He doesn't know what he wants."

"Awfully harsh, Sidey."

"You haven't been around here for the last eleven years."

"I talk to him on the phone when he'll take my calls."

"Anyone can sound relatively normal on the phone for a couple minutes."

"I take it, then, you've heard about the Muenster moon?'

"You kidding me? Yeah, I've heard about the rind in the sky. I've heard about the bubbling peanut-butter-and-jelly core at the center of the earth that's going to erupt sometime tomorrow morning. I've heard about the replica presidents. The great portal in the electromagnetic field that dogs and cats use to travel into and out of our lives. Aliens in the embryos, money embedded with antipodean microchips, cybernetic ants, the senator with the glass brain. I've heard it all."

"You have to admit, though, that all this color really brightens a life, spices up all our drab twenty-four-sevens."

"If you like living in a cartoon world."

"You see your father a lot?" said Ambience. This whole family was a wonderhouse of limitless wings.

"When don't I see him? He wants me to drop in here every other day at least or he's out at my place every other night. He could call, but he won't. You know about him and the phone, right?"

"He won't get a cell."

"The rays it gives off cause brain cancer."

"Of course they do, but what about a landline?"

"He hears weird sounds on it, so of course it's probably tapped."

"And who exactly's interested in hearing what a hick barkeep stuck in the sticks has to say about anything?" said Graveyard.

"Who isn't? That's his view, anyway. Don't you know he's in possession of dangerous info nobody should be in possession of? That's why he's being surveilled every minute of every day. As a matter of fact, we all are."

"We all are what?" said Ambience.

"Being surveilled."

"By whom?"

"I don't know. Them."

"And who's them?"

"Those who want to know, I guess. Ask Dad. He can explain all this horseshit better than I can. It's something about total control and, of course, total money. All I know is the fix is on and we're all fucked."

"Can you imagine the load?" Ambience said. "Carrying all that stuff around in your head every day?"

"You know, Graveyard, you wised up and skyed on outta here while the getting was good."

"I did what I had to do."

"I really really hated you for a long, long time."

"You could have done the same."

"I was too young and too broke. And who else was going to hang around, make sure Dad wasn't going to fry another wire or two?"

"Mom?"

"She couldn't make a coherent grocery list. No, I'm afraid the only logical possibility was yours truly."

"Farrago?"

"C'mon," SideEffects said. "She has trouble opening a door. No, I was the lucky winner of this lottery. And you know why? You know why I won? I was the only one in the fucking drawing." He picked up his drink, drained the remaining half in one continuous swallow, then with meticulous care placed the empty glass on the precise spot in the center of the table where it was obviously supposed to go. He looked at his brother and his sister-in-law in measured turn, as if daring either one to speak a single word. Then he turned and sat silently and stared flatly at whatever happened to be offering itself up for consideration outside the window: car, tire, gravel, girl, tree, road, sky, each object displayed in about that much detail. He really wasn't at the table anymore. Then he turned again and contemplated his brother for several slow seconds. "You know," he said, "I think I need some money."

"Dad said you were doing so well," Graveyard said.

"Dad doesn't know everything."

"How much do you need?"

"More than I can comfortably ask for."

"What is it? Gambling, girls, booze, or drugs?"

"It's complicated."

"Not something boring like bad investments or bad loans?"

"Try all of the above."

"I can't believe what I'm hearing," Graveyard said. "So little brother has been living a secret life all these years." He caught Ambience's eye. "Can you believe this?"

"He always looked shady to me," she said. She felt as if now they were in a movie together and he was the guy's guy and she his tagalong girlfriend. It was stupid and silly to be thinking that, but she couldn't help it. He gave her the proper expression back. Up one on the Fuck-O-Meter.

"Can we get any details?" Graveyard said.

"I don't think so. Fill in the blanks."

"How much do you need?"

"How much did that lottery pay out?"

"I think that's a matter between me and the state. And I can't believe you even dared to ask."

"Dad got a high-end SUV."

"Is that what this is about? You don't want to be the one who drew the short straw?"

"I think I'm owed something."

"You do, huh? What about your get-out-of-jail-free card?"

"Haven't seen that yet."

"And how much will it take to make you shut up and go away?"

"I figure half would be about right."

"Really? And through what bizarre accounting practice did you arrive at that particular sum?"

"It's a fair number."

"For an inbred crime family."

"You don't know what it's been like, stuck in this hellhole with a sister who occupies a permanent position on the spectrum, a mother who's about as substantial as a piece of fluff, and a father who's the self-appointed mayor of wigtown."

"And for that you demand half my money?"

"What's half a life worth?"

The stolid gray dome that had been covering this particular patch of earth since sunrise opened suddenly for no apparent reason, allowing a shaft of brilliant bright light to penetrate the dirty front window of The Crevice, ricochet off a copper mug sitting on the third shelf above the bar, and into Ambience's left eye at the precise instant the perception passed through her—though it may have been the BroomDusters speaking, too—how random that right now (1:11 by her watch) she had been placed in this strange bar in the nowhere upcountry, trapped in unforeseen family crossfires, wondering what time the feature ended, or that, frankly, how random right now to have been placed anywhere at all. What she needed most at the moment, she abruptly decided, was a sweet hit of ellipsis. Under the table she began rooting around in her lambskin bag.

"As the oldest"—SideEffects was speaking in that funny little carnival barker voice of his he sometimes fell into—"it was your duty to watch over the family."

"Like a shepherd?"

"Like a son."

"I wouldn't describe either one of our parents as infirm."

"You know this place hasn't been doing so well lately, either."

"He hasn't said a word about it to me."

"You know his way. Also, he takes some thirty pills a day."

"For what?"

"You name it, he's got it. And someone's got to stick around to make sure they all go down. He gets confused sometimes."

And the boys went on as boys do, blah blah blah, blah blah blah. Sometimes when Ambience found herself in a situation like this, a hijacked innocent to intense convos that were not her intensities, she felt herself beginning, step by step, to thin out a bit. It must be like consciously losing one's hair, if one could actually feel the loss of each separate strand. She supposed she was still visible, but only in the most superficial sense. She entered into one of her ghostly selves, which had always seemed to her to be a place where she saw things she didn't ordinarily see and where whatever it was that rolled ceaselessly through her mind and let her know she was alive spoke more loudly than usual. Since she was an only child with only a single parent, this persistent abrasiveness between blood relatives was something novel and intriguing to her. After a while all this friction must become quite exhausting. Are all families of more than two just like this? Probably. She didn't know anyone her age who had a healthy or even a relatively communicative relationship with their parents. Everyone was tense and unhappy, though few would admit it. To start, everyone needed more money, especially those who already had more money than they could waste in a lifetime. Greed was an insatiable mouth. Next, everyone needed numerous hugs and kisses, an infinity of x's and o's. Then, most of all, everyone needed not to need. Good luck, everyone, with that one. She opened the pillbox under the table, plucked out a pill between thumb and forefinger, raised her hand to her mouth, and slipped the magic between her lips. Then, reaching under the table, she tapped Graveyard on the thigh three times and slipped him a dose, too.

And blah blah blah the insistent background noise began rising steadily back into audibility:

"You were the one took that big chip out of Dad's favorite driver, not me," SideEffects said.

"I certainly did not. I wasn't even allowed to use those clubs."

"Didn't keep you from doing so whenever you damn well pleased."

"So *you* remember."

"And I'm the one took the paddling for it."

"Well, I took the hits for letting the dogs out."

"You deserved it."

Brothers. What a vicious mess. Ambience could now see quite plainly that they were truly related. The shape of their bodies. The shape of their minds. No wonder they disliked each other so much.

"When we went to Funtastic," Graveyard said, "you were the one got to ride with Dad on the Whirly-Ball. Twice. In the front car, yet."

"It was my birthday."

"And what did I get on my birthday?"

"Beats me."

"The Big Box of Brain Busters."

"But you always liked mental games that no one but you could solve."

"I hated those. You had to have a graduate degree from Porcupine U. just to open the damn package."

"You went to Porcupine."

"That's why I had trouble opening the box."

"He did leave with a master's in Patterns of Concomitance and Contingency in Ancient Rhetoric," Ambience said.

"Which catapulted me into the high position I hold today."

"You didn't need no degree to get where you got," SideEffects said.

"Let's not go through that door again. Just tell me how much you want."

"I ain't begging for nothing."

"Seems to me that's exactly what you're doing."

SideEffects stared steadily at his brother as his expression slowly hardened. Then he glanced away for a second, turned back again, and just as Ambience was beginning to slip ever so languidly through the mist into that other world, abruptly tossed his fresh drink directly into Graveyard's startled face. "Hey!" said Ambience, reaching out a hand too late. Without a pause Graveyard leaped across the table, seized his brother by the neck with both hands, and began shaking and throttling him as furiously as he could. Glasses went flying, alcohol splashing onto everyone. Back at the bar the woman with the ombré hair screamed. Ambience jumped from her seat and quickly backed away as the table collapsed and both men went crashing to the floor. Roulette came rushing over, loosing a torrent of incoherent obscenities and accompanying spittle over all. "Stop it!" Ambience was yelling. "Stop it! Stop it!" It was all she could say. As she got on her knees, down on the floor herself, trying to pull one of SideEffects's hands from around her husband's neck, he batted her away, then hit her a second time hard in the face with his fist, and she got really angry. "Fuck you, you bastard!" she said, then punched him with her own fist, at which point Roulette grabbed her by the shoulders and lifted her out of the fray. "Now, you," he said, "you stay here!" The brothers were tangled together on the floor, pummeling each other as best they could, both their faces beet red, trading insults neither of them heard. Roulette squatted down, tried to get between his two sons, pry them apart, when suddenly, out of nowhere, a clenched fist (it wasn't entirely clear whose) caught Roulette in the jaw, and instinctively he started hitting back at both of them. He was serious now and punching for keeps. In seconds there was blood from somebody all over everybody. Ambience simply could not believe the chaotic scene now spread out before her: father and sons reduced to a welter of thrashing limbs on a gummy floor. Everybody was hitting everyone else, everyone grunting, panting, cursing. Then suddenly, for no discernible reason, all the swearing simply stopped at once, as if the voice track had been abruptly cut, and all that could be heard was the dull, sickening sound of fist on flesh, over and over again. Ambience began to shout, without any awareness whatsoever that she was the one doing the shouting: "That's enough, you fuckers! Enough!" No discernible response. So, surprised by her own strength, she simply reached down and with seemingly no effort whatsoever simply lifted SideEffects off her husband's body as easily as she would have picked up a large dog. Probably that emergency adrenaline she'd read so much about. Roulette delivered a last light tap to Graveyard's cheek, let out a groan, rolled over, and slowly struggled to his feet. He wiped at his mouth, then stared at the blood on his fingers. "I didn't want to do that," he said. He looked down at his sons. "You two…" He had no more words. "I didn't start it," SideEffects said. "You didn't do anything to stop it," Roulette said. "He threw a drink in my face," Graveyard said. He got up off the bloodied floor and wiped his hands on his pants. Roulette turned, waving a dismissive hand toward them all, and walked away, back to the safe place behind the bar. "The drink in my face," Graveyard said. "Did you happen to see that?" Without turning or speaking another word, Roulette waved his dismissive hand again and kept walking. "You can get up now," Graveyard said to his brother, who remained prone on the floor. He appeared to be studying something he now found of deep interest up on the ceiling. "We've got to replace those tiles," he said. Then he got to his feet with a clumsiness he pretended was purposeful.

Graveyard had a nasty smirk plastered on his face. "Forget about that money," he said. "And the get-out-of-jail-free card. And if I never see your fucking face again, I'll die a happy man."

"You're not the only one."

They glared at each other, a moment promising that this calm was only a temporary truce.

"Go ahead," Graveyard said. "Try me."

SideEffects examined his bruised knuckles and appeared to be seriously considering the suggestion. Finally he said, "Not in front of Dad again. But let me tell you, I don't easily forget."

"And let me tell you," Graveyard said. "I don't scare easily."

"Might not be talking that way if you were broke."

"I don't need a heap of paper certificates to tell me who I am."

"Fuck you," SideEffects said. "And fuck you again." And he turned and walked out of the place like the proverbial stoic hero through the saloon door, and through the window they could see him get on his bike and jump on the kick-starter and see the bike roar to life and tear out of the parking lot and the huge backfire it produced rattled the windows and gravel shot out from beneath the rear tire and pinged against the glass. And that was that.

"You get any boost from the ell?" Ambience said.

"Not that I noticed."

"Me, neither. You know, if the stuff had kicked in the way it was supposed to, this last twenty minutes would already be gone. Erased. Permanently. Like it never happened at all."

"Imagine if there were a pill that could do that to your entire childhood."

Back in the secure, peaceful world behind the bar Roulette tried to reclaim interest in the ever-present hearing, but after a while spent glued to the screen and registering nothing, he realized that's all he was doing, zoning out over a screen, and he picked up the remote and turned off the set. He lost himself gratefully in the routine of the bar. He knew how to make a drink. He knew how to crack a joke. For a while he was in charge. When LostSequin arrived a couple of hours later to take over the night shift, Roulette retreated into his office and sat down and stared uncomprehendingly at the beautifully gaudy cover of the comic book lying on his desk. Patchman depicted in a life-and-death struggle with his archnemesis, Monochromo, on the observation deck atop the Stiletto Tower in Mercy City. His guts were still a turmoil of unfocused images and blurred emotions. The fight kept replaying for him in a badly edited montage of jump cuts and frozen frames. A real fight, an authentic exchange of blows with his own sons. He couldn't understand how such a monstrosity could have even occurred. He couldn't say for sure what this internal muddle it had left him with actually meant. For that matter, even after all the difficult years of his life he had already somehow traversed, more or less successfully, he didn't really know what anything meant. While he was living it, he was carrying around somewhere inside him the curious notion that his own life, at least, had always seemed to be guided by some sort of propulsive drive aimed toward some genuine target where, he supposed with slightly vague conviction, the true meaning of everything he had experienced, everything he had learned, would finally be revealed in a grandiose explosion of sound and color. But creeping up on him, more and more lately, was the growing sensation that he had already missed the target. It had been hidden all along in those little disposable moments he had failed to take sufficient notice of while focused naively on a horizon he couldn't see clearly, one that perhaps had never existed at all. But what he did know at this quite real, quite specific, quite urgent moment was that he was drowning in a dark pool of profound disappointment. And he just felt so damn lonely.

CHAPTER 22

AT HOME WITH MISTERMENU

SO AFTER ALL THIS time MisterMenu and DelicateSear had gotten back together. Who knew? Each had sampled plenty of other genitals in plenty of other places and had found that theirs fitted together just so. Neither was all that clear on how or why, exactly, their reconnect had taken place. They'd gone out one evening to SilverSettings on what each initially believed to be a routine friendly business dinner. Halfway through the entrée (bloody buckhorn stump for him, cosseted cabbie claw for her), MisterMenu began replaying the dramatic season-ending episode of what he called the MissusMenu Show. DelicateSear'd heard it all before in minute detail, but he couldn't seem to keep from rerunning it. In a nutshell, he and the wife had begun dinner that evening with a verbal spat over drinks (subject: did it even matter?), a shouting match during the entrées, and by dessert a full-on food fight that ended in the kitchen with most of the imported Mannaware in pieces on the fifteen-thousand-dollar nugget-parquet floor. She'd sued for divorce the following day. The day after that he'd settled more or less permanently into his not-so-secret pied-à-terre in the monied elevations of the MinisteringArms. Smiles for all. Cue the theme.

"I remember," she said. "About three months ago. When you changed."

"No. I didn't change."

"Oh, drop your pearls. It wasn't anything really you could even put your finger on. Like a subtle new seasoning added to the ragout. That's all."

"Did I seem down? Was it anything apparent?"

"No, no, not at all. Nothing visible."

"Because that can destroy you in negotiations, you know. They're predators out there, all of 'em—they sense weakness in an instant, then go in for the kill."

"Not to worry. Never occurred to me that your claws were ever anything but razor sharp. It's just that a small part of you, an infinitesimal part, might have seemed a bit distracted."

"But it wasn't noticeable?"

"Not at all. I'm sure most people, in fact, didn't detect a thing. It's just that ever since I was a little girl I've been fine-tuned to other people's internal weather. Don't know why. My grandmama was like that, too. You couldn't lie to her about anything."

"That's why you're in charge of Context and Control."

The waiter appeared tableside as if by magic. MisterMenu ordered another magnum of the Grand Marque TickleWaterReserve2009 ($1,100).

"I'm not used to such heights of extravagance," DelicateSear said.

"You'll adjust," said MisterMenu. "And I think you've been acclimating to the altitude quite professionally." He offered her a toast. To the bestest, the grandest, the loveliest, the sexiest, you know, the estiest of everything.

"Guess what? I'm already thoroughly acclimated." And she toasted him. To the richest, the handsomest, the sexiest, the kindest, the whateveriest, etc., etc.

Their eyes locked. And it was tempered Dura-Bolt.

"You know what?" MisterMenu said.

"What?"

"I think we need to repair to my collateral crib."

"Well, listen at you, Mr. DaShiznit."

"I may be an old wrinkle mask, but I've still got a pulse."

"Next you'll be rattling off your fave beats."

"I was serious, though. We need to check out those sheets."

"We do, huh?"

"I think they might need changing."

MisterMenu called for the check, paid, and in minutes they found themselves out on the sidewalk, blinking into the setting sunlight. The GalacticCloudTouringConfiguration glided noiselessly to the curb. Trefoil, in his tailored black uniform with gold piping, exited the driver's seat, came around, and opened the rear door.

"Good evening, madame," he said. He gave her a crisp salute. "Pleasant to see you again."

"Nice to see you, too, Trefoil."

MisterMenu and DelicateSear slid onto the commodious rear seat, assumed their respective look-at-me-I'm-being-driven-around faces, and settled back into the intoxicating glove leather. Trefoil guided the Cloud into traffic with hydraulic grace. In less than a minute the passengers' mouths were squirming wetly around all over each other. DelicateSear's hand moved reflexively toward MisterMenu's zipper. Gently he touched her arm and unglued himself from her face. "Not yet," he said. "Like to have something left in the tank for the bedroom."

She couldn't help but smile. "When has that ever been a problem for you?"

"Like cigarettes—first one of the day is always best. Rather not blow it in the back seat of a car. We're older than that, right?"

"If you say so." Her expression shifted slightly toward the business end of the spectrum. She slid back a panel, revealing the well-stocked liquor cabinet. "Drink?"

"Know how to make a GoldenRubySpikedPlatitude?"

"Sounds out of my pay grade. What's in it?"

"Twenty-year-old Maccloister, tomb vodka, volcanic-rock-filtered gin, aurora borealis nectar, dawn-harvested master melons, speckled tummerl eggs, and a generous sprinkling of gold flecks up top."

"Sounds rather yummy."

"I'll have Sinisteria prepare you one. You'll like it."

"I need something now." She grabbed the most interesting-looking fifth within reach, the decorative amber cylinder of historic Lickerlich, unscrewed the cap, raised it to her lips, tossed back a slug right out of the bottle.

"You're such a peasant. I love it."

She turned and stretched her legs across his lap. He stroked them all the way home.

Since the separation MisterMenu had resided in the presidential penthouse of the MinisteringArms, in midtown. DelicateSear had already been there on numerous occasions so was thoroughly adjusted to the manifold conveniences that invariably and deliberately wowed first-timers. She headed straight for the bathroom and the shower that adjusted itself to the user's preprogrammed preferences regarding water temperature, force of spray, and number and positioning of various nozzles during the "aqueous clarify." On exiting the cleansing pod you controlled the air temp through verbal command. Which DelicateSear did. She liked being naked, so she didn't even bother enfolding herself in one of the lamb-soft fleece bathrobes hanging freshly laundered in the robe closet. She found MisterMenu in the odeum, lounging on his favorite viewing berth, staring at some ratty old picture with all the men running around in hats and all the women draped out in ugly gowns she couldn't believe anyone actually wore in real time. She also couldn't believe MisterMenu looked at these yawners for any other reason than to impress what few friends he had with the fact that he'd actually endured watching them.

She stood before him, languidly drying herself. "I simply cannot believe these towels," she said. "They feel so good they should be illegal."

"Take a couple."

"I couldn't. I'd like to but I couldn't."

"Why not? I can get more."

"All right. Maybe I'll pick out a few before I go."

MisterMenu pressed a button in the armrest of his berth. He

had barely lifted his hand away before a tall, slim woman of obvious tropical origin appeared in the doorway. She was wearing a curious royal purple uniform consisting of a pleated miniskirt and an usher's bolero jacket with a large *M* embroidered in white above each breast. DelicateSear, who had made not the slightest effort to conceal her exposed body, stared steadily at the woman as if she were the one who was starkers.

"Sinisteria," said MisterMenu, "would you please be so good as to mix us a couple SpikedPlatitudes?"

"Yes, sir." She was answering DelicateSear's stare beat for beat.

"And make one for yourself, if you'd like. You may serve us in the dream chamber."

"Yes, sir." She turned to go.

"And Sinisteria," DelicateSear said.

"Yes, ma'am?"

"Wouldn't you like to get a bit more comfortable? Aren't you hot in all those icky, sticky clothes?"

"Thank you, ma'am." And she softly exited.

"Has Sinisteria lost weight since the last time I was here?"

"You'll have to ask her, I'm afraid. She's always looked quite smokin' to me."

"There you go again. The older you get, the younger you seem."

"Thank you. Shall we adjourn to the dream chamber?"

"Capital idea, Fussbutt."

So they did.

MisterMenu liked women. He liked having them in his life. He liked them in the boardroom (within reason). He liked them in the bedroom (without reason). He was a woman's man. In fact, he never felt more himself than when he was in bed with a woman or women, as the case may be. He liked to think they liked him. Except from his wife, he had never heard differently.

The master dream chamber, MisterMenu's preferred lair, was decorated in a style best described as "nouveau primeval mystique."

The full carpet was an absurdly thick white alpaca, the walls were a dark blue suede, and the few spare pieces of outer-space-safari furniture had all been custom-crafted by Halcyon of Planisphere. The sole painting, a multimedia piece, actually, mounted precariously over the bed, was entitled *Veiled Lagoon*, an original fabulation by the trending BluntShears. The bed itself, a circus-ring-size monstrosity that actually revolved, he'd had specially constructed after reading in *SumpTown*, a periodical he never admitted to anyone he even glanced through, that this was the very type of bed that Razzlapin famously cavorted upon. MisterMenu wanted the exact same model, only bigger. Now he had it. Which was where MisterMenu and DelicateSear artfully arranged themselves after MisterMenu relieved himself of his workaday costume, tossing each bespoke item wherever it happened to fall on the insanely soft and insanely expensive carpeting. He stood before her in complete unselfconscious exposure, including his penis in all its unadorned whatever-the-hell-it-was. He caught DelicateSear staring markedly at it. Rightly or wrongly, he interpreted her gaze as a sign of avid affection.

"Do you want me to shower also?"

"You needn't bother. But what you could do, though, is pop into the powder room and give your asshole a quick scrub."

"I assume you've performed the same courtesy on yourself."

"Certainly. I believe in always being well prepared."

"I'll get right on it, then. And by the way, I love when you give me orders."

"I know you do."

So he obeyed.

By the time he returned, Sinisteria had brought the drinks and joined DelicateSear on the bed. They were busily engaged in talking about their children. They each had a two-year-old, and each child was experiencing similar difficulties conforming to the demands of the porcelain god, DelicateSear's girl bursting spontaneously into tears whenever the phrase "toilet training" was even mentioned,

Sinisteria's boy running out of the room to seek refuge beneath the dining-room table.

"My girls glided through the whole issue with hardly even a single complaint, both of them," said MisterMenu.

"All well adjusted and psychologically fit," DelicateSear said.

"Of course," said MisterMenu. "Mental health runs in the family."

"You've all been so very rich in every department," Sinisteria said.

"There's the proof. What greater evidence of sanity than the acquisition of vast amounts of the ever-ready?"

"Let's change the subject," DelicateSear said. "Talk about money is such a real bringdown."

"And what subject interests you?" He believed he knew the answer to that question.

"I don't know. Knitting?"

He emitted his short, sharp laugh. "My favorite subject, too. Let's knit my body to yours." He grabbed her arm, pulled her toward him. He appeared to be about halfway there on the occasionally rocky road to maximum hardness. But only halfway.

"Think somebody needs a bit of assistance. Want me to get you an EverTrue?"

He shook his head. "Takes too long. How about a manual?"

She reached down between his legs and began jerking him off. After a while he stopped her arm. "Let's save it for the closing bell." He turned and rolled heavily on top of her. He parked his now suitably firm thing inside her. Then, without further ceremony, he pistoned it quickly in and out until he came. Which didn't take all that long. He, of course, was not wearing a condom. He never did. He sprayed his paste all over the interior of her warm oven. He sighed and rolled off her.

"All right, you two," he said to the women, "have at it."

Like most good heterophiles everywhere, MisterMenu could often achieve the height of erotic arousal by watching a couple of hot women cover each other. Which he now proceeded to do. They were on each other's mouths in an instant. It was as if a private membrane deep inside each one of them had risen to the surface to expose itself for the sole purpose of rubbing furiously against its adjacent twin. They rubbed until the kindling burst into flames. Their bodies merged and burned up altogether. Mouths and nipples and pussies and assholes. Gone. MisterMenu watched. As if the heat were emitting rays that could warm his heart and tan his skin. And it did. He wanted to say something suitably piquant, but nothing occurred to him. Where had those girls just gone? They'd obviously been somewhere not of this world. Where was that? What was that? He wanted to go there, too. Could he? Would he? Probably not. They were women. Natural emonauts to other planets.

"All right," MisterMenu said. "Enough. I think you girls like each other a little too much." His voice coming from such a far distance that he barely recognized it as his own.

DelicateSear turned a groggy, dazed expression toward him. She was wearing that loose, gray-dawn drunken face of hers. He could tell she wasn't even seeing him.

"What?" she said.

He grabbed her, pulled her toward him, and planted a Mister-Menu buzzbomb right on her wet road-worn lips. She kissed back. Then they mixed it up for a while with their tongues. Suddenly Sinisteria's mouth was there among them, too, joining in enthusiastically, and it became impossible to know who, exactly, was kissing whom. This round of saliva guzzling lasted until their face muscles wore out and then gradually slid to an end. They couldn't stop smiling at one another.

"I need another drink," DelicateSear said.

"Second that," said MisterMenu.

"Hit it a third time," said Sinisteria. She rose to go make them. "No," said DelicateSear. She pushed her back down. "I'll go." DelicateSear left the warm bed and, still naked, ambled to the full bar at the end of the room, where she busied herself with a lot of clinking activity.

Gazing in that direction, MisterMenu said to Sinisteria, "Got a dynamite ass, doesn't she?"

"Yes, sir."

"Let me ask you something. That bother you, calling me sir all the time?"

"No, sir."

"I was going to ask you not to do it anymore, but then I realized I liked it. It even excites me sometimes."

"It excites me, too, sir."

MisterMenu leaned over and tried to kiss Sinisteria in a frank imitation of DelicateSear's full-on, go-for-broke manner. It seemed okay, but the charge was of a decidedly lower wattage.

"How about a replay?" he said.

So they did. Same result.

"I think you like DelicateSear better than me," MisterMenu said afterward.

"She's a very fine lady."

"Yes, she is. And so are you."

"And you're a very fine man."

"On my fine days."

DelicateSear arrived with a tray full of drinks. "And what are you two gossiping about so intensely?"

"You, of course," said MisterMenu.

"Well, I am an endlessly fascinating topic." She passed out the drinks and joined them on the bed.

MisterMenu took a sip from his glass, rolled it around in his mouth. "Your Platitudes are as good as Sinisteria's."

"Who do you think I learned from?"

"My two girls," MisterMenu said. "Here, let me get closer to both of you." He set his drink down on the red teak headboard and wedged himself in between the women. He placed a firm arm around each of them. "Feels like we're a family now, doesn't it?"

"A family that every time they're together again they immediately get naked and screw one another's brains out," DelicateSear said.

"Well, what's a family for?"

"Fighting and making babies," said Sinisteria.

"Well, we're making a sandwich," MisterMenu said. "And I'm the cream in the middle." He turned to his right and kissed DelicateSear. He turned to his left and kissed Sinisteria. It was like sampling wine. Who hit the best notes, possessed the most lingering finish? He couldn't determine. So he decided to simply get wasted on both. Consume *their* fire. Wallow in *their* practices. So he did. All the while reveling in *his* lust. There was no end to the body. It was a universe unto itself. You could learn more by exploring the frantic turmoil of skin and flesh than you could scrolling through the compuverse of all your days. Later, when he surfaced for air, he realized it might be actually possible to drown in the physical, in this unfathomable sea of sensation. Or was it? Maybe there was no death here at all, maybe the struggle to keep one's head above water simply conveyed you to some unimaginable place where all was safety and contentment. In addition to cleansing the body of toxins, indulging in carefree sexual activity provided, at least for MisterMenu, a blue-chip corollary: it also sparked his mind. He became, for a crucial interval, at least, a philosopher of the sheets. As far as he was concerned, there wasn't a single human endeavor he was aware of that couldn't be finessed in order to yield a lucrative return of some caliber. In fact, some of his best perceptions had been slough from an enthusiastic fuck. So what he needed now were supple mouths servicing his stick, and, unusually for him, he surprised himself by actually asking the girls if they wouldn't mind taking turns, one after the other, polishing the pole with their tongues. Without even the slightest demur, they applied themselves to the task with convincing enthusiasm, feigned or not. The middle finger of his right hand, seemingly having acquired a will of its own, found the opening to a nearby asshole, he didn't know which one—did it matter?—and deftly inserted itself inside. All shiny and warm. He explored the walls of the cave. Then his finger became a dick and began moving like a dick. Someone moaned. Maybe it was him. He removed his finger and tapped the top of each girl's bobbing head. "That's enough," he said. "Main event." He rolled over onto DelicateSear, but his dick was already beginning to lose some air. "How about an assist?" he said. DelicateSear obligingly reached down and stroked him until the balloon was inflated again. MisterMenu worked it until he was about to cum when he pulled out and turned his attention to Sinisteria. She seemed slightly tighter and wetter and he liked that. Again he was mounted bareback. His preferred ride. Condoms were for ordinaries. He didn't really care all that much about disease or babies. They were problems that could be taken care of. What mattered in the moment was supreme. The skin-on-skin vibe and the indiscriminate mixing of fluids. Then, just as he began to melt and drop his load inside Sinisteria, he stopped, pulled out, and switched back over to DelicateSear. And that's how it went, back and forth, in and out, for as long as he could stand and then some. Then he was struck by one of his patented fun notions: why not figure that whichever female he finally happened to ex-plode inside of was obviously the one he liked best? And truly, he didn't yet know who that particular contestant would be. Ever the reliable gamer (no such thing as a trivial game), he was interested in the outcome. He was always interested in outcomes. But for a true, honest verdict, he would have to let the body, not the mind, decide. He was well aware of all the devious snares the "objective" mind was capable of devising, being a grand master of emotional chess himself. He closed his eyes and, in the heat of the moment, lost track of which side of the bed he was occupying, so that when the finale finally arrived, he wasn't even sure which squirming lady happened to be the lucky depositee. He had to examine the flushed face beneath him for several seconds to be certain, and—lo and behold!—the winner was (fevered drumroll): Sinisteria. Who knew? He bestowed upon both women a series of plentiful kisses as equally as he could, maybe a few more for the loser, DelicateSear. "My girls," he said. His plummy voice abundant with all the attributes of untarnished gratification. He sighed. Deeply.

"You can take a well-deserved rest now," said DelicateSear. "After such a full, productive day."

Sinisteria was playing with his soft dick, wiggling it back and forth, obviously testing her ability at a bit of manual resuscitation. He kept pushing her arm away. "All right," he said. Now thoroughly refreshed, MisterMenu clapped his hands. "Back to work." He and both women jumped simultaneously out of bed. He seized Sinisteria by the waist, pulled her tightly against his chest, leaned down, and whispered in her ear for several beats longer than the usual allotment of ear-whispering time. Her tall, slim body seemed to actually lengthen in height as she listened. They stepped apart. "Okay?" he said. She nodded her head.

"Should I get my pad?" DelicateSear said. She had that arch look in her eye, but MisterMenu preferred to ignore it. "Sinisteria," he said. "Coffee, please, in the bridge." Which was how he referred to his home office. He and DelicateSear got dressed and retired to said room. MisterMenu assumed his position in his supercomfortable custom-made chair behind his supercomfortable custom-made desk. DelicateSear stretched out on the long, long couch. MisterMenu pondered her for a long while. As if stringing together the words of something important he wanted to say. Or waiting for her to do the same.

"Am I supposed to inquire now exactly what you were whispering to Sinisteria?" she said.

"If you wish."

"All right, what were you whispering?"

"None of your business."

"Touché," she said.

MisterMenu riffled through some papers on his desk. He paused. He studied her in silence. He riffled his papers again.

"I believe I'm going to have to terminate FiberFlywheel," he finally said.

"Congratulations. What took you so long?"

"I don't know. I keep thinking of Marginalia. You know, the daughter."

"You fucking her, too?"

"Only a little."

"You dog."

"Damn thing is, who do I replace him with?"

"RevenueWarts?"

"His closet's so jammed with skeletons it bursts into a chorus of 'Dem Bones' every time you walk past the door."

"NonAlignment?"

"He's best friends and co-owner of SteelCalipers with Loyalty-Oath."

"LensFlare?"

"He's got that upcoming wire-fraud thing."

"ThermalExplosion?"

"Bad breath."

"Looks like the executive holding pen at NationalProcedures has taken a net quality hit. Go outside? Bring in some new blood?"

"Competition's generally worse off. They're all trying to pick off our people."

"Or the whole company itself. What're you going to do about VariancePanoply?"

There'd been rumors for weeks that Variance, their major rival in the prevalent trade of making money out of money, was preparing a hostile takeover bid. NationalProcedures was on edge. Staff were updating their résumés. Checking the ConnectTheDots website during working hours for job possibilities. Routine corporate hysteria.

"Those clowns don't know what's coming to them."

"Which is?"

"I'll lay on my jiggery-pokery double thick."

"And how does that differ from your legendary fiddle-faddle?"

MisterMenu explained.

"Sounds like, if all those dots fall properly into place, you might even end up in a position to buy *them*."

"Presto change-o. The abiding rule of global capitalism. Modern business is medieval alchemy, my dear. Embrace that truth, never stray too far from the primal core, and you can do no wrong. You know, a great man once defined happiness as 'a clear horizon.' Are my old peepers deceiving me or is that the very scene unfolding spectacularly before us?"

"Somewhat. There is, unfortunately, a slight blemish at the moment threatening to depreciate the market value of that particular picture."

"Yeah? What?"

"BlisterPac is dead."

"Who he?"

"The guy who's been tracking down the whereabouts of your missing bag o' money for all these months."

"My bag o'?"

"Your bag o'."

"What happened?"

"Well, so far as we know, he either slipped or was pushed off a cliff into a giant gorge, apparently a big tourist attraction outside some shithole upstate named Randomburg. He'd traced the money to that area, which, not so coincidentally, is the boyhood home of our mark, the illustrious Graveyard, the lowlife who scooted off with the bag to begin with."

"Local law enforcement on it?"

"Of course, but that's all ordinaryland up there, so we don't know yet the level of competence we're dealing with."

"I miss my money."

"I know you do. And we're working overtime to get it back."

"Whatever you have to do. Subcontract it out, if necessary."

"I know just the right people."

"Fine. But don't tell me their names. Don't tell me any names. Or any details about the operation. Just retrieve the bag."

"Think of it as already being back home in your hands again. Think of how it feels. Think of how it smells."

"I'm thinking." He had actually closed his eyes. "I'm smelling." Now he opened his eyes. "Visualization of desire is the force that manufactures wealth. Do you know what the eleventh of this month is?"

"A Friday."

"My birthday. I like birthdays. Especially my own. I like presents."

"This should be a memorable one."

"I can already feel the four-leaf clovers popping up at my feet."

"You deserve them."

"You know what?" He raised his arms above his head in an athlete's triumphant victory-lap salute and then beamed a full-on psychic charge of pure MisterMenu directly into the center of DelicateSear's receptive gaze. "I should just like to announce, with absolute conviction, in full chief executive authority, that I do, most certainly, like being me."

CHAPTER 23

SHYSTER SPECIE

TO HIS VAST ANNOYANCE Graveyard was awakened before noon by the chattering of his cell phone. It was his mother.

"Your sister's been arrested," she said.

He managed to mumble something in response that probably wasn't even an actual word. He carefully opened one sticky eye. He checked his Elaboration. He couldn't read the dial. The hands and all the numbers were blurred.

"Are you even awake yet? I've been up for hours. What is your problem? No wonder you can't hold down a real job. I said, your sister's been arrested. If you can rouse yourself to pretend you care."

"What happened?"

"I don't know. There's more than one charge. They're calling it domestic abuse or spousal abuse or assault or something worse. The lawyer said attempted murder's been mentioned." At which point she broke into tears.

"What—her boyfriend try to beat her up?"

"No, she beat *him* up."

"Blood oranges and farrago beans," he said. "Where is she now?"

"Here with us. Your father bailed her out. She wants to see you."

"Be there in ten." And he hung up and turned to Ambience. "Get dressed. We've got to get over to the house."

"What's up?"

"Major howdy-do at the ranch. My sister's been busted," he explained.

They struggled into yesterday's clothes. The instant Ambience was outside the door she immediately lit up.

"So now we have to wait for you to smoke a cigarette?" Graveyard said.

"Just a couple puffs."

"Give me a hit."

She passed him the lighted butt. He inhaled deeply. He exhaled slowly. He handed it back. "Wish this stuff didn't kill you," he said.

Ambience shrugged. "We all have to go sometime." She banged a couple more pulls, let the butt fall where it may, rubbed it out with the sole of her RavenMistressSideLaced boot. "Okay," she said. "Let's go spring the kid from the slammer."

When they arrived at the old homestead, Roulette, fronting full paternal mode, was buried in his big chair in the living room, dressed in his underwear and hiding his face behind a newspaper.

"Hi, Dad," Graveyard said.

His father grunted. The paper rattled.

Carousel was in the kitchen opening and slamming shut cabinet doors in apparent random order, constructing a meal of some kind or other. The phrase "in a dither" came to Graveyard's mind.

"Hi, Mom," Graveyard said.

She looked as if the oxygen in the room had just run out. "Your sister's upstairs locked in her room. She's expecting you."

Outside Farrago's closed door Graveyard paused, then quickly knocked twice.

"Yeah?"

"It's me."

The door immediately opened, releasing an enveloping cloud of thick leaf smoke. Farrago stood before them, holding a neon-green glass bong in one hand and a lighted joint in the other. "Fuck me," she said. She looked like she hadn't slept in days and like there wasn't a mattress in the world comfortable enough to provide any relief. She passed the bong to Graveyard, who took a healthy hit and passed it to Ambience, who seconded his judgment.

"Come in," she said. "Welcome to private hell number ditto fuck. Excuse the mess. Maid's day off." She dropped onto the stained couch, peppered with cigarette burns, and began busying herself with the mouth end of the bong. She inhaled more than it seemed possible for normal lungs to contain. "I assume you've heard all the gory details from at least one of the parental units." Extended breathy exhale.

"Actually, no," Graveyard said. "Mom babbled out something about you beating your boyfriend up."

"That's the noodle version."

"So," said Graveyard. "Give us the restored director's cut."

So she did. Last year she'd begun detecting other scents on Loophole's clothes and skin, scents not originating with her. Loophole explained the aroma as a by-product of his new job. He'd supposedly been hired as a part-time bartender at TheRancidSaddle, out on the NobodyGoesThere Pike, where staff and patrons were all "superfriendly huggy types." Okay. Dubious, but conceivable. Then his hours began getting unexpectedly extended and he'd have to go to work on nights he'd already claimed he had off. So she finally called the place on a Thursday he was supposed to be subbing for someone named FaultyBrakes and they'd never heard of him or FaultyBrakes. He hadn't even had the respect to deceive her with an inventive lie. She waited until the next gaming session, when her mother was out at her stupid book club gossiping about the who's-on-who erotic byplay of *Good Girls at Home with the End of the World* or some such shit and when Loophole was thoroughly locked into the meanest section of Level XII of that ultimate fanboy favorite, *The Ruby Caskets of Melanthia*, to initiate her interrogation. He ripped off into a rage, blew the game, which made him even madder, and then started threatening her like she was one of his curb puppies or something. Then he called her an ungrateful cunt and bitch-slapped her across the mouth. She slapped him. He slapped her again. So she clocked him across the face with a game controller, cutting his right cheek. His face went all red and he grabbed her by the throat with both hands and started choking the life out of her. She was gasping for breath but still managed to knee him hard in the nuts and after he let go of her and while he was doubled over in pain, she seized the entire game console, lifted it high above her head, then brought it down with all her strength onto the back of his skull. He dropped to the floor like a side of beef. She was so mad; she'd never been that mad in her whole life. She couldn't see, she couldn't think. She just yanked the game's power cord out of the wall socket, wrapped it around his neck, and began tugging on the ends like she was trying to kill a rabid animal. Which she was. He made some sort of pathetic gagging sounds. When the sounds stopped and he quit squirming around like a stuck pig, for good measure she bashed him in the head with her favorite giant glass ashtray. He groaned and blood started running out of his hair. Then she pulled his cell out of his back pocket, threw it on the floor, and stomped on it until it cracked. When he started moaning and trying to get up, she clobbered him again in the head with the ashtray. Then he stopped doing anything. She ran out of the house, hopped into her MileWolf, and fled the scene. She raced on over to Dad's place, where the cops picked her up two days later. She'd been locked up, slapped with all kinds of fake charges, and it didn't look good.

"But he assaulted you first," Ambience said. "What you did wasn't anything more than self-defense."

"Not according to his lawyer."

"Fuck lawyers," said Graveyard. "All these ridiculous charges should be dropped immediately."

"That's what Dad's trying to do."

"Who'd he hire as an attorney?"

"FlintyWhiteShoes."

"From across the street?"

"Yeah."

"He doesn't know how to put on a pair of pants. We need

to introduce some crisp lettuce into this settlement sandwich. His office still located above the WhoDoYouTrust? bank downtown?"

"How the fuck should I know?"

"What about this Dupehole or Asshole or whatever the hell his name is? Can he be bought?"

"He likes money."

"Who doesn't? Where's he live?"

She told him.

"Listen, Farrago. No more worries, okay? This problem is solved. Give me a hug."

So she did.

FlintyWhiteShoes was old. He was as old as the word *old* ever meant. His skin was like papyrus. His voice a creaky whisper. His body an assemblage of bones. His hair was white. His spottily shaved beard was white. Even his eyes were white, the irises so pale as to appear colorless. His office was a collection site for teetering heaps of paper, all important documents, no doubt. Dust drifted in heavy slow-motion curtains through shafts of sunlight falling from the unshaded windows. The room smelled of the past. Graveyard actually found the overall effect rather impressive and reassuring— in a movie-feel sort of way. Here was a real attorney. This was what authentic acquired experience looked like. Didn't it? And above all, FlintyWhiteShoes was convinced that Farrago's case was, if not rock solid, at least plaster solid. "Or I wouldn't have accepted it," he said in a voice so weak that both Graveyard and Ambience had to lean physically forward to even catch it. "But I have represented the law for the whole of my adult days and I might as well admit to you that the law, as you may or may not know, is not about truth or justice. It is about the law, and that is often something else entirely. It is a specialized game with its own unique set of rules and its own peculiar language. And I happen to be somewhat adept at playing said game. Still, having said all that, the outcome of any case is far from assured."

"Yes, sir," said Graveyard, "that's the reason we're here. We've come to assist you with the case."

"I don't ordinarily require much assistance."

"I'm sure you don't. But if you could just let me explain. I'll try to be brief."

He did and he was.

In response FlintyWhiteShoes was, well, flinty. But the sheer amount of cash Graveyard offered in support of his proposal was sufficient to produce a suitable spark. WhiteShoes, who appeared to have no staff or aides of any kind, personally typed the agreement Graveyard had requested, guaranteeing the document was all legally dank and aight and like that. Graveyard left him a packet of fresh Benjamins as a tip. Which he accepted with much polite cordiality.

"For one as green and untested as yourself," he said to Graveyard, "you do seem to possess an innate grasp of the fundamentals of the law. I predict much success in your adventure."

"You know what?" Graveyard said. "I do, too."

"Thank you, sir," Ambience felt compelled to say. And she meant every word.

"I liked him," she said once they'd returned to the car.

"I did, too. It's not often you meet a fictional character in real life. But if my scheme goes according to plan, we probably won't be seeing him ever again."

They then stopped at the nearest Pens, Paper, and Panoply, out on Round Moon Road across from Liquor Auditorium, purchased the most expensive black attaché case in stock, and drove around to the deserted parking lot in back. As Ambience kept watch, Graveyard stuffed the case with as much crispy cash as he could fit inside.

He settled himself behind the wheel and turned to Ambience. "Ready?" he said.

"Do it."

He and Ambience peeled out of there like people either escaping from or entering into if not an adventure, then at least a knotty situation. They found Loophole in his rathole of an apartment, as described, above the GrinAndBearIt Medical Supply Store. He only answered the door after Graveyard refused to quit knocking. He was also still in his underwear past one in the afternoon. There was an ugly cut on his left cheek, which was inflamed and swollen, and a couple of nasty ligature marks around his neck.

"Yeah?" he said. The door had been opened only wide enough to reveal his head. "Whaddya want?"

"We'd like to talk to you."

Loophole's eyes, attempting to take in the presence of strange visitors, seemed to shift in and out of focus. "Who are you?"

"I'm Graveyard," said Graveyard. "This is my wife, Ambience."

"Aw, hell," he said. He closed the door and they could hear the lock click.

Graveyard stepped closer and began banging on the door.

"Go away," said the voice behind the door.

"We need to talk to you."

"I don't need to talk to you."

"It's about your case."

"Talk to my lawyer."

"We'd like to speak with you. We'd like to offer you a proposition I think you'd be very much interested in."

"Listen, there's absolutely nothing your sister can say or do to make me change my mind. Only thing I'm interested in is getting that bitch behind bars, where she belongs."

"It's about money."

There were a couple more clicks and the door opened wide. Loophole stepped back, allowing them just enough room to enter. "This better be good," he said. He picked up a pile of dirty clothes off the couch and tossed them carelessly into a corner. "Sit," he said. So they did. He took a seat on a duct-taped leather chair, *his* chair, facing the too-big-for-the-room TV tuned to *Dollars for Dumps*, a trending afternoon game show in which contestants were shown color photographs of assorted apartments in Mammoth City and asked to guess the actual inflated market price on each rental. The game was harder than it looked. Big winners were almost always slightly certifiable. That's why it was so popular. And hilarious. Once seated, none of them in the room could stop watching that hypnotic screen. They tried to talk anyway.

"So what's this all about?" Loophole said.

"We're here to bring a touch of closure to this unfortunate incident," said Graveyard.

"Don't know how you're going to manage that. As I've already explained—to the police, the prosecutor, your father's attorney, the news media—there's nothing Farrago can do or say to make up for the enormous pain and suffering she's inflicted upon me. Nothing, understand?"

"We do and she does. The hideous extent of your physical injuries is clearly obvious. I can only try to imagine the severity of your invisible wounds. And Farrago agrees. She wishes to apologize. She wishes to convey to you how sorry, deeply sorry, she remains to this day."

"Lot of good that does me sweating in pain at three in the morning."

"Yes, I know. The apology is only words, but it is sincere. And we are prepared to offer further restitution if you'd be willing to drop all charges against her."

"Twelve hundred," said Loophole.

"What?" said Graveyard.

"I'm sorry," said FerretCheeks, the porcelain-toothed host of *Dollars for Dumps*, from inside the TV. "That's incorrect. The actual monthly rent on that particular item is a shade higher, at twenty-two fifty."

The audience groaned.

"Twenty-two fifty for that piece of shit?" Loophole said. "I could lease an eight-room house in Randomburg for less than that."

"But you'd still be in Randomburg," said Ambience.

"How much do I have to pay to live in a decent place in that fucking Mammoth City?"

"You don't want to know," said Ambience.

"But we're here today," Graveyard said, "to help lighten your burden."

"I'm going to need a lot of lightening."

"We understand. Would, say, ten grand help?"

"To do what?"

"We're serious. I'd hoped you be, too."

"You want your sister off the hook, right?"

"Why we're here."

"You love your sister?"

"Of course."

"Know who I love? Me. That's who. And I'm lucky to have such a devoted lover. See, I've got no family rushing to my side to fix things up, to fix *me* up. I've got to do all that shit for myself—the bed, the blankets, the chicken soup, the tuck-in, the hugs, the kisses. So I need something special. I need to be wrapped in dollars. Understand? Suffocated in them. Ten grand's only enough to cover my knees."

"I'm not MondoBank."

"Didn't say you were. But I understand that lottery you won buys a lot of clover."

As Loophole talked his legs had spread slowly apart, causing the cloth halves of the fly on his boxers to slowly part. Ambience found her attention being drawn again and again to that dark opening. Although she really couldn't see much of anything at all, she continued to peer brazenly, curious about what might be lurking in there. She couldn't help herself. It was an area of interest.

"She tried to kill me," Loophole was saying. He noticed Ambience checking out his junk. He smiled back at her.

"She was defending herself," Graveyard said. "Anyway, let's not replay the incident over and over again. It's done. In the can. I've got money here with me." He held up the black case. "Cash on hand. Let's not haggle anymore. It drains us needlessly. It's more than ten grand, more than double ten grand, more than you can

multiply by ten grand. Sufficient salve to heal all your wounds."
He opened the case, displayed its contents. The multitude of fresh,
clean bills seemed to be smiling at all of them. "I will ask you to sign
a statement promising to relinquish all further legal and criminal
claims against Farrago. Okay?"

"Let me see the money again."

Graveyard opened the case and turned it toward him. Loophole looked extra hard. "Pass it over," he said. Graveyard did. The
case propped open on his lap, Loophole gazed admiringly at the
contents. He picked up a stack, ran his thumb along the edges.

"Please note those are all hundreds," Graveyard said.

"I'm noting."

"Deal?"

Loophole continued to stare into the case. He seemed in a
trance. Seconds passed. And passed. "It is cash in hand, the stuff in
this case you're willing to hand over, not a check."

"That's correct."

Finally he stopped studying the money and looked over at
Graveyard.

"Yes?" said Graveyard.

"Yes."

Graveyard reached out a hand and they shook. Then he passed
Loophole the agreement and a pen.

"I'd also like you to pay special attention to clause number five,
which stipulates that should the prosecution decide to proceed
with the case, even after you've informed them you refuse to press
charges, you will also refuse to testify against Farrago."

Loophole leaned forward and read.

"Fine with you?" Graveyard said.

"A-okay."

"Now, if you'll just autograph the dotted line."

Loophole did. Graveyard took the paper, folded it, and placed it
in his shirt pocket. "I detest clichés," he said, "but sometimes they're
the perfect way to button up a situation, so I'll say it anyway. It was a

pleasure doing business with you, Loophole. I would even go so far as to say I hope we may meet again under better circumstances. And I mean that. But you and I both know that's never going to happen. So I'll just say good day and goodbye." They shook hands again.

"Nice to meet you," Ambience said.

"Same here," said Loophole.

Outside, as they approached the car, Graveyard said, "The legerdemain of money. See it once, see it twice, see it forever. Works every time. Problems, like stubborn stains, go away justlikethat. Poof!" He spread his fingers dramatically before him and then waggled them with what he hoped was as mysterious an air as he was capable of producing. "You can break into applause at any time."

"With repetition, though, the trick loses its luster, don't you think?" Ambience said.

"You kidding me? I can explain what I'm going to do, explain how I do what I'm going to do, do it, and they'll always be like, 'We've seen it before, we want to see it again. Now.' Impossible to wear the shine off the hocus-pocus of boodle. A perpetual crowd-pleaser."

"For the rubes in the cheap seats, maybe."

"For the rubes in the box seats, too. Count on it."

After they left, Loophole opened the case and again peered inside. The sight of all that lovely cash made him feel ravishingly alive. He closed the case, popped a beer, sat down in his chair, and tried watching TV again for a while. And what was on TV now? Nothing, nothing, and nothing. The case was lying on the table in front of him. It had the clean, sleek, elegant appearance of the sort of case that movie bad guys always left in restaurants, offices, banks, or whatever enclosed space they wanted blown up. He picked the case up and balanced it on his lap. He couldn't contain himself. He could literally feel the money with his eyes. He was trying desperately to get his churning mind used to two separate things: (1) the sheer size of the amount of loose cash spread out before him and (2) the simple and amazing fact that all of it was his and his alone. He closed the case, stood up, walked back into the bedroom with it. He set the case down on the bed. He stretched himself out beside it, pulled down his boxers, and proceeded to give his jerky an award-winning Loophole Special—that's long and slow, long and slow, until the sweet bomb explodes and covers the sky in sugar. When he finally came, the cum shot into the air higher than it had ever gone before.

CHAPTER 24

A WOMAN AT LOOSE ENDS

AMBIENCE HAD MADE THIS appointment with herself more than a week ago, about a half hour after learning that Graveyard planned on spending much of the weekend backpacking along the BurningThigh Trail in the Bric-A-Bracs with CancelledStamp, an old buddy of his from Tip O' The Wedge, for no convincing reason she could see other than a futile attempt to recapture high school glories she did not share and had no interest in. Graveyard and CancelledStamp had both been expelled for painting, on Senior Day, the statue of the school's founder, Old White Guy, a remarkably lifelike shade of black. They also planned on concluding their vigorous weekend with a Sunday visit to the ArmsAhoy GunGala in picturesque UpperDingervale. Ambience's reaction to these two days of action-packed fun: bring me back a tasty piece of bullet.

Thirty minutes after Graveyard left Saturday morning she lit her first sweet cigarette of the day. Inside. Let the air-conditioning deal with the effluvia. Then she began her telephoning. First call to Mom. Rub the tender guilt spot for a couple of therapeutic minutes.

"Amby," Mom said when she finally picked up after about a dozen rings. "I was up in the attic going through the old picture books. Remember how cute you were when you were six and your father was still with us?"

"Some people think I'm still cute, Mom."

"Oh, no, dear, I certainly didn't mean to imply anything any different. It's just that you were the best-looking child anyone had ever seen. It was commented upon everywhere."

"Yeah, I remember, and you used to drag me into town to show me off to everyone you met."

"Well, I was proud of you."

"That's not what a little kid feels when old coots she doesn't know bend down to drool over her."

"Amby, I'm surprised at you. Those were my friends."

"They weren't mine."

"Well, I can see you're in one of your snits now. You know I don't like to talk to you when you're so knotted up like this."

"I'm not in a snit."

"I can hear it in your voice."

She became acutely aware of the volumes of air that lay between them, that had always been between them. "What's that noise in the background? I keep hearing this metallic rattling."

"My blender."

"Well, it sounds like it's coming apart."

"It's always sounded like that."

"What are you making?"

"My health drink. It's a refreshing combo of flowering man-gletops, bilge nuts, moonfruit sections, pared canker root, ahoya extract, and jasper buds."

"Sounds absolutely awful."

"I've never felt so full of energy in my entire life. I've spent the morning tidying the living room and the den. I'm finishing up the attic this afternoon. And tonight I'm taking in my first play in years, maybe ever. It's called *Marbles in the Batter*."

"Good for you."

"I'm going with AllocatedDraft. You remember AllocatedDraft?"

"No."

"Sure you do. I used to drop you off there every morning on my way to BonusBrands."

"The crazy lady. The house smelled of celery."

"And she hated celery. Never touched a stick of it."

"Her rosterchip cookies were great, though."

"You'd spoil your dinner filling up on those."

"She had a funny dog, too. With only one eye. And it always came no matter what name you called it."

"It's a TorsoWhisk."

"What? What is?"

"My drink. That's what it's called. A TorsoWhisk."

"I suppose I should try one, too."

"I'll send you the recipe. How's Graveyard?"

"Getting along."

"He found a job yet?'

"That's one of the reasons I'm calling you. His uncle died."

"Oh, I'm sorry to hear that."

"Uncle Parsnips."

"Was he sick?'

"Not so far as we know. Graveyard didn't even know him. It was all rather sudden. And he left Graveyard some money."

"Gosh, nothing like that ever happened in our family."

"And not just some money. I mean a lot of money. A substantial amount of money."

"Is it enough to make me nervous?"

"Yes. Graveyard's not too concerned about finding a job right now."

"My goodness."

"Yes. A life-changing amount of money. So what I was wondering was, how you doing right now? Need any help?"

"I'm flattered he'd even think of me, but no, things are good here. The flies are still selling real well, my government check comes every month, and I go into BonusBrands when I can, a couple days each week. I'm fine."

"I'm sending you a few bucks tomorrow."

"Amby, really, that's not necessary."

"But I want to, Mom."

"I love you, baby."

"I love you, too, Mom. Listen, Graveyard's just come in and he's making strange signs at me. Better go see what he wants."

"You do that, honey."

"Talk to you later, Mom. Bye."

"Bye."

And she hung up. And she wanted a cigarette. Badly. So she had one. She sat on the hard, uncomfortable motel chair, staring blankly into space for several minutes, processing that call. It was like shuffling through a deck of playing cards without any suits. No winning at that game. Then she picked up her phone again. She called Warranty.

"Hi," Warranty said. "So how's it going up there in Peckerwood?"

"It's shadowland here, kid. This is where the country goes to die. Everything's about twenty years behind the rest of us. The women are still wearing puntpushers."

"That's so junior high."

"And the kids are all trading flip rings."

"Nooooo!"

"The other day I actually had a squelchburger. Deluxe."

"Gosh. Haven't had one of those since the last BeefBar place in town shut down, about a millennium ago."

"Like I said, it's a real living history museum up here."

"How's Graveyard?"

"You know him. As long as there's a TV to watch and a gun to shoot, preferably at the same time, he's happy."

"And have you watched TV and shot a gun?"

"Does the president pick his nose when no one's looking? Only thing, all the TVs around here are too small for Graveyard's taste. But we went to a range the other day."

"How'd you do?"

"Like riding a bike. It all came back. I killed the rest of them, including the owner of the place."

"Well, a girl, too."

"Shit, yeah."

"What's the family like?"

"You know, a family. Dumb and fucked up. His sister's kinda cool, though."

"Aren't the sisters usually cool?"

"One hopes. How's things in the big metro?"

"Bangin' and boomin'. We had a water main on the street blow last week. Flooded the whole basement. You got anything stored down there?"

"Not that I know of. I'll check with Grave. How's Herringbone?"

Warranty blew out some air. "Into full-on Herringboney. He's given up all pretense of being a quote, nice, unquote person. I haven't really seen him in a week. We're on different schedules now. He's got some kind of phony-baloney job at some kind of phony-baloney night operation he won't tell me about. He's hardly ever even here anymore. I can smell the other women on his clothes. There's always a strange pair of panties in his pocket. I think he must be collecting them or something. The other night I caught him with his face buried in a pair of leopard-skin Ultra-Slims that were definitely not mine. Like he was doing a bump of ellipsis."

"When's the story ever going to change?"

"Beats me. How're the skies?"

"Nothing. Dishwater gray."

Besides collecting tolls at the entrance to the Conundrum Bridge, Warranty was a ninja fangirl of clouds. Yeah, those fluffy white things hanging spookily over all of us. She loved them. She wanted to live in them. She wanted to be one. She took pictures of them. She drew pictures of them. She made models of them out of cotton balls. She collected books about them. But most of all she simply liked lying in a quiet field and staring up at them. She could do that for hours. And often did. The world's beauty. The world's peace. The world's violence. The world's terror. All bound up within these mysterious concoctions formed out of nothing more substantial than air and water. Contemplate that. She had occasionally dragged Ambience out with her on her cloud excursions to WoodenSandal Park, north of the city, where there were several infrequently traveled meadows relatively free of picnickers and dog poop and offering almost un-limited sky vistas for prime atmospheric observation. So far, despite all her efforts, Warranty had failed to win Ambience over to her own level of enthusiasm for these adventures in cloudlarking. But still Ambience was coming along quite nicely. On their last outing she had even surprised Warranty by blurting out the proposition (stale copy to veteran sky scryers but a revelation to noobs) that clouds were like thoughts passing through the mind of God or whatever that thing was that had thoughts that big. "Or maybe it's you," Warranty said. "Maybe those are visible manifestations of your inner reveries."

"Cool," Ambience said. "I can ride with that." The real fun, though, lay in regressing into that childhood favorite, picking out recognizable shapes in the burgeoning aerial cavalcade. Once Warranty claimed to have spotted a winged dragon emerging from a nondescript lump of white vapor. And in one productive day Ambience saw both an old-timey western locomotive coming round the bend, dark smoke spouting from its stack, and an arrange-ment of raggedy cumuli that reminded her of the grouping of the Neverquesas in South Agenda, after she had visited the big island, Toodleloo, the previous spring as a location scout for *Paradise on Hold*, or so she said.

"How're celestials down there?"

"Good and clear yesterday," said Warranty, "but I had to work. Aside from today, any luck at all up there?"

"Pretty much a nephophile's holiday. A couple rainy afternoons, but mostly one cloud extravaganza after another passing in forma-tion everywhere you look."

"Nephophile. I'm impressed with your vocabulary."

"You taught me the word."

"Listen, Ambience, how about a favor? Shoot some pix for me. As many as you can stand. Text them when you get a chance."

"No problem, Warranty. I'm out practically every day. And clouds love to pose for me."

"They like you. They're your fans."

"Cloud groupies. Great. Maybe I should throw in a couple extra selfies for good luck."

"Do, Ambience. I especially want to see those."

"Okay, Warranty. Look, it's been great talking to you. I'll try and call again at least once before we leave."

"I love you, Ambience."

"Love you, too, Warranty. Bye."

She tried calling CarnyDoll but, typically, no answer. And Ambience hated leaving messages. She hated talking to machines and didn't believe anyone else should talk to them, either. CarnyDoll didn't especially like talking to people. Ambience understood.

Then she called FurryFarm. She wished she could talk to Nippers. She wished he could talk to her. But it was good to know he was doing well and eating well.

She loved her cat. She wished he was with her now.

Now she was tired of holding the phone to her ear. And her hand was sweaty. She put the phone down on the bedside bureau. She lit another cigarette. She pulled the half bottle of LaughFrogg from their rented cupboard. She took a slug. She took another. She ran a poorly edited montage of half-baked notions and video snippets from her life through her mind. Nothing made any more sense than it had the last time she paused to rewatch this review. She needed a new edit.

She went into the bathroom, opened the medicine cabinet, took out the brown plastic vial of prescription zephyr, unscrewed the cap, and shook out a tablet into her hand. It wasn't zephyr, it was ellipsis. Tab clutched in the palm of her hand, she walked into the bedroom and lay down on the bed.

She dropped the ell.

Probably she fell asleep for a while.

Then she was outside in the parking lot. She was searching for the car. It was missing from its spot. Then she remembered. Grave-yard had taken it.

Then she was folding her clothes and placing them neatly in the drawer.

Then she was sitting in the living room, watching TV. What was going on? She never watched TV when she was alone. Especially not during the day. She stared uncomprehendingly at the screen. She was trying to figure out the name of the show. She was trying to figure out what the show was about. It was all nonsense.

Then she was down on the grotty floor, engaged in a vigorous set of sit-up reps. She was getting so fat. She'd done zero exercise the whole of this wasted trip.

Then there was a row of real people lined up behind a white picket fence with only their heads visible and their faces all rubbery and unreal and in constant spastic motion running through a strained series of grotesque expressions never before seen on any real human faces. Had she been able to she might have screamed.

Then she was across the street, seated at a window table in the WaffleGym. She was staring at the tiny holes in her pancakes. So many holes. There wasn't enough syrup to fill them all.

Then she was scrolling through the photos she had taken on her cell since they'd left Mammoth City. Nothing, nothing, and nothing. A couple of okay snaps but little else. What was the point, exactly, of a vacay escape if all you had to show for it was little more than a measly handful of stupid pictures? What was the point?

Then she was in the motel office, chatting with the nice lady in charge. She had comforting russet hair. Ambience didn't know what they were talking about.

Then she was studying her left hand with scientific intensity. All these stubby fingers. What the fuck was that all about?

Then she was folding her clothes and placing them neatly in the drawer.

Then she was cleaning the kitchenette with a roll of paper towels and a spray bottle of Xall she found in a cupboard under the sink.

There was a stubborn red stain on the counter that no matter how hard she tried could not be rubbed away. What was going on? She hated cleaning house.

Then she was running through the corn in a white peignoir. It was night. The corn crackled all around her. She was being chased. By whom? By what? Her eyes came open. The jagged network of fine lines revealing the botched paint job on the ceiling overhead popped sharply into view. She was drenched in sweat.

Then she was bending over, pulling a tray of hot brownies from the oven. What was going on? She hated baking.

Then she was folding her clothes and placing them neatly in the drawer.

Then she was lying on the bed, her pants pulled down to her knees. She was caressing her pubic hair. Her pubic hair felt so nice. So slippery smooth. So beautiful. Then she was touching the button. She began caressing the button. The button liked being caressed. Beneath her a deep rumbling began. It grew and grew until the earth split. She smiled then and she couldn't stop smiling. We need more catastrophes like that, she said to herself.

Then she fell asleep and dreamed she was holding Graveyard's hand.

CHAPTER 25

THOUGHTS AND PRAYERS

IT WAS AMBIENCE WHO realized that morning they were out of ellipsis. She'd looked everywhere. Her old zephyr prescription vial in the medicine cabinet was empty, as was the mother lode, the repurposed mayonnaise jar under the dirty clothes on the floor in back of the closet. She thought for sure she'd hit paydirt in the pockets of her Pear&Pumice bouclé jacket. But no, nothing. There wasn't a single cap to be found anywhere in the suite or the HomoDebonaire, which she'd also searched diligently. What she really couldn't understand was how she'd allowed their chemical situation to reach such a serious defcon level. What could she possibly have been thinking? Where had her mind been? Forget that last. She knew the answer.

"We're out of ell," she said. She told Graveyard where she'd looked.

"No worries," he said. He knew a place. The Rock Pile, an old-timey boutique down at the south end of Mess O' Stuff run by a cool green-card dude named BackAlley, who'd once had a lively business in cartridges, cassettes, and CDs until all the music became free. Now you could go there to score rare movies, oop comic books, and various popular substances that would never be free. The place always smelled of incense and zits. "I don't know," Graveyard said. "The store may not even exist anymore, maybe the mall, either, but let's give it a try."

"I'm horny," Ambience said.

"Yeah? A second ago you were ready to tear up the carpeting cause you couldn't find any ellipsis."

"What do I know? You think I understand myself?"

"You're rich. You don't have to."

"I have my people do it for me?"

"Now you're working it like a bullion freak."

"Round me up some people."

"In a minute." He was already undoing the porcelain cabochon buttons with the burned-leaf motif on her HeavenlyConcourse hand-embroidered silk blouse. "My God, sweet aubergine, you've got nothing on underneath this rag."

"I believe in going commando top to bottom."

"I like your taste." He kissed her on the neck. He licked her neck. "And in fact, I like your taste." And then the carapaces came off and they slipped seamlessly into a space beyond words, free of comment or commentary. Now it was all about the feels. But after a while the rented living room, for Ambience, at least, ever sensitive to the tone of things, seemed entirely too constricted, and she guided them to the rented bedroom, which, though not as large as the master version back home, contained a bed of at least sufficient cubic feet to absorb the size of their emotions. They rolled around for a while on the stale duvet. First they were groping, then they were making love, and then they were fucking. Ambience's skin a quilt of knitted nerve endings. The air a pool of warm oil. Her tongue a phantasmagoria of color. She was bathed in metaphor. She was rich.

"I liked that," she said when they had finished.

"I did, too," Graveyard said. "Let's do it again sometime real soon."

"Capital idea."

What if, Graveyard said to himself, and not for the first time, lying quietly in an agreeable postcoital reverie, the moment of greatest pleasure you've ever experienced in your entire life, the very peak of bliss, was only the mildest hint of what it was possible to achieve on the spectrum of physical euphoria, that there were no limits whatsoever to the boundaries of ecstasy but the intensity you could personally bear, that you and you alone controlled how much good you allowed yourself to tolerate, and that once your private quota was fulfilled the excess was converted instantly to pain. Imagine that. And not the first time he had done so. Changes the face of the whole planet, don't it?

They showered, adorned themselves in brand new sets of shamelessly expensive clothing, and refreshed, relaxed, and ready to face their public, ventured out into the seasonably cold twilight, loaded the bag of money and the bag of guns (those perpetual twins) onto the rear floor of the HomoDebonaire, climbed in, and exited the parking lot of the Stay 'N' Pay.

"Think I'll take the scenic route," Graveyard said. "It's shorter and there's much less traffic. In fact, there is none."

"Rush hour a real bear out here?"

"You never know. CorrugatedDreams is up along the interstate and Equidolt and probably plenty more pop-up businesses I haven't even heard of. That's a mess of people letting out at once. The way we're going will be short, quick, and hassle-free. Plus you get to see the country."

"Do it," said Ambience.

Sound track for this late afternoon's drive was Dub Coroner's *Casanova Hymn*, the track in play at the moment, the slammin' "24K Luv Scraps." Ambience soon found herself nodding to the beat and singing along with the trippin' chorus: "You say it ain't me, so you saying / Pack that piece, now you damn chigging / Milly, flush that fortune down, flush that sweet fortune all the way down."

The song ended.

Ambience turned to stare out the window into the gathering dusk.

"My God," she said. "I see cows. Those are actual cows. There's cows out there on the hill."

"Lordy me, Maw," Graveyard said in the appropriate bad accent, "they got real critters on real farms and everything." He dropped the accent. "You sure those might not be deer?" He glanced quickly over to his right but couldn't see anything. It was getting darker and darker. "Aren't cows supposed to be brought into the barn at night?"

"They're big and fat and standing still and lying down and they're in black and white."

"Cows," Graveyard said.

"That's what I said."

"Those are farms over there. We're in farm country."

"Where nervous white people huddle together to vote for other nervous white people?"

"Whining always enjoys a big chorus. You know my father is local district chair of the Flying Freedom Freedom Party."

"You've told me often enough. You must be so proud."

"I used to get free stuff at the annual Liberty roundups."

"What—a kiddie StreetCleaner and a Make The World Go Away baseball cap?"

"Mostly divinity fudge and unlimited servings of frosted flake crumble."

"Everything a growing boy needs."

"Couldn't get enough."

"Listen, there any real stores at this so-called mall? Places where you can get real stuff worth buying? I haven't gifted myself a single party favor on this entire trip that was both ludicrously priced and completely unnecessary. And I'm beginning to suffer serious withdrawal symptoms."

"Used to be a pretty good Synapsaurus outlet there, but that was twenty years ago, so who knows if it still even exists today?"

"I need to buy something, Grave. Soon. Seriously soon. I'm getting the shakes."

"Don't worry, we'll find some sort of uselessly stupid and glamorous knickknack that'll get you well again."

"That's why I love you, Grave. You always know how to say just the right thing."

"Well, sometimes."

"And you were certainly right about this route. Talk about the road less traveled. I haven't noticed another car since we turned onto it."

"Sautéed kale and broiled ramps." He kept glancing up into the rearview mirror.

"What's wrong?"

"You might've spoken too soon. This dickweed's been hotdogging us for miles now." He reached up and twisted the mirror off to one side. "Like to shoot out those brights, too."

Ambience turned to look back through the rear window. "He's gaining," she said.

"We'll see about that." Graveyard hit the accelerator. But the tailing car not only kept pace, it also moved up to about a foot off the HomoDebonaire, then began knocking repeatedly against the rear bumper, at the same time leaning on an abrasive, persistent horn.

"Didn't know small-town hicks could be such rude drivers," Ambience said.

"I don't think those are small-town hicks."

As he spoke, the pursuing car began grinding against the rear of the HomoDebonaire, attempting to push it forward. Metal complained and shrieked. Graveyard sped up. The trailing car cut abruptly to the left, moved up rapidly from behind, and began trying to pass him in the oncoming lane. It was a shiny black late-model Fustian XL with darkly tinted windows and an invisible driver who obviously liked its horn. When Graveyard sped up to keep the vehicle from cutting him off, the SUV swerved suddenly to the right, bumping into the HomoDebonaire, scraping its side. More metallic screeching. It pulled away for a moment, then immediately came back again, grinding relentlessly against them. "Jellied liver and lima bean relish," said Graveyard. His grip on the steering wheel tightened.

"This roach is definitely getting on my nerves," Ambience said. "What's he think he's doing?"

"Well, I think he's trying to run us off the road."

The black SUV, which had fallen back behind them for a few

seconds, now began accelerating again for another pass. Graveyard reached out to his brushed steel Navigation Gallery, lightly touched an icon on the display screen, and instantly the HomoDebonaire's deluxe Ultra-Drive function was activated. They easily zoomed out ahead of the receding Fustian.

"Okay," said Ambience, "that may have done it. You've dusted 'em."

"Thanks to the Homo's five seventy hp."

But then, despite their lead, the trailing headlamps began growing ominously in size. "Think maybe you might want to take up a position in back," Graveyard said. "Just to be on the safe side."

Without a word Ambience climbed over into the back seat and immediately turned around to face out the rear window. "Those blinders are like arc lamps," she said, blinking against the glare. "What's—he got his high beams on?"

"Yeah, they're probably customized HIDs, and god knows what he's got under the hood."

"Who do you think it is?"

"Well, it's pretty obvious they're probably associates of Mr. BlisterPac. And they're not in party mode."

"Here they come again," Ambience said.

The light from the approaching SUV magnified in intensity, eventually filling the HomoDebonaire's interior. Then the Fustian began bumping again and again against their tail fender as its driver leaned without mercy on his horn. The Debonaire swerved slightly to the left, then slightly to the right. Despite the Ultra-Drive, Graveyard couldn't seem to shake them.

The first shot struck somewhere in the trunk of the Debonaire. It made a dull thump.

"You hear that?" said Ambience.

"Not good," Graveyard said. And he already had the pedal to the floor. Ambience pulled the bag of guns onto the seat beside her and began sorting through them. "What did I tell you?" she said. "I knew it was eventually going to come down to something like this. Money and guns. Guns and money. What did I tell you?"

"We can handle this. We've got the car and we've got the firepower."

The next shot cracked the rear glass. "Shit!" said Ambience. She ducked down in her seat. Graveyard checked the dash. The digital read on the velocity amplification was flickering up and down around the hundred mark. Suddenly several shots hit the body of the car simultaneously. "Shit!" Ambience said again, ducking again. "Whoever Mr. Big is, it appears he wants his money back real bad."

"Unfortunately, they always do," Graveyard said, fighting to maintain control of the rattling wheel. "We've arrived at the butt end of the corporate life." He couldn't depress the accelerator any further. Under him the car felt alive, an animated being of blood, muscle, and heart that moved in sync with his will. He was no longer looking at the gauges. He had never driven so fast in his life and he was riding on sheer car jockey's grace. It was like he was flying, the road slithering around like an angry snake before him. And still he couldn't seem to shake the Fustian. What had they done to that engine? No machine should be able to pace a maxed-out HomoDebonaire. Yet here they were. And this service road hadn't been built for such speed. So far the stretch had been a relatively flat straightaway, though the steering column was vibrating and so were his arms. What he tried not to think about were curves. How would he handle those? Up ahead, out there in the darkness, beyond the reach of the headlamps, hovered the Red Hole. He was hurtling toward it at max acceleration. But he blinked once, twice, three times, and the Red Hole went away.

"What do you want me to do?" Ambience said. "Lean out the window and let off a few caps?"

"Yeah," he said. "Give that a try."

Ambience powered down the left window. A hard wind came howling in. She picked up the first weapon at hand, a converted Gibe & Cloister 418, stuck out her head, hair whipping across her face, pointed the gun in the general direction of the Fustian, and popped a half dozen rounds, which were immediately answered by a return spray of automatic fire that peppered the Debonaire to the accompaniment of sudden pocking sounds. Ambience pulled her head back inside. "Holy shit!" she said. "They got major clout."

"I've had it with these people," Graveyard said. "Break out the LampLighter."

Ambience fumbled around in the bag, eventually producing the short, stocky shape of the ever-reliable LampLighter 505, the weapon she'd stitched her initials with into the paper zombie back at Bullets 'N' Brunch. It felt pretty cozy in her arms. Before she could raise it into firing position, though, several more hostile rounds came bursting through the rear window. She fell flat onto the back seat, heart in overdrive.

"Knock out the rest of the glass and give 'em a big kiss from me," Graveyard said. This wasn't really real. This was a flick he'd seen before. Many times before. With an audience. In a darkened theater. Actually being in the cast—in a starring role, yet—occupied an entirely different level of being. A picture of a gun was not a gun. A real bullet was as hard as reality could get.

Ambience used the barrel of the gun to break out the remaining bits of window glass and once she'd gotten a clear field of fire she propped the weapon on the top edge of the back seat, took aim, and let loose. A whole magazine's worth. One of the Fustian's headlamps went dark. She reloaded and shot off a volley into the black space above the remaining light, where she imagined the windscreen to be. She fired and fired.

"I'm trying to take out the window," she said, "but nothing."

"They've probably got that freaking Hexigard sheeting with spall face. If you can, keep knocking at the same spot. Might weaken the glass enough to get in."

So she did. No dice. The Fustian kept coming. The Fustian kept shooting.

"Go for the tires," Graveyard said.

So she did. And, for a moment, the Fustian appeared to actually begin slowing.

"They're dropping back," Ambience said. As they did, they released several additional bursts of fire, the flashes speckling the night.

Then, up ahead, at the very forward edge of the Debonaire's headlights, a sharp curve began bearing rapidly down upon them. "Hold on!" Graveyard shouted. He tried braking. He tried twisting the wheel. But it was too late. At terrific speed the luxury sedan slid sidewise off the road, bounced off a telephone pole or a cable pole or an electric pole or whatever the hell kind of pole it was, crashed through the guardrail and on down into a dead cornfield, the dry, brittle stalks thrashing against the grille and side doors of the career-ing car until it came at last to a shuddering stop somewhere in the midst of the field, dust, tiny bits of dirt, and withered leaf settling over the ruined body of the car.

"You okay?" Graveyard said.

"Yeah, I think so," said Ambience. "The fucking gun bag slammed into my face. I think my nose is bleeding."

Graveyard tried restarting the engine. Nothing. He tried again. Still nothing. He leaned forward, turned off the headlamps. The clear sky was utterly moonless. Except for the faintly illuminated windows of a farmhouse in the far distance, there was absolutely no light. It was the darkest dark Graveyard had ever experienced, country dark.

"Ready for what comes next?" he said.

"Bring it on," she said.

The Fustian had slowed, turned off the highway, made its leisurely, crunching way down onto the tattered field, and edged up to a position somewhere between unnervingly close and eerily distant from the rear of the Debonaire, where it came to a delib-erate stop. Its remaining headlight switched off. Its doors remained closed. Silence.

"Give me the MojoMaster," Graveyard said. "If you can find it."

Ambience felt around on the floor. "The MojoMaster the one with the HiggledyPiggledy rails?"

"No; other."

She passed him the rifle over the seat. She turned around to scan the quiet darkness framed in the busted-out rear window. "What're they doing? No one's gotten out of the car yet. At least that I can see."

"Old mob technique," Graveyard said. "I read about it once. Or maybe I saw it in a movie. They want to give you plenty of time to contemplate all the pretty stuff that's going to be coming your way shortly." He retrieved a box of rounds from under the seat and got busy loading magazines.

A cold wind had begun blowing in through the open back window. Ambience could feel the chill through her clothes. "Should've worn a heavier coat," she said.

"Don't worry," Graveyard said. "We'll all be sufficiently warmed up in a couple minutes." He inserted a full magazine into the MojoMaster, clicked it into place. He looked back at Ambience. She looked at him. They didn't need to exchange a word. Then Ambience heard a sound and quickly turned back toward the window. "Somebody's getting out," she said.

"Try giving them a sweet wake-up call."

Ambience opened up with the LampLighter, let it run for a few deafening seconds. In the dark at least two people answered, the muzzle flares clearly visible and shockingly long. She immediately answered, aiming right toward where the last flashes had appeared. Out there somebody yelled something.

"What'd he say?" Graveyard said.

"Fuck if I know." She fired off more rounds into the dark. "How many you think there are?"

"As many assclowns as could fit in that tacky circus car of theirs. Or, more likely, as many as BlisterPac's mysterious overlord is willing to shell out for. I wouldn't be surprised if, on the grand all-encompassing spreadsheet, we haven't already been written off as an unfortunate minor liability. We're probably not worth anything more than an economy mission. I'd say four at the most, if that. Give them a friendly 'Hi, there.' See what happens."

Ambience let off a five-second stream of rounds. Loud and bright. Silence. No response.

"Maybe they're already out of the car and slipping toward us," she said.

"You'd think we would have heard a door opening or something. Give me a turn. These shitholes are really pissing me off." Ambience crouched down in her seat. Graveyard pointed his MojoMaster over her head and out into the night, squeezed the trigger, and held it until his ears hurt too much. Again, there was no reply.

"Time for a recon," Ambience said. "I'm going out."

"In the open? You'll lose your cover."

"Number one rule in the Rangers: keep moving." She opened her door as cautiously as she could. From out of the dark came a sudden violent eruption of intense fire that made lots of twinkling lights and plunking sounds. Ambience and Graveyard ducked down behind their seats.

"Did you see where it was coming from?" Graveyard said.

"I've a good idea." She raised up and fired off into the night. Nothing came back.

"Cute," Graveyard said. "They're playing with us."

"I've got no patience with games." She took out her pack of Daredevils, lit up, and proceeded to smoke what she hoped would not be her last cig. The effect was better than ever.

"Give me one of those," Graveyard said. She did. She lit his for him. He noisily exhaled. "I'd forgotten what these can be like," he said. They sat smoking together in silence. When Ambience finished, she tossed the still-glowing butt off into the night. Then, clutching the LampLighter, she started to climb almost delicately out of the car. "Time to woman up."

"Where you going?"

"To do what has to be done."

"Maybe we should both go."

"You stay here, sit on the money. You're good at it. I'll do the moving around. I'm good at that. Remember Bubu Bugaboo?"

"Where you almost got killed?"

"But I didn't."

"Yeah, truffle mouth, you should most definitely try to remember that."

They shared a look, all their lives summed up in the silence. "See you in hell," she said. She'd always wanted to say that. Now she had. She slipped back toward the front of the car and then stepped silently off into the night. Graveyard leaned over his seat back, grabbed the bag of guns, yanked it into the front with him. He picked out his favorites—the BoxcarSystem 20/10, the StreetCleaner, the trusty HoiPolloi, along with the MojoMaster—and, balancing the unwieldy weight as best he could, exited the driver's side of the Debonaire with a surprising amount of stealth and made his way to the front of the car. He wanted the solid cover of the engine block. He leaned against the warm hood, metal still ticking like a can of trapped insects, cradled the Boxcar in his arms, and sighted down the barrel. He couldn't see a thing. Should have sprung for a fancy pair of those night-vision specs, but frankly he hadn't ever planned on needing them. Live and learn. Without those lenses there wasn't anything to see but total night. Trick, of course, was to keep focused in the proper direction and wait for the darkness to begin breaking apart into pieces that moved around in a suspiciously humanlike manner. After a while he started seeing white spots, and of course they were moving all over the place. He wondered how Ambience was doing. If anything happened to her...Then suddenly there was a rapid burst of light off to the left. Then another burst even closer. As soon as Graveyard shifted to the left side of the hood to cover that action, someone opened up on him from the right side. He crouched down behind the engine. He could hear the rounds pouring in like a bucket of pebbles being tossed against the car. Bits of window glass showered onto his head. And whoever was shooting was shooting seriously. Even when Graveyard thought the blistering fire was going to stop, it didn't. Then abruptly it did. In the interval the silence seemed deafening. My turn, Graveyard said to himself. He stepped out briefly into the clear, raised the Boxcar to chest level, and let go. He put all of himself into the machine rattling between his arms. It felt good. But before he could finish, something bit him on the left calf. Ow! he said to himself. That hurt. Then something bit his right arm. Ow! again. He was being nibbled to death. Then, just as he was ducking back behind the safety of the car, he took a sudden kick straight to the gut. Scones and smoked marrowbone, he said to himself. Definitely not good. He didn't want to, he couldn't help himself, but he went down. He could feel himself falling and knew the ground was going to be hard before he even hit it. It was. Scallop crudo and apricot cream cheese, he said to himself. I am fucked. He felt wet, so he touched the front of his jacket. He didn't need to look at his hand. Everything seemed to be running out of him. And if this was the part where his life was supposed to be fast-forwarding through his screen, why wasn't it? No memory train whatsoever. What could that mean? The show must not be over. Maybe there was going to be another beat or two and several more after that. So in this important climactic scene, he would act it extra. Before the martini shot there would be at least one other random player, maybe more, who would find his parts unexpectedly and brutally trimmed. Bracing himself against the body of the car, he rose by separate considered stages to his feet. He stared out into the armed obscurity. As he watched, a firefight broke out off in the distance, stopped, then started again. Kill them, Amb, he said to himself, kill all of 'em. Then some pieces of the darkness got loose and came charging toward him. He didn't even aim. He didn't have to. He just fired. The MojoMaster did what the MojoMaster was built to do. The piece of darkness on the left tumbled to earth. Then the piece of darkness on the right. He settled back against the front fender. His chest hurt. His right leg hurt. His left arm hurt. It was all hurt. Pictures of Ambience came stuttering through his mind. If anything happened . . . Then he decided it would be a good thing if he could just lie down on the ground and rest for a while. So he did. He lay there listening. All he could hear was his own heartbeat, strong and steady, and his own rasping breaths, short and weak, and then, beyond that, heavy feet stumbling clumsily across the frozen ground from behind. They neared. They stopped. He tried to turn to see who it was, but he couldn't move. "Ambience?" he said.

"No," said a voice and put a cold barrel to his head and pulled a trigger.

And the final astonishment passing through his mind before the final astonishment: casu marzu and lutefisk, none of this is at all what I thought it was.

Gun in hand and scuttling along close to the ground like one of the Lower Marginalians in *Planet of the Speckled Souls*, Ambience made her stealthy way up around the roaches' right flank. In the distance she could just make out a boxy, squat shape darker than the surrounding dark: the damn Fustian. No movement around it that she could see. All was tensely calm. She pressed on. She hoped to surprise the roaches with a classic end around and hoped the result would be equally classic. She had never wanted more to propel hard bits of metal into a deluxe assortment of soft, juicy targets. If only the ground weren't so broken and rocklike and covered in all these horrible mangled stalks. It was like trying to traverse an expanse of rubble from a demolished building. She'd already tripped and nearly fallen an embarrassing number of times. What a klutz. Suddenly flashes of light began cracking the darkness around the Fustian. These were immediately answered by similar flashes off in the direction of the Debonaire. Graveyard, she said to herself. Do it. Then the lights started talking back and forth to each other for several minutes, and then they stopped. Now her turn. She could see shadows detach themselves from the night and begin shifting around the larger shadow of the SUV. She got onto one knee, aimed, let off a crackling torrent of fire, and immediately threw herself forward onto the ground just as the angry response came whizzing over her prone body. When it stopped, she got up, ran about twenty yards to her left, aimed in what she hoped was the proper direction, fired, and before she could flatten herself completely against the ground took a hard blow to her right thigh and collapsed between the stony furrows. I am shot, she said to herself in amazement. She couldn't believe what was happening. More bullets looking for her began exploring the clods of dirt scattered randomly about in front of her. Something searing brushed furiously against the side of her face. It felt like a length of hot wire being drawn sharply across her cheek. She was shocked. Then she was angry. I am not dying here, she said to herself, in a crappy shithole, in the crappy dark, in the crappy middle of total crappiness. Somebody called out. She couldn't understand a word. She didn't move. She didn't speak. Somebody called again. Then what she'd been waiting for began to happen. Something was coming toward her in the dark. She didn't move. She waited. Under her finger the comforting curve of the trigger of her LampLighter felt hard and cool. She waited until the dark shape was close enough to talk to. She quietly raised the weapon and pointed and squeezed the hard trigger. Everything lit up and got quite loud. When she let go of the trigger, nothing was moving anywhere around her. For a while there was a brief twinkling of light coming toward her from off in the distance near the Fustian. Nothing too serious. Then it stopped, too. She felt her leg. It didn't feel good. But it didn't feel all that bad, either. It was one of those infamous "licks from Satan's tongue." You probably wouldn't die, but depending on where that tongue had been recently, you might wish you had. She began paying attention to her breaths, counting them methodically off, one by one. Breaths were energy, and when she determined that her tanks were near full again, she decided to risk rising to the vertical. It wasn't as painful as she'd expected, and she discovered she could actually put a surprising amount of weight on the injured leg. She could even move forward, even if it was only by way of a pronounced limp. Thank goddess, she said to herself. Time to reset. She moved off about thirty yards from where she'd been, eased herself down flat onto the ground, and focused through the sights of the LampLighter, seeing what she could see. Which wasn't much.

The night refused to break up into recognizable moving pieces. And then abruptly it did. Two, possibly three, figures were fidgeting about the Fustian. She slowly zeroed in on one moving blob, aimed directly into the center of the mass, and squeezed the trigger. The blob stopped moving. And when a second blob began shooting back in her direction, she simply centered on the muzzle flashes and kept firing until the flashes stopped. Then she lay there waiting until the silence became complete. When the silence had lasted long enough for her to feel safe, she gingerly climbed to her feet. The leg had begun to stiffen. Limping badly, she cautiously approached the dark Fustian. She found two bodies sprawled near the rear of the car. They were both decidedly dead. She didn't look at either one of them for very long. She didn't care what they looked like. Then she saw the flash off in the dark back near her car and heard the sharp crack. Without knowing, she knew instantly what that light and that exact sound meant. She went on. Out in front of the Fustian she found two more bodies, one of them still struggling for breath. The sound was like a clogged drainpipe. Don't bug me, she said to herself. I'm shot. She let him struggle. She had taken only a couple more steps when she caught another flash out of the corner of her eye and heard something nasty whizzing past her right ear. She dropped to the ground. She looked away from the point where she thought he'd be and, sure enough, caught him in her peripherals: a single figure frozen in a half crouch out in front of the Debonaire. She aimed the LampLighter and fired and continued firing until the figure wasn't there anymore. When she got to where the figure had been, she found him motionless between the furrows. She didn't look at him, either. She walked on past. How many was that now? Four? Five? We were worth five whole roaches. Imagine that. Behind the HomoDebonaire she came upon what she had expected to find: the remains of Graveyard lying on the ground behind the right rear tire, ominously still, severely silent. She looked down at the knotted wreckage of what had once been her only husband ever. Never suspected she'd be confronted with this version of him. Her eyes filled and she got down on her knees and then fell helplessly across his bones and began kissing his cold cheek again and again. She couldn't help it. He'd been an entire third of her life. After she'd worn herself out with her grief, she slowly struggled to her feet and turned and pointed the LampLighter in the general direction of the Fustian and started firing and kept firing until the magazine was empty. She was crying now and realized she'd been crying for quite some time. Then she opened the back door of the Debonaire, pulled out the bag of money, and, dragging the bag and her leg behind her, started hobbling toward the road and the nearest house on the road with lighted windows. It seemed awfully far away. It had numerous strings of multicolored bulbs framing its eaves and windows. It's Christmas, she said to herself. She'd forgotten it was Christmas. As she watched, the porch light came on. She headed for that light. She tossed the LampLighter off into the darkness. It landed with a satisfying thump. She struggled on over the rough, uneven furrows, cursing her leg and the pain and the night. She was now, she supposed, occupying the role she had always secretly imagined for herself: The Last Girl. Halfway to the house she softly opened her hand and allowed her end of the bag to fall limply to earth. She didn't know why. In the far distance she could hear the approaching sirens and she could see the flashing lights. Society come to make everything better.

CHAPTER 26

PRECIP

THAT DAY MISSUSMENU SLEPT until a couple minutes before noon, which was fine with her because now she could say to everyone she met throughout the day, "When I got up this morning…" and she would not be lying. She hated having people perceive her as a worthless layabout. Even if she was.

She slipped into her favorite robe, the silk twill one adorned with ostrich and peacock feathers she bought on their last trip together to Pantaloon, and made her way to the kitchen. She paused for a moment in the doorway, again pleased by the kitchen's appearance, the strict bareness of its counters, the antiseptic shine of its floor, the emptiness of its sink. Now that *he* was gone, she didn't mind spending time in the kitchen, sitting quietly at the clean table with her hot coffee, letting her mind ramble on where it would without any interruption. It had become once again *her* kitchen.

That "morning" MissusMenu made the coffee the way she wanted, not the way *he* liked it. The routine was comforting, the result ethereal. She began by placing two tablespoons of magic sprucenut oil into her personal FOREVER DERVISH cup. Then she ground her freshly roasted high-elevation Majestica beans in her JavaMill conical burr grinder, put the resulting grounds into a filter, poured hot water slowly over grounds, watched the grounds bloom, finished the pour, added two tablespoons of grass-fed yak butter, combined everything in her Mushamatic DigitalBrain ProChef blender, waited thirty seconds, and savored the high-octane result.

She was now ready to assault the day. A day she planned on bringing to the mat. She needed a victory because she needed this headache to go away. MissusMenu had a headache. She had a headache yesterday. She had a headache the day before that. And the day before that. And all the days in an unending chain back to who knew when? She now existed in a near-permanent headachy mode. And she was fresh out of her achy medicine. She would've sent Mix'N'Match to pick up a refill at DrugTemple but she'd fired that obnoxious tart in what seemed like another life now after discovering her using MisterMenu's dangler as her personal lollipop. Since then she'd declared their residence a female-free zone, which had translated, distressingly, into a help-free zone. As in the enlightened life, the best men were already taken. After untold months she'd been utterly unable to find a single adequately trained male who'd lasted longer than a quarter of a year in her employ. Her best friend, ElongatedVowel, who'd also converted to all-male help for similar reasons, had recently suggested she contact the agency she swore by, GuysWhoDon't, but MissusMenu had been so distracted lately by her impossible domestic situation and, of course, the headaches that she'd been unable to assemble the energy or the time to implement further changes, no matter how necessary, to her steadily deteriorating household.

Whenever she pictured her husband in her mind she saw him in midfuck, and the fuckee was not her. It was never her. It was never her in image or in fact. For a long time she didn't believe she could bear the anger these images induced, but after a while the fantasies of murder deliquesced into scenes of extended torture and then into physical beatings. Lately her reveries had become preoccupied with elaborate schemes of financial revenge—any one of which would kick *him* in the nuts with greater force than any boot. She actually found herself sometimes quietly smiling to herself as she watched imaginary banknotes flying up the office flue. In fact, she actually found herself becoming physically aroused during such daydreams, more aroused than *he* had ever made her.

Now, though—this very day, in fact—the first step was going to be undertaken that would result in *him* being permanently removed from her life and from as large a portion of his precious capital as possible. She had an appointment at Crotchet & Swole at two this afternoon with Mr. Crotchet himself—founder of the firm; adviser to presidents (except of course that ghastly MadeForYou); successful defender before the Supreme Court of the Personal Sequestration Act, in which any funds deposited on the eleventh of each month in confirmed Rainy Day accounts were, after a year and a half, exempt from all future federal, state, and local taxation; overseer of the tsunamically complex merger between LightningStrike Industries and AllTheMoneyInTheWorld, Ltd.; and, most important, LadderedStockings's representative in her nasty marital breakup with the mega-everything MahoganyBreath, winning the largest settlement in the lengthy recorded history of divorce. Now, there was a record worth shooting for.

For her meeting today with Mr. Crotchet, the "initial strategy session," as he called it, she was looking to make a midimpact impression, something suitably poised between what she'd wear to the Sticks and Shadows gala and an Emerald Noose Conservancy fund-raising. She elected to go with the black BabyVendetta open blazer with notched lapels over a burgundy faux sheath midi dress with statement sleeves and her knee-high CastleFlambeaux boots. She studied herself for longer than she should have in the full-length mirror on her bedroom closet door. She liked what she saw. No doubt Crotchet would, too. Probably he'd want to fuck her. That was fine, too. Every inch of erection length translated into God knew how many inches of fresh banknotes. The conversion rate was so variable. One way or another the man was going to get *her* money. Count on it.

She checked the digital read on the outdoor thermometer. Eleven degrees Fahrenheit. When was this damn global warming finally going to kick in? She'd been waiting forever. Now she was going to have to wear the Glamorama force-vector suede embellishment, too. Not the finest complement to her overall presentation, but it was deliciously warm.

She glanced at the Tri-Gem Elaboration (inscribed on the back: M&M) strapped to her left wrist. She had hoped she might be able to squeeze in a quick finger rub before she left, but there probably wasn't adequate time. Her cell chimed. It was BurnishedBrass. Should she take it? Without thinking much at all she pressed the Talk button. BurnishedBrass was worth almost a billion and her life was a mess. Her youngest son was entangled in something involving the internoodle and douchy checks and shell companies and banks with funny names in countries no one had ever heard of, an infinite web of schemes his mother couldn't begin or even care to understand. Her daughter had disappeared into the dark cultic labyrinth of the Order of the Happy Sun. The eldest son had devoted what remained of his life to completing the entire run of Convection & Isobar cloud jigsaw puzzles. The middle son, who lived in a giant gourd on the Great Plain of Quasiland, hadn't been heard from in three years. BurnishedBrass had, of course, shifted to an all-male staff the instant it had become recognizably fashionable and then, shortly thereafter, discovered her husband in bed with the recently hired bearded napkin folder. Today she wanted to complain, of all things, about what she regarded as the sketchy jewelry selection in the tenants' discount boutique. MissusMenu had no time for such nonsense. She hung up on BurnishedBrass in midsentence. Her cell chimed again. It was Roustabout. The car was out front. She slipped into her embellishment. Such a heavy coat. She entered the gold-trimmed elevator and plummeted smoothly, soundlessly, the fifty-two sublime stories to the central atrium. She said hello to Firmware and FinalNotice, who were manning the desk. She said hello to Rheostat, the smiley doorman. Outside the wind was blowing. Ordinaries scuttled past with their heads bowed, their hands in their pockets. Roustabout stood at attention by the open rear door of the MagnusMotivator. She said good afternoon to him. He said good afternoon to her. Then, just as she stooped down to enter the plush interior of the limo, she felt something quite light, quite delicate, fall onto her shoulder. She touched her shoulder with a gloved hand. She looked at the whitish goop now stuck to the tip of her pointer finger. It appeared to be a bird dropping. She glanced upward. The sky was blue. The sky was clear. There was nothing there.

ABOUT THE AUTHOR

Stephen Wright is a Vietnam veteran, an MFA graduate of the Iowa Writers' Workshop, and the author of four previous novels. He has received a Whiting Award in fiction, a Guggenheim Fellowship, and a Lannan Literary Fellowship and has taught writing and literature at Goucher, Princeton, Brown, and the New School. He was born in Warren, Pennsylvania, and lives in New York City.